KRAMPUS TALES

A KILLER ANTHOLOGY

Edited by
TIFFANY CURRY, TARA JAZDZEWSKI, SEAMUS
KING, AND ALEXA ROSE

Printed in the United States of America

First Printing, 2020

ISBN 978-1-7357905-5-8

Jazz House Publications
300 Lenora Street # 1119
Seattle, WA 98121
www.JazzHousePublications.com

Supervising Editor: Tiffany Curry
Cover art: Mike Kessell
Formatting: Nicole Scarano

CONTENTS

DARK HARMONY

E.D. EDWARDS

A mystery infects musical instruments, especially guitars. Some people collect guitars like fine art or baseball cards. For serious musicians there's a deeper connection. A guitar is more than just something to collect or play around on. A genuinely dedicated musician can have an uncanny link to his instrument. Let me give you an example. Somebody stole my friend's bass guitar once. About eight, almost nine years later, along about Christmas time, I see his bass in the secondhand section of a music store. I'm in there looking around, thinking I might buy myself something nice, give myself a little holiday present, and I see that guitar. Bam. Immediately I know that guitar belongs to my friend. Guitars are like people. The older they get, the more they develop a distinct personality. That particular bass guitar has dings, decals, cigarette burns, and some unique repairs. Even after nearly nine years, I can still recognize it. I help my buddy get his guitar back. He didn't realize it, but my buddy had been mourning that bass guitar the entire time it went missing. A musician can grieve for an instrument almost in the same way he grieves over a lover when she's gone. My buddy tells me that his bass starts vibrating when he touches it again, like it was glad to see him or something. Maybe the little vibration in the strings is the guitar's version of a puppy dog wagging its tail. After he gets his base back, all my friend's gigs just seem to go better. Like a piece of his soul came back to him. That bonding explains how guitars become haunted.

I need you to appreciate this before I tell you my story.

So, I'm with another good friend of mine, Hoyt Owens, at this creepy old bar in Kentucky. This is Currituck County somewhere around the mid-1990s on the Saturday night after Thanksgiving. Elvis Presley is singing "Blue Christmas" on the jukebox. Again. Christmas music gets played to death and there's no choice but to endure it 'til January. Hoyt buys us some beers. We watch the bartender sling some ugly Christmas lights over the antlers on a moose head hanging on the wall behind the bar. It's his attempt to be festive. This bar has a fair amount of decorative taxidermy, but the moose head is the only taxidermy getting Christmas lights. The bartender shoves a menorah in the window next to the neon liquor sign just to show he's inclusive. That'll be the extent of his holiday efforts.

My buddy and I are just hanging out, having a cold one, when this old guy limps into the bar. He's grimy looking, wearing a baseball cap and a muddy windbreaker. His jeans are smudged with dirt and motor oil. He comes up to us, just swaggers on up to Hoyt and me, acting like we're all good friends. There's a rank smell to this man and a weird glitter in his eye.

"Hey, fellas." The guy starts telling dirty jokes, acting like he's our private stand-up comic. Hoyt's expression is pure annoyance. He's got no interest in this weird old guy or his depraved puns. I guess the guy senses that he's losing us, so he changes his tone and gets to the point. He says he wants to show us something outside. He's insistent. It's pretty clear that he's not going to leave us alone.

Hoyt downs the last swallow of his beer, puts his empty glass on the sticky bar, and gives me an exasperated shrug. "Come on. Let's go see what all the fuss is about."

So, we follow the guy out of the bar and around to the back of the building. It's night and cold. Powdery snow floats in the darkness. The guy points to this rusty old van parked in the alley under the dim glow of a streetlamp. The snow wafts about in the light above the van, feeble little flakes too flimsy to assemble on the ground.

"Over here, Guys."

I'm feeling there's something not kosher about this whole thing, but there's only one of him and the two of us. Hoyt is an ex-marine. I was on the wrestling team in high school. I'm not too worried the guy will jump us or anything. I'm more curious about whatever it is this guy seems so desperate for us to see.

We follow him to his van and the guy slides the doors open.

It's like Santa's warehouse in there. Carpets, television sets, electronics, collectibles, bicycles, golf clubs, just boxes of crap crammed in that van. He opens a fancy lacquered box with a wad of jewelry inside…chains, rings, bracelets. He claims none of this is costume shit. Every trinket is valuable, estate quality jewelry.

"All this stuff goes up for auction tomorrow, but you guys get first crack at anything you like." The guy reminds us several times of how close it is to December, to Christmas and the need for presents. "Two big, strapping young fellows like you probably have girlfriends, right?" He shakes the jewelry box a little, holding it out like he thinks he's tempting us, like we're a couple of hungry stray dogs and he's got a plate of sirloin steak. Hoyt is recently divorced. The last thing on his mind is buying jewelry for his bitch of an ex. Hoyt glares at the jewelry box like it's a carton of fresh turds. At this point in our lives, neither one of us is in a relationship. I don't have any use for fancy jewelry either.

Hoyt keeps telling the guy we don't want anything. We're just about to ease away, to go back inside the bar for another beer, when I see this guitar wedged between some boxes inside that van. It's an old acoustic guitar that's been beat all to hell. I don't have the best view, but it looks like a badass blues man or rugged country music singer might have owned that guitar. Anyway, the guy can see my interest, so he tells me I should hold the guitar, check it out. He reaches over some stuff, grabs the guitar by the neck, and yanks on it. The guitar is wedged in tight. There's a weird howling noise when the strings scrape up against something, almost seems like a cry of pain. He tugs harder, jerking the guitar free with a hollow thump against the body and a sad twang of strings. The old guy stands there triumphantly, holding the guitar up so I can get a better look.

It's an old Harmony archtop with a murky, tobacco-colored sunburst and F-holes on the face like a violin. I know Harmony came out with this model sometime around the depression era. My great uncle had one similar to it before he died. This guitar is probably 60 years old or older. I really want to play it.

The guitar feels warm in my hands, when I take it from him. It's been sitting around in a cold van for god knows how long, but it feels warm, almost alive when I touch it. I run my hand across the body. The center front is all scratched from aggressive strumming and the fingerboard has some light splitting in the grain but it's sturdy. No broken strings. I strum a chord. Weirdly enough, it's in tune. There's a hair-thin crack along the back of the body, but that doesn't affect how it plays. It has nice action and a deep, resonant sound. I strum a couple more chords. Definitely in tune. Not what I would have expected.

On impulse, I play a version of that old Led Zeppelin tune, "Stairway to Heaven," not singing or anything, just playing the lead melody. The music sounds good out there in the dark with the light snow falling around us, layering a thin, pale dust over the gravel and asphalt of the alleyway. I get caught up playing and before I realize it, I'm plucking the last note on the last cord of that song. I can almost see the sweet sound hanging a moment in the cold air, like breath, before the final echo dissolves into the night.

I look over at Hoyt, who nods and says, "Real nice."

I shrug nonchalantly but I'm feeling proud. My ex-marine buddy doesn't often give out compliments.

"Yes sir-re." The guy takes off his baseball cap and runs stubby fingers through his greasy hair. "You sure know how to play that thing." Then the guy says he'll sell the guitar to me for a hundred dollars. He talks it up; telling me it's a relic, a one-of-a-kind antique. "Just a hundred dollars," he repeats with a pleading tone in his voice. "You know that's a good price."

It *is* a good price. This is a solid wood guitar with all birch construction and faux-binding lines along the body edge. It's in decent shape. The age gives it character.

All I have on me is forty-seven dollars. I ask my buddy if he has any money. He says he spent his last dollar on beer. I know Hoyt is lying but I also know he isn't about to lend me fifty-three dollars for a guitar. It doesn't matter to Hoyt how good that guitar sounds or feels in my hands. In Hoyt's mind there are better things to do with fifty-three dollars on a Saturday night than pitch in to buy an old beat-up guitar.

We're about to walk away when the guy calls me back. He sells me that guitar for the forty-seven dollars in my wallet. After the guy leaves, when he's driving away in his van, Hoyt says it looks to him like all that stuff in the van is stolen.

"You probably bought yourself some stolen property."

"Well, she's mine now." I rub the neck of the guitar, itching to play it again. The guitar still feels warm even though it's freezing in the parking lot.

"Yeah. Better hope you don't get charged with a felony or end up on Santa's naughty list." Hoyt spits in the snow. "All I'm telling you is that nothing good comes from buying shit out of the back of a van."

That's how I came into the possession of the Harmony.

I consider myself a professional musician, but I mostly just pick up a random gig here or there. I don't belong to a band. I have a regular job as a groundskeeper at the big hospital complex. I mow laws, prune hedges, shit like that. Even in winter they keep me on a steady paycheck to shovel ice or blow snow. You know, to keep sidewalks and the parking lot clear. So, I'm not anxious about money. I'm certainly not rich, but I pay my bills. What I am anxious about is losing my connection to the music scene. I barely get a couple gigs in a month and usually it's with a band that's temporarily lost a guitar player. The rhythm guitar player gets sick, so I fill in. The lead guitar player gets an attitude, so I take his place until things get worked out, the guy finds his humility, or the rest of the band decides to tolerate the bullshit arrogance. So, yeah, people know me in the local music scene, but I'm a drifter. I drift from one band to another. When it seems like I might land a permanent position, something happens to screw it up. Bad breaks, I guess.

Normally I play electric guitar. I have two. An Epiphone Les Paul standard with a classic mahogany body and a Fender

American Telecaster in a sweet metallic ice blue with a rose-wood neck. Both set me back a super cute chunk of change. But buying that forty-seven dollar Harmony stirs a strange ambition in me. I get to thinking maybe I'll put a little acoustic group together. Do something radically different. I decide to talk with this older woman I know, Laura Broadnaux, to see if she'd be interested. Laura sings vocals and plays a jazzy clarinet when she isn't styling someone's hair or rescuing feral cats. Laura is open to the idea of an acoustic group.

"I think there's real potential for an acoustic music group," she says. "Especially now with all the holiday parties. Some people don't want anything loud and electric at Christmas. Holidays are a time to visit with each other. People want to hear themselves talk. And not have to scream above the music. Yes, an acoustic group might work out nicely, but I think we'll need a third instrument for a cohesive sound."

She tells me to talk with Clifford Peach to see if I can get him on board.

Cliff plays upright bass when he isn't selling hardware or dealing with his family's issues. When I talk to him, he gets all excited about a three-piece band. Cliff says he thinks he can get us a party gig if we whip up a couple sets with a few Christmas tunes scattered in for a holiday theme. I'm not exactly thrilled to be playing a Christmas party, but it's a gig. We set a time to practice. Cliff says he'll coordinate with Laura.

When I get off the phone with Cliff, I pick up the old Harmony and start picking around on it. The next thing I know, I'm playing "Silent Night" and it's a beautiful thing to hear, full of longing and shit. Now I'm usually a hard rock kind of a guy. I like music with edge to it. I like it loud and aggressive. I don't normally do sweet and harmonic, but here

I am playing "Silent Night" and feeling emotional about it. It's at about this moment when I realize there's something odd about that old Harmony guitar.

Cliff, Laura, and I practice at my apartment because I don't have any kids or cats. My apartment is close to downtown in an old stone Victorian that didn't get torn down when all the other old houses did. Instead it was partitioned into eight different apartment units. My unit is on the third floor, no elevator. Cliff hates carrying his base up so many stairs but being up on the third floor gives my apartment good separation from the neighbors. I don't want to annoy them with our practice sessions. My landlord doesn't much care what I do as long as I pay my rent. So, we assemble at my place and get tuned up. The old Harmony is already in tune. I just sit around waiting for Laura and Cliff. When we finally get down to it, we decide to do original arrangements of familiar songs. That's easy. It's all stuff we know. It's more about choosing what to do than actually practicing it. Then, just messing around, we accidentally work up an original number. The song just spirals out of nowhere. I start playing this tune and Cliff starts jamming with me. Then Laura writes lyrics. I say she "writes," though she never puts any pencil to paper. Her lyrics are spontaneous. She just sings out emotions straight from the gut.

She calls the song "Cold Solstice." It's about a distant midwinter sun, long nights, and emotional starvation. A creepy tune but lovely in a brooding way. I'm proud of the guitar solo, which is powerful. I'm not bragging. These are seriously potent riffs for an acoustic guitar. After that one practice, I feel like we're ready. We sound good.

That week I go to work at my regular job and come home to find the guitar moved. I'm living alone. No girlfriend, no roommate, no cat. There's no logical reason for that guitar to get moved around in the apartment. Nothing else seems touched, not the Telecaster or the Les Paul. This happens more than once, so I start keeping the Harmony in a second-hand guitar case I shove under the couch. But then I come home to find the case open on the floor and the guitar leaning against the couch like somebody's been playing it.

Maybe I'm just forgetting to put it away.

Our gig is on Friday, December 2nd. It's a four hundred dollar gig. Even split three ways that's some nice pocket change. The party is at this swanky house in a gated neighborhood, a mansion decorated in that minimalist way rich people have of doing Christmas. Fresh evergreens and tiny twinkling white lights. The place smells like a pine forest. There's an open bar. Waiters walk around with trays of expensive party food, hors d'oeuvres with shrimp or meatballs on toothpicks.

We set up our gear and start playing. When our first set is over, there's maybe about seventy guests all decked out in swanky clothes. Suits, ties, and glittery cocktail dresses everywhere. After a short break, we start the second set, the one with the most holiday music, the stuff that hasn't been played to death on the radio. We open with a version of Pearl Jam's "Let Me Sleep," then Charles Brown's "Please Come Home for Christmas," and our adaptation of "Have Yourself a Merry Little Christmas." I have to give her some credit, Laura's pushing fifty and not much to look at, but she has some pipes on her and an expressive way of singing. She also plays a wicked clarinet. Laura has the talent for a genuine music career, but she's just not young or pretty enough for success. Besides, she's devoted to her cats. Cliff is just as talented. He's versatile on the upright bass. He can play jazz and classical, then turn around and slap out some dirty blues. But Cliff has his family life to deal with. There's the wife, three kids, and a forgetful father-in-law who lives with him. Of course there's his hardware store, too. It's the family business, so Cliff has to run it. Hardware before music.

I'm the only serious musician of our group, but I've had some tough breaks.

The guests at this fancy party become aware of us during that second set. These people are the type so preoccupied with collecting the luxuries of life that they don't notice much else. I'm surprised when they finally pause in their power conversations to listen. Now that we have their attention, our music seems to affect them. They start gathering closer in a cluster, their bragging mouths shut down and their eyes wistful. We aren't just ordinary musicians hired to make the pleasant background noise that hides awkward silences. Even their affluence-blunted souls can tell that our music is special.

We close the evening with "Silent Night." It's a version of the song no one has ever done. Cliff's playing has wistful jazz undertones and Laura is amazing. But I have to tell you, my old Harmony guitar is magic. Pure, sweet magic.

When the party is done, the host comes over, shakes our hands, pays us our money and a bunch of compliments. Some guests toss tips in my open guitar case, mostly ones and fives, but a few tens and twenties, too. Another guest comes up and books us for an event the very next night. I leave that mansion breathing the cold winter air, feeling truly rich. Not just loaded in my wallet but a soulful kind of rich.

"That was a good gig," Laura mumbles as we load our gear in Cliff's truck. It's an understatement. When she turns to look at me, her face is pale and there's a hollowness around her eyes. "You've been practicing."

Maybe I have been practicing. Maybe I've been getting so lost inside the music that I forget how much I've been playing, taking my old Harmony out of its case, leaving it on the couch, leaving it on the bed, leaving it leaning against a wall, or on the countertop in the kitchen. Calluses on my fingers are thicker than they've ever been. Instinctive riffs just come out of nowhere. I haven't touched either the Telecaster or the Les Paul since I brought that old Harmony into the apartment. I have this odd feeling that I've been disloyal. It's like I'm hooked on this potent new music, get stoned playing it, and the Telecaster thinks I need an intervention.

I'm not ready to sober up.

Cliff names our group 'The Holidaze.' When I complain about the asinine name and remark that Christmas will be over in a few short weeks, Cliff reminds me that there's always a holiday coming up that needs music. After Christmas and New Year's, there'll be Valentine's Day, Mardi Gras, St. Patrick's Day. There are celebrations all around the calendar. The marketing possibilities are endless. So, we become 'The Holidaze' and word gets out. 'The Holidaze' get booked for every Friday, Saturday, and Sunday left in December and a fair number of weeknights, too. We're booked for Christmas Eve and Christmas Day and then solidly through to New Year's Eve.

There's something dreamlike about all these gigs we play. Office parties, private parties, the special events at the mall, even the bar gigs… they all seem surreal. There's intensity to the seasonal stuff, a kind of violence. I don't mean the regular violence like a bar fight and a stiff upper cut to the face. Our music is layered with a dishonestly gentle, emotional kind of violence. It's the kind of brutality people never fully recover from once they've been doomed to experience it. Our audiences seem mesmerized listening to us and maybe a little depressed afterward, but they keep coming back for more. We've already got some fans. We're even celebrated in a music review in the local paper as a "seasonal sensation."

There's a picture of us next to the review with me in front playing the Harmony, Cliff on my right with his upright, and Laura on my left playing her clarinet. I'm looking pretty good. I could be a teenage girl's wet dream.

Christmas Eve after we play our bar gig, I come home to relax in the chair by my bedroom window. The moon is distant and pitiless, casting a mean light on the boxy fifties era apartment building across the street from my Victorian. The colorful Christmas decorations hanging in the windows of those apartments seem vulgar. A spotlight shines on the blow up vinyl Santa Claus leaning against the sign, "Pleasant Gardens Luxury Apartments. Vacancy. Inquire within." The Santa seems floppy and deflated. The manager needs to get the air pump out again before the Santa melts down to a miserable puddle of plastic. But then, maybe not. The season is nearly over.

Staring at the stupidity of Christmas decorations, I feel restless and maybe a little sad. Cliff is home with the wife and kids. Laura is with her cats. I'm alone. The Harmony is packed away in its case. The Telecaster and Les Paul hang on the living room wall, where they've been gathering dust these past few weeks. It's truly a silent night.

I yawn and eventually fall asleep sitting in my chair and looking out the window at odious Christmas lights.

I don't know how long I've been sleeping sitting upright in the chair, when suddenly I'm yanked to consciousness. My bedroom is dark. Neighbors must be in bed. Christmas lights are off. It's quiet. But then I think I hear somebody playing guitar. It's faint and seems to come from my living room. I get up and feel my way down the dark hall. There's a light on in the living room. The old Harmony's out of the case, sitting on the couch, nobody around it. But I hear music. It's a dreadful, malignant music and it comes from inside me. I pick up the Harmony and start playing. I don't know if I'm playing the guitar or if the guitar is playing me. My nerves vibrate. Calloused unseen fingers pluck away at my spirit, dragging me deep inside a cavernous, malevolent melody that's as satisfying as it is dreadful.

I wake when the phone rings.

It's morning. I'm on the couch with the Harmony in my lap. Weariness clouds my head like a hangover, though I haven't been drinking. Not much anyway. The phone keeps ringing but I'm slow to recover. When I'm finally awake enough to answer, it's Laura. She sounds haggard and nasal, like she's been crying.

"It's Cliff," she moans. "I just talked to Cliff 's wife. He went home last night after our gig. He kissed his sleeping kids, put the gifts under the tree, watched a bit of *It's a Wonderful Life* on the tube with his father-in-law, and then he went to bed. But sometime early on Christmas morning, before anyone else was up, Clifford walked outside the house barefoot and in his boxer shorts. He carried his bass with him and laid it out on the snow-covered driveway. His wife woke up when she heard him running over it in his truck, backing up and running over it again and again. She ran outside yelling at him, but it was like Cliff was possessed or something. She said there wasn't much left of that bass but strings and sawdust. Then Cliff took off, barreling down the icy road, skidding until his wife said it seemed like Cliff deliberately swerved and drove his truck straight into a telephone poll. She just stood in the front yard screaming, not knowing what to do. Cliff is at the hospital now in critical condition." Laura whispers over the phone. "Why would he do this?"

We have a gig scheduled for that afternoon. It's not a paying gig but a radio thing on the local college station. It was something Cliff lined up because he thought the exposure would be good. It's only a college station with students deejays, but it has a solid reputation and a following among sophisticated types who like alternative music. Some of the local music critics have described our sound as "alternative," because they don't know another category where we fit.

Laura wants to call the station and cancel.

"No. We can't cancel at the last minute."

"Play without Cliff?" Laura seems appalled.

"It's not like either of us have family we need to spend Christmas day with," I growl. I don't mean to sound hateful, but it comes out that way. I take a deep breath. "We can handle it," I say more gently. "We owe it to Cliff. He would want us to carry on."

It takes some persuasion on my part, but Laura finally agrees.

The kid who runs the radio show has the makings of a decent deejay. I listen to him on the drive to the college. He has a deep, resonant radio voice. He plays recorded music, talks knowledgeably about it, and begs listeners to call the station to make requests. He also promotes us.

"Stay tuned, because coming up at two o'clock and live in our studio, we'll have that popular new group, 'The Holidaze!'"

I wonder if anyone would be listening to a college radio station at two o'clock on Christmas Day. I also wonder what kind of pathetic college kid spends his winter break at school doing unpaid work that probably doesn't even earn him extra credit on his grades.

The campus is pretty much deserted when I arrive and walk across the snowy lawn to the student center. Laura waits for me in front of the building. She seems morose and I'm a little worried if she'll be able to perform up to standard. I remind her we're doing this for Cliff. Maybe guilt will inspire some musical genius. We're just a few seconds waiting, when through the glass doors I can see the kid deejay walking toward us. He's everything I predicted he might be. Fat and pimply. He also looks like he's more than a little stoned. He unlocks the door for us and ushers us across the empty lobby of the student center and into the area of the student radio station and the little studio. Microphones on boom arms have already been positioned in front of some stools for us. The kid seems to know what he's doing.

When we're about to do a quick sound check, Laura tells him, "We won't need that third setup. Our bass player had an accident this morning. He won't be coming."

Laura and I do the radio show without Cliff. We play all our "alternative" spins on traditional Christmas music and our original song, "Cold Solstice." My guitar and Laura's clarinet are a strong duo. In-between songs the kid deejay interviews us, asking about our background and our inspirations, shit like that.

We close the show with "Have Yourself A Merry Little Christmas." It's the bleakest interpretation of that song Laura has ever done. When she sings the lyrics, "From now on our troubles will be far away," you can hear from the sound of her voice that troubles are sharpening their teeth on Laura's psyche. As always, the old Harmony comes through. Every lick fills the room with a mind-blowing resonance. When the show's over, the young deejay seems impressed but a bit unhinged. When he blinks, tears crawl down his pimply cheeks. Then he turns his head away from me, embarrassed. It's satisfying to know that your music is powerful enough to make someone cry.

Laura and I leave the radio station and go our separate ways. I drive home from the deserted campus to spend the rest of Christmas at the apartment playing my old Harmony. The music is impulsive and angry but beautiful.

So beautiful.

While I'm alone playing my guitar, Laura goes home, puts away her clarinet, feeds her cats, and then deliberately overdoses on prescription painkillers. Laura's cousin finds her dead body the next morning when he arrives with his annual after-Christmas fruitcake. Laura left him a note begging him to please take care of her cats. I learn about Laura from the two detectives who appear at my apartment to question me.

"We usually see a spike in suicides this time of year, but it's odd to see a suicide and one attempted suicide who are both members of the same band," the older detective says. There's a delicately accusatory tone to his voice.

"Suicide does tend to come in clusters, especially around the holidays," the younger detective adds with more obvious sympathy. "It's called suicide contagion. This has been a bad year for it."

The detectives grill me about Laura and Cliff. They want to know if I saw any signs of depression, if there were unusual pressures on the band, if we were all getting along, if there was anything going on between Cliff and Laura. Shit like that. Before they leave, the younger detective cautions me to take care of myself.

So, there's nothing left for me to do but cancel all our remaining gigs. That's the official end of 'The Holidaze.' Our career is over just as we were about to do something big in the local music scene.

I suppose there isn't a guitar in this world that isn't haunted by its owner's disappointments, but the frustration I suffer with the old Harmony is profound. I brood around, playing tragic tunes. I barely sleep, but when I do, I have these weird, repetitive dreams. Not nightmares in the usual sense. I mean, it's not like goblins come screaming out from under the bed or anything. Nothing overtly scary. There's just a singular scraping noise, somebody moaning, and then music. I always wake up sweating and feeling a little sick.

Then I dream about the guitar player.

It's a lucid dream, a waking dream, but I have no control over it. I'm surprised to see that my guitar player is a woman. If I suspected that the old Harmony was haunted... and maybe I did have those suspicions... I never would have considered a woman as the ghost. I guess there's Bonnie Raitt and Joni Mitchell, but usually guitar players are men. The competent ones anyway. I always believed that if the old Harmony had a spiritual connection to a previous owner, it would be the superior attachment to some universally recognized musical talent and not the residue of some ghastly female spook. It's sobering to think that this woman is the spirit inside my remarkable guitar. But there she is, sitting on my couch, her head bent over the old Harmony just fingering away.

The woman is grim, gaunt, and dimly familiar. I can't imagine why she seems familiar or how I can possibly think I might know her. Long hair tangles around her shoulders like a cape. She wears an old fashioned dress, a drab long-sleeved thing buttoned high on her neck. The length of the dress extends to her feet. Its hem gathers around the scuffed toes of black shoes. This is garb from another era or the austere clothes of a woman held captive to oppressive religion. She plays music that has an emotional depth to it I can only describe as scary. It's like knives to the gullet but with soft melodic blades traveling seductively through the auditory canal before taking a deadly slice at my essence. Her long fingers strum, pluck, and chord with passion and precision.

I'll admit it, this gruesome woman has a dexterity and expertise I'll never achieve. I don't like to consider that the skills I've polished over these last few weeks might have originated with her.

When she looks up from the guitar, her rheumy eyes glare at me, the rims pink with grief and resentment. I remind myself that I'm dreaming but I'm also thinking that the music industry would never welcome this woman. Even though she's a chillingly capable player, there's nothing soft or sexy here. Never in a million years would the commercial music business make a place for the likes of her. Of course, I'm dreaming.

Suddenly the creature jumps up from the couch, howling. Her voice sounds like heavy fingernails pressing hard and dragging across the entire length of a guitar's low E-string. She rushes me, swinging the old Harmony in the air above her head. Her hair and the long dress billow around her like dark smoke. When she gets close, she smashes the guitar across my head like she's Pete Townshend. She batters me with it. Wood splinters and guitar strings fly in my face. Then she's all over me. I'm so stupefied, I can't defend myself. She bites. Her teeth are hot in my cheek. The smell of her is sharp, as if I'm breathing in splinters of cold glass. She claws me, screaming and ripping my shirt with long, calloused fingers. She stabs me with the broken neck of the old Harmony, using it like a knife. Then she kisses me. Her cold tongue in my mouth is putrid; triggers my gag reflex.

I think I fainted.

The next morning, I wake up on the floor, sore and bruised. I can see my reflection in the blue surface of the Telecaster. There are bite marks, cuts and scratches along my face and neck. But when I look away from the Telecaster, I see the Harmony sitting propped against a chair like nothing happened. The guitar was never smashed over my head, though the pain I'm feeling says differently. I limp to the bathroom and check myself in the mirror. It looks like I was mugged. My clothes are all bloody. The biggest bite mark on my cheek is pretty nasty like it might be infected. I'm bruised and scratched. I consider driving myself to the emergency room, but I don't know what I'll tell the doctors. If I tell them what really happened to me, they'll have me committed.

I take a shower instead, dry off, and lather on some antibiotic lotion and a few strategically placed Band-Aids.

When I'm clean and bandaged, I put the Harmony in its case. I hesitate to touch it, but I take a deep breath and quickly get the guitar in the case with the clasps shut tight. I decide to drive north to a pawnshop in the neighboring county. I'll get rid of her there.

The shopkeeper whistles when I walk inside the door. I know I look awful.

"You must have had an impressive night," the man says.

"Good times," I tell him grimly and get down to the business of pawning the Harmony. At first the shopkeeper doesn't seem too interested in an old acoustic guitar. He already has four hanging on the wall. When I open the case, his expression changes. He recognizes this guitar as a valuable antique, but he complains about the general wear. He takes it out of the case to inspect it. The way the shopkeeper handles the old Harmony I can tell he's a musician.

"Just strum it," I urge him.

The guy props his foot on a stool and puts the guitar over his knee. He plays a simple G chord. The old Harmony's in tune. It's eerie the way that guitar is always in tune. The man plays a song and it's an exquisite little melody. There's a look of wonder on his face at the guitar's pure tone. He plays another song, some sort of classical thing. The guy has talent.

I feel a little stab of envy watching him play. It's something like seeing an ex-girlfriend with her new lover, realizing just how beautiful she is and how deeply I'll miss her, but also knowing she'll gleefully rip out my heart if it gives her some satisfaction.

"Okay," the shopkeeper says finally. "I'll give you fifty for it with the case."

I agree. It's not about the money.

The guy is still plucking around on the old Harmony when I leave. After I close the pawnshop door, I can still hear her music from the sidewalk outside. It sounds vindictive, ominous, and yet so lovely. So lovely.

With grim resolve I get in my car and drive to a liquor store to buy a fifth of Jack Daniels. I go back to my apartment, pour a drink, and raise the glass to the Telecaster and the Les Paul.

"I promise. I'll never ignore you again for any bitch of an acoustic guitar." Then I thoroughly baste my throat in the heat of hard liquor. Before I take my Telecaster down from the wall to dust it off and rock out on something sunny and uplifting, I get that pawn ticket from my pocket and tear it up. I'll never go back to that pawnshop.

So, here I am.

It's been years. I survive. Back in '08 during the financial bad times, I had to sell the Telecaster and the Les Paul. I own a second hand Gibson Firebird now. I don't miss the Telecaster or the Les Paul as much as I thought I would. I don't even think about them so much. But that old Harmony still shadows me. I think about her all the time. Even in Spring, when skies are vivid blue and everything blooms with optimism, her sad music lingers. Something dark squeezes my chest. Those melodies of exquisite melancholy are rooted deep in a corner of my heart. I cannot dig them out. Maybe I don't really try. I feel her dark connection all year long. Spring. Summer. Fall. Winter. But the bond is most intense during winter months, especially in December, when the nights are long, the solstice is cold, and the soul is sincerely troubled.

THE MAIN EVENT

KELLY GOULD

I t had been a long day. Jack Androvsky sat on the metal bench in the poorly lit locker room. His reflection in the dirty mirror on the wall showed a tired old man. The white tank top was stained in several places and clung tightly around his ample belly. His black boots and red pants showed less signs of wear. This locker room belonged to Green Valley Mall Security but they let him use it to change into and out of his work uniform. Jack had also been showering there since his hot water heater at home stopped working. His stomach growled and he thought of Uncle Don's Pizzeria. Maybe tonight he would splurge and pick himself up a pepperoni and sausage pie on his way home.

He knew something felt wrong as soon as he saw Wayne Herbert, along with the two security guards on either side of him, enter the locker room. The Kid, as Jack thought of him, had to be at least thirty but still less than half of Jack's age. The Kid still had on his shirt and tie, but he had removed his jacket and rolled up his sleeves.

Wayne Herbert, aka The Kid, aka Jack's Boss, never worked this late.

"Hey there, Jack. How are you?" He leaned his back against the wall next to Jack's open locker. Folding his arms across his chest, he tried to appear casual and comfortable.

"Not bad, Mr. Herbert. You?"

"Well, actually," Herbert replied, "there's something I needed to talk to you about. Not going to beat around the bush. I'm really sorry about this Jack, but we're going to have to let you go."

"What do you mean?" Jack said. "It's only the sixteenth." Nine days until Christmas meant at least nine more days of employment, or so he had thought. He tried to keep himself calm and respectful, but he could feel his fists clenching tighter.

"I know, I know." Herbert held his hands out in front of him. "It's just that I wanted to tell you in person, you know, that we're going to go a different direction. Nothing against you, of course. I think you've been doing a fine job. It's just that, um, we've been getting complaints."

"Complaints? About me?" Jack didn't know the mall manager, Mr. Herbert, very well. He'd only started working at Green Valley this season. He picked up from their few interactions that Mr. Herbert possessed little spine and even less intelligence. Even now, as he was firing Jack, he wouldn't look the older man in the eye.

"Well, yes. Some of the parents-"

"What the hell kind of complaints would they have that I never heard over at McKenzie River?" The McKenzie River Outlet Mall had employed Jack each of the previous three Christmas seasons.

"As I was saying," said Herbert, clearly annoyed, "some of the parents don't think you fit their idea of what a Santa Claus should be."

"How's that?"

"Jack, how do I put this? We have a higher level of clientele here at Green Valley. Higher income families come here instead of places like McKenzie River. No offense."

Jack snorted and shook his head. Like those classy people didn't eat at the same fast food places and crap in the same toilets as the ones who shopped at the outlets.

Herbert ignored Jack and continued on. "Some of the comments were about your nose. It looks like it's been broken a time or two."

"Seven. Broke it seven times," Jack muttered.

"See? Santa doesn't have a broken nose. More importantly, parents who pay for Christmas photos don't want that kind of thing framed and hanging over the fireplace next to the stockings." Herbert spoke slowly, as though offering an explanation to a child.

"Can't help that, I guess. That there's over and done with." Jack thought back to the last time he broke it. He'd set it back into place himself, much to the disgust and admiration of the rookie referee. That had been one of the less severe injuries he sustained over more than twenty-five years in the ring. He'd been hurt far worse many times but the permanently bent and slightly off-center feature in the middle of his face stood out the most.

"It's not just the nose, Jack. Your demeanor isn't exactly kid friendly. You scare the little ones sometimes. Not your fault, it's just how you've always been, I'd bet. Maybe you could take some acting classes? Work on that, grow the beard out some more, get it to a better shade of white, and maybe we could talk about coming back next year."

Jack nodded slowly. Now he found he couldn't look the other man in the eye. Looking into the dirty mirror again, he had to admit that his beard could have been a little thicker. That, and his hair held more dirty gray than Santa white, only reinforced what Mr. Herbert said. His pride kept him from begging for the job no matter how much he needed it. He knew it wouldn't do any good. The boss had his mind made up.

"Ok, Mr. Herbert. If it's all right with you, could I have a few minutes to get cleaned up, pack up my stuff, you know?"

"Sure, Jack," Herbert said, nodding at the security guards. "Take your time. These guys will walk out with you when you're ready. If you could just leave the suit in here when you're done, that'd be great. It is mall property, after all."

"No problem, Mr. Herbert."

COURTNEY FELT NERVOUS BUT EXCITED. The Winter Ball had been just like she imagined it would be. The music, the decorations, and the mood lighting seemed like something out of a movie. Travis held her hand and told her how pretty she looked - he actually called her beautiful! - all night long. Then, on the dance floor, he kissed her as they rocked back and forth in each other's arms.

The kiss, tender and loving, made her heart soar; she would remember it for the rest of her life.

Now they walked in the damp grass together through the park a few miles from the West Irvington High School dance. She held his hand once again. In her other hand, she carried the heels she'd awkwardly worn to the dance. Travis had a blanket tucked under one arm. The air felt frigid; Travis draped his jacket over her shoulders, but she still shivered a bit.

They knew they shouldn't be here. The signs they passed told them the park hours ended hours before. The darkness aided them, allowing the couple to creep through unseen.

Only the basketball court, way over on the other side of the baseball field, provided any illumination that could possibly get them caught.

"You think here's good?" Travis asked.

Courtney nodded. "I think so." She'd turned sixteen a few months ago but she had a pretty good idea why her boyfriend had brought the blanket along with them. They had been together almost five months and she already knew she loved Travis. She didn't think their first time would be tonight but she had thought far enough ahead to wear her matching black bra and panties, just in case.

Travis spread the blanket out on the ground. The large blanket provided plenty of space for them both to sit comfortably. Courtney leaned against his shoulder and he put his arm around her.

"Damn," he said, "it's cloudy. I was hoping the stars would be out."

"It's still nice. Look, the moon's poking through over there. See?"

Travis looked down at her. "You're right. It is beautiful out here tonight."

"Oh, aren't you a smooth one," she said.

He leaned in and kissed her, bringing his other arm around to complete the embrace. Neither of them felt the chill of the night air anymore. Stars shone in their eyes when the kiss finally ended. The two teenagers sat, gazing at the moon.

"It's kind of spooky out here at night," Courtney said. "I'm glad it's not Halloween."

"It doesn't have to be Halloween to be spooky, you know. Christmas has plenty of scary stuff too."

"Oh yeah? Like what?"

"Well, there's Krampus. You've heard of him, right? He

goes around punishing the wicked children while Santa gives gifts to the good ones?"

"Uh-huh." She'd seen the movie but hadn't been impressed.

Travis continued, "But there's other ones. True stories of Christmas evil-doers and their dastardly deeds." He grinned at her. "If you're not careful, you might meet one of them, out and about during the holidays, searching for naughty children in need of punishment."

"Lucky for me I'm a good girl. If I do meet one, I won't have any problems."

"We'll see about that," Travis said and they both laughed.

He thought it couldn't get worse than being fired from his seasonal mall job by his weasel of a boss. Wrong.

Jack took his time, just like Mr. Herbert had told him he could. The water in the shower felt hot and someone had been kind enough to leave behind some soap and shampoo for him to "borrow."

Those two security guards never once poked their heads into the locker room to hurry him up. He knew they were still right outside, waiting. They hadn't looked too excited at the possibility of fighting with the old man to get him to leave. Jack figured he weighed in at three-eighty, more than both of them combined. He'd never been a small man and the passing years had added inches to his waist. Jack knew, though, just like those kids outside the locker room knew, that underneath the extra weight and deteriorated muscle existed enough iron to give them a fight they wouldn't forget.

Jack didn't have any fight left in him.

Ducking out of the *other* locker room exit, he successfully avoided Herbert's would-be escorts. He didn't want a fight, but he knew if they saw him still wearing the familiar red and white suit - complete with fuzzy hat - they would be forced to do something about it. Herbert should have got the suit back *before* he fired me, Jack thought. Consider it a severance package.

Jack went to where he parked his car, at the far end of the otherwise empty parking lot. Midnight approached and only security or custodial staff had the misfortune of being at the mall at such a late hour. He limped across the asphalt, cursing at Herbert under his breath for making him park so far away.

"Excuse me. Mr. Brody?" He was almost to his car when a voice from behind made him jump. Jack spun around clumsily, almost falling as his chronic knee pain flared to life. He winced but kept his feet under him.

He relaxed as he realized mall security hadn't followed him, coming to retrieve the stolen suit. He should have known better; only one group of people still called him by the name of Brody.

Wrestling fans.

This one stood at a respectful distance, wearing a thick jacket and blue jeans. The jacket looked warmer than the Santa suit Jack had on and he felt a momentary flash of jealousy. Next to him stood a boy who looked to be about fifteen or so. He shivered, wearing only a hoodie and a pair of sweatpants.

"Sorry to bother you, Mr. Brody. We're big fans."

Jack looked the pair over. This kind of thing still happened now and again, nostalgic fans looking to remember their childhood through rose-colored glasses, bringing their kids along to meet the Scourge of the Pacific Northwest. He could tell the dad had been a fan for a long time, his demeanor showed that, but the kid didn't look old enough to have been alive the last time Jack had stepped into a ring. He supposed the boy could've watched him on that video website the kids talked about. The internet age made it possible for a whole new generation to see his matches.

"This is my son, Rudy. I'm Neil." He offered his hand but Jack only stared at him until he lowered it. "Rudy, this is Grizzly Jack Brody."

Jack Androvsky, wrestling as Grizzly Jack Brody, had been a mainstay of the Pacific Northwest Wrestling Federation in the 80's and 90's. Standing at six-foot-three and weighing in at three-hundred-fifty pounds in his prime, Grizzly Jack fought his way all up and down the west coast. From Vancouver, British Columbia to Tijuana, Mexico, he earned his reputation - one grueling night at a time - as a tough as nails, take no shit, mean as a bull professional wrestler. With his perpetual scowl, he intimidated the men and scared the women and children in the crowd. Sometimes cheered, sometimes booed, Jack pushed himself to his limits every night, making sure everyone who bought a ticket to see him wrestle got their money's worth.

"Mr. Brody, I was hoping you'd sign my belt." Neil held out the leather belt adorned with metal plates. He had a silver sharpie in his other hand. He visibly relaxed, but only a little, when Jack took them from his hands.

"The first show I ever went to when I was a kid," said Neil, "was down at the Irvington Fairgrounds here in town." Jack quickly scrawled his signature on the brown leather as the man in front of him continued to reminisce. "Before the matches, you pulled that semi-truck in the parking lot a hundred feet all by yourself. The news was there, I was on my dad's shoulders. It was the most amazing thing I had ever seen."

Jack remembered Don Simmons, the promoter/owner of

PNWWF, talking him into doing that truck stunt. "Think of all the publicity," he'd said. "It'll definitely put butts in the seats." Some people still remembered it thirty years later.

The belt in his hands, he noticed, felt like a quality replica. Genuine leather, shined and stiff like it had never been worn, with thick silver metal plates adorning the strap, made him pause and admire the workmanship. He hadn't seen one of those in a long time. Stamped in the metal on it was PNWWF WORLD HEAVYWEIGHT CHAMPION. It was a championship Grizzly Jack never won. That same Don Simmons who had strapped him to an eight-ton truck had also told him that he wasn't exactly "championship material." Apparently, he made an excellent monster, the guy who could lift other men off of their feet and hurl them across the ring. He just wasn't good enough to hold the strap himself.

Jack handed the belt back. "There you go. Thanks for being a fan," he said begrudgingly. He felt a little bad for being such an asshole with the guy. He and his son had nothing to do with his shitty day.

"Thank *you*, Mr. Brody. Thank you for all the memories." Neil examined the signature with a smile on his face.

Jack nodded and turned back to his car. He only made it a couple of steps before Neil spoke up again.

"Mr. Brody, one last thing if you don't mind. Do you think you could roar for us? You know, like you used to in the ring?"

The older man narrowed his eyes and stood silent for a long moment.

"Fuck off, dude."

Not bothering to hang around to see the look on the man's face, Jack walked away and got into his car. Lowering himself into the old hatchback took a lot of time and emphasized the aching in his joints. His body no longer folded into the small car as easily as it used to, but he owned it free and clear. By the time he looked up, the autograph seeking duo were on the other side of the parking lot, trying to put distance between them and the grumpy old has-been.

He shook his head and muttered to himself as he turned the key in the ignition. Instead of the familiar rattle of the engine coming to life, he heard only a click, followed by silence. The battery died.

"This day just keeps getting better." The smart play, Jack knew immediately, would be to go after Neil and his boy. Surely, they had some sort of vehicle with jumper cables. If they couldn't give him a jump, they could give him a ride. For a ride, he would even be willing to give them the roar they had asked for.

Pride kept him from asking for their help. Jack thought his pride died a long time ago. Once upon a time, his mountainous ego prevented him from even imagining a scenario where he felt this sorry for himself. Other wrestlers feared and respected him. Grizzly Jack Brody kept the boys in the locker room in line. He knew how to enforce the unwritten rules in the ring in case anyone forgot.

Sometimes one of the guys would, either because they were too excited or too angry, get a little reckless. In wrestling, you depended on your opponent to not only make you look good, but also to help keep you safe. That relationship required trust. Taking liberties with the man across from you drastically increased the chances of someone getting hurt.

One of the ways Jack kept that from happening in his matches involved popping the other guy in the mouth for real. Not a full shot with his mammoth fists, but something hard enough to knock out the occasional tooth. That, along with a tersely worded, "Knock it the fuck off," kept things in check.

Jack only remembered one time that the unwritten rule

enforcement necessitated a stronger response. This rookie thought a little too much of himself. He started grandstanding during a tag team match, trying to make the other guys look bad. Jack took exception to this and decided to hand out some informal justice on the spot.

In front of more than three hundred fans, Grizzly Jack lifted the man off of his feet and into his finishing move, the Bear Hug. This time, though, he meant it. He locked his right thumb between his left index and middle fingers, creating an iron grip. Next, he slowly squeezed the breath from the other guy with his gigantic arms and whipped him around like a rag doll. The rookie flailed and bucked, powerless to break the hold. Jack held onto him until the man blacked out in his arms. Only then did he release the hold, letting the unconscious man fall limply to the canvas.

Jack's partner quickly pinned the fallen wrestler for the victory. Jack never saw the guy again. After the match the rookie just packed up and left, not even bothering with good-byes. Don Simmons never said a word to Jack about it. Everyone agreed that it took a special type of person to do this job.

Being the enforcer worked well for Grizzly Jack, but the injuries piled up, and getting older made it harder for him to bounce back the way he used to. His weight - always an issue - fluctuated wildly. Life on the road with too much beer, whiskey, and late night greasy spoons, took a toll. At one point, he wrestled a match at a weight closer to four-hundred pounds than his listed three-fifty.

Don Simmons had died and the PNWWF had gone out of business in the years before Jack wrestled his last match. He didn't expect it to be his last match as he laced up his boots and went over the details with his opponent for that night. Jimmy "Pretty Boy" Norton was new to the business but already on the fast track to being a Chosen One. He had the look: muscles seemingly chiseled from stone, long, flowing locks of blonde hair, and perfect teeth to go with a panty-dropping smile.

Jack knew this young man would be a main-eventer for whatever promotion he wrestled for. The young man knew it, too. Being a Chosen One gave him an unhealthy arrogance that got under Jack's skin.

The match called for Jack to lose, of course. At his age and mileage, the time-honored tradition of passing the torch to the next generation of wrestlers meant Jack's losses vastly outnumbered his victories. Putting the younger guys over - letting them gain a name for themselves by beating him - made them bigger stars while he still got to collect a paycheck doing what he loved to do.

Jimmy Norton had no respect for Jack's twenty-five years. He thought he had it all figured out and barely listened to the older wrestler's suggestions for the match.

When the bell rang, Jack led off with a monstrous-looking punch to the Pretty Boy's face. He made it his goal not to cause any damage but still make it look believable. Jack had done it thousands of times and no one did it better. This time, instead of rocking back with a grimace on his face, Norton looked him right in the eye, smirked, and flexed his muscles for the crowd. They ate it up, hooting and cheering; they worshiped Norton. Jack gritted his teeth.

"No-selling son of a bitch," he said under his breath.

The match continued. Jack let that first one go, but then it happened a second time, then a third. Every time Jack threw any kind of offensive strike at his opponent, he reacted as if he had been hit by a four-year old. He made Jack look weak on purpose.

They traded some stiffer shots as the match slowly turned

into a fight. Jack weighed his options and decided to risk his paycheck to teach this punk a lesson.

He grabbed Norton by his long hair, holding the man's head up while he delivered a mean right cross to his jaw. Jack smiled wickedly at his opponent's grunt of pain. Following the punch, Jack moved in closer, wrapped his massive arms around Norton, and began to squeeze. The crowd popped for the Bear Hug. His grip felt good, like always and he thought maybe, just maybe, this would teach the little shit some respect.

The two men, nose-to-nose in a combative embrace, stared daggers at each other. A smirk emerged on Norton's face as he began to resist Jack's hold. Slowly, the younger wrestler flexed; first his arms, then his chest. He arched his back and Jack felt his grip, ever so slightly, start to slip.

Jack bore down. Veins bulged in Norton's neck as he flexed muscles seemingly made of coiled steel. Jack grimaced and held on, straining to keep his opponent under control.

No way you're breaking out of this, he thought. *You'll remember the night you crossed Grizzly Jack, you little shit.*

"Over my dead body," Jack grunted.

Norton took a deep breath, something that should have been impossible. The smirk had become an arrogant sneer. He bent his elbows and pushed his arms outwards as Jack struggled to keep them trapped at his side.

"You fucked up, old man." With one last, great effort, Norton broke free. Jack felt it going but refused to believe until his own arms were thrown wide from the show of strength.

He tried to get his hands up to protect his face, but the punch landed. Norton hit him in the mouth with a quick jab, knocking out a tooth. A swift kick to his left leg put Jack down to his knees.

Holy shit, this guy can hit, he thought. *I might be in trouble.*

Holding his injured knee left his head wide open. Norton took advantage, raining blows down rapidly and with great satisfaction. Jack lost another tooth and felt his jaw break under the onslaught.

If it had been a boxing match, the referee would have stopped it. In professional wrestling, the referee couldn't stop the fight, even if he wanted to. The beating continued. Jack's vision swam in front of him as Norton threw a monster kick into his ribs, knocking him flat on his back.

Looking directly up at the lights in the rafters, Jack barely had a moment to register the pain from his freshly broken rib before Norton strutted into his blurry sight. The man stood over Jack, fist cocked back.

"You don't belong in my fucking ring." The haymaker connected with a sickening crack. Jack fell unconscious, his face covered with his own blood. Norton put his size-fourteen boot on his fallen opponent's chest in one last show of disrespect. With that, the referee counted one-two-three and Grizzly Jack Brody's wrestling career ended.

Jimmy Norton beat the pride out of Jack that night. Now, as he watched the two wrestling fans he had been so rude to walk away and disappear into the darkness, he knew he must have some dignity left. Enough, anyway, to keep from asking for their help.

"Shit," Jack said to the empty car. Sometimes it didn't pay to be a proud man.

"HANS TRAPP," said Travis as he reached into the jacket covering Courtney's shoulders, "was a German lord in the fifteenth-century." He pulled his wallet from the pocket and removed a dollar bill. "Hans was a rich man, filthy rich. He was also wicked and sinful down to his core. Legend has it that he was caught worshipping the Devil and got kicked out of the Church for it. Lost everything: land, title, money, family name."

Travis carefully folded the bill in half, then half again.

"This punishment did little to curb his evil deeds. Now penniless, he would stalk the forest, usually dressed as a scarecrow, searching for children who had wandered too far from the safety of their homes."

"Why a scarecrow?" Courtney asked.

"I don't know. To blend in? Because it's creepy as hell?"

"And why was he searching for kids? To kill them? Why? They didn't do anything to him."

Travis shrugged his shoulders. "He was evil, okay? That's why. Now let me finish my story."

Courtney rolled her eyes and giggled.

"One day, just as he was about to capture a young boy wandering alone in the forest, he was struck down by a bolt of lightning. Truly Divine justice."

He picked up one of Courtney's heels from the blanket. "Hey, what are you doing with that?" she objected. "They're my only pair."

"I'll show you. Relax," he said. Using the heel, he quickly dug a shallow hole in the grass next to them. "Since his death, Hans Trapp has been known to show up now and then, but only for children who didn't make the nice-list. Children who need to be punished."

"You mean like kids who trespass after the park is closed?"

"You shouldn't worry. Didn't you say you were a good girl?"

"I *am* a good girl."

Now it was Travis who rolled his eyes. "But sometimes, on certain nights near Christmas, he will appear if you know the right way to call him." Travis held the folded dollar bill up. "First, you need money. Coins work but bills work better. Hans was obsessed with money and that continues even into the afterlife."

He cupped the bill in both hands and held it out to Courtney.

"Next, it needs to be imbued with the breath of the innocent. Like the boy in the forest, he will seek out the blood of the virtuous."

Confused, Courtney frowned at him.

"Blow on the dollar," Travis explained.

"Oh." She closed her eyes and gently blew on the bill in his hands.

"Now we recite the Dirge of Suffering.

> *"Wicked is your way*
> *Tonight, and through the day*
> *Look upon us from your hellish tower*
> *And hasten here this very hour"*

When he finished, he placed the dollar bill into the hole and carefully covered it with the damp dirt.

Travis looked expectantly into the darkness surrounding them. Courtney followed his gaze even though she didn't know what they were looking for.

"Well, he didn't show. Maybe you are a good girl after all." Courtney playfully punched him in his arm as he laughed. "It *is* his job to punish the naughty kids. Good kids like us don't usually get to see him."

"You are such a dork," she said as she laid her head on his

chest.

"What, you've never heard this story?"

"Not one bit. Sounds like the old 'Bloody Mary in the mirror' urban legend."

"You need to get out more. I first heard about it in elementary school. Maybe it was just the cool kids who tried it." She hit him again for that one.

"Don't be mean," she said. "You *were* scoring boyfriend points tonight."

"Really? How many?"

She batted her eyes at him. He leaned over and kissed her. His hand drifted down to the top button of her dress. Eyes closed, he deftly undid two of the buttons before he moved down to kiss her neck.

"Mmmm." Courtney craned her neck to encourage him. "Now you're putting points back on the-" She opened her eyes and gasped. Travis, single-minded and unaware, kept up with his task at hand.

"Travis," she patted the back of his head frantically. Her tone changed as cold fear clutched her insides. She pushed his lips away from her skin. "Travis, stop. What is that over there, down by the trees? Is that a man watching us?"

THE EX-MALL SANTA limped slowly down the sidewalk in the general direction of his apartment. Cold crept into his joints, stiffening them painfully and making him wince with every step. Jack still fantasized about having a whole large Uncle Don's pizza all to himself. Hell yeah, he'd get extra cheese, he deserved it. Things changed quickly for him, though, and the deep dish he'd craved for days faded like a distant memory. For one thing, he headed away from Uncle Don's in the direction of his apartment. He would have driven there, even if it meant driving out of the way. The temperature dipped into the forties, warm for December but cold enough to avoid walking outside any more than necessary.

The loss of his job weighed on his mind, more pressing than the chill in the air. Jack's income being suddenly and drastically reduced meant that dinner would be mac and cheese; maybe he would add hot dogs if they hadn't gone bad.

Jack wore the stolen Santa suit. It kept him warmer than anything else he had with him. He pulled his hat as far down as he could get it, but the cold air bit at the parts of his ears still exposed to the winter weather. He was glad he decided to take the suit when he left the mall. He read once that ninety-percent of body heat escaped through your head and hands. At the rate he was moving, it would take him quite some time to get home, and he couldn't afford to give up any of that warmth.

The pain in his knee had spread to his hip like a blossom of agony slowly unfurling. His lower back tightened up and even the arch of his foot began to cramp. Jack knew he hadn't walked more than a mile straight since he retired from the ring. The two-plus miles remaining until he reached home discouraged him, especially since his body began betraying him after less than half that distance.

Jack's breath came in ragged wheezes. Bent over, hand on his knees, he stopped for a rest. He would have killed for a bench to sit on but he didn't see any nearby. The park he walked by held a brightly lit basketball court, but everything else appeared shrouded in darkness.

"What kind of park doesn't have a goddamn bench?"

Straightening back up, he grunted at the audible pop from his back and hip. Right on the heels of that, he heard the girl's piercing scream. To his right, from the darkness of the grassy field, he could make out the two shadowy figures running parallel to him. The girl screamed again as she stumbled and fell to the ground.

Jack's eyes slowly adjusted. The girl, looking out of place in her formal dress, was getting back up with the help of the boy with her.

"Where is he? Travis, do you see him?" she cried.

"C'mon, Courtney. Get up, get up!"

Confused but wary, his eyes searched for a threat. He couldn't see what they fled from, but he could hear the terror in their voices. He stepped off the sidewalk and slowly hustled over to investigate. The kids, Courtney and Travis, saw him coming.

"Oh, thank god," she said. "Do you have a phone? There's someone chasing us, he was right behind-" She pointed back toward the empty field where they ran from. A figure, shrouded in black and gray, stood motionless about fifty feet away, staring at them. In the near darkness, the man appeared to blend into the shadows, but Jack could make out the man's tattered clothing. He wore a dirty burlap hat along with a dark bandanna covering his face. Straw stuck out haphazardly from under his hat and out of his sleeves. His clothing - dark, wool pants and matching coat - hung loosely on his frame. The material, torn and frayed at his wrists and ankles, fluttered in the soft breeze. To Jack, he looked like some sort of homeless scarecrow.

"Hey!" Jack yelled. "Knock it off. Leave these kids alone."

Suddenly, the scarecrow-thing broke into a slow, shambling run. It kept its arms at its sides as it headed right for Jack and the teens. Courtney screamed and Travis let out a soft whimper before the two of them took off running again, leaving Jack behind.

Jack decided to put a stop to whatever this weirdo planned. The guy had a lot of nerve, playing dress-up and scaring people. He forgot his pain for a moment as righteous indignation took its place in his mind.

"You sure picked the wrong night to mess with me, freako." Jack moved forward to meet the approaching threat, but he had to side-step to block the scarecrow's path. He beelined past Jack, running in a direct line toward the escaping kids.

"What the hell is your problem?" Jack asked as he intercepted the scarecrow, grabbing him by his shoulders and twisting him around to face him. Immediately, his eyes watered and bile rose in his throat at the smell emanating from the thing. The overwhelming scent of rot and dirt washed over him, causing him to reel backward and lose his grip.

This close together, Jack could see the bandanna covering the scarecrow's face was made from the same kind of filthy burlap as its hat. Shadow obscured the rest of its face. The scarecrow took hold of Jack's collar and delivered a vicious head-butt to his jaw. He struggled to keep his wits as he tasted his own blood. Winding up like a pitcher throwing a fastball, Jack retaliated with a solid right cross that would have taken the head off of a normal man. The scarecrow's head whipped to the side with the impact. Jack screamed. He felt the bones in his hand break in several places. Punching the man felt like hitting a brick wall.

Jack expected to see the scarecrow's unconscious body fall to the ground. Instead, he watched as the thing recovered and stood silently in front of him. It reached up and adjusted the hat Jack had knocked askew. The scarecrow tilted its head, regarding Jack with unseen eyes. He didn't even see the blow coming. The backhand felt like a baseball bat to his face. The next thing he knew, he lay flat on his back in the damp grass, fighting to keep conscious. For the second time that night, he thought of Jimmy Norton and his last match. The moon lit the night sky; he preferred it to the lights in the rafters. The feeling of failure stung the same way.

Except this time, the finishing blow never fell. The scarecrow left him behind, refocusing on the fleeing couple. Jack had bought them a little time, and they used it to run for their car. The thing ran with a speed it hadn't displayed until now, closing the distance faster than Jack would have thought possible.

Despite its awkward gait, the creature's preternatural swiftness allowed it to circle around instead of pursuing its prey directly. Jack saw what it planned to do. The scarecrow moved to block them from getting to their vehicle.

Pushing himself up with his one good hand and sheer willpower, Jack got first to his knees, then his feet. "Not on my watch, you don't."

Jack ran slowly and gracelessly. His hand, knee, and hip throbbed with every plodding stride. Courtney screamed up ahead as the scarecrow successfully stopped their escape, forcing them to retreat towards the basketball court. Her scream urged him on, even as his body screamed at him for relief.

Travis tripped and fell hard underneath one of the hoops. The scarecrow, moving slower now, stalked them from the other side of the court.

"Run, Courtney. Leave me," he shouted. She dropped to her knees and threw her arms around him. They looked up helplessly at their approaching doom.

A thunderous roar shook the night and washed over the

basketball court. The scarecrow stopped his advance and looked for the source. Grizzly Jack Brody stepped onto the court, head held high and limping like an injured monarch. He took his place at the foul line, facing the creature and protecting the couple. Staring icily at his opponent across the empty space, he removed his fur-trimmed red jacket and let it fall to ground behind him. Even in just his tank top, he didn't notice the cold. Not anymore. Jack focused solely on the thing in front of him.

"Not on my watch, asshole." He said it again like a mantra. "You got one chance to walk away."

Without a sound, the scarecrow lurched forward. It held its arms out like it intended a malevolent hug. Unfazed and with a steely dedication, Jack moved towards center-court to meet it.

When they collided, the scarecrow grabbed Jack around his throat with both hands. The grip tightened, and he immediately felt the effects of the restricted blood flow. Jack shot his hands up and between the creature's arms, pushing them apart and breaking the choke-hold. He followed that up by reaching around to the back of his opponent's head and pulling it down to his chest. Supporting his weight with his one good leg, Jack delivered a violent knee strike to the thing's torso. Sharp, fresh agony exploded through his leg. With a grunt, he fought through it and drove his knee into it two more times, driving it backwards.

Jack smirked as a high-pitched whine issued from the scarecrow. "You feel that one? Yeah, you did. There's more where that came from."

The wrestler saw the punch coming this time. He braced himself and managed to turn just enough to avoid getting hit straight on. Even the glancing blow to the hardest part of his forehead stunned him for a second and darkened his vision.

With the scarecrow so close, Jack made his move. He wrapped both arms around the thing and squeezed with every ounce of determination he had left. The broken bones in his right hand ground together as he threaded his thumb through the fingers on the opposite hand, locking the hold tight.

The creature began to thrash and strain, trying to free itself. Keeping it trapped in the Bear Hug required all of Jack's remaining strength and concentration. No backing out now, he thought. If I can't finish this fast, it's the end. Not just for me, but for those kids, too. He felt his energy waning. The shooting pain from his hand was the only thing keeping him from passing out from exhaustion. A feeling of light-headedness came over him, and he tightened his grip a little more, creating searing waves of agony that cleared his head and kept him in the fight.

He recognized the creeping heaviness slowly permeating his chest. The heart attack five years ago had started the same way. Not a blinding burst of hurt but rather a more subtle numbness and loss of breath. Jack knew he had to end this fast.

Pushing his own feet apart and widening his stance gave Jack more leverage while putting his head against the scarecrow's chest at the same time. He struggled to maintain the Bear Hug against the monster's attempts to break out. Now in position, he used his legs like pistons, propelling himself over and through his opponent. The scarecrow, off-balance and unprepared for the sudden momentum shift, stumbled as Jack pushed forward.

The combatants fell to the asphalt together. Jack's hands, still secured behind the scarecrow's back, hit the ground first, followed an instant later by the crushing weight of the two bodies. The whine of pain from the monster became a scream. Jack's grimace became a mask of blood and desperation. He felt himself fading. Only his own weight, pinning his arms beneath his opponent, kept the thing from escaping.

"Ohmygodohmygodohmygod," Travis repeated as he clung to Courtney.

Wide-eyed, she hugged her injured boyfriend's head against her chest. The scarecrow's screams continued to get louder.

"What is that?" Courtney asked. In the midst of the fight that potentially held all of their lives in the balance, she noticed it first. Thin, yellow smoke began to pour from the scarecrow. What began as a trickle quickly became a flood. The smoke flowed from its sleeves and pant legs. The yellow cloud obscured the two fighters, hiding them from view and dampening the sound of screaming scarecrow.

The scream faded, eventually disappearing into nothingness. Courtney held her breath and Travis dug his fingernails into her arm. Their hearts pounded. "Is it over?" he said.

The cloud hung in the air, dissipating at its own pace, keeping the couple in agonizing suspense. Peering intently, they both saw the image of the victor emerge.

"Oh, god, he's dead." They both stood, Courtney supporting Travis and his hurt ankle. Jack lay on his stomach with his arms still hidden beneath his body. The scarecrow disappeared without a trace. "Travis, he's not breathing."

Tentatively, the teens approached the fallen fighter. Courtney reached out to touch him, maybe check for a pulse. They both jumped as a low growl, followed by a severe coughing fit, came from the man. The hacking and spitting went on long enough to make Courtney think the man would pass out on them again.

"Holy shit," Jack said after he finished coughing up more yellow phlegm than he would have thought one body could produce. He rolled over to his back and grabbed his left arm.

The numbness had spread down to his fingertips. Jesus Christ, he thought, I've been in car wrecks and felt better than I do now. Travis and Courtney stood over him, still concerned.

"Hey, guys," said Jack in a gravelly voice, "you got a car, right?" The teens both nodded. "Well, I might need some help to get to it but do you think I could get a ride to the ER? I'm in a bit of a bad way right now."

Relieved, Courtney gave a nervous laugh and pointed. "Of course. It's right over there. We'll help you up."

It took several dozen grunts and muttered curses, but Jack got himself to his feet. The heaviness in his chest increased. He had to speak slowly in between labored breaths.

"Uncle Don's Pizzeria is on the way to the hospital. If you spot me money for a pie, I'll pay you back. I'd kill for a pep and sausage right now."

THE BEANFEAST

SINEAD MCCABE

Oliver, Paula and little Daniel Ormerod drove up from London on Christmas Eve to spend their first real English country Christmas at Oliver's family farm. Roads bright with sodium orange and crowded with seasonal traffic dwindled into tracks slick with black ice, so dark and quiet that Daniel fell silent in sympathy. When Oliver finally pulled up at his parents' farmhouse, the night sparkled with frost. Daniel sat tongue-tied with awe as Oliver helped him from the car; the sight of the old farmhouse nestled into the dark tree-furred hollow and the soft noises of animals from the nearby yards transfixed him.

The huge kitchen felt so warm and crowded and heavy with scents in contrast that the three of them swayed, a little faint, as they walked in. Every picture frame, wooden beam or bannister had been trimmed with gleaming holly and ivy. Fairy lights glimmered among the dark green leaves. Tinsel glittered on every surface, even framing family photos. Steam richly-scented with roasting meat and pudding, and the babble of happy chatter, rose all around them. Daniel was picked up and kissed by each relative in turn, while Paula smiled in the background. Oliver and his older brother Simon, a very large and stocky man who strove to take up at least half of the space in any room, confronted one another with a white-knuckled handshake.

"So how's your lot doing?" Oliver smiled with his mouth only.

"Oh, doing good, mate. Doing good." Simon's hand was much bigger, and he bore down on his brother's fingers, grinding the bones.

"Great. Isn't that great," said Oliver, as he flicked his white hand out of Simon's grip.

Oliver didn't like Simon, never had. Paula didn't like Simon either. He drank too much, he boasted too loudly. He undressed every woman he met with his eyes, while his quiet and colourless wife Veronica kept her eyes on the floor.

Veronica greeted Paula now with a damp kiss and an "Oh! Hasn't Danny got big!"

"Paula, my sweet, you're finally here. It's a dream to have you all here at Christmastide." Oli's mother Cathleen bore down on her, round and cheery as one of her own puddings.

Paula blinked. *Had Cathleen said Christmastide, really? Truly they were not in Kansas anymore, or London anyway.*

Cathleen beamed, rubbing her arms with hands that felt like sandpaper.

Time and tide wait for no man, Paula thought, *maybe she just said Christmastime and I need to stop being such a city brat and deal with the way people talk here. Oli used to have this accent, I bet, he must have worked hard to lose it.*

Veronica said something about schools and their holidays. Paula smiled distractedly and watched as her husband and his brother engaged in a hand crushing competition, under the guise of brotherly love.

"Mum, look!" Daniel was pointing out of the window, not down at the twinkling festival of light in the long and winding valley, but up the looming hill above. The topmost crags glowed with snow and dozens of bonfires dotted the crown.

"Wow. Look at that, Oli!" Paula peered from the window at the red flowers blooming in the black and white night.

"Yeah, it's a local tradition. Every Christmas. We'll go up later and start our own bonfire, eh Dan?"

"What, like Bonfire Night?" asked Paula, feeling timid.

Cathy beamed at her again. "Exactly like that, but no ghoulish effigies on the fire; no, these are happy fires, Daniel!"

"I like fires on Christmastime," announced Daniel.

"Me too," Paula said, leaning down to smooth his hair.

"Mum?" Daniel began to squirm under her touch, bouncing from foot to foot.

"What, love?" said Paula, with a soft restraining hand on his shoulder.

"I really really need a wee."

Oli's mother Cathleen swung Daniel up into her big arms and carried him off to the bathroom. Her husband Michael sat silently smoking a pipe by the great black range. On the four occasions Paula had met him, he'd uttered exactly eight words to her; "Congrats, Paula" (twice, once on her wedding day and once when they came to meet Daniel for the first time) and "Pass that corkscrew there." Oli said he had never been any different. Paula once trained as a therapist, although she never practiced, and she suggested a deep-rooted past trauma, still resonating on a primal level through her father-in-law. Oli considered it for a while, and then said, with apology in his eyes, "It might be, love, but I honestly think he just doesn't like talking to people very much."

"Shall we go through?" Simon boomed over the sounds of homecoming, with a regal wave in the direction of his mother's living room as though the king of his own private castle. Veronica trailed him, head bowed, eyes roaming as she fingered her lace collar.

"So," Oli collapsed into a velvety armchair and Paula politely accepted a glass of Veronica's sickly eggnog, perching on the arm at his side, "how's it been, bruv?"

"Best year of my life, Oliphant," grinned Simon, "best year of my life. Got not one but three new contracts, ka-ching! New conservatory on the house – oh yeah. Two weeks in the Seychelles, don't mind if I do!" He was counting off his good fortune on his hairy, sausagey fingers. "Kiddies at private school now, they'll be heading for Oxbridge one day!"

Paula caught Oli's eye and had to look away, biting back the giggles. Simon and Veronica had twins, drab little things as dull as their mother. Simon was usually reduced to boasting about their wins at the Egg-and-Spoon race.

"But – where are they, Veronica?" Paula turned with reluctance to look at Veronica, who was staring at her own glass, eyes darting to Simon and then back again.

"Oh- they're with my parents, Simon thought it would be best -"

"It was her dad, the old swine, promised them a trip to Disneyland if they went to Gloucester this Christmas, bribing them, you know. Well, they wanted the trip and I want to see the old swine pay for something for once. Rather them than me anyway, listening to the old fool's stupid jokes for a week,"

Paula watched Veronica carefully, noting the red rise in her cheeks and the feeble little fist she half-clutched, listening to her husband run down her father. Paula felt a twinge of unease; she'd never seen Veronica separated from her kids before. Veronica was what Oli called a drone parent, like a helicopter, but less fun.

Had anything happened to the kids? Paula realized, dully, that if Simon turned out to have harmed them in some way, it wouldn't surprise her, and his wife would never stand up to him about it.

"Pay for something, *for once?*" Oli was saying, his colour high, and Paula gave herself a mental slap and forced herself back into the room. "I seem to recall Veronica's dad made the down payment on your first house-"

"Oh that, no, he wanted to. It was a wedding present," trilled Veronica with an idiotic giggle, and Simon turned toward her and scowled.

"And didn't he in fact finance your business for the first three years?" Oli went on, despite Paula pinching his back where they couldn't see.

"No, Oliver, no he bloody didn't, I don't know where you even got that-"

"Oh I think he did-" Oli laughed, big and broad, but the bitter edge to the laughter made Paula wince. She could see no good humour in it all. Oli and his brother had always fought, but this was more, this was like stags clashing antlers, driving in, crashing heads-

"And how's your business then Oli? Oh right I forgot, it folded after a year, dumbest idea for a business I ever heard, what a joke-"

Oli stood up. He actually stood up, like a man in a pub who wants to take it outside.Paula simply gawked, while Simon sat stolid in the biggest chair in the room, a red velour throne, and sneered at his brother. Then Cathy walked in with Daniel in her arms, and she pointed a large rough finger at each of her sons in turn.

"There'll be no quarrels," she said, "at Christmastide. Bad

enough you didn't even bring your children to your family, Simon. Oli, sit down and let me put Daniel in your lap. Come on! Paula, you'll be needing a proper drink." She poured Paula a generous tot of golden rum from the '70s bar in the corner of the great dim room while Veronica flushed, her eggnog disparaged. "Daniel, ask your dad about the day the pig escaped."

"There's a Christmas fire inside, too!" Daniel pointed, dimpling with pleasure, "Daddy, tell me about a pigiscape."

Paula kept her eyes on Simon, who kept his stone cold eyes fixed on the fire and his knuckles white and tight around his glass. Oli seemed like himself again, though.

A commotion in the hall and Oli's sister Melissa, husband Mustafa and daughter Shahnaz arrived bearing shining gifts for under the tree, more laughter and greetings.

"Uncle Olipants!" shrieked Shahnaz, and jumped into Oli's waiting arms.

"Shahnazadingdong!" Oli lifted her high in the air to make her giggle. Paula smiled and shook hands all round, while Shahnaz danced Daniel in circles, both twinkling in the firelight like Christmas-card kids.

"I like Nanna's toilet, Shahnaz. It's got ships in it. Mum can we get toilet ships?"

She smiled for real and swung him up high. "Twenty ships if you like!"

"Thirty!" chimed in Oli.

"Thirty-two!" shouted Shahnaz.

"Forty-nine," decided Daniel.

"Dinnertime," laughed Cathy, and everybody cheered. Even Simon.

It was almost a relief, after dinner, to escape the stifling heat and meat-fragranced steam of the big farmhouse kitchen, into the dead black of the night sparkling with frosty stars, to drive in convoy up the massive slope of the hill in convoy and start their own bonfire.

Paula, Oli and Daniel drove behind Simon's enormous SUV.

"Just help me not kill him Paula. That's all I ask."

Paula tucked Daniel's hair under his red hat. "It's three days. Focus on that. Don't let him under your skin, you know exactly what he's like. Three days of weird Christmas bonfires and loud, obnoxious boasting."

"I mean did you hear him? Oxbridge? He's such a pr-"

"Don't listen to Daddy, darling. Look at the Christmas lights! Look! A fairy! Yeah I know. He's hideous. And if he tries to rub our faces in his remodelled bathroom one more time, I'll drown him in his wife's disgusting eggnog. But we have got to play nice here. Do you think Sonia and Mark are really at their in-laws?"

"Yeah, I suppose they must be. Why not?"

"Well you know how Simon is about Veronica's family, it's always been all about your family – and Daniel coming up for the first time, too, you'd think- woah! That was a big rut."

"Sorry. Yeah, the ground's hard-frozen, it gets like iron."

"Did you really do this every Christmas when you were kids?"

"Twelve nights, finishing on Christmas Day," Oli nodded.

"Why?"

"Tradition. You know what it's like around country places like this. Everyone's got to wear one purple sock and drive a tractor into a wall on their birthday and nobody has a clue why. It's traditional. Anyway, I don't mind this one so much. It's pretty, seeing the fires at night from your bedroom window when you're nine."

"Didn't you go up too? Help build the fire?"

"Yeah, sometimes. Any night except Christmas Day itself. Kids aren't allowed up on the last night, strictly adults only."

"Why?"

"No idea."

"But what about church? Didn't you go to church on Christmas Day?"

"Nah. We've never been a church-going family. Traditions, that's what Mum and Dad are all about. Okay, here's our family ledge!"

"Oli. Nobody has a family ledge. It's not a thing that is done."

Nevertheless, they hopped out and Daniel let out a little shriek at the cold, the wind like ice-water down the neck, frost glittering on every leaf, rock and branch. Paula tucked another blanket around him as he goggled up at the ice-shard stars, eyes wide with wonderment.

"Little city boy," she whispered into his muffled neck. They turned together to look at the Christmas lights in the valley, a broken rainbow far below their feet. The lights seemed inexpressibly cosy and human in the howling blackness of the deep midwinter night. Simon issued orders at the top of his lungs while Oliver argued back at the top of his Veronica scurried to do whatever she was ordered while Melissa and Mustafa played around like children. Mr and Mrs Ormerod, sullen and cheerful respectively, ignoring their offspring entirely, cut and dragged branches into a rising cone-shape in their own sweet time and way.

Paula held Daniel close, listening to the boom and rush of the fir trees in the wind, which smelled of snow and endless winter. Idly, she fingered a little arrangement of mistletoe hanging in the tree over her head, thinking it was a serendipitous natural phenomenon. Then she saw several other such arrangements. She realized someone had made these little mistletoe antlers, and attached them to acorns like tiny heads.

"Hey Cathleen! Did you make these?" she called.

"I certainly did," Cathleen yelled back, hauling a petrol can from the back of her truck. "Why, don't you decorate trees at Christmas down in London, love?" Cathleen chuckled at her own joke.

Paula didn't find the little ornaments funny. She'd never seen anything like them- they made her uneasy all over again. She felt too aware of the black hole of forest behind her back, deep and unknown, surging and swaying in the wind. Her back prickled; she felt watched. She turned and stared behind her. She could see nothing but the ghostly pale branches waving a foot from her head and then, only the dark.

A whoosh of flame made Daniel jump and then clap as the welcome, crackling heat climbed. Paula turned with a glad smile to the light, and she clapped too. Oli came over, smelling like cold smoke, and put his arms around them both as his family joined hands and began to skip around the fire, self-conscious and snickering at first, but then with more abandon.

"Mum! I wanna go too!" Daniel wriggled to get down and Paula glanced at Oli.

"Yeah, go on, it's fine. I used to do it all the time. Look, Shahnaz is dancing too."

Daniel ran to grab the hand of his cousin, and together they pranced about the rising flame, roaring with laughter.

"Do you wanna dance too?" Paula shivered in her husband's arms.

"Nah, I haven't done that for years," Oli kissed the top of her head and watched his mother and sister, fondly. They sang, all except Mustafa, who didn't know the words yet, but danced extra wildly in the freezing air.

"What are they singing, Oli?"

Oli paused for a moment, listening, remembering. "Oh yeah -hold on- "*Winter be long, but one day be done. Winter be long, but one day comes the sun. Winter be hard, but one day shall fall. Winter be death, but death shall not reign over all.*"

Paula's shiver became a shudder. "Very... er.... Well, less Deck the Halls and more Wicker Man, if I'm honest."

Oli laughed. "It's a really old song, yeah. Listen to Simon roar it out! Like a rugby chant."

"Not as loud as he roared about his three new contracts," murmured Paula. "*Best year of my life! Best year of my life!*"

Oli sighed. "Yeah. Still, next year it'll be our turn. I feel it. Then come Christmas we'll be stuffing our best year up his fat arse. What do you say?"

"I say aye," said Paula, and turned up her face for a kiss. Oli's lips were ice cold, and his red hair glowed in the firelight.

"I like dancing with the fire, mum," shouted a voice that tumbled into her leg. "Can I keep this nissletoe man?"

"Er- best not, Big Dan," Oli took it from him gently. "Best leave it on the tree. It's part of the magic."

"What magic?"

"The magic to make Santa come!"

Daniel's eyes and mouth were three big O's of awed belief. He ran to put the "nissletoe" back where he found it.

The fire flared and spat, and then began to die. The dancing dissolved into a panting, giggling, wheezing ring of figures, orange and black, still holding hands in a ring around the fading flames. Off to the side, Paula shivered and dug her hands deeper in her pockets, stamped her boots and winced at the pain in her feet, rememberg for a moment that yesterday she walked in the heaving crowds and sparkling glare of Regent Street. The image flared in her mind her brain like a faraway dream as the fire fell into embers. They stood alone again in the icy dark, with the strange distant screams of hunting and dying animals flying in the black wind past their frozen ears. For a moment, a silence fell, which Simon inevitably broke with a roar.

"Brandy! Rum! And Mum's mince pies!"

"Ooh, I wanna mince pie, I'm starving!" shouted Shahnaz, and they began to stumble back to their cars. Michael fell behind the others as he methodically stamped the last embers to death, muttering something rhythmic as warmth died under his driving heels.

"What you got there, Daniel?" Paula asked. Daniel was shoving the last of his mince pie into his mouth with the flat of one hand, and holding a case like an old Etch A Sketch in the other. His gaze flicked to hers for a moment, but he was too entranced by his find to answer her. Paula leaned over him and squinted at the screen. Daniel had found a rolling diorama which moved when you turned the heavy black knobs at the bottom.

"Oh, that was my grandma's," called Cathy from her armchair where she sat with Shahnaz on her knee, "He found it in the airing cupboard, didn't you love? Haven't seen that thing in years."

Daniel nodded again, but still couldn't tear his eyes from the thing; he reached the end and wound it back to watch it again. Paula watched it with him, angling her head so the reflections of the fairy lights didn't obscure the screen. As the painted woodland unscrolled, faded and cracked, a company of men and women with big smiles and rosy cheeks set out through the summer forest. Animals flashed by as Daniel turned the knobs faster; a fox, a little stoat, a badger, a boar, two stags locked in battle, their antlers wild with strings of moss. The company disappeared and reappeared, and then a shape appeared ahead of them. They chased it into a forest buried under deep snow.

Paula stirred on the arm of the chair, unsettled; this was no animal she recognised, though it went on all fours. It was just a hunched, dark shape; another boar? No, the thin leg thrust out at the stiff unnatural angle of an 18th century painting was too thin and pale for a boar, it looked like a skeletally thin human limb. The image turned too quickly for Paula to see, and the gleaming leaves of holly flashed colours onto the screen, obscuring details. All she saw were the layers of beech-foliage growing darker and more secret as the painted night fell and the painted moon rose. The merry band of – hunters? Hide and seek players? - went around and around through after the running shape, the distance closing every time, until the final scene showed… Paula blinked. There was no sign of the running shape. Now in the cracked and faded black of painted night, a ring of chuckling, rosy-cheeked folk danced in a ring about a bonfire in the woods. The End.

A hard shiver went through Paula then, and she gently took the thing from Daniel, who relinquished it yawning, glancing up to see Oli watching them both from under his lashes. He stared for a moment longer, and then smiled. She smiled back. She waved the thing at him.

"Did you used to play with this as a kid, too?" Oli consid-ered, his eyes still lost under the shadow of his lashes.

"I don't think I bothered with it much," he said, "but I remember Melissa used to really like it." Paula smiled again and turned to her son.

"Okay little man, it's time for beddybyes. It's sooo late," she said, picking him up. He was too sleepy and full of pie to offer even a token protest.

She carried him up to bed in the smallest room that he would share with Shahnaz. She thought he might be nervous about the room, cloaked in holly and ivy like all the others, or disturbed by the diorama and the weird echo it contained from their own evening, but all he wanted to do was look for Santa out of the window, and went peaceably to bed when he began to shiver. Paula stared for a moment from the diamond-paned, deep-set old window. The lights in the valley seemed to shiver in the cold night. The wind had dropped, but it was colder than earlier. Staring up too long at the sky, she suddenly recoiled with a gasp. Luckily there was nobody from whom to hide her irrational terror. Daniel snored peacefully in his bed.

Not too long after she went back downstairs, Paula made her excuses and turned in herself, leaving the bedside lamp on. *Oli will need it when he comes up. That's why I'm leaving it on. Not because I'm scared.*

In the night, she struggled up through layers of heavy sleep, pulled out of her dreams by strange sounds in the hillside woods outside her window. In the dark and cold of the smaller spare room she lay, with a rime of fear over her prickling skin, feeling very solemn, very small, vulnerable as a child. She wanted badly to put her head under the pillow and will herself back to sleep, as she did when she woke up on Christmas Eve as a child, afraid to see Santa. If you looked at Santa, he wouldn't give you toys, but would take you back to the endless winter of the North Pole, where you'd have to work in his toyshop and stay a kid forever.

What are these thoughts going through your head? Are

you afraid of Santa, Paula? Thirty three years old with a child in the next room and lying here not daring to breathe because of Santa?

No, she didn't fear Santa. She feared those sounds. The unearthly faint squeals in the distance and the distant yelling and crashing in the underbrush terrified her. Someone laughed and whooped. She was sure it was Simon.

What time is it? 2.50a.m. What the hell? How drunk are they, and who is out there? Everyone except she and ..... Paula turned her neck, hearing it crack with tension in the dark, but she already knew that the bed was empty. She'd left Oli downstairs among the holly and the ivy, drinking and arguing. She'd thought he would shortly follow.

Paula realised that she was probably the only adult left in the house and the thought horrified her. Then she remembered Mustafa, who didn't drink and had retired before she had. She felt weak with relief. Just family then. But it sounded like more, so many more, there had to be at least ten people shouting out there. The sounds of branches and bracken crashing and crunching under blundering feet, and whoops and hollers and wild squealing, were getting nearer every minute.

Slashes of silver light on the bedroom ceiling flew and vanished, flew and vanished. She almost screamed at the first flash then realized it was torches from the party outside.

Doing... what? Paula asked herself. *Chasing something? What is it? What screams like that, like nothing human?* Waves of cold nausea rolled through her. She willed herself to get up, open the curtains, look. Like a grown-up.

She did not move.

The screams became wilder, frantic with fear.

And then there was a howl and a thud and the screaming stuttered, shuddered, and stopped.

The deep, slow, satisfied hum of many united voices which followed carried all too clearly on the frosty air. It made her bones feel sick.

Shaking so that she almost fell, Paula crawled from the bed and crept to the window. The party returned, dressed in darkness, breathing fast and deep. She counted fifteen or so. Not just family then, she had known it; a neighbourhood affair, though she spotted Simon, laughing, and Oli, who had his head down. Michael Ormerod, Oli's sullen and silent father, headed the pack, and he carried a dripping sack. Paula's heart flew into a gallop.

Why didn't Oli wake me, or tell me this was going to happen? Why are there so many of them, what were they doing? What the hell is in that bag?

In the morning she woke to Daniel bouncing on her back and shrieking with joy, his Christmas stocking landing on Oli's groaning face. The house already smelled like roasting meat and Christmas spice, cloves and sweet ginger and cinnamon. Paula oohed and cooed alone over Daniel's gifts because Oli was still groaning, half-asleep.

Paula glanced over, frowning, and once he began to surface from sleep, she asked oh-so-casually as she dressed Daniel in a hundred and one layers: "I woke up in the night and missed you, what went on outside? I heard some absolutely mental noises."

"Oh," and Oli blushed all over his face, mortified. "I'm sorry you missed me, love. Another fu- another effing tradition, I'm afraid. Si dragged me into it, wouldn't let me off. Never will."

"Wanna share?" she asked quietly, beginning to dress herself, and he rolled his eyes and lay back down.

"Not really love, to be honest. It's not worth it – a load of nonsense really, but it keeps Mum happy."

"Okay," said Paula, still quiet, making it clear it was not ok at all, but Oli offered nothing more, only comments on the glorious weather. It was a sparkling clear blue day, glittering with frost. Icicles as long as Daniel's arm were hanging from the eaves, the sun turning them into diamond daggers. Oli reached out and snapped one off to give to Daniel.

Paula watched them both as she battled her way into dress tights, and wondered. *What was in that dripping bag?*

At Christmas dinner that afternoon she found out, when Michael proudly bore in the enormous head of a pig on a platter. The neighbours, invited around to share the feast, cheered and thumped their cutlery on the enormous wooden dining table, already groaning with meat and fruit. Oli rolled his eyes in metropolitan disgust.

Simon caught the expression on Oli's face now, and leaned over, eyes gleaming with hostility above the red slabs of his cheeks. "What's up with you, bruv? Ten years up the city and you've forgotten your roots? Too slick for your own home and your own traditions, is that it?"

Oli snarled back in real hatred, to Paula's alarm. "That's my damned roots, is it? That – pig chase? Grow up Simon. Grow up and let go of mum's apron strings."

Simon opened his mouth to roar, but Daniel finally realised what the strange thing on the plate was, and let loose a horrified wail. Shahnaz burst into sympathetic tears.

Cathleen leaned over, "Eh, loves, you must have a boar's head for Christmas, it's just tradition, but there's no need for you to eat it. Here! Let's pull our crackers, shall we? Look, you've won! Let's put on our hats!"

The children cheered up in their paper crowns but Mustafa looked as though he was struggling not to vomit as his wife loudly claimed the pig's cheeks, saying "I was, after all, the one who brought it down in the end. Eh, Simon?"

The neighbours cheered again for Melissa, and the stem of Simon's wine glass snapped in his meaty hand as he stared at his sister, queen of the hunt, her glasses steamed with triumph.

"Never mind, eh, Si? Your sister might be more of a man than you but you definitely bought a conservatory and that's what counts, eh?" Oli laughed in a malicious way that Paula had never heard before. The neighbours stood all round, solid farmers of both sexes, dressed in antique shades of green and brown with tinsel and holly around their necks or heads, their faces almost as red and round as the pig's. The noise and laughter and clinking of glasses became louder by the minute, a thickening miasma of wine and ale in the air. There was a feeling growing in the air, too; an expectant feeling.

Shahnaz chattered to her auntie about her presents.

"And I got three plushies, Auntie Paula, and I only even asked for one. But I guess Santa thinks I was a really good girl this year."

Paula nodded and spoke on automatic. "That's awesome, Shahnaz, and you're always a good girl, aren't you." She tried to identify the feeling inside her.

Something is coming.

She seemed to catch glances flying across the table; Cathleen and Veronica, Melissa and Cathleen, even Oliver and Melissa. The pork congealed untouched on her plate as she watched and listened, trying to understand what was going on. Her head started to lurch and spin.

For a moment she heard the squealing terror in the black night again. For a moment, the bright, crowded kitchen became as thin as gauze, nothing but a painted surface over the dark. It felt as though, if she were to turn her head quickly to the left or right, she would see not the farmhouse kitchen, but some other, much older scene.

Cathleen stood up for the toasts as the dusk fell.

"To Simon!", she cried, "and his wonderful year! To Melissa, and Mustafa! To Daniel, and Sonia, and Mark, and Shahnaz - all the little cousins! To Paula and Oli, and their first Christmas on the farm!" *Clink, gulp!*

"Wishing us all success this year,, and another fine harvest to come!"

Clink, cheer and gulp!

Then they sent the children upstairs to play with their toys before bedtime, and the adults began to prepare for the bonfire.

"Just a local affair, my love, hope you don't mind," said Cathleen, taking a shrugging Oli by the arm.

"Oh," said Paula. "Oh right. I - completely understand." She tried to catch Oli's eye, but he left the room without looking back.

From the bedroom window she watched the scarlet flowers blossom again in the snow far above, the tiny black figures dancing and singing around them under a bone-white crescent moon that she wouldn't look directly at for fear of seeing a crooked winking face.

Her knuckles tightened on the sill. Her breath came too fast, too shallow. Her heart stuttered in her chest and throbbed in her ears. She could still smell the cloying scent of the roast pork, and she swallowed hard on her nausea. Slow waves of dizziness washed over her head and blurred her vision. Her palms, slick with sweat, slipped on the sill.

Please, Paula thought, *don't let me pass out.*

Some of the figures seemed to be wearing headdresses of antlers. She could almost hear their bells ringing above the soughing of the wind in the trees.

The wind had risen again, never seeming to fall for long

on this bleak hillside, blowing day and night, making the red ribbons of the flames stream first one way, then the other. She could swear that she saw Oli, swigging from a bottle and dancing in wild circles, silhouetted against the strange Christmas bonfire.

Was that Oli? – running hard head down against his brother to clash antlers with a crash of furious bells? Was it really? There were so many now on the hilltop that she couldn't count them. They were such a whirling mass that no individual could be distinguished. It became impossible to understand what was going on, but the whirl was frantic. Her heart gave an awful leap in her chest as the wind seemed to blow screams to her, screams both fierce and supplicating. The sounds died down to thin whistles, and she decided it had only been the sound of the wind. She let herself breathe again. Her breath was still too fast. Her palms were still sweating as she let go of the sill.

I don't want to go back down there. I don't want to be here. I'm not coming here again. Next year I'm going shopping on Regent Street, under the blazing lights among the crowds.

She lingered at the top of the stairs when they all poured back into the kitchen, stamping and panting, and Paula heard Michael roar out- Michael! She barely recognised his voice.

"Here's to the spring, back before we know it! And here's to the King of the Bean!"

King of the What? she wondered, but Oli was calling for her.

"Paula! Where are you? It's time for the cake!"

Oh no, she groaned privately, *not more bloody food, I'm about to puke as it is,* but she set a smile on her face, while her insides roiled with unease, as she ran down to join them.

Sitting in a circle, under a great bough of holly and mistletoe so dense it looked as though the forest had invaded the house, the people of the neighbourhood cut a great cake, rich with fruit and nuts, into thin slices.

"Come on Paula!" Oli grinned at her, but it was a strange grin, not one she'd ever seen before."Come and choose a bit."

Upstairs, the children were laughing; a sweet sound, tinkling like silver bells.

"Come and choose!" They roared it, like a chant.

She jumped in terror, and Cathleen laughed, putting a soothing hand on her arm. "Sorry love, a bit loud I know. It's only a tradition, you know. For luck. Luck, and a fine harvest."

It came back at once, the cry: *"Luck, and a fine harvest!"*

Cathleen began to offer the cake around, and Paula suddenly realised: "Where's Simon?"

Did that flurry of exchanged glances happen again, behind her back, around her shoulders? Things were being said, she could feel it, and she couldn't hear them.

"Oh, don't worry about Simon," said Veronica, brightly. "He's had a good year, you know. The best."

Paula stared. Veronica looked happy. She smiled a real smile, wide and joyous, and her thin shoulders seemed laid back and calm. This was the first time she'd ever seen Veronica look-

The cake platter was under her hand and she took a slice blindly, without looking; moist crumbs fell between her fingers, the scent of oranges and lemons and seasonal spice made her stomach churn faster. Everyone had a slice now, and they all watched each other as they ate. Veronica sat with that contented little smile, looking more relaxed than Paula had ever seen her. Melissa, with her jaw stuck out in determination. Mustafa, flushed and damp from the dancing. Cathleen and Michael calm, chewing like cows. The neighbours, red and plump, catching crumbs with their hands. Oli, eating away through a sick little smile, his face white and oddly twisted, watching her with sidelong glances under his lashes..

She lifted the cake with extreme reluctance, for one polite mouthful, and bit. Almost at once she yelped: "Ouch!" and spat her mouthful into her hand as politely as she could. Some hard, strange little object glistened in her palm.

A strange sigh passed around the circle, a sigh of awe, and satisfaction, and relief.

"The bean!" Oli's face appeared more oddly twisted and sick-looking than ever. The smell of evergreen rose above the taste of the rich cake. The two mingled in her mouth and Paula knew she was going to be sick soon.

Cathleen beamed; the circle tightened around her. "Oh, great luck, Paula! Great luck, to the King of the Bean!"

"The – what?" She choked. The strange little lump still sat warm in her hand. Even as Cathleen answered, she could see that it *was* a bean, dark and hard, baked into the cake and now it was hers.

"Great luck for a year to the King of the Bean, Paula," Cathleen gave her a congratulatory hug, "and now, you're it!"

They all closed in, shaking her hand, grinning and nodding. The kitchen turned thin once more, and something very old peered out at her from behind the evergreen. The wild night howled around them; they were so far from the city and the light.

Paula tried to speak and found she could not. Upstairs, the children still laughed, playing games as old as time.

Veronica beamed at her, happy and free. "A Happy Yule-tide and a joyous year to you!"

"Who," Paula croaked, looking at Veronica's sly wide grin

and the tight circle with no place for Simon, "Who was 'it' last year?"

Oli's white face grimaced at her, trying to smile. "Can't remember," he said, "it doesn't matter any more."

Michael nodded. "That's tradition. We forget."

"Indeed," said Cathleen. "The old King is dead. Long Live the New!"

TRINKET THE ELF

K.A. MILTIMORE

Terrance hadn't attended her funeral. He lived in Seattle, and Aunt Mae lived across the country in some tiny town called Painted Post, New York. He probably *could* have attended if he had been willing to take a plane into La Guardia airport in the middle of December during a snow-storm. He'd decided against it moments after getting the call from his cousin, Hazel. He'd mourn the old gal's passing from afar.

"Other than your cousin, she was your last living relative, Terr. Don't you think you should pay your respects?" Gina said, peering at him over the pages of her Vogue magazine. She came from a loud and boisterous family, with cousins that outnumbered fingers and toes. Naturally, she thought they should attend the funeral. Plus, they would have the added benefit of Christmas shopping in NYC. Gina loved her fashion.

"Mae wouldn't want me to break the bank. She wasn't much for ceremony and such. I've sent a lovely bouquet to the service and besides, we weren't really that close."

Gina arched her penciled eyebrows at him but said nothing, returning to her magazine. He knew she didn't approve, but they hadn't been dating long enough for her to say that statement out loud.

Terrance hadn't given his aunt another thought until the package arrived on his doorstep three days before Christmas. He monitored his deliveries for Gina's gift - a must-have Coach bag due to be delivered. Instead of the sturdy cardboard box he expected, he found a shoebox wrapped with packing tape from corner to corner. At first blush, he thought it looked like a bomb.

"What is this? Gina, did you order something from that auction site?" he called to her over his shoulder. She was too busy singing along with the Christmas carols blaring from the wireless speaker to hear him. He squatted and took a look at the return address. *Painted Post, New York.*

"Lord, did Mae send me something?" He picked up the box, expecting some heft to it. Instead, it felt light and squashed beneath his grip on one end. Guilt crept into his gullet at the thought of his old, sick aunt mailing him a final gift. *And he hadn't even bothered to go to her funeral.*

"What's that? Did you order some shoes? The box is all smashed. You should file a claim." Gina peered over his shoulder, and he could smell the garlic on her breath. She'd been sampling his marinara simmering on the stove. He made a mean marinara.

"No, I didn't order shoes. It looks like something from my aunt." He heard Gina take a sharp breath and step back from him. *Great minds think alike*, he thought.

"Well, open it up. It must be special for her to send it to you." He heard the disapproval in her voice. *You're a cheap man and an ungrateful nephew*, her tone said.

"Yeah, let's see what it is," he said, following Gina back

toward the kitchen. Whatever it was, he knew it would make him feel guilty.

Terrance took out a small knife from his kitchen junk drawer, taking care to slice through the layers of packing tape without plunging the blade too deeply. Gina held her glass of Cabernet, clicking her red nails against the crystal rim. The speaker on the mantle had moved on to a new tune - "Christmas Time is Here" by the Vince Guaraldi Trio. *"Christmas time is here. Happiness and cheer. Fun for all that children call their favorite time of year."*

He peeled back the tape and lifted off the smashed New Balance lid, revealing a sheet of tissue paper that had been used and reused several times by the look of it. Pulling it back, he saw a plastic face grinning back at him. A wide, Y shaped grin, with a deep red tongue poking just over the lower lip. Crinkled blue eyes looking up and toward the right, as if something hid under the green felt cap that covered the painted brown hair. The foot-tall doll wore a felted elf costume.

"Aww, she sent you an Elf. It must be a family heirloom. A Christmas Elf," Gina said, letting her fingers graze against the molded plastic hair. A red-felt onesie embroidered with holly sprigs and candy canes covered the doll's body from neck to toe.. His feet were presumably inside the pointed and curly tips that ended in two small pom-poms missing much of their fluff.

"I don't remember this doll at all. I can't imagine why Mae would have sent it to me," Terrance said, picking out the small piece of notepaper nestled next to the ugly thing.

"'Dear Terrance, we wanted to send you a little something from Mother's collection. Something that you can remember her by. She always said that Trinket the Elf must be displayed with pride each and every Christmas. I thought you and your children might enjoy him. Merry Christmas. Love, Hazel.'"

"Children? What's she talking about?" Gina set her wine glass on the granite countertop. He could have kicked himself for not reading the note to himself first. *At least she isn't throwing it*, Terrance thought.

"She's confused. My ex-wife had two kids from her first marriage. I haven't seen them since they moved to Arizona, almost nine months ago now." Terrance set down the box next to the wine glass, tossing the note over the hideous face of "Trinket." He hadn't told Gina about the kids, only that he had been married before.

"You should have told me, Terrance. Your somebody's step-father. Two somebodies, actually. You should have told me." Gina picked up her purse from its resting place on the stool at the edge of the counter. *Dinner was off, apparently.*

"Gina, don't be upset. I wasn't hiding anything. It just didn't seem like something to just blurt out. I was going to tell you when the time was right." She furrowed her brows, squinting her eyes at him in that way she had when she was angry. Most of the time, that anger was directed at someone else.

"Sure, whenever the 'right time' would have been. Anyway, I'm not hungry. I'm going home. See you later." Without another word, she walked to the front door and slammed it behind her. He knew better than to try to convince her to stay or to chase after her. Gina needed time to cool off or things would be ten times worse. She had a quick temper, but he knew she would calm down. At least she had said 'see you later.' *It couldn't be all bad*, he thought.

He picked up the shoe box and headed toward the garage. Trinket, along with Hazel's note, would go straight into the trash. He didn't want a reminder of this night, and besides, the ugly doll held no special memories for him. He lifted the bin and held the box above the plastic sacks, but his hand wouldn't release it. *What would Gina think of him tossing out his aunt's prize doll? He'd look like an even bigger jerk than he did already. If he tossed Trinket, Gina might just toss him.*

"Damn it," he said, pulling the doll out of the box and tossing the New Balance box into the recycling bin. "Guess I am stuck with you for at least one Christmas."

"Good morning, all you Christmas elves. It is December 23rd, so if you haven't finished your shopping yet, you are running out of time. Speaking of time, it is ten passed the hour." Terrance swiped the button on his phone to shut down his second snooze alarm of the hour. He'd spent half the night writing texts to Gina that he then deleted, and he woke exhausted.

Climbing out of bed, he let his feet tap the wooden floor, seeking his slippers. His right foot found it easily enough, but his left foot was struggling. He scanned the floor, but he couldn't see the leather leftie

"That's weird. I left both of them right there," he muttered before kicking off the right slipper and padding to the bathroom. He'd find it later. Right now, he needed coffee and a "good morning" text to Gina. He wanted to be the one to reach out first.

His programmable coffee pot had his French Roast waiting for him when he came down the stairs barefoot. Thanks to his preset timer, the Christmas tree lights had popped on, as had the "nice and easy coffeehouse blend" radio station on his wireless speaker. Terrance lived in a house of automation, and he loved it. Voice commands controlled everything from temperature to the light dimmers, to his front door locks. Sleek modernity everywhere except for the elfin monstrosity set upon the mantle.

"Trinket, you stick out like a sore thumb," he said, pouring his coffee. He needed a jolt of caffeine, a little something to wake him up and get him logged in to work. The aroma teased him as he drew the Star Wars mug to his lips and he let the temperature-perfect brew into his mouth. He tasted the salt.

Terrance leaned toward the sink and spat out the coffee, spraying it all over the clean porcelain. The grit from the salt rimmed his teeth.

"What the hell?" He opened the coffee pot's filter chamber and saw the damp remains of coffee covered in a pile of white crystals.

Gina. It had to be Gina and some kind of prank. Had she done it when he had gone to the door to get the package? Maybe her family did Christmas pranks, and he was meant to brew it last night before he had read that damn note out loud. That had to be it, he thought.

He filled a glass with water and guzzled some to swish out the remaining salt. *What a wonderful way to start my morning,* he thought. He hoped work would go better than this.

MANY OF HIS colleagues had already taken off for the holiday, but Terrance planned to work right up until Christmas. He'd pause to put in the prime rib roast he wanted to make for Gina to celebrate their private Christmas; Gina was going to be with her family after that, and their relationship was too new for meeting the parents. They'd celebrate tonight and exchange gifts. Tomorrow, he'd binge-watch his favorite zombie movies and eat leftovers. A perfect Christmas Eve.

Terrance settled in with his laptop, which he'd left on the kitchen table last night. He lifted the screen, reaching for the wireless mouse that wasn't there. *Had he left it on the charger? No, it wasn't there. Had he knocked it on the floor? No, the robot vacuum would have bumped into it.* He couldn't find it, and Terrance felt a vein throbbing at his temple.

"What is happening today? My slipper, the damn coffee, now the mouse. Jeez, I've had it and the day has barely started." Before he could continue his tirade, his phone buzzed. Gina had sent the first message. *Damn it.*

<We still on for tonight? If so, I'll be there at six. G>

He reread it, trying to infer her tone. No heart emojis, no XO, no smilies with a colon and a parenthesis. Still, she planned to be over, so things weren't completely screwed up. He could fix it up tonight with a delicious meal and her Coach bag. He realized with a start that her gift had yet to be delivered.

"That will be next, I suppose," he said, pulling up the email with the tracking number. One copy and a paste later, he saw that the box had been delivered late last night.

Except it wasn't there. There was nothing on the doorstep. Not a trace that anything had been there at all.

"Seriously? Come on!" He slammed the door and headed back to the laptop. He'd check the outside camera footage to see if anyone had taken the box or if it had even been delivered. If it hadn't, he'd contact customer service and give them holy hell.

The outside camera pointed away from the house, showing the steps leading up to the covered porch but not the door itself. He'd be able to see anyone who had approached the front door, along with a date stamp of their arrival.

Scrolling through the footage, he saw Gina storm out, and then three hours went by before a harried delivery carrier climbed the steps with a package in hand. The man scanned the box, set it down out of view, and then left the porch at 10:30PM. After that, nothing had come to the porch - not a stray cat, not the neighbor's dog, and certainly not a package thief.

"That's it, I'm losing it. It has to be out there." Terrance huffed back to the door, slamming it open to inspect every cranny of his porch, every square inch of space between the front door and the steps. Nothing was there. From inside the house, he heard a high pitched sound, almost like a little laugh. *It has to be the neighbor's kid. Had he left a window open?*

"I don't have time to deal with this. I need a gift by tonight," he said to the empty hallway, slamming the door. He needed something in the next few hours. He'd deal with the missing package later when his nerves weren't shot.

TERRANCE DIDN'T HAVE time to order another Coach bag or, in fact, to order anything else. He needed something right then, and that meant going out to get it. Terrance had constructed his life so that he rarely had to leave the house; his groceries were delivered, he worked from home, he shopped at home, he downloaded movies. He avoided going out at all costs, let alone during the mayhem of the day before Christmas Eve. But he wasn't about to put the nail in his relationship coffin with Gina by not having something wonderful for her to open on their first Christmas together. He'd just have to get dressed and hit the stores.

Layered up in a flannel jacket and a pair of jeans that

were close to too small, thanks to too many holiday treats, he grabbed his wallet and stuffed it in the pocket of the coat hanging from the rack. *If he could just find his car key, he'd be all set.* He was pretty sure he'd last used the car around Thanksgiving, so the key could be anywhere. Luckily, after rummaging around on his desk, in the kitchen junk drawer, and in the little bowl he kept by the front door for spare change, he'd found it.

He opened the front door, and rain smacked him in the face from the fierce wind blowing from the north. "Jeez, almost forgot my coat," he muttered, backtracking inside to grab the wool peacoat off the rack. Sliding it on, he heard a scuffling sound behind him, and he spun to look. It almost sounded like a dog or some creature shuffling across his wood floors. *Had something followed him in from the porch?* After a quick scan of the room, he was sure the house was empty, and he could leave.

He slid the Japanese import out of the garage, down the impossibly steep hill he lived on, and navigated toward Queen Anne Avenue. Busy with pedestrians, buses, and honking cars throughout the year, a rain squall made it nightmarish. His nerves were worn already, nevermind driving in fierce weather on a slick street in downtown Seattle.

"She's worth it, she's worth it," Terrance muttered, finding a pay lot near the Queen Anne Jewelry shop. *They better have something because he wasn't about to drive anywhere else.*

"What can I help you find, Mister?" The older gentleman behind the counter sported a cheery red and green plaid vest. His face had a broad smile and crinkled eyes reminiscent of Trinket, and Terrance fought the urge to scowl at him. *It wasn't his fault that he resembled a hideous Christmas doll.*

"I need something for my girlfriend, something nice but not..."

"Not an engagement ring, right?" The older man chuckled and took out a huge ring of keys, unlocking the cabinet in front of Terrance. "I have some very nice bracelets. If it isn't too serious, you don't want to go with a ring. Earrings are good for mothers and sisters. Bracelets can be just right for special ladies." He pulled out a tray of sparkly bangles nestled on dark blue velvet.

"How much for that one?" Terrance pointed to a slim bangle crusted with diamonds and sapphires. The jeweler chuckled.

"You have expensive tastes, son. But then, I bet she is a special lady. That bracelet sells for $1,500 normally, but I'll sell it to you for $1,000, plus tax." Terrance took a sharp breath; he hadn't planned on spending quite that much. He took a quick glance at the clock and decided the extra money was worth it to get out of this shop and back home.

"Sold," he said, reaching his hand into his wool coat pocket. The pocket where he had placed his wallet before leaving the house was now empty. Terrance thrust his hand deeper as if there were another layer to the pocket, but his knuckles grazed the satin lining. He shoved his left hand in the other pocket, sure that it must be there but pulling out nothing but air. He had two pockets in his coat, and neither of them held his wallet. *Could it have fallen out in the car*, he wondered?

"Wrap it up, please. I'll be right back." He hurried out the door of the shop, into the blowing wet wind, and clicked the lock on his car. Crawling around on the seats, peering inside cup holders, even looking under flat floor mats all yielded the same result. No wallet.

"What the everloving f..." He paused the expletive when

he saw the children on the sidewalk next to him. *What was he going to do now, with no way to pay for the bracelet?* His phone vibrated in his back pocket, and he pulled it out before covering it with his sleeve.

Back in the shop, the jeweler was waiting for him, looking less jovial than he had before. Terrance pulled up the banking app on his phone and stepped back to the counter.

"Can you take payment from my app? I've lost my wallet, it seems."

The jeweler's gaze transformed from skeptical to puzzled. Terrance could tell the man had no idea what he was talking about

"If you can explain it to me, and I can see the money in my account, I'll take it. No tricks, though."

Terrance sighed silently, pushing the frustration out his nostrils in a blast of air. Teaching this man how to do e-commerce was the only way he was getting his bracelet.

"Okay, let's get you paid, sir."

FIVE-THIRTY PM and the crisis had been averted. He'd only just pulled into the garage after spending the better part of an hour with the jeweler, getting him set up to accept e-commerce transactions, and then paying for his own purchase. To his credit, the jeweler was grateful for the help and asked if Terrance would help him set up a website in exchange for a discount on another purchase. Terrance thanked him kindly and said he would think about it, knowing he would never take the gig. He hadn't done tech support in ten years for a reason.

He put the wrapped package in his flannel shirt pocket, and he kept patting the bulky square to make sure it was still there, despite feeling it every time he moved. It would stay in that pocket until he gave it to Gina because nothing was going to happen to it, not if he could help it.

The doorbell rang, and he wondered why Gina didn't use her voice recognition access to just come in. He patted the box once more and moved to the front door. Terrance opened it wide for the lovely face he saw through the peephole; his girlfriend holding a bottle of wine and a red and white poinsettia.

"Hey, you could have just come in. I'm glad you came," Terrance said, leaning in to give her a quick kiss before taking the plant from her.

"I tried, but the voice recognition isn't working. Sorry you had to make the trip to the front door just for me," she said with a small laugh, but Terrance wondered if she was more serious than she was letting on.

"Just another thing I need to handle around here. Things have been crazy today. You wouldn't believe it. Come in out of this rain."

"I see you have your aunt's Elf by the tree. It looks cute." Gina tossed her wet coat on his leather sofa, and he bit his lip but said nothing. *He'd hang it up when she wasn't looking.*

"Yeah, old Trinket is spending Christmas with me. Look, babe, I'm sorry about yesterday. I just…"

"Forget it. I don't want to talk about it tonight and ruin our evening. Let's have our Christmas." Gina leaned in and kissed him gently. He forgot entirely about the wet raincoat.

"HEY, Terr, I think you forgot the forks," Gina called to him as he brought the prime rib to the table on a silver platter.

"Very funny, Gina. Almost as funny as the coffee this morning."

She grinned, scrunching her shoulders under her ears in a "who me" gesture that Terrance found adorable.

"Alright, I'll own up to the coffee, which in my defense would have been funnier if I was here when you sipped it. But I swear, I haven't touched the forks. We only have knives here." He placed the tray on the trivet and then stood behind her, scanning the table. There were no forks anywhere. He knew he had placed them by the plates, right next to the knives because he couldn't remember the proper side of the plate where they should be placed. There had been forks, and now there weren't.

"G, don't tease me, seriously. I've had a bad day. Don't gaslight me, I might just lose it." He rubbed her shoulders, and she tipped her head back, looking up at him.

"I swear, I didn't touch them."

Terrance took a deep breath. He was tempted to call her out to tell her he didn't believe her. But the new peace between them remained fragile, and he didn't want to screw things up by getting angry over something as dumb as missing silverware.

"Well, how about you look at this while I get forks," he said, drawing the box from his flannel pocket. He placed it on the center of the china plate as she murmured, "Oh, Terrance."

It might not have been the Coach bag she had been dropping hints about, but she didn't seem to mind. After several passionate kisses, Terrance broke away from her embrace. *Maybe this day wasn't so bad after all.*

"I'll get the forks," he said, as she modeled the diamonds and sapphires in the candlelight.

DINNER behind them and with fresh, non-salty coffee on the table by the couch, the pair snuggled in the dim twinkling light of the Christmas tree. *White Christmas* played on the TV, but they hardly watched it. Terrance's luck seemed to be improving.

"Hey, babe, gentle on my hair, okay?" Gina chuckled as she broke her lip-lock with him. He had no idea what she was talking about, but at that moment, he didn't care.

"Shall we take this party upstairs?"

Gina chuckled again at his question, this time rising from her seat. *Yes, the evening was definitely on the upswing.*

"Let's finish the movie, and then we'll see. I'm going to hit the powder room."

Terrance nodded, hiding his disappointment. But he refused to betray his thoughts that Bing Crosby wasn't as exciting as his romantic suggestion. He rose and picked up his coffee cup for a refill.

"Okay, I'll meet you back here in a few."

Gina gave him a playful slap on the shoulder, and he headed for the kitchen.

The coffee had barely hit his cup when he heard the scream. He ran to the living room, still clutching the coffee cup when Gina barrelled up to him and knocked it from his hand, splattering the hot liquid all over his couch.

"You ass, I can't believe you did this. What is wrong with you? Are you some kind of serial killer freak?"

"What are you talking about?" Terrance watched her grasp her dark hair behind her head, holding it up in her clenched hand. A huge chunk of her hair was cut off just a few inches from her scalp.

"What happened?" He took a step toward her, but she held out her hand in a "stop right there" motion.

"You know damn well what happened. You cut off my hair when I was on the couch. You son of a bitch. What a psycho!" She dropped the patch of hair and clawed the bracelet off her wrist, throwing it at him hard enough to impress a baseball scout. Before he could respond, she grabbed her coat off the coat rack and slammed the front door.

"Jeez, what the hell..." He stooped and picked up the bracelet, placing it back in his flannel pocket. He wasn't about to lose a thousand dollars as well as his girlfriend tonight.

"Holy crap!" he said to the empty house over the sound of Bing's crooning. He didn't even bother turning off the TV. Instead, he stalked upstairs to bed.

CHRISTMAS EVE DAWNED, and Terrance considered staying in bed all day. He had no one to get up for, no gifts to open, no pet to take for a walk, no reason he couldn't hide his head under a pillow until this nightmare holiday ended.

His bladder, however, wouldn't comply. Shuffling out of bed, he calculated whether he could take a pee and go back to sleep before fully waking. But years of being an early riser conspired to make him wide awake for the whole damn day.

"Might as well work," he muttered, finding his robe on the back of the bathroom door. At least he could impress his boss with his devotion; he didn't need to know that Terrance would be all alone and losing his mind.

Terrance heard voices downstairs, and for a moment, he felt his breath catch in his throat before he remembered the

TV. He'd drink his coffee, turn off the TV, and bury his head in his laptop for the day. *It was the best plan that he had.*

Terrance scrolled through his phone as he walked down the stairs, hoping that maybe Gina had sent him a message, though he doubted she would have. His eyes darted across the texts, finding a few from coworkers but nothing from Gina. He felt his foot touch something that wasn't carpet, but by the time his brain registered the fact, his foot had twisted on it, and he found himself flailing down a flight of stairs, crashing into the hardwood floor below. His phone skittered out of his hand, the glass cracking on the banister, before sliding out of sight under the couch.

For a moment, he took a mental inventory of his arms and legs. *Was anything broken? No.* All four limbs hurt like hell, but he could move. He had landed on his hands and knees, and both throbbed. With gingerly movements, he found his way to his feet. A phone rang, but not the familiar chirp of his cellphone. It was a buzzing ring, and he looked around for the source before he remembered the landline that he never used.

The phone rested on a shelf in the kitchen, and he shambled toward it, keeping his wrists moving in slow circles. No one called the landline. He couldn't remember the last time it had rung.

"Hello?"

"Terrance, is that you?" The voice sounded unsure and somewhat familiar. It almost sounded like Aunt Mae.

"Yes, this is Terrance." A dead aunt calling him on Christmas Eve would be the cherry on his psychotic break sundae.

"Merry Christmas. It's Cousin Hazel. I wasn't sure if you still had this number. It was the only one that Mother had in her phone book. How are you?"

Of course it was Hazel. No crazy calls from the grave.

Just an obligatory holiday call from his cousin. "I'm alright, Hazel. Well, actually, that isn't true, I just fell down my stairs, but how are you?"

"Oh, dear, are you alright? What a terrible day to take a tumble." *As if there is a good day to fall down and almost break your wrists.* "Did you get my package?"

He paused for a minute and then remembered the Elf. He glanced over toward the mantle, and the doll's ugly face stared back at him with that horrible grin.

"Yes, I sure did. It was very thoughtful of you to send it to me. I know how much Auntie Mae loved her decorations. I'm surprised you didn't want it, Hazel." His knees were throbbing, and he needed some ice. *Maybe he could convince her to wrap up the call quickly.*

"I'm glad Trinket arrived safely. I have a confession, Terrance. Mother left me her collection, but I had memories of Trinket from my childhood, and I couldn't quite bring myself to bring him into my home." Hazel's laughter caught Terrance by surprise.

"What do you mean? I know he isn't the most attractive thing, but…"

"Oh, it isn't that, although that is true, he is a bit of ugly mug. No, I remember being afraid of Trinket. There was always something about him that I found unsettling. Whenever Mother would put him out for the holidays, I would start missing things - little things, a button, a slipper, my favorite barrette, my cereal spoon. I swear, one year, I found a snip of my hair was gone. Mother always told me I was foolish to be upset, but then she'd say something absurd like Trinket had only borrowed my treasures. Anyway, I didn't want to give him to someone outside of the family, so I thought you might like him, or at least your kids might."

Normally, Terrance would have set Hazel straight about

his step-kids, but his knees throbbed, and he wanted to end the call. He turned back toward the living room, scanning his mantle for Hazel's hand-me-down garbage. The shelf was empty.

"Hazel, I have to go. Thank you for the call and Merry Christmas." Before she could respond, he lowered the phone and placed it on the cradle. *Where was Trinket?*

"Can't be," he said, walking over to the shelf. *The doll must have fallen from the mantle, hidden behind the tree.* Terrance looked among the artificial branches, behind the wrapped present that Gina had tucked for him to open on Christmas, but Trinket wasn't there.

"I'm going crazy. There is no way that doll got up and moved around the house." The TV was still on, and he needed to think, so he reached for the remote on its charging station, but it wasn't there.

"Of course, it's gone too." He forced himself down on the ground, taking care to avoid putting pressure on his hands or his knees so that he could search under the couch for the remote. He saw it, deep under the furniture, but it wasn't alone. Other things were clustered near it. He reached in, feeling the plastic of the remote. The next thing felt cold, like metal. There was a cardboard box wedged under there too; he could feel the smooth edges and packing tape. Then he felt something like hair.

Terrance pulled each item out from the couch and stared at the morbid collection. The missing forks, his leather slipper, the box with the Coach bag, his missing computer mouse, his wallet, the strands of Gina's hair.

"Naughty," said a voice, high and piercing. "Naughty boy. You found my treasures. Trinket doesn't like naughty boys. No presents for you."

Terrance scrambled to his feet, hobbling away from the pile on his carpet.

"Who is there?" he called, backing up toward the kitchen.

"Naughty. No children here for Trinket to play with. No children for his frolics and games. A house without children at Christmas is naughty. Trinket doesn't like naughty."

The voice wasn't in the room, but he could hear it coming from somewhere nearby.

"Show yourself." Terrance stepped toward the granite countertop where his butcher block rested. He pulled a chef's knife from the block.

"Come and find me, naughty boy. I have your treat waiting." The voice peeled into a squeal of laughter, high and horrible to Terrance's ears. It seemed to echo and reverberate against his almond-painted walls and sleek furniture.

"Trinket," he said, but he couldn't finish the sentence. He couldn't speak to an inanimate doll that had to be a figment of his breaking mind. If he started speaking to it, he knew all hope would be lost.

The voice's laugh trailed off, and the room fell silent again. Clutching his knife, Terrance made his way along the hallway, opening closets and peering into the powder room. Nothing.

He thought he heard something, upstairs, a loud thunking sound on the floor. Careful step by careful step, he moved up the stairs, feeling the pain in his knees with each tread. He left the landing and headed into his bedroom.

In the center of the room, he saw his other boot; the mate to the one that had sent him crashing down the stairs. Sitting neat and tidy in the center of his white carpet, nowhere near where he kept it buried in his closet for the rare snowy Seattle days. *Another gift from Trinket.*

He picked up the boot and placed it on the dresser; he

didn't need to trip again. Other than finding the boot out of place, everything looked just as he had left it. He grabbed the blankets, giving them a rough tug to strip them from the bed. *No demonic elf was hiding in their folds.* He opened his closet door, using the blade of his knife to move the clothing about, rather than bend over to peer into the darkness.

Under the bed. It was the last place left to look. Terrance set the knife on the dresser so he could use his hands to get down on the ground. Sprawling on his belly, the right side of his face pressed to the floor, Terrance peered under the bed. The grinning leer of Trinket stared back at him. He'd found the doll.

"Naughty boy has found Trinket. Well done, naughty boy. Now, for your treat." Terrance lifted his left arm to grab the doll, but it moved, darting toward him. He smelled peppermint and saw the flash of what looked like a striped candy cane before he felt the pressure against his open eye. The popping pressure and then the horrible burning pain as the candy cane pressed into his eye socket.

"Enjoy your treat," Trinket said as Terrance howled in agony.

———

CHRISTMAS MORNING and the family was already bundling up for the trip to Grandma Jones' house. With two small kids in the house, the family had no luxury of sleeping in anyway. They might as well get moving while the roads were quiet.

"Did you pack the gifts?" George asked, zipping up the toddler's coat. "Don't forget the fig pudding in the fridge."

"Yes, the car is packed, and I have the pudding. Let's go grab a mocha on the way," Stephen replied, taking little

Aimee's hand and leading her to the front door. George and their daughter, Mabel, were coming behind them.

Stephen opened the door, and there against the doorframe, lay a doll. The ugliest Elf doll that Stephen had ever seen. It had a huge grinning smile and a worn felt hat, cocked jauntily on its head.

"Look what Santa left for us!" squealed Aimee, snatching the doll from the ground before Stephen could stop her. It was old, but it looked clean.

"Yes, what a surprise," Stephen said, glancing back at George, who shrugged his confusion back at Stephen. *Someone had left this Elf on their doorstep. Maybe it was Mrs. Tanaka from down the street; she sometimes babysat for the girls when Stephen and George went out.*

"Daddy, he has a tag on his suit. What does it say?"

"It says 'Trinket.' That must be his name." Stephen stepped toward the sidewalk, and Aimee clutched her prize to her puffy pink coat.

"Trinket, we're going to Grammy's house. Let's go!"

UNWRAPPED PRESENCE

DM DAVANTI

The two hooded figures ignored Dom as they slowly passed. One carried a candle, the other a steaming pot. Keeping a safe distance, he followed them through the cobwebs in a narrow passageway. The air tasted of rust, a dull metallic attack on his lungs; he swallowed back a cough so as not to arouse the pair ahead and delicately proceeded past vague debris on the ground. They arrived at a blackened door covered with claw marks. He stopped, holding his breath as one of them removed a large set of iron keys from the folds of the robe. They inserted the key and turned it. The click echoed throughout the passage loud enough to make Dom want to cover his ears.

The door opened. The stench made him gag and he recovered just in time to duck the cloud of flies escaping as the two entered. Swatting them away, he kept going and stopped at the door. The sharp pounding of his heart thundered in his ears as the door slammed hard against the wall.

From beneath their hoods, two sets of red eyes leveled harsh stares at him. One of them emitted a sickening chuckle, more like a choked gargle with its wet raspiness. The other held out the steaming pot, sending another battery of flies toward him.

More hoarse laughter and he stepped inside.A deathly chill filled the air, stone walls and a stale stench surrounded him. He turned to the left and felt his heart sink.

"Dom…" Brenda stared at him with baleful blue eyes. The tears froze upon his cheeks immediately.

Her body lay on the bed, twisted at an obscene angle on the bed, legs twisted behind her as her head pressed against the exposed mattress where the yellow fitted sheet had pulled back off the corner. Wayward strands of her dirty blonde hair stuck to her reddened scalp.

"All mine," she said forcefully, the sting of it echoing in a loop that rendered his eardrums raw.

The hooded pair disappeared and he realized he held the steaming pot. The idea of looking down terrified him, the rank odor growing with each rising rancid bubble.

"Dom…Dom…Dom.."

"Stop! Stop it!" the thin, youthful tone of his voice sounded foreign to his ears and laughter erupted behind him, and he shot around but no one stood there.

"Dom…"

A cacophony of feral giggles grasped him abrupt terror and he turned to find himself surrounded, the room full of foxes, all silver with dripping fangs, yellow eyes twinkling with maniacal zeal.

"Dom!"

"What?" he cried, turning back to Brenda.

Now sitting up with one leg crossed over the other, Brenda sneered at him, tongue slightly poking from the corner of her thin mouth like she always did when she felt upset.

"What, Brenda? What do you want from me?"

"DOM!"

It became hard to breathe; the air was replaced by dank rot, burning his nose making him dry-heave.

A round of faraway laughter drew his attention to the narrow window, where rich green grass glistened beneath summer sunshine. More raucous laughter carved a deep ache as he made out his own voice within the mirthful choir.

"Go ahead, Dom, just go ahead..."

He turned back to Brenda but only a blue marble urn sat on the mattress. Something sat on top of the urn, and as he bent over to get it, one of the foxes leapt in front of him. It fixed him with a feral smirk, its jowls dripping with something that seared the ground and left an acrid stink and black smoke that curled into a dragon. The smoke quickly overwhelmed him, tearing the air from his lungs.

"DOM, WAKE UP!"

He opened his eyes to the sight of Roberta standing over him clutching an irritated cat, gray fur standing up at all ends.

"He was right on top of you, your face! Never seen him do that before!" she said.

"Vito, what the hell? Trying to kill me over here?"

The feline let out a strangled howl and managed to slip Roberta's grasp, but not before scratching her cheek.

"Aw jeez, let me get some ointment! Vito what the hells the matter with you?" he bellowed as he rose.

"Never mind, just get up already! Of all days, Christmas morning, you decided to sleep in! Tomorrow you'll be back to getting up at the crack of dawn and..." Her voice trailed off as the gravity of the following day hit him.

Three years since Brenda's passing and it never got better, the sting never alleviating as some say it does. He thought of Dominick, down in Pennsylvania with her, silent in death as in so much of her life.

"Dom...*Dom*...DOM!"

He turned up to her and she recoiled with a grimace on her too-burgundy lips.

"Don't look at me like that! Are you even listening to me? I was trying to tell you...so tell me what was I talking about just now? Hmm?"

He got up and walked toward the bathroom.

"Where are you...between you and that damn cat I don't know what's going on around here anymore!"

Dom returned, wearing a befuddled glare.

"Where's the, you know, ointment?" he asked.

She held it and wiggled it in her hand before smearing some on her cheek.

"How bad is it?" she asked with a wince.

He stepped toward her and wretched.

"Aw God, you look *terrible*! Can't be seen in public with you no more! Sorry!"

She squeezed out a dollop of ointment on her finger and flung it at him. He jumped back in horror but it landed on his white tank top.

"It's not going to kill you Dom! Why all the fuss?" she giggled, watching him recover from almost falling backward on the bed.

"Oh, that's funny? What if I would've got hurt? You know what..." he stopped and rubbed his lower back.

Her smirk sloped and collapsed as he bent over, wincing.

"Oh for the love of God, no..."

He stood up and laughed, prompting a ragged exhale from Roberta.

"Don't do that to me!" she cried, squeezing more ointment onto her finger.

"Stop it! That stuff leaves a stain! It's all greasy!" he protested, shuffling out of the bedroom.

When he realized she failed to pursue him, he re-entered the bedroom and stopped at the full-length mirror on the inside of the closet door.

"Silver fox..." he said under his breath and smiled at himself.

As a young man caught up in the gang fights of 1950s Queens, he genuinely never expected to live past twenty-one, much less forty. Never mind seventy. However, he wouldn't have been surprised how well he'd aged;his hazel eyes sharp as ever, and a full head of peppery hair that gave him an air of sophistication. Roberta had even talked him into visiting a dermatologist to tackle his psoriasis once and for all.

Roberta took great pride in her "winds of change" campaign. He'd even taken to wearing a peacoat, as opposed to his leather blazer, plaid in lieu of black and gray.

A sheer flood of change swept away all but photos, trinkets and the occasional awkward phone call from what his life used to be; more plaid, less black, cacophony of overhead El trains, street music and car horns of Astoria for the dense silence of Woodsend, Connecticut.

The silence, more ominous than even what he encountered in his brief stay in Pennsylvania, proved to be a nemesis in his new home. Somewhere in the recesses of his mind, he could still hear the steady hum of the Grand Central Parkway, brakes and noise from Hillside Avenue and the laughter and profane chatter of his neighbors.The memories felt so immediate but they existed a lifetime away, much like his son, Dominick, way down in Pennsylvania with Diane.

Despite cozy nights watching television and frequent visits from her three daughters and grandchildren, the house felt empty. He and Roberta enjoyed pool parties and the raucous laughter of the kids. but once summer ended, the silence crept in.

Autumn arrived with a sudden unnerving thud; for hours, he'd find himself staring at the barren field on the other side of their triangle-shaped half-acre.

He didn't know what drew him, other than a vague sense of anticipation. There just had to be more to than a bland barren field other than the occasional deer. Sometimes he thought he heard whispers when the wind picked up, but could never make anything out.There was something beyond the trees.

So he waited for something to appear, something to happen.

Roberta told him about the place once, and said that the Smyth family owned it, priding themselves on having the biggest wheat field in the area. A steady gray pall seemed to remain over the Georgian Colonial house, matching the dull pallor of the weathered façade still visible behind the overgrown, craggy tree branches and network of wisteria. On a clear day, when the fog took a rare day off, he could see past the house to the desolate woods beyond, row after foreboding row of dead trees.

Roberta abruptly hugged him from behind, and he smiled to conceal his surprise.

"Don't you go getting all conceited on me now, mister!" she chirped, blonde perm tickling his ear as she rested her head on his shoulder.

He smiled and looked at their reflection.

He still saw the way she looked thirty years ago; a dancing riot of high heels, teased hair, black Dior, him in his V-neck Gucci sweater and gray Member's Only jacket. Steamy Friday nights at the Kew Motor Inn followed by wistful mornings, avowing that one day they would be together.

He remembered Brenda's dry resignation when he told

her he got stuck at work, or had a managers' meeting and the mirage faded, and felt a lump in his throat. Swallowing hard, he attempted a smile when she suddenly pulled his head toward her.

"Merry Christmas by the way!" she said with a smirk and planted a kiss on his cheek.

The wisp of a disembodied cackle raised his neck hairs, echoing in his ears for a few moments.

"What's wrong?" she asked, blonde perm bobbing in befuddled curiosity.

"Nothing...just thought I heard something."

He offered a quick smile and went downstairs to the kitchen. Pouring himself a cup of coffee, he hoped she wouldn't follow him outside.

Their first Christmas together in Connecticut should have been magical. Yet no matter how much he wanted to enjoy it, his unease and disorientation endured, reminding him that the tumult he experienced in such a scant span of time allowed him to feel that way.

So many questions that slipped through the cracks, volumes of things left unsaid to both his wife and son. So many random questions...

The fate of his Saint Joseph statue haunted him, and he just couldn't shake it. Following superstition, he'd buried one on his front lawn. Family and friends alike swore by the practice, stating they'd sold their houses quickly and profitably after doing so. Months later, after the house had been sold, he tried digging it up to no avail. Even with help from others, they practically dug it up entirely and found nothing.

Standing in the slight chill, he tried redirecting his thoughts to the day ahead: children tearing open gifts, merriment in his growing relationship with her family, more cookies... But, as always, framed by those skeletal trees, the vast emptiness drew him back.

Devoid of passing deer, the dead field loomed. The trees seemed farther away, as if it had shrunk away from them at some point during the night. After a few minutes, he spotted something. It appeared as a distant black dot at first before he could make out the clear human form. Nearly dropping his coffee mug, he backed away.

A phone rang from inside, and he turned back reflexively, recognizing his ringtone. When he returned his stare to the field and the desolate woods beyond, the figure disappeared.

He opened the door to a shrill peal of laughter that froze him to the spot. It definitely didn't resemble Roberta's chirpy chuckle and it didn't sound like the television.. A silhouette greeted him on the living room wall, curling and spreading and he laughed to himself.

"*Vito*, come here, you crazy little..."

When he walked inside, neither Vito nor the silhouette awaited him. The air in the house felt icy cold and he put down his coffee mug to warm himself.

"Vito..." he called softly.

Another cackle. He turned the lamp on, but the bulb popped in a quicksilver flash, leaving a black burning odor that stung his nostrils.

In his peripheral vision, he noticed something dark by the brown sectional to his right. He turned and the sight of a shadow struck him as absolutely wrong; it was too dark, almost shiny. There was nothing casting it, no light from the window that he just closed.

The walls seemed to close in, and for a moment, he smelled the dank rot of the dungeon room. He thought of Brenda and could practically smell Elizabeth Arden wafting in the air. A rapid whisper alerted him to the fireplace.

He made a move to the left and the shadow scampered back to the wall, shifting, pulsing. The whisper faded and he turned to leave. Before he could, the mahogany bookshelf tilted, and the ornate stone name plaque slid off the top. It crashed with an awful thud, halving the word FAMILY in a perfect split.

Roberta called him but it sounded so far away. The echo trembled and dissolved into a light whisper, then a rapid scattershot, leaving his ears hot with countless tiny voices

The shadow danced and he blinked but there it remained, curling and sliding along the wall. He thought to look back at the curtains but found that he was frozen to the spot, unable to move or look away.

The sound of his ringtone made him blink again. When he looked back the shadow shrank into the thin trail of vapor and disappeared, leaving the living room muted in its natural overcast glare from the windows.

He heard the ringing again, somewhere in the house. Backing out of the room, he slowly made his way upstairs, knowing he wouldn't reach it in time to pick up once he found it.

Out of breath, he stopped at the foot of the stairs, warily glancing at the living room. He wanted to chalk it up to dirty glasses, except he wasn't wearing any. He rubbed his eyes, and tried to recall what he'd eaten the night before and when. Then he remembered the cookies.

Nearly retching at the thought of the cookie swap the night before, he hoped against the onset of some terrible condition that would further curtail holiday merriment. No explanation existed for what he'd just witnessed, so it had to be something with him, some internal disconnect, an issue attributed to overindulgence of some kind.

The ringing returned at the same time Roberta called him,

uniting them into a sonic calypso whine. She cast a quizzical glance as he joined her at the bedroom armoire.

"Are you alright? You don't look good!" she said, placing her palm to his forehead.

"I'm alright, I tell ya. Now where's that phone?"

"Wasn't it downstairs?" she asked, red fingernail tapping his cheek.

"I was just…down there."

Turning away from him, she scoffed. He pretended to ignore it but she did it again. He even caught her sneaking a sideways glance, pursing her lips in mock annoyance.

"I bet you it was him" he snapped defiantly.

"At this hour? Probably Margaret! Wanna bet?" she smirked.

"Bet? It's Christmas! That's sacrilegious! Probably call right back"

"Thank goodness he's not much of a talker! We've got to head over Pam's soon!" she informed him with a stern glance over the top of her glasses.

"Berta, it's only eight! Let the kids open their presents, we have some coffee then you call," he sighed to her eye-rolling annoyance.

The phone rang again and relief washed over him. He suddenly felt the need to speak to his son.

"Probably Dom," he said hopefully, and raced downstairs to snatched it off the table on the third ring.

"Merry Christmas, son!" he exclaimed to the requisite five or so moments of silence.

"Morning," Dominick muttered, harshly clearing his throat.

"So, what you got going on today?"

More silence, followed by a distant sigh.

"We just brought offerings to our departed," he intoned.

"Ok...so you guys made the whole spread huh? Macaroni, the meatballs, the ..."

"How's the weather up there?" Dominick almost snapped.

"It's, I don't know, fine, I guess. Everything okay with you? You sound, I don't know..."

"I don't know..." his son repeated in a deep croaking voice.

Before Dom could respond, his son emitted a slow sinister laugh.

"I don't know...I don't know...I don't know...I don't know..."

"Dominick!"

The phone felt hot to his ear and he pulled it away and saw the screen flashing in a riot of numbers and letters, pulsing green with a black border encroaching in all sides. Laughter squawked from it and he put it back to his ear in time to hear a guttural growl fading into a croak.

"Hey Dominick, what the hell is..." he yelled.

"She's glad to see you happy."

"What?" Dom snapped back, but his son had hung up. The phone suddenly felt cold in his hand, like a freezer pack and he tossed it onto the hallway table and went downstairs.

Shaking his head, he walked downstairs. Roberta fixed him with a cockeyed glare.

"Now what? You always look like that when you get off the phone with him!"

"Weird...he was just telling me...pretty much what I was just dreaming about, he'd just done. I don't know...that's just strange."

"What do you mean? What'd he say exactly?"

"Something about how he just brought offerings to the dead, just like in my..."

"Always so morbid," she cut him off, and turned to the window.

He started to talk again, but she did a double-take and clutched her heart as she stared out the window.

"What's the matter?" he asked and joined her at the window.

"Holy mackerel!"

Snow fell so heavily that it seemed to rain down in chunks,creating a near white-out as they looked out the window. From what he was able to see, a few inches had already accumulated.

"Where'd all that snow come from?" he asked.

"Same place it always does," she cooed, hugging him from behind.

He suddenly felt hot and itchy, and squirmed from her embrace.

"Oh poor dear, that psoriasis of yours acting up again? We'll have to get you back to Dr. Perkins. I'm in the mood for some more coffee," she chirped and kissed him on the cheek.

He smiled and handed her his cup, making sure she was out of sight before wiping the lipstick from his cheek, an old habit from when he was a younger man with many ladies to keep track of.

A shrill howl startled him and he couldn't tell if it was from inside or out. Music suddenly filled the room, loud brash opening notes, so familiar.

"Only You"

He turned to see Berta frozen in horror, steaming coffee mugs, titling precariously in her trembling hands.

"It just…"

"Seriously, Dominick! I understand that you miss her and tomorrow is…"

"Roberta, swear to God I didn't even touch it!"

Pursing her lips into a tight grin, she handed him the mug and walked upstairs.

"Roberta!" he called after her with no response.

The lights went out, falling snow leaving a silver-blue sheen on the room. The music, however, continued to play.

The hairs on his neck went up as he heard a series of jagged breaths, followed by the whistling cackle. Standing alone in the darkness, his rapid heartbeat only grew more furious. Relief flooded him as he heard the sound of Roberta's careful footfalls down the stairs toward him.

The lights suddenly returned and the song switched to Bing Crosby, "White Christmas".

She stopped at the edge of the room, small brown eyes fixed him on him in cockeyed curiosity.

"Okay, I know you just didn't do *that*!" she said, trailing off into nervous laughter.

"I'm *telling* you Berta! Freaking thing just came on! Then the lights…Weird!"

"Better call Joanne, let her know we might not be able to get over there if this keeps up," she said, gesturing toward the window and the snow falling outside.

She dialed and beamed when her daughter picked up.

"Merry Christmas, honey! Guess you guys won't be stopping by because there's no way we'd make it my little… what's that? What do you mean? It's a blizzard out there and…hello? Hello? Joanne…hello…"

Roberta looked at her phone, then outside. She tried dialing again, but the phone went dead.

"I charged it overnight! What the heck is wrong with this thing?" she said before tossing the phone onto the coffee table.

The lights flickered for a few minutes then stopped. He

held her close enough to smell the toothpaste on her breath, minty fresh frantic prayers spewing forth in his ear. He waited a moment then exhaled.

"I think we're okay..." Dom whispered.

The lights went out altogether and the house got cold all at once.

"Why'd you have to even *say* that?" he whined, vapor emitting in the frigid room.

"I didn't..." she said sheepishly.

"Yeah, I know, I was talkin' to myself, keep up there Berta! Damn thing'll probably come on in five, four, three, two..."

He pointed to the ceiling and groaned after a moment.

"Dom..."

Without responding, he rushed out through the kitchen and to the garage. He flipped the breakers to no avail and returned to a trembling Roberta.

"So cold..." she whispered, holding herself against the visible chill in the room.

"I'll go turn on the generator," he said and quickly donned blue work pants and Timberlands to face the storm.

The moment he unclicked the latch to head outside, the sound of frantic scampering noises stunned him. Before he could react, Vito squirmed his way outside and took off down the deck steps.

"Vito! No!" Dom bellowed into the icy howl of the storm.

Rushing out, he nearly slipped on the icy deck but managed to steady himself and make it down the stairs safely. Hand bracing against the storm, he managed to arrive at the generator only to find the gas tank empty.

Then, in the garage, he kicked the three plastic containers when he found them bone-dry. They'd been filled just before

Halloween. Returning inside, he watched Roberta's face grow crestfallen.

"Not gonna believe this…" he grumbled, kicking off the snow onto the cat-patterned floor mat.

She opened her mouth to speak but a booming roar from inside interrupted her, a man's voice. They both ran into the living room and he nearly slammed into her when they both stopped abruptly.

"What the hell is going on?" he muttered, tossing his gloves off.

"I'm sorry Dom but I…" she trailed off, wringing her hand as she gazed off.

"What? What'd you do Berta?"

"I might have done something I wasn't supposed to. I… think I *opened* something I shouldn't have…"

"Berta, for the love of God, would you just tell me what the hell it is you're talking about please!"

She did an indignant double-take, pursing her lips.

"You don't have to be like that with me. I'm telling you ok?"

"Just tell me, would you please?" he replied, hoarse with exasperation.

"That old trunk, I…opened it."

"Okay…"

"As soon as I did, it…I don't know, got really cold and then I felt this strange chill," she said and made the sign of the cross.

Dom's hazel eyes opened wide and she took a deep breath.

"It passed through me and then I heard the voice…"

"The voice?" Dom asked.

"A woman's voice, talking…I don't know, I think it was

Irish or something. It was so fast, almost like she was singing..."

He rubbed his mustache and shook his head a few times.

"What...*exactly* made you open the trunk?" he asked, eyes narrow in suspicion.

Stepping back, her eyes opened and narrowed repeatedly back at him.

"Why? What's wrong with it? I love that trunk, I've always loved that trunk!" she spouted a little too quickly, almost frantic.

"Nothing... wrong with it, just..." The words stopped at his lips and he looked away.

The Woodson's old trunk had always spooked him and he couldn't figure out why. The fact that their family retrieved the rest of their belongings but not the trunk always stuck in his craw. When it came time to pack up the house after closing, he gladly got rid of it.. Diane had always loved it so he promised it to her.

Then Roberta caught sight of it and pined for it. The amorous glaze in her eyes at the sight of the trunk stuck with him, and he felt defenseless when she asked to keep it when he agreed to move in with her in Connecticut.

He fixed her with his sternest glare where his thick eyebrows nearly joined in a serpentine wave of disapproval.

Her hurt pout tightening into a worried coil, Roberta took a step back from him.

Brenda would always chuckle and gesture to Dominick:

"Look he's brought out the DiNuzzio Cobra!"

For a moment, Dom had to remember to keep a straight face.

"Roberta, what's the story here? What's up with the trunk?"

Her jaw trembled, red lips opening and closing repeatedly before emitting a shrill sob.

"I was looking for a ring, *okay*?" she wailed.

"A what?" he asked with a grimace, like he'd never heard the word before.

"I just thought...I don't know, maybe, you were going to do some grand romantic gesture, like propose to me in front of everyone...Christmas..." she broke down into choked sobs, and removed her glasses.

"At the family *'cookie swap*?'" he said in sing-song sarcasm.

Her eyes opened then narrowed just as quickly. With a slight nod of her head, she wagged her finger at him.

"You told me you had a good time!" she said in a deep sinister rasp.

"I did!"

"You told me you had a good time, and I *believed* you!" she said through gritted teeth.

He stepped back, then wondered why. He'd never felt threatened by Roberta before. He liked that about her. She didn't challenge him the way Brenda did, leaving frail scraps of his arguments in her fiery wake. Thoughts of her piling up in his mind, he tried to channel her; that indefatigable pluck, resourcefulness in the face of calamity.

What would Brenda do?

"Should we, I don't know, call the parish maybe?"

"And tell them *what* exactly?" she said, followed by the hint of a laugh.

"This is...I'm saying, they know how to handle this type of stuff! Especially the, oh God, what are they called again? The movie, the..." he stammered, snapping his fingers.

"The Jesuits?" Roberta asked, with an amused grin.

"Yeah! There you go! The Jezyooitts!" he tried to get it out, nearly choking on his dentures, as they jarred loose.

"*Holy Water*!" she exclaimed, and rushed to the glass display case in the dining room.

Dom laughed nervously in spite of himself. It was kept in the same place as it was at his old house, near the family bible.

A frigid swirl of air enveloped him. He stepped toward the wall but it followed him, whispers whipping up rapidly in some language he couldn't understand.

"*Whaddya youse want*?" he whined.

It grew quiet and Dom felt heat slowly rise back into him from the floor.

Roberta returned with a small crystal vial and began frantically sprinkling water all over the floor, most of it landing on the exposed tops of Dom's skippered feet.

"What the hell Berta? Come on…"

"You *said* to get holy water!" she shot back.

"All right, let's not get silly all right? Freaking ghosts… Seems like everything's all right now, so…"

Turned to Roberta, he paused, disquieted by the sight of her staring intently at the wall. Lips slightly parted, her eyes twitched, almost in indignant accusation. She made the sign of the cross and casually grabbed a cookie from the dish on the coffee table.

"At least we have the cookies," she offered hopefully.

"Yeah, that's a…that's *good*!" he said.

The night before, excitement filled him as they attended his first Holiday Cookie Swap. Roberta went on and on about it.He enjoyed it too, but he'd already sampled just about each and every variety of cookie imaginable. Just about. Among the dizzying array of chocolate chip, sugar, butter, oatmeal, sprinkled vanilla, and other cookies, nobody brought his beloved *Tricolore*.

He coveted rainbow cookies; growing up poor, he only saw them on the tables of more well-to-do Italian neighbors. Naturally, he missed the family spread of shrimp, meatballs and macaroni, but he enjoyed the Christmas Eve cookie swap.

Things, however, got slightly awkward when he corrected seven-year old Jeremy to call him Dom and *not* Grandpa. Earlier, he'd overheard Roberta tell her gaggle of grandchildren to do so and spent most of the evening bracing himself.

Roberta pulled the tray closer to the edge of the table and took a powdered butter cookie.

"It goes great with the coffee," she said, offering him one.

"No thank you," he said to her slight sigh.

"Get the blanket so we can cuddle up!" she said, pointing to the other end of the couch.

Dom stared at it for a moment, the haphazard blanket balled into a spray of Patriots' blue, red and gray.

"You know what? Too small! I'll get the quilt from…"

"What do you mean? What's wrong with…oh, *you*!" she chirped with a pinch on his arm.

"What? It *is*! Why you pinching me over here?"

"Because I know why you don't like it- it's the *Patriots*! Am I right? Tell me I'm right!"

Dom rose and she sat up straight.

"Don't leave me alone down here!"

"What Berta? I'm just going upstairs!"

She called after him but he'd already walked off. The remaining light seemed to drain from the room and it grew painfully colder.

The strands of lights on the Christmas tree flickered and she sighed in relief, awaiting the return of electricity to the rest of the house. There was a steady buzzing in the room; she could feel it before she heard it, a deep chill that made her teeth instantly ache, and a sharp metallic taste formed in her mouth. Then a fog appeared, spectral, almost static in nature. It quickly gained matter, and began to coalesce into a clear form. He was tall, gaunt with dark pits for eyes, raising a long finger at the Christmas tree.

"You dare mock the birth of our Lord with pagan idolatry?" he roared.

The tree went alight with a mere touch of his forefinger as he grew closer. She found herself sliding off the couch, hiding behind the coffee table.

"Hide, the harlot does, like a serpent through heathen sands? Show yourself, witch!"

She backed away and bumped her head on the end of the sofa.

"The harlot reaps ill begotten bounties while blood kin suffer, whittling for scraps and the serpent with you shall forever lurk, slithering around the bones of your eternal soul and you descendants and their descendants forevermore! Shall ye choke on the venom of your sin, shall ye bathe in the sweat of swine in the swelter of hell itself serving your dark master, your false lord, vermin excised from the rafters of the hereafter, cast out to be scorched by the light of the Lord!"

"I'm not afraid of you!" she shouted, much to his amusement, breaking into an awful laugh that echoed loud enough to dislodge the quilted prayer made by her grandmother from the wall with a sharp crash.

"Repent!"

"YOU repent, you, you, you...after what you did to my ancestors? Who do you think you are? What makes you so high and mighty? Huh? So afraid of a woman... a woman with spirit and spunk and skills...skills of which you can't conceive!"

The preacher shirked back, holding up a hand in defense. His form dissipated for a moment before returning with a static fury. Behind him, the skeletal remains of the tree glowed almost blue, blinding in some incandescent light.

"REPENT!"

A book flew straight at her. She tried to duck but wasn't quick enough. It hit her on the forehead, knocking her glasses off. She tumbled backward, bracing herself against further attack. Trying to catch her breath, she reached around for her glasses.She managed to grab them and put them on in time to avoid the book slamming her from above.

She saw it as it landed before her — the Holy Bible. She reached but it felt hot to the touch. She backed away but it followed her, singing the carpet. Electric pulses made the air quiver before her as he grew closer. When the inevitable smack of the wall struck on her back, she took a deep breath and slid up the wall, never tearing her eyes from his furious opaque glare. Extending her forefingers and pinkies at him, she leaned toward him.

"Qui vocat spiritum…"

Upstairs, Dom heard Roberta yell and ran to the door but it slammed shut just as he reached it. The unmistakable aroma of Elizabeth Arden perfume immediately flooded his nose. He turned, half-expecting to see Brenda sitting on the bed, ready with some wry observation or wiseass remark but he found himself back in the tunnel, the hooded figures a few feet ahead of him

This time, he felt no fear, the dank odor familiar along the path, the debris now clear to him - family pictures and old Christmas cards. He closed in on them and they removed their hoods and stared at him impassively. Dominick and Diane carried a tray of traditional Christmas hor d'oeuvres to Brenda's sky blue urn.

"*Glad you're having such a good time*," Dominick said sharply, landing hard on each syllable, eyes narrow.

"*So glad you're even enjoying yourself,*" Diane said softly, dark eyes opaque, accusing. She was bent over and rested one hand on her back.

"*So glad,*" Dominick concurred, stirring a pot of beans.

He wanted to ask her if she felt okay and felt silly for even thinking about it. Diane wasn't okay, wouldn't be okay but he went up to Connecticut anyhow, not even waiting for her surgery.

"*No you didn't,*" Dominick said and made him step back with the terror that his very thoughts were laid bare.

"*He had enough. He didn't want to deal with another sick woman,*" Diane said sadly, her doll face framed by her mass of black curls.

"*He had to live his life*", Dominick replied solemnly, without taking his eyes off his father.

"*Have some meatballs,*" Diane said, offering him a steaming tray of Swedish meatballs.

Before he could refuse, his son held out a tray of shrimp cocktail to him. The sight of his own hazel eyes staring back at him wrenched his stomach and he felt himself make a fist.

Diane produced a glass tray of deviled eggs, paprika resting ever so delicately on the bright yellow egg yolk nestled in its bed of white.

"*Deviled eggs, your favorite. We want you to have a good time.*"

"*Yes, We want you to enjoy yourself.*"

"No…"

"*Macaroni and cheese. Just like Grandma used to make. Remember back home, Dad? No of course you don't. You don't want to remember.*"

Diane nodded and put the tray down to rub her back.

"He doesn't want to remember. Stop making him remember."

"I won't. I won't make him remember. I know what he wants. He doesn't want any of this. He doesn't need any of this. Not anymore."

Dom slapped the tray out of his son's hand. Dominick fixed him with a grave stare and shook his head.

"Sorry. So sorry for not giving you what you want. So very sorry for not completing you. I know what he wants."

"How do you know what I want?" Dom cried.

"What does he want?" she asked, ignoring him.

"He wants cookies."

"Cookies," Diane repeated blankly.

They faded into smoke and he began coughing. The air cleared, and the room became bright, the lights garish and blinding, and it smelled like fresh bakery. A riot of laughter made him look around and as the smoke cleared, he saw an army of smiling children running at him...

Children, children everywhere running, rushing toward him, all offering cookies, laughter deafening as they grew near. They were facsimiles of Roberta's grandchildren,boys with neat blond parted hair and girls in pigtails with green and red ribbons but with only ragged black holes where their eyes should be.

"Grandpa, here!"

"Have a cookie, Grandpa!"

"You're the best, Grandfather!"

"I'm not Grandpa!" he boomed. They disappeared, and he walked back into the living room. Blackened cheeks stained with mascara bisected by rapidly flowing tears, Roberta nodded and wiped her face.

"I know, it's all right, it's not your fault! I shouldn't have pushed so hard, I shouldn't have..."

He enveloped her in an embrace and noticed she stunk of smoke, the ends of her sweater singed.

"Come on," she said softly and led him across the hall, to the third bedroom that had been designated his trophy room.

The trunk stood open.

"When I first saw it, that first time I visited you in Pennsylvania, I couldn't believe it. I was drawn to it immediately and, to be perfectly honest, I haven't been the same since. Look, I'm still a good Catholic – I mean we go to church, right? But Dominick, I might as well tell you…" She took a deep breath and folded her hands.

"In my family, way back in my family line, there were women who…who had *certain* talents. Bakers, healers, the sort of women who used their gifts for the betterment of the family, and of their village too, for all the *good* it did them!"

"You and all these secrets? What the hell, Berta? What does any of this have to do with the trunk?"

"Funny, I really *was* looking for a ring too…" her voice cracked as she reached into the trunk and removed a stack of letters tied in a white ribbon. They aged in progression from the yellowed, weathered ones on bottom to more crips and whiter ones on top. Dom warily scanned them as she shook her hand toward him until he took them.

"Brenda's handwriting…" she said softly with a shudder.

They felt like a brick in his hand. That perfect cursive, those immaculate loops… He wiped his eyes, not caring if Berta noticed or not.

It all happened so fast and before he'd known it,Brenda died and he'd moved twice, to two different states and started wearing peacoats like a suburban yuppie. He had a cat.

"Dominick…"

Although standing mere feet away, Roberta's voice sounded like an echo from another dimension. The unfamiliar pitch was a cosmic callback to a joke he only pretended to grasp. Everything suddenly felt forced. It was a flimsy construct at best, an escape plan written on a receipt.Whether they got married or not, they would only be playing house.

He'd never left Queens, not really; he still sat at Brenda's bedside, sheltered from the storm but not the silence that followed.

The empty house once full of laughter and conversation and arguments and yelling, doors slamming echoed with only well-wishes from neighbors, the creak of the fridge opening to welcome yet another foil-wrapped casserole, platters and platters of platitudes... A teardrop fell onto the top letter and the rapidly-spreading smudge roused him from the ache of it all.

"Here, I *can't* ..." he choked, handing them back to her.

Roberta gently took them and tucked them under her am as she reached to him. He stepped back, wiping his eyes, barely registering her deep sigh.

"She... *Brenda* wrote these letters to..."

"Wait, hold up... you *read* them?" he asked, face twisted into a disgusted grimace.

"I, well...I *did*, ok? And I apologize, Dom, but..."

"But *what*?"

"I didn't know what else to do. I thought she could help us. He won't leave us alone! He'll *never* leave us alone!"

"Whoa, whoa, whoa...*slow* down! Who? Who won't leave you alone?"

Eyes closed tight, she remained silent, turning away as he neared.

"Dominick, we don't have enough time to explain *everything* but, to answer your question, he was a preacher..."

"Ok, hold up, what the hell Roberta? I'm not liking this..."

Leaning in close, she fixed him with a sober glare.

"Like I said, we *don't* have time but I need you to know that I'm a good Catholic and I love you, I always have but like I was saying…"

Agape, he just shook his head, blankly motioning her to continue.

"So, as I was saying, he was a preacher. The Honorable Reverend Wilford Smyth, Witchfinder General around these parts."

"Witch…*what*? I'm sorry, I'm sorry …" he stopped himself, placed his hands on his hips, and twirled his fingers for her to go on.

"Wouldn't leave them alone, hounded them, tortured, killed them! *All* because, because…"

Still registering everything in his mind, Dom didn't interject. He'd already learned more than he ever needed to know. But he'd lived long enough to learn that the only way out is through.

"All because of *cookies* Dom! Because people liked their *cookies*!" she cried.

She took a deep breath and stared away before turning back to him.

"The survivors, the ones who'd hidden in barns in the woods, they swore vengeance. So they buried him headfirst, so he'd head to hell instead of heaven…"

"Right, right, of course, makes sense" he cracked with a knowing nod, prompting a narrow glare.

"…Out past the field, before they burned it."

"Holy…" he exclaimed, before ceasing at the sight of her grave stare.

"…On Christmas morning."

Moments passed before a crash came from downstairs, a guttural rumble that rapidly approached them.

"What do we do now Roberta? We got something for this or what?"

Wiping her cheeks on her sleeve, she nodded and pointed to the trunk.

"I'm going to need you to just *trust* me," she pled "You might get the heebie-jeebies but just...*please* trust me, okay?"

"Ok, alright sure," he replied.

Carefully navigating around the wreckage of the room, she stopped at the upended mahogany table. Groaning as she bent over, she opened the middle drawer diagonally, distrusting its contents on the floor. She snatched a white candle, hurried back to him and lit it.

"Qui vocat spiritum..."

"What's that? *Latin*? Damn, been a long time, I don't remember nothing ..." he said, scratching his head.

She cast him a sharp glance and he fell silent.

"Qui vocat spiritum..."

She launched into a rapid chant and he felt the air swirl about. A thick silence hung in the room but he felt a presence.

"Our Lady of no name, please help us..."

The room fell silent for a moment, so quiet that Dom could hear the wind outside. Then came a wail, a horrid shriek that pierced the skull, and made the heart stop, shattering the glass panes on each display case as it rose in furious intensity.

The trunk flew open and an iridescent pulse spread through the room. The glow fluctuated before the foreboding scowl of the preacher until it settled into the form of a petite woman. She had bright green eyes and blonde hair and looked to be in her twenties. A smirk fixed to her full lips, she casually looked the preacher up and down.

"Cast your brittle soul back to whence it came, charla-

tan! You wouldn't know about Christ if he beat you at billiards!"

The preacher growled, waving his hand frantically as if attacked. The lady just smirked and snapped her fingers. Cookies flew from the table at him, *through* him, perforating his static form at jagged angles as he roared in crackling rage.

"Dominick, stand back..." Roberta said, fixing her aching fingers into a hex sign.

"By the blood of my ancestors, I cast thee out! Back to an earthen abyss condemn you to forever stare into darkness... into the eyes of the devil himself, to never befoul this house again!" she cried.

The lady unleashed a wail that blew Smyth apart, sending white-hot gray matter scattering through the room, until it collected on the floor. Instantly regaining shape, he grew even taller, barely an inch below the ceiling. Towering over them, his nostrils flared. Dom heard something behind him, and almost too terrified to look, he forced himself, bracing for untold horror. The sight of Vito, casually sauntering past him, simultaneously offered relief and blank confusion. The cat slowly walked right about to the preacher, who cast a disgusted grimace.

"Foul creature!"

Vito looked up and opened his small maw and unleashed a caterwaul that shook the house with the roar of a thousand throats. The preacher's eyes opened and grew until its form collapsed into itself in a fury of screaming shadows. Berta ran to Dom and they cowered away from the throb of the energy and wrenching shriek.

The lady flew at the preacher and joined in song, uniting as a skull-splitting chorus that made the shadows explode one by one until nothing remained of the preacher but faint trails of smoke. Vito emitted a soft purr and laid down on the couch. He offered a white paw to her and she returned a broad smile with a wink. She bent over to pet the purring feline.

"Good job, my little friend!"

She caught Dom's bewildered stare and smiled gently.

"She wrote me letters, long lovely letters. Addressed me as Lady, she did," she tittered, eyes twinkling as she nearly blushed.

The shock of a teardrop on his cheek and, for the first time since he could remember, he felt embarrassed and he didn't know why.

"Don't you go getting sad, mister! You loved each other for a long time," she said, beaming from above. With a warm, sly smile she winked at him.

"Oh and another thing mister, that statue of Saint Joseph? You were about two feet off and a foot shallow!" she cracked with a hearty laugh. A green light circled the room and enveloped her in its swirl. Then she was gone.

The lights returned and Bing Crosby picked up "White Christmas" right on cue, the Christmas tree twinkling in a riot of color.

Roberta's phone rang and she bounded away, exploding into excited tears when she picked up.

"Joanne! Joanne, honey! Is that you? Yes...well, you wouldn't believe what happened after I talked to you! In the middle of the storm, the power goes out! and then ...what? Of course I talked to you! Earlier this morning when the snow got heavy and...What do you mean 'what snow'? It's a blizzard out there, it's a..."

She turned to the window and met Dom's blank gaze as he looked out. Not a flake of snow drifted from the sky, the sun shone through the trees beyond the field.

"Okay…well never mind dear. We'll be over soon okay!" She hung up and wiped her brow.

Dom shook his head then made a face at her sheepish grin.

"Want to open our gifts?"

"Why the hell not?" he sighed.

She grabbed a long package in holly-patterned wrapping paper and offered a terse smile.

"Guess this one's for *me*…" she said, voice betraying an artificial lilt.

Taking her time to carefully remove the wrapping paper by unfolding each sharp corner, she eyed him sharply.

"Great job on the gift-wrapping hon," she chuckled.

"Yeah, I'm pretty good at it actually! I have my special technique!" he said with a smile, but she didn't pay attention. Focused on sliding the paper off the white box, she appeared to be in no hurry to see what it was. Dom applied a smile nonetheless, maintaining it as she removed the top of the box, set the delicate tissue paper aside after examining it for a moment, or three.

"Really nice, Dom! Really, really nice, thank you." she said in a monotone rasp.

She stood and held the black ankle-length Shearling coat in front of her, looking down at its decorative buttons.

"Try it on," he told her.

She looked up at him at him and they exchanged a quick glance devoid of mirth.

After sighing under her breath, she donned the coat at a glacial pace, fully extending her left arm into the sleeve before inserting the right, then flexing both as he nodded.

"Fits perfect right?" he asked hopefully.

"It does, thank you so much!" she said, and offered a flat smile.

Wasting no time, she took the jacket off and returned to the tree. Taking some effort, she lifted a rectangular package wrapped in solid green paper with a mistletoe attached to the name tag.

"Now, I cannot wait until you see this!" she said, eyes sparkling behind her Donna Karan frames.

"Damn, this sucker's heavy! What the hell you got in here, Berta?"

She shrugged with a slight curtsy, then shook her head as he tore the warping off in one haphazard yank.

Inside lay an ornate carving of DINUZZI, like the one that hung for decades on the wall of their foyer in Queens.

He felt the muscle in his face rise and from a smile as he lifted the hefty piece, following Roberta's jubilant smile as she walked to the empty space adjacent to the front door.

"We can put it right here!" she pointed.

She stood before almost the exact same spot where the name hung in his old house. He smiled and visibly exhaled at the sound of his ringing phone.

"It's probably..." he began.

"I know, Dominick," she said softly and walked to the kitchen.

Dom cleared his throat and picked up. It was Dominick after all.

"Merry Christmas, Dad! How you all doing up there?"

Stunned by the jovial banter and his softened tone, Dom sat silently for a moment, staring at the sun-dappled tree in the backyard.

"Dad?"

"Oh sorry, I'm here! Well, glad you're in a better mood than before!"

"What do you mean?" Dominick asked with a chuckle.

"When we talked earlier, you were all, I don't know…you kinda had an attitude."

"Dad, I didn't speak to you before…" he said, voicing trailing off with growing concern.

Dom walked outside and stared at the house next door. The faintest hint of light shone between the rotting boards covering the windows.

"Dad? You okay?"

He choked back the onset of tears and cleared his throat.

"Yeah, I'm just… glad everything's all right. How's Diane?"

A CRACKED NUTCRACKER
CHRISTMAS

DELLA SULLIVAN

As Christmas drew closer and closer, panic forced the three Harrison sisters to set up an emergency luncheon date to discuss how the traditional family holiday would unfold. They reserved Christmas Day for intimate family. They held the festivities for the entire clan on Boxing Day, though they could be flexible. Every relative within 800 miles traveled to Toronto to spend family time with all the cousins, second cousins and satellite members who were close friends. Reminiscing and mulled wine became de rigueur as part of the celebration. With only 15 shopping days left before the big elf came, they needed to make decisions about location, menu and guest list.

The location gave them the most trouble. Charlotte, the oldest sister, had hosted the last 6 holiday celebrations and refused to do it again. However, the constant pressure from her sisters reminding her that her house in Rosedale, with its six bedrooms and two-family rooms suited the large crowd to a tee had her shaking her head no, while her mouth said yes.

This year Charlotte vowed to say no, not this time. An uneasy resolve twisted her stomach.

The menu was always turkey with all the standard trimmings; green bean casserole, pumpkin tarts, and pumpkin pies, in addition to all the sweet and savory dishes brought by their guests. Cousin Louise, from Quebec, always brought a large larded homemade Christmas pudding that was admired, but never eaten. When she walked around the room presenting it, everyone made signs of full tummies and a promise to take some home. In contrast, the fiery Italian chorizo pasta dish cooked by Uncle James disappeared quickly as nearly everyone gulped down large portions with gusto.

The guest list of aunts and uncles and cousins varied, depending on who had divorced, reconciled or tried out the opposite sex. Great Aunt Josie, now in her 95th year always knew who had been naughty or nice. Not much missed her inquisitive nose and her grapevine was vast and accurate. This required a patient and gossipy phone conversation with her in early December and every year Charlotte hung up with a list of the "not invited" according to Aunt Josie

Charlotte asked her sisters to meet her in a restaurant in Yorkville in the middle of downtown Toronto. It had been a favorite lunch spot of her mother's, loved for the soothing smooth jazz that constantly played. She enjoyed the privacy the large leafed green potted plants arranged artfully around the small tables afforded the diners. Charlotte picked a window seat, and allowed herself one glass of wine rationalizing that this didn't break her sobriety vow.

She thought back to a comment her husband made. "One glass of wine doesn't make you an alcoholic." She had been drinking too much since the funeral and had gone to a couple of AA meetings.

I can control myself. One or two itty bitty glasses of Chardonnay helps me relax, she thought.

The stress of the holidays, so soon after her mother Kathleen's funeral made her feel dull and sleepy. Her mother had been a widow for 20 years, and she had a very close relationship with her girls, especially Charlotte. She had involved herself in all her children's lives to a greater degree than she had when their father was alive. She hoped her mom and dad were together again. She quickly wiped away the thick buildup of tears that overflowed her eyes. Her mother died from complications of emergency gallbladder surgery just days before Thanksgiving. She was only 69 and had been in perfect health.

Her mother's death still hit her at odd moments, grabbing her and leaving her grasping her stomach. The fear of life never being the same again mixed with a now constant fear of impending disaster kept her from sleeping well. The pressure of taking over her mother's matriarchal status settled heavily on her shoulders.She had a prescription for anxiety pills, but never wanted to succumb to their siren call. She feared if she swallowed one pill, she would down the rest gulping a good Chianti. The expectation of being eased into the great beyond enticed her. Better not to start down that slippery slope.

She glanced outside barely registering the vista of a winter wonderland with soft fluffy snowflakes drifting over the seats in the courtyard. The snowy skies promised a white Christmas. She hadn't purchased a single gift. Normally her closets overflowed with presents for her four children; Tony, Bertram, Olive and Philip. She kept a holiday book, and as she wrapped each gift, she recorded it and made sure the numbers of gifts for each child were equally fair. She took great care selecting unique gifts for her two sisters and two brothers and bought still more gifts for aunts and uncles, teachers, piano teachers and other last-minute gift exchanges.

Each year since the beginning of their 15-year marriage her husband, Angus bought them a Caribbean or Greece cruise. Just the thought of that holiday kept them sane over the holidays, knowing that when the snow at home became streaked with grit and browning salt, they would be on their mini honeymoon with nothing to do but enjoy cerulean waters and fruity cocktails. They had agreed on their first honeymoon, relaxing in a catamaran in Bermuda, that this yearly vacation would substitute Christmas gifts for each other.

Much like her mother had been, Charlotte prided herself on being organized. She most resembled her mother with her soft round body and cinnamon coloured hair with sparkling light brown eyes. Tossing her head, she brought herself back to the moment. Once they finished lunch, she would start shopping. She planned to hit the stores hard and fast. If that failed, there was always Amazon to fall back on.

Second to arrive was Jane, the baby of the family. She had not even taken her coat off or put down the bulging shopping bag before she wailed, "We are orphans now." As she settled her tall frame into her chair, tears crawled down her cheeks. She would be twenty-eight years old on New Year's Day, had a good job as a flight attendant and a new girlfriend, Ursula.

Charlotte thought Jane could be a bit spacey, and although very competent in the air, not much good in a family emergency. In times of trouble, she could be counted on to freeze in position and shrug her shoulders helplessly. A result of being the baby of the family, she never learned to "fight her way out of a paper bag," as her mother liked to describe her. However, her strong, true soprano voice sounded great leading the Christmas carols. Her favourite carol, "Jingle Bells" got plenty of air time.

"Jane," asked Charlotte, "Is there anything you'd like to bring on family day?"

"I love decorating gingersnap people cookies for the holidays," Jane said.

"Do you have time with your heavy flight schedule this year to make them?" asked Charlotte.

"Yes, I will find the time. It is so much fun to bake sweets," Jane replied. "I will make enough cookies to package extra for everyone to take home."

Though pretty, her cookies always contained too much sugar, making them hard enough to break teeth. Jane was pretty, too. She possessed a long neck, round blue eyes, a trim figure, and a stunning smile. Men watched her wherever she went. She learned how to deflect their advances because she knew before she turned six that she preferred women.

The middle sister, Amber, late by 20 minutes, waved away Charlotte's deliberate glance at her gold wristwatch.

"Oh, honestly Char, not my fault, the salon was so slow." Amber worked hard to keep her figure. Monthly salon visits kept her red hair vibrant. She spared no expense when dressing herself. For this luncheon, her green Versace blouse made her stand out, even in this high fashion area.

Jane whispered, "Is that Heidi Klum? Sitting right over there?"

"Don't point, for goodness sake, Jane!" said Charlotte. "No, I'm sure it isn't. Well, it could be. Don't stare."

Amber tapped her jade green bullet proof nails on the table top. "I had a facial and a Botox treatment planned, but canceled in order to be here. Being forty is no picnic." Glancing at the table, she asked, " Oh, are we all having wine?"

Charlotte looked at Amber and opened her mouth to respond, but Amber sang out, "Waiter, two bottles of whatever they are drinking. I probably need a stiffer drink. Those boys of mine are so hard to control. The school put them on probation, apparently for spray painting the lockers of all the jocks pink. The boys say they didn't do it but...."

Amber's twins, Dwayne and Dwight, became collectively known as D-boy when they were younger. Even on the cusp of adulthood, people found it next to impossible to tell them apart. They had handsome faces, with dark curly hair and violet eyes reminiscent of Elizabeth Taylor. She took a big gulp of her wine, and declared, "The older they get the harder it is to discipline them. Not that their father is any help. He has them half the time, and insists their bad behaviour is just boys being boys."

Jane piped up and said, "I'm only going to have girls. They are so easy to raise."

Charlotte laughed as she said, "That is exactly what Mom said."

Amber knew this was not the time to tell them what she found under their beds. Pages and pages of disturbing drawings of grotesque beheadings. Swirling around the edges were great twisted horns and open screaming mouths. The spatters of red all over the papers told her where her expensive red nail polish had gone.

"Did I tell you I have nightmares of a big bad wolf who constantly stalks us?" Amber asked. The wine loosed her tongue and she continued. "He often disguises himself, sometimes sporting huge curved horns but these don't terrify me as much as where behind the hairy visage, the features look like my D-boys. Something evil and tentacled slithers on the ground, and that wakes me."

"That sounds really scary to me," Jane whispered back.

Charlotte looked at Amber and said, "Remember when your boys locked you in the bathroom?"

"That was horrible," Amber nodded. "Thank goodness I keep my Keto snacks in the adjoining closet."

When Charlotte had been unable to reach her sister by phone for two days, she found herself in her car, her bedroom slippers still on her feet, driving to Amber's house.

"I found you crying on your closet floor. I made you some chamomile tea and then I called the police because it was time those boys of yours learned some consequences."

"Yes, but that didn't help," said Amber, anger making her voice quiver. "The old judge reprimanded them and released them into their father's custody."

"I called Aunt Josie yesterday and we talked about the invitation list. Almost everyone is available this year. We can send out 36 invitations." Even as she said this, Charlotte experienced a spasm of fear. She poured herself another glass of wine and it helped to ward off her feelings of impending disaster.

"Jim and Tammy might come, but Peter is going on a third honeymoon with his new trophy wife," said Charlotte.

Their two older brothers did not live in the city. Peter lived in the south of France. Jim, and his wife, Tammy lived almost off the grid. Their home, far to the north in Ontario, required a 6-hour drive each way to come visit. The closest neighbour lived two miles away. A series of trailers haphazardly attached at weird angles made up their home. Several old and discarded truck trailers came with the purchase, and littered the west side of his forested property. His nephews and niece delighted in moving from one trailer to another, and found evidence of long dead chickens and one was still tainted with the gagging aroma of a slaughterhouse. Something old and rancid-smelling attached to their clothes long after these visits and the sisters learned to throw out the clothing worn while visiting Uncle Jim.

"That drive up north takes the whole weekend." said Charlotte. "I asked him why they chose to move there and he told me they liked the quietness of being isolated and the raw natural beauty of the woods made the frequent sewage problems and the mosquitoes worth the effort."

Jane said, "I only visited him once."

She refused to drive up there again after her first visit. She swore that there was something unholy living in the woods that surrounded Jim's maze of a house. For weeks after her visit, she would call Charlotte, her voice trembling, "Please come, Char, I think the devil is at my door."

Their mother had called her youngest, "tender-hearted," meaning too delicate for the rude and rough things in life. Charlotte always went to her, and often rocked her to sleep. This malevolence lasted about six months, until one call late at night, Jane whispered to Charlotte, "it's gone, I don't feel the demon's presence anymore."

Every other year, Jim and Tammy skipped his family party to visit Tammy's family who lived in another province. Tammy was stunningly beautiful. She had chocolate coloured eyes, an oval face and jet black hair. When he and his wife did come, he gathered all the children and started contests of who could burp and fart the loudest and longest. The children hooted with delight when they saw him. His sisters loved him dearly, too. All three of them had great burp skills honed by competitions with him as they grew up.

"I received an email from Jim." Charlotte filled up her wine glass, ignoring her inner voice that said she'd better eat something, "They are planning on coming this year if we can hold family day on the twenty-second. They want to fly to

Red Deer to celebrate with Tammy's family on Christmas Day."

Jane and Amber toasted glasses and said simultaneously, "Fine, the 22nd" and all three giggled.

"Oh, yes," said Jane, picking up the huge shopping bag, "remember how dad used to have that big collection of nutcrackers and how Mom said they just made her sad and she threw them out when he died. I found these four nutcrackers at a yard sale, and bought them as a remembrance of our family." She lifted them out one by one, the figures taking up all the space on the table. Two feet high with red jackets and white tufted hair with bushy mustaches hiding their levered mouths, the nutcrackers were noticeably damaged.

Charlotte looked at Jane, and said, "All of them are missing paint chips and one of the nutcracker's hair is smudged with orange. It looks like it has been in a fire."

"No worries," replied Jane, "I will spruce them up and make them festive. Please, for Dad? They will look great on a fireplace mantel. I'll bring red baubles and silver trimmings."

Amber jumped in and supported Jane. "Yes, let's. It would make Mum happy, if she is looking down from heaven."

Charlotte groaned aloud. "I wish she was still here. I don't know how I'm to get through the holidays without her. But if you think this makes her happy, I'm okay with the nutcrackers."

Amber picked up one of the least damaged nutcrackers, and as she tipped it to see if the hinged mouth would open, she fumbled and it knocked over her wine glass that then splashed onto Charlotte's black shirt.

"No worries," sang out Charlotte, "we can always get another bottle of wine."

"If Petey isn't coming, maybe we could invite his first wife? "asked Jane. The sisters heard the yearning in her voice as she inquired about their oldest brother. He was pushing fifty and had begun to lose his hair. He was six foot seven and weighed well over three hundred pounds. They still called him his nursery name, Petey, behind his back.

"Gosh, no,'" declared Charlotte, "remember the last time we included Janet, Petey was outraged, demanding his family side with him on every issue that had anything to do with his first ex. He called us all kinds of names; disloyal, selfish, and ignorant. I'd rather not stir up that kind of rancor again. I'm afraid Janet will have to celebrate without us."

"Charlotte, you have to host," exclaimed Amber, "your house is the biggest, and most able to hold our huge family crowd. More importantly, you have the park with the big toboggan run just steps out your back door."

"Remember how Angus likes the kids to make snowmen? And last year, he had silly carrot noses," laughed Jane. "The young ones used them as floppy noses, and the older ones put them down lower."

"It seems those noses are missing this year," giggled Charlotte, "I put them in the trash."

Amber smiled at the memory, but asked again, "You will host, won't you, Charlotte?

Her resolve nothing but a sour memory, Charlotte shook her head, but sighed, "Okay, just this year, but next year it has to be someone else." As she rose to go, she had to clutch the table to keep the room from spinning.

Her sisters gave her quick hugs goodbye, and promised to call later. Amber left the restaurant to go back to the salon. Jane followed her, clutching her bag of nutcrackers. Charlotte sat back down, and when the waiter came with the bill, she looked at him with red rimmed eyes and asked for a Cobb salad and a carafe of coffee.

THE TWENTY-SECOND DAY of December started out with a magical feeling of anticipation. The morning sun glinted and sparkled on four inches of fresh snow so brightly that one could not look at it for long. Charlotte looked forward to a day of peace and goodwill, filled with anticipation for the special laughter that came when her family reunited under happy circumstances. Ignoring a shiver of doom, she put on her apron and began breakfast. Angus put on the stereo and soft classic Christmas music ran in the background. Amber and her sons came early to help, setting up extra tables and chairs. The twins didn't last long and made their way downstairs to roughhouse with Charlotte's two oldest boys.

Jane and her partner, Ursula, arrived with bags of gifts and the refurbished nutcrackers. Charlotte sighed when she saw them. Jane, true to her word, had repainted and buffed up the tall sentries and their mouths moved easily up and down with the cantilever in the back.

"Oh no, that one still has the singed hair," said Charlotte.

Jane said, "Nothing I did took that color away." The women set down the nutcrackers and went to the car for another load of gifts and cookies.

"Where do you want me to put the gingerbread people?" Jane hollered as Charlotte no longer stood in the entryway.

"I'm in the family room, putting your nutcrackers on the mantle and arranging evergreens and red baubles around the soldiers. They look lovely with silver tinsel. Mom would approve," Charlotte yelled back.

With the decorations now complete, the sisters began the

serious job of stuffing the turkey, making the casseroles, peeling potatoes and setting up a table for the food that came with each new guest. Her daughter, Olive, dressed in a velvet red dress with a scarlet hair bow in her dark hair, stood at the door and welcomed their guests. She took their coats and politely told them where to put their feast offerings.

When her female cousins arrived, she left her post, calling out to her mother, "Emily and Jill and I are going upstairs to play."

The three great aunts and four younger aunts busied themselves with setting the tables and bossing the nearest males to go find the chairs. Philip circled the tables placing tubes of red and gold pull crackers on each of the plates. Red linen napkins held the silverware. Philip was proud of his crayoned name place cards and although some of the names were nonsense, most of them could be understood. Soon, the oohs and aahs at the sight of the huge well-cooked turkey being carried to the main table had everyone scrambling to find their place.

Charlotte looked over the festive table and enjoyed the lighted candles flickering in the red and white rose centerpieces. She knew her mother would have approved. She smiled as she heard Jim's voice announcing a burping contest would take place after the meal, and she sent a silent thank you to the Gods that be for watching over and caring for her family. But instead of feeling warm and cozy, a shiver of dread moved up her spine.

The thirty-six family members and three guests enjoyed the delicious meal, laughing at the table cracker fireworks, and how silly they looked with the coloured paper crowns on their heads. The conversation lulled as everyone tucked into the feast. Gradually the rumble of voices started up and soon grew so loud Charlotte rose and left the table to start the coffee. The kids took this as a sign to skedaddle and soon had the adults laughing as the kids' joined bodies made runaway trains that bumped into walls and rocked side tables without incident. Too full for pudding everyone gathered in the formal living room with its elegantly decorated fake tree. It was time to open their secret Santa gifts. In a coincidental moment, all three sisters' eyes met and a ripple of fear zipped as fast as electricity through them, leaving them feeling breathless and lost. They felt relieved when the wrappings were gathered up and the kids went outdoors to play.

Most of the older folks knew to move to the family room, a welcoming and gracious room with sliding doors to the back yard. A fire burned brightly in the fireplace next to the grand piano.

As Aunt Myrtle settled herself into a loveseat, she commented, "This is a lovely Christmas tree! How clever to decorate it with only white and blue lights. Those blue decorations are just marvelous."

Aunt Edith sat beside her and said, "That real tree just smells like Christmas, doesn't it? Makes me remember when our kids were small."

Charlotte, a tea towel between her hands, stepped into the family room and her heart mourned that her mother was missing this Rockford moment. A feeling of foreboding still nagged at her; something was wrong. Dropping the cloth on the floor, Charlotte made a bee-line for the wine fridge.

Nothing is going to go wrong, she thought. *If it does, it won't be big enough that a little wine won't make it better.*

All of the children, even the D-boys, wanted to go tobogganing.

"Come on, Dad," said Tony, "I will help the younger kids put on snow suits, and we can get the sleds out of the back shed."

Angus asked,"Uncle Harry, will you keep watch over the fire while I get the kiddos ready? There is more firewood behind the tree."

Uncle Harry waved him away and made his way straight to the bar. The adult men not doing dishes or handling the children helped themselves to Angus's Scotch and poured healthy rations into crystal glasses. Boxes of chocolate circled the room, and the ladies needed to see the pictures of what each chocolate contained.

Great Aunt Josie declared, "Now, every cherry cordial is mine, by right of being the oldest. Hand them over if you find one."

"Now, Josie, last year you got your way. This year you will have to share some of those ooey good cordials." Aunt Sarah made a motion to slap Josie's hand away from the delectable candies.

"You can have the cordials, I want the caramel ones," shouted Aunt Edith. "I might have hearing aids, but there is nothing wrong with my eyes. I know a good caramel when I see one."

Not so playfully, Aunt Myrtle said, "My favourite are the chocolate ganache ones. I could eat them every day."

With everyone busy pouring drinks and arguing over the chocolates, no one watched the fire. No one noticed the D-boys re-entering the room and fussing with the nutcrackers, or how they each punched the other in the shoulder before smirking and gliding out the sliding doors to join the rest of the children. Angus usually kept a close eye on the fire, but the kids kept him busy. If he had been watching, he would have stopped Uncle Jim from putting those last two logs on the fire.

Jane and Ursula helped Great Aunt Josie with her walker

and patiently guided her to a comfy wingback chair close to the new roaring and crackling fire.

The remembrance nutcrackers stood tall and proud on the mantle. A wide red and green plaid ribbon wove its way around and through the thick garland of fresh evergreens that curled around the nutcrackers. Big pine cones and large red Christmas ornaments scattered here and there completed the fireplace decoration.

"I think there is something odd about the nutcrackers," said Great Aunt Josie. "I can't figure out what is wrong, but something just doesn't look right to me. Does anyone else see what I see?"

"Looks like a dog bone hiding under the mustaches," rumbled Uncle Bill in his deep voice.

"You old fogies, you can't tell a walnut from a dog bone?" remarked Uncle Harry, "they are nutcrackers. They are supposed to look that way." He picked up a walnut from the bowl of mixed nuts on the coffee table. "See, just a walnut." He used the small pincered nutcracker to open the walnut and munched contentedly.

The ten-foot Douglas fir sat close to the fireplace. The edges of the nearest branches curled upwards as if to get away from the heat. No one noticed anything askew. If they did, nobody said a word to Charlotte. She basked in the after-glow of a good meal and several extra-large glasses of wine. She received lovely compliments about her decorating, reminding her she had her mother's gift in that regard.

The holiday reminded her of her own childhood. All of their family traditions were duplicated and enjoyed once again. Even the three late additions to the bulging guest list didn't spoil the day. Aunt Edith throwing up eggnog in the hallway outside the bathroom didn't bother her. She felt sorry for Jane's girlfriend when Uncle Harry tripped her with his walker, but that didn't ruin it. The twins' habit of popping up from behind furniture to scare cousins and aunts alike, didn't phase her. She thought it was hilarious when Aunt Jewel's little lap dog dragged the turkey carcass over her new carpet.

Charlotte smiled to herself and thought, *Nothing is going to mar the joyful warmth of the day.*

After they divvied up the leftover food and a vast collection of plastic food containers holding the take home remnants of turkey, gravy, green bean casserole and packages of rock-hard gingerbread cookies made its way onto the blue-veined granite counter, bedtime arrived for the little ones. They upheld the rule that everyone under the age of 16 had to go to bed, or at least amuse themselves upstairs. The adults congregated to sing everyone's favourite carols in the beautiful family room. Great Aunt Josie placed her teacup on the top of the piano and sat down and played a few scales to limber up her fingers.

Jane and her girlfriend stood in front of the fire and began singing a rollicking Jingle Bells. As the family raised their voices in song, happiness filled the room before chaos erupted.

The nutcrackers blew up and flew off the mantle, spraying shrapnel from the oddly shaped walnut bombs into all corners of the huge room. The explosions caused the Christmas tree to burst into flames. Jane and Ursula instantly disappeared. Charlotte stood the closest to the imploded sliding doors. Ignoring the shattered glass that burst from the pressure of the bombs, and the blood flowing from her face and arms, she shouted over her shoulder for everyone to follow her. She grabbed the closest person to her, her sister-in-law Tammy, and ran out the sliding door. Just a few steps away from the burning house, she came face to face with Angus, his arms full of snow covered sleds.

He dropped them immediately, and shouted as he ran, "I'll go around front and get the babies out."

Later, Angus confessed, "I thought I'd be too late. Running as fast as I could, I tripped and fell twice. I was screaming for the kids to get out of the house and thankfully, the older ones heard me. Every child waited at the top of the stairs." Tears rolled down his face, as he recalled, "I could smell the smoke, and all the children were crying. I skipped steps on my way up the stairs and scooped the three smallest into my arms, and without being told the older kids grabbed hold of a little one. Tony grabbed a bunch of blankets from the bed Emily slept on. He told me he shook her awake and then just ran towards my voice, clutching the little girl, and the blankets. I'm so proud of my boys. They followed me to safety. Just as we crossed the road, Bertram whispered to me, 'I am praying, Dad.'"

Angus broke down and sobbed before continuing his story, "We stood on the neighbor's lawn, watching as the fire curled around the bottom windows. It was a bad moment when the flames licked their way upstairs. The whooping sounds of the fire trucks was a great relief."

Charlotte was hiccuping with grief. "Once outside I pushed Tammy away from the back of the house, and told her to put snow on her head. Her hair was on fire. I went back into the family room, and the flames and the smoke were so thick I couldn't see a thing beyond that greyness. I could hear cries and screams and the snarl and snap of the fire. I bumped into Harry's walker, and blindly reached for him. Aunt Sarah was right there, and together we took an arm and hustled him out the door. Jim was right behind us carrying Aunt Josie. He didn't realize she wasn't alive."

She wiped her eyes, and whispered, "Jim and I ran back to the doors but it was too hot to go inside. We reached into the inferno and blindly felt around. Each of us grabbed a body. We dragged out Aunt Myrtle and Uncle Bill and immediately threw them on the snow and rolled them over to put out their burning clothes."

Charlotte took a shaky breath, "We tried to go back in, but the fire was so aggressive. It was so awful. We couldn't hear anyone screaming anymore. We knew what that meant. It felt like we were moving in slow motion as we moved around the house. We could hear Angus and the children from across the street. When we reached them Jim gently placed Aunt Josie on the snowy ground, alongside Aunt Sarah, Uncle Harry and Aunt Myrtle and Uncle Bill. They were badly burned. Tammy's arms were bloody and burned but she would not lie down. She kept a death grip on Jim's arm."

Charlotte's face contorted as she heard Angus say, "There was an awful moment when Philip ran out into the street, crying that he wanted his teddy. He was going to run back into the burning house. I caught him just as he reached the other side of the road. He struggled to get down but I squeezed him tightly. I was afraid I was hurting him. After the shock of this drama, it was hard to keep everyone calm."

Hours later, after the fire died down, the police asked Angus again if he had seen or heard anything. Angus's voice quivered as he said, "Just before the sing-along, I was in the backyard, picking up the sleds to put back in the shed. I thought I heard someone laughing and moving around in the backyard. Curious, I went to check and saw nothing of note; no one was on the swings; no neighbours out in their backyards." Angus rubbed his forehead and continued, "I saw the D-boys slide out the family room doors. When they saw me, they ran away and disappeared around the corner of the house." Angus's body was shivering from shock. Even the fireman's blanket over his shoulders couldn't warm him. "It was just seconds after seeing them that the house exploded."

Charlotte clung to his sleeve and recited over and over, "I had a bad feeling that a disaster was coming. I thought about cancelling. Something evil was happening and I could not stop it. Jane and Amber are gone, all gone. Great Aunt Josie, gone. Dust. Where is my family?" Angus patted her on the shoulder as tears streamed down their soot blackened faces.

The early edition of the Toronto newspaper reported the house fire, the worst in the history of Rosedale. The dwelling burned to the ground. All the children were declared safe and unharmed. The distance from the fire and the quick rescue made by Angus saved their lives. Sadly, only eight of the adults survived including the home owners. Jim and his wife and four senior relatives, two with critical 2nd degree burns. The police issued a be on the lookout warning for teenagers Dwayne and Dwight Krampson, alias D-boy. They were wanted for questioning in the Christmas Nutcracker Fire.

THE HOUND OF HOLY NIGHT

ALYSSA CUMPTON

Something wet and almost slimy worked down the inside of her ankle, resting for a long moment against the top of her foot before finishing its downward descent into her boot. A crunch echoed from a collapsing drift of snow, and Emily Peterson sighed, resigning herself to wet socks for the remainder of the afternoon.

The land around her was a nearly unbroken swath of white, the snowstorm from the previous evening having dropped another few inches of fluff on top of an already impressive base layer. Despite the resort and ski lodge standing like watchmen off in the distance, the towering mountains and silent forest were her only company as the hazy winter sun bathed the world in hues of pale yellow.

With a muttered growl, Emily kept walking, resolutely shoving one boot clad foot into the next icy berm. Heaving herself forward, she continued her slow trek towards the line of dark pines visible across the open meadow. Glancing over her shoulder, she frowned at the swath of destruction she'd wrought on the pristine wonderland, a torn canyon of disheveled snow and footprints lying in her wake.

With Christmas Eve upon the world, Emily found it hard to scrounge up even a scrap of goodwill or holiday spirit. She'd mistakenly thought that buying herself an expensive Sierra vacation would at least dull the ache that settled in her chest each December.

The ache had other ideas.

The memories of past holidays gleamed in her mind like forgotten bits of tinsel left to linger in the carpet long after the world had forgotten all about good faith and charity. The more she tried to think of something else, the harder her thoughts struggled to drag her back to a time she'd much rather forget.

Teeth aching from the chill in the air, Emily forged on as the dark line ahead of her began to split into individual tree trunks, the scent of pine lingering in the wind. She forced the frown to slide from her face.

No.

This year, she would enjoy her holiday.

The snow draped boughs were silent as she entered the cathedral of trees, the world still in its icy stupor as she made her way to the top of an embankment. Pausing to catch her breath, warm plumes of air wafted across her cheeks as she exhaled, sweat trickling from under the edge of her beanie. She pulled off her gloves to whisk away the slickness from her cheeks, contemplating the frozen landscape.

It was cold. It was quiet.

And Emily hated it.

"So much for communing with nature," she muttered under her breath. It was late afternoon and the dappled sunlight cast dingy gray shadows across the white. The silence unnerved her and she'd just started to turn away from the tree line when something burst from the undercover, sending rooster tails of silver into the air as the stillness of the moment shattered.

The deer that bounded at her was a study in elegance despite Emily's sudden shock at being faced with several hundred pounds of fast moving animal. Taking an involuntary step back as the doe bounded past a little too close for comfort, the heel of her boot caught on the edge of a submerged rock.

Balance hopelessly lost, Emily had just enough time to brace herself before her back slammed into the snow, her misstep sending her cartwheeling down the slope amid her own personal avalanche. The world swam in a yin-yang of white and black and she eventually squeezed her eyes closed against the monotonous whirl.

Something hard caught her in the ribs, adding breathlessness to her list of troubles.

In the end, the trunk of a sturdy aspen won out against momentum, bringing her to an abrupt halt.

Her head rang out like the proverbial Christmas morning bells as the world continued to spin against the inside of her eyelids. It was a long moment before she chanced moving again, something wet and warm running fingers through her hair.

Emily moaned as the adrenaline faded, each ache and pain slowly registering its presence with her brain. One eye opened, the white nearly blinding as she steadied herself against the ground with a palm. The other hand investigated her face,and came away red.

"Great."

From the bottom, the embankment she'd so gracefully traversed looked like Everest. Several spots of red dotted the slush around her like ripe holly berries, and she pulled her hat off to further investigate the gash along her temple.

She gave it another few minutes before she pulled herself to her feet, beanie requisitioned as a compress for her still bleeding head wound. Under the cover of the forest, the day seemed even darker, and she wanted to be anywhere but where she was.

Three steps up the hill, she hesitated, glancing over her shoulder.

A shiver ran down her back, one she was certain had nothing to do with the temperature.

The feeling only intensified as she worked her way back up the slope until it felt like eyes were crawling along her flesh. The sensation drove her mad, and she turned once again, sinking down to her haunches as she let her eyes rove the trees.

A black dog stood not twenty yards behind, head up and tail pointed to the sky as it watched her, thick ruff blowing in the slight breeze. It was big, far larger than the Labradors and Shepherds she normally saw, coat so dark that it seemed to absorb the surrounding light. Emily sucked in a breath, her mind immediately jumping to wolves.

The canine did nothing, and although he was an impressive specimen, he didn't seem inclined to attack. Emily's rational mind began to overcome her nerves as she stared back at the creature. She was no wildlife expert, but she was fairly certain wolves didn't stand around staring at random hikers. Slowly pushing herself back to her feet, she began to back away without taking her gaze off the dog.

It never moved, staying almost unnaturally still, eyes so dark they were almost lost amid the waves of fur. Although she couldn't say why, Emily felt uneasy at the animal's odd behavior.

They never broke eye contact, not until Emily crested the final ridge and trotted back out into the open meadow where the weak sunlight beat back the shadows that seemed to have grown in intensity. She waited for a moment to see if the dog was going to follow her, but it never appeared.

Shrugging at her own foolishness, Emily turned and retraced her footprints back towards the lodge.

———————

EMILY DIDN'T EVEN BOTHER to clean the blood from her temple, merely shoving her hat as low as she could before parking herself at the expansive bar in the lodge's front ball-room. Gesturing for the bartender to bring her something alcoholic and hot, she noted she'd lost a glove somewhere along the way. In the warmth of the room, sensation slowly returned to her left hand with tingles of fire.

"Looks like you had a fun afternoon."

Emily looked over at the man sitting two stools down and shrugged, gratefully wrapping her hands around the hot drink placed in front of her, trying to ignore the bartender's horren-dously red and green sweater. "You could say that."

He gestured to his own head. "You alright?"

"Yeah," Emily muttered, enjoying the scalding liquid as it burned her throat.

"That gash might need stitches."

When Emily turned to glare at him, he merely shrugged. "I'm a paramedic."

Emily laughed under her breath although the sound held no humor. She hated being out of control, and the day so far had left her feeling like she was trying to corral snowflakes with a butterfly net. "Of course you are."

"John," the man said, sliding over a stool to offer his hand, seemingly unperturbed by her lackluster attitude.

"Emily."

"Mind telling me what happened?" He asked as Emily finished off her drink and called for another. "Looks like it was quite the story."

"I went on a hike," Emily replied. "Fell down a hill."

"How'd you manage that?"

When she thought back on it, Emily began to realize how ridiculous the whole thing sounded, like she was starring in her own comedy of errors. She began to chuckle, the sound building in her throat until she laughed so hard she could hardly take her next breath. "It was a deer."

"A deer?" John replied, watching her carefully.

Wiping tears from her eyes, she nodded. "A damn deer scared me and I lost my balance, tripped on a rock and well," she gestured to her head.

Her drinking partner grinned at her. "Now I see what you're laughing about." He snorted. "Did you see which one it was?"

At Emily's blank stare, he continued. "You know. Dasher. Dancer. Maybe Rudolph."

She waved a hand. "Very funny."

The whole room smelled like cinnamon, and Emily took a deep breath, the final dregs of her unease drifting away. It had been a long time since she'd just sat and talked, and she found a reluctant smile beginning to drift across her face. "I guess I'm not really meant to be a hiker."

"You ski?" John asked.

Emily shook her head and immediately regretted the motion, pressing a hand to her forehead. "Not really."

"Then I have to ask," John said. "You know this is a ski lodge right?"

"I never would have guessed," Emily replied, rolling her eyes. "I think the chairlift gave it away."

To Emily's surprise, nearly an hour drifted away as they

sat, tossing back jokes and jibes, watching the endless rotation of people that came and went at the bar. It was nice. Nice to talk to a stranger who didn't know a thing about her past.

Didn't know a thing about what she'd done.

The smile faded from her face nearly as fast as the sky outside darkened to indigo.

"Everything alright?" John asked, catching the shift in mood.

"Yeah," Emily said. "Head's just starting to ache."

"You should really have that checked out," John said. He glanced down at his watch. "I've got a family role call to attend, but I'd love to continue this if you're going to be around later. I've been coerced into that Christmas Eve celebration later tonight and I wouldn't say no to some company that's at least drinking age."

Emily glanced up, ran the thought around in her mind a few times and figured it was better than moping around in her hotel room. "Why not?"

"Great," John said, offering her a grin as he slapped some bills down onto the bar top. With a wave, he disappeared into the flow of people making their way in from the slopes.

Turning back to her drink, Emily lazily watched the sky darken even further, the long winter nights robbing hours from the sun. The outside lights clicked on, adding a warm yellow glow to the already homey ambiance.

The grand strings of greenery and holiday bulbs strung across every available surface were every inch the perfect holiday scene, and Emily wouldn't have been surprised to see Frosty wander in from the cold and burst into song. Even the long suffering custodian doing her best to keep the floors clear of snow and mud had jingle bells tied to her mop.

The bartender returned to interrupt her thoughts. "Another one?"

Emily waved him off. "This is fine."

He turned back to his other customers and Emily made to swallow the last of her drink when the spicy tang of Fireball abruptly became something else.

Choking, she nearly dropped the tumbler as she slammed it back down onto the bar, the taste of iron exploding across her tongue, the drops of liquid in the glass a deep, cherry red instead of gold. Gasping back a scream, she frantically wiped her hand across her lips, the taste of blood still overwhelming every coherent thought.

She felt bile rise in her throat as she pushed away from her seat, stumbling back into the flow of people, several of them grumbling at her disregard. Emily couldn't even reply, swearing that she could still feel the unnatural thickness clogging her throat. Darkness closed in around her, and it took gouging her fingernails into her flesh to keep from succumbing.

"Ma'am, are you alright?"

The words were fuzzy and far away, but Emily grabbed onto them, squeezing her terror down until it finally settled. The bartender stared at her, as did everyone else in the immediate vicinity, and when her eyes finally drifted back to her glass, she found only golden remains staring back at her.

"Sorry," she managed to choke out, her voice an octave higher than usual. Shame burned across her cheeks and she wanted to hide amid the branches of the nearest fake tree, if only to avoid the onlookers.

"You sure you're okay?" The elven barkeep asked again, not looking at all convinced at her apology.

Emily nodded. "Yeah. Yeah I'm fine."

"Right," he replied, sweeping the glass away. "I think we'll call that a day then."

Emily settled her tab, leaving an exorbitant tip before

practically sprinting for the safety of the hotel elevator. Alone, the tinny sound of an instrumental Jingle Bells filling the air, she closed her eyes and rested her head against the wall.

It had felt so real.

It *had* been real as far as her mind was concerned. Although the sharp taste of iron was fading, she fully expected her teeth to be stained red like a Christmas vampire when she chanced a look at them in the mirrored metal of the elevator control panel.

Humming nervously to herself, she tried to slow her heartbeat to something resembling normal, writing the whole thing off as an unfortunate caveat to her encounter in the forest.

"It's just the head wound," she said aloud, the words echoing as Jingle Bells moved seamlessly into White Christmas.

Despite the festive notes, holiday cheer was the last thing on her mind.

THE BOILING hot water of an extraordinarily long shower managed to rinse away some of the residual unease from her strange day. Braiding her hair back as she gingerly inspected the gash on her head, Emily tried not to wince as she poked a little too close to the still forming scab. It wasn't a bad wound, but it hurt. She dug through her toiletries until she came up with an aspirin bottle.

The foggy mirror reflected only exhaustion, her eyes the color of weak coffee. She pulled at the dark circles that seemed to have taken up a permanent residence above her cheekbones and winced.

Resting her hands against the edge of the counter, she frowned, considering the deep green sweater and pair of jeans she wore. The outfit wasn't fancy, but it was as festive as she intended on getting. Foundation concealed the lines beginning to form at the edges of her eyes and lipstick a shade too red made her at least look like she'd come to celebrate.

Older, she realized. Not quite the kid she sometimes felt like.

The nagging memories were knocking again, and she flipped her golden braid back over one shoulder, stalking back out of the bathroom in search of her water bottle. Instead of the fancy hotel room she'd expected, she found herself face to face with the same monstrous black dog from that morning, the creature perched atop her bed like an overgrown labradoodle. The pill bottle still clasped in her grip hit the floor, rolling under the bedside table with a clatter.

Stumbling back, Emily dove for the cold porcelain sanctuary of the bathroom, slamming the door behind her even as she expected to feel the thud of claws against cheap wood. A dog in the forest was one thing. A dog in her hotel room was something else entirely.

Not a sound came from the other side of the door, but she flipped the lock just in case, pressing herself back against the towel rack as she searched for something she could use as a weapon.

A quick pat down of her jeans assured her that her cell phone was still charging on the nightstand where she'd left it. Cursing as she pulled the shower curtain rod down to the floor, she tore the plastic free and hefted the bar in her hands. It wasn't nearly heavy enough and as an afterthought, she grabbed her can of hairspray.

"What is going on around here?" She muttered, trying to keep her hands from shaking. She contemplated screaming for help, or waiting for the maids to walk in on what was sure to be the shock of their lives, but she didn't want to be stranded in bathroom purgatory for who knew how long waiting for rescue.

Her nerves wouldn't take it.

It took her a good five minutes to work up the courage to flip the lock, and it was another two before she threw open the door, lunging out even as she expected to feel teeth and claws sink into her flesh. The swinging shower rod shattered the glass on one of the generic paintings above her bed and she let loose with the hairspray like it was a can of mace, shouting at the top of her lungs.

It was a long, long moment before she realized she was alone.

Standing in a cloud of hairspray fumes, Emily dropped the can as though it was aflame and began to search.

Clawing through the clothes she'd hung in the small closet and checking under the bed left her with nothing. Growling, she crossed the room and assured herself that the window had been locked before she threw it open, letting the frigid air bellow into the room.

She wasn't certain why she cared if the window was locked or not as her room was on the third floor of the resort. As far as she was aware, canines weren't known for their climbing abilities. There was no way a dog had made it up the flat side of the building.

The heater clicked on in response to the drop in temperature and Emily let herself sink down onto her glass covered bed, blinking as she stared around at her destroyed room.

"I'm not crazy," she muttered to herself as she ran a hand over the bedspread, checking for traces of hair or snow, unsurprised when she came up with nothing.

"I know what I saw," she shouted to the walls, not caring if anyone had heard her. "None of this is real!"

Jesus. Was it finally happening? She'd wondered before, whether the mental illness in her family was catching. Was it her turn to lose touch with all reality and turn into a gibbering nut job? She felt like crying but forced herself to her feet, groaning as her bruised ribs protested the movement. No. She'd made a promise to herself years before that she'd never be like that. Her mind was her own and resolute in that fact, she picked up the hotel phone and made a call to the front desk requesting maid service.

Grabbing her cell, she found a Christmas playlist and cranked the volume as high as it would go. She certainly didn't feel festive, but she sang along at the top of her lungs anyway, hoping that some faux Christmas cheer might chase away the fear that lingered in the back of her mind.

HE WATCHED THROUGH THE WINDOWS.

The humans were celebrating, loud and boisterous as they danced in merriment, food and drink abundant and flowing. The shadows had been banished to the outside, where the first flakes of snow began to drift down from swollen clouds, the slopes empty and the clanking machinery silent.

He moved in the shadows, four feet silent as they left nearly invisible prints in the faint gold light of the hundreds of tiny bulbs that adorned each eve and window. Every building stood as a perfect gingerbread house, outlined with frosted white, gutters thick with icicles as children's laughter crept out from inside.

The pointed black ears that tipped forwards didn't hear the caroling or the piano or the clinking of glass and china.

The black eyes didn't see the red and green or how each face glowed with merriment. The black dog searched for something else, for something far more primitive.

The one he sought had not yet appeared, but being older than time itself, he could wait.

Patience, they said, was a virtue.

He certainly didn't have many.

Settling back on his haunches, he tilted his head upwards to catch the scent of decay in the air. Sometimes he wondered how the humans could stand it.

All of them were dying. Each and every one suspended in a slow descent towards rot. Some were worse than others, skin worn and hair dull as life slowly bled from their fleshy forms. The stench began as soon as they were born, and although it had been a long while since he'd been this close to humans, their scent remained as familiar to him as every corner of his shadowy realm.

He would return to that familiar darkness soon enough, but only when his task was complete. He'd never failed in such an endeavor, not since the beginning of time itself, and he had no intent on starting a new tradition. With a huff, he swished his thick black tail along the snowbank, unused to his heavy mortal form.

He rarely came to the surface to personally collect one of his charges. More often than not, he caught them wandering in the in-between, where everything existed in murky gray. Some were heavy with sorrow, others tasted of bitter longing, but he took them all along, leaving them at the edge of the black where things even he feared to speak of waited with open arms.

He didn't know what happened once he abandoned the souls at the dark place.

He wondered briefly if he'd see his counterpart. He had a

feeling that the white wolf wouldn't want this particular soul, but he'd been surprised before. Once they had both run untethered through the mortal realm, dancing in an endless battle as they tricked one another and fought over the fleeting remains of each human life.

A doggie grin just a little too wide to be entirely comfortable reflected back at him from the window pane where he admired the white fangs that filled his mouth. Some souls existed only for the dark place, and he knew his current charge was beyond the reach of the white wolf.

The thought made his snap his jaws at an errant snowflake.

Time was growing short.

The faintest whisper of corruption drifted over him and his attention focused back through the window as a tall woman in green emerged from the elevators, glancing around before straightening her shoulders and heading into the main ballroom where the revelers had begun to dance around the base of a massive pine. He watched her go, her soul calling to him like a siren as he sank back into the shadows, black eyes flashing red beneath the Christmas bulbs.

It wasn't yet time.

He could wait.

EMILY JOINED the party by staking out a forgotten table in the corner.

The pounding in her head finally quieted to a distant ache, she forewent alcohol in favor of hot apple cider. Although the bartender shot her a funny look as she passed, he said nothing, barely able to keep up with the patrons pressed two deep against the polished wood of the bar.

At the furthest end of the expansive room, a glittering tree of gold and silver lorded over all, the branches heavy with the weight of balls and bobbles. The revelers all smiled as they laughed and ate and sang, and Emily found she'd never felt quite so alone.

She didn't deserve to be there. She dropped her gaze to the worn tabletop in front of her, tracing the lines of the false wood grain with a fingertip.

"Looks like you could use another drink."

Glancing up, she offered only a wry smirk in response. "I think I'm already cut off."

John slid into the chair opposite her and propped one elbow on the table, angling himself so he could keep an eye on the room. "I don't think they're cutting anyone off tonight. Another storm's rolling in, so it's not like anyone will be going anywhere."

"Right," she muttered.

John pinned her with a stare that made her want to shift in her seat, like she was a specimen under a particularly powerful microscope. "How's the head?"

"Better," Emily said. "Still hurts."

"No more deer?"

"Not unless someone's seen Saint Nick up on the roof," Emily replied.

John laughed.

The silence between them existed somewhere between the oddness of perfect strangers and the comforting familiarity of old friends. The minutes lazed away as they watched the rest of the room spin around them, a pair of teens stopping by to check in with John every so often before dashing off again.

It was everything a Christmas Eve should have been.

Emily tried to relax, reminding herself that she wasn't crazy and that everything was going to be fine. The things she'd seen all had perfectly reasonable triggers and she wasn't showing any other symptoms of insanity. She ran through a few mental relaxation techniques she'd learned and raised her eyes to her companion.

"Are you from around here?" Emily asked abruptly.

"Down in the valley," John replied, taking another sip of the drink he'd arrived with. "I grew up about an hour away. I guess that means I'm a local."

"Do you know if they have wolves around here?"

"Wolves?" John said with a frown. "Not that I've ever heard of. Why?"

Emily twitched one shoulder towards her ear. "No reason." She tapped the heel of one boot against the floor. "I saw a stray earlier and it made me wonder."

"I suppose it could be possible," John said. "It's a big forest out there, but if I was a wolf, I certainly wouldn't be hanging around a noisy ski resort."

A staff member dressed as a sugar plum fairy interrupted their conversation, offering them both candy canes from a basket, informing them that the next round of Christmas caroling would be starting shortly. They both declined and she moved on to the next table.

"What about you?" John said. "Do you have family here?"

Emily felt herself freeze, watching as several children dashed by. The volume of the room seemed to skyrocket and each laugh seemed to stick into her like the sharp point of a knife. She didn't have any family.

And it was her fault.

"Excuse me for a minute," she said, slipping out of her chair and making a beeline for the buffet table. She heard John yell something after her but she didn't bother listening.

Something tightened in her chest. Shame burned behind

her tired eyes. Jesus what was happening to her? She went to clutch at her temples but hissed as the pain in her head flared up again. Heading back up to her room seemed like the thing to do, but the thought of being alone sent shivers through her.

Emily leaned back against one cool wall, just off the edge of the dance floor. Some Christmas it was turning out to be. She was supposed to be happy, to forget all her troubles and worries and just be, at least for one night. It seemed that she couldn't even manage to do that right.

The faint scent of sweets finally drew her attention, and hoping that calories would settle the unease that seemed to have taken up permanent residence in her gut, she moved to grab a plate.

She'd just added a sugar cookie to her collection of confections when something large and dark loomed at the edge of her vision. Head snapping up, she felt her plate slide from boneless fingers, the holiday treats scattering across the floor as she froze to the spot.

Blinking, she felt a whimper escape her throat.

When she moved again, she did so with purpose, bisecting the room as she strode across the dance floor and back to her abandoned seat. John looked at her in surprise, one eyebrow inching towards his hairline as she pulled him from his chair.

"Easy there," he said, offering apologies as dancers swerved around them. Emily didn't say anything until she'd parked him directly in front of the buffet table, releasing him to cross her arms over her chest.

He glanced at the table and then back at her. "You're going to have to elaborate."

Something hard stuck in her throat, but she refused to bend. It was there. Right *there*. "You don't see it?"

"See what?

"Please," Emily said, grabbing at John's jacket sleeve as she glanced back at the food. The deer still hung there, tongue lying limp between flaccid lips as dark red furrows slowly leaked fluids down the tawny hide. "Please tell me you can see it."

"Emily," John said, grabbing her around the shoulders. "See what? What's going on?"

"The deer," she choked out. "It's right there." She pointed at the carcass as though it was a simple misunderstanding.

John followed her arm and she felt the rest of her self-confidence shatter when his forehead creased in confusion. "There's nothing there."

They were starting to draw a crowd and Emily felt each curious gaze like a brand burning into her skin. None of them could see it, she realized. To them, she was just another loon, jumping at shadows and providing a little entertainment for their Christmas Eve. Someone else to feel sorry for while they opened gifts and sang Joy to the World.

"No," she said, shaking her head and pulling away from John. "I'm not crazy."

"Never said you were," John replied, holding his hands up. "But I think you need to get checked out."

The deer remained, staring back as a steady reminder that Emily couldn't ignore. She wasn't hallucinating. She wasn't dreaming. It was right there. A gory Christmas decoration plastered between Santa's workshop and the cheese tray, entrails and organs slowly oozing down onto the buffet table, coating fruitcake and stuffing in red.

"Emily please," John said. "I can help you. I think you knocked your head harder than you realized."

"No," Emily said, backing away. "No. You won't put me somewhere and forget me."

And the secret, the one she'd tried so hard to ignore,

floated in front of her mind like the Christmas star. Her own mother, locked away because Emily couldn't bear to watch her fade from reality, a slow, lingering death in a strange place with strange people, her own daughter never visiting. She'd preferred to ignore the reality of it, living her life until guilt had nearly suffocated her.

Her mother had died alone.

On Christmas Eve six years before.

Remorse was something that Emily was familiar with, and the heavy sensation struck her hard enough to bring tears to her eyes. She didn't deserve to be forgiven for what she'd done. It was her penance, she supposed, to now know what her mother had felt, when eyes looked back at her with confusion and pity instead of understanding.

Now she knew what it felt like to be the crazy one.

"Please," John said, following after her as she slowly retreated. "You need to let me help you."

"No," Emily said, shaking her head. "You can't help me." She spotted the swinging doors that led back to the kitchens and she bolted, shoving startled patrons out of the way and upending trays of food as she pushed past confused waiters.

The kitchen staff looked up in confusion as she stormed past, elbowing aside anyone who didn't yield to her quickly enough. An abandoned butcher's knife caught her eye and she snatched it as she passed, hardly slowing as she followed a glowing green exit sign out the back and onto a loading dock.

Hopping down to the pavement, she crept along the building until she came to the end of the loading zone, dashing across the open parking lot and out into the snowy night, just as the first heavy flakes began to drift down from the starless sky.

HER FEET TOOK her and she let them, unable to focus on anything but movement. The snow grabbed at her legs but she kept going, running as though she could escape the truth that seemed to be intent on drowning her with its inevitability.

She felt like she had lost her mind.

Fear and frustration eventually morphed into anger, which kept her going until sorrow tempered her rage, her body refusing to continue on as the drifts reached up to mid-thigh.

She fell, the wet powder seeping through her jeans as her knees folded, head hanging low as she gasped for breath. It was cold enough to feel the frost in the air with each inhale, and the sweat drying to a crust on her skin licked away each molecule of warmth. Emily felt her hand grow numb as the knife she clutched burned with ice, and after a moment she forced her fingers to open, the silver blade sinking into the snow.

The forest loomed around her, dark and deep and unfamiliar.

Between the creeping exhaustion and her mental turmoil, Emily doubted she'd have the wherewithal to get herself back to civilization. A sheen of snow fell in the silence and she reluctantly forced herself to stand, intending to follow her tracks back the way she'd come.

Taking a deep breath, she began her trek.

It didn't take long before she realized the sound of crunching snow wasn't matching up with her footsteps.

Straining her eyes to see into the black, the trees around her seemed far more sinister than the threat of hypothermia.

Up ahead, a black mass peeled itself away from the shadows.

The black dog stalked forward, shoulders hunched as

snowflakes began to gather like frost on the ends of the midnight pelt. He circled and sat, chest out, watching her as she floundered in the deep snow. Something within her whimpered in submission, but Emily pulled her shoulders back and held her ground.

It wasn't real.

No matter how many times she told herself the truth, the specter refused to fade, remaining as a steadfast silhouette against the pale snow. It was just a dog. A mirage, created by her guilty mind to drag her even deeper into a make believe hell. The eyes were too dark, deep ebony orbs that seemed to flash milky white when they caught the faint ambient light of the sky through the canopy of trees.

Too horrible to be real.

"Get back," Emily shouted. "I'm not afraid of you."

The dog stood again and continued forward, coming to a halt just ahead of her. A pair of pointed ears perked up, and Emily swore she saw a black tongue dart out from between gleaming white teeth.

"What do you want?" Emily shouted, no longer certain if fear or anger coursed through her blood. The shadows between the trees seemed to be growing, clawing their way across the white snow until they circled around her, piano keys played by invisible hands. "You're not even real."

The dog did nothing, but the strange black eyes never wavered.

Emily took one step back, then another, suddenly realizing how very stupid it had been to take off into the night. Her feet moved independently of her brain and before long she scrambled on hands and knees, fingers digging into the snow and ice as she turned to run.

"Not real," she muttered under her breath like a mantra, dodging through branches that caught in her hair, stumbling over rocks and through a partly frozen stream. "I'm sorry, I'm so, so sorry."

Every sound became a gunshot in her ears as she struggled through the snow, the drifts grabbing at her soaked clothes. The air felt like a thousand daggers scraping across each lung, and the gloomy trees seemed to block her every path.

She ran like a woman possessed, only stopping when a familiar black silhouette appeared in her path, patiently waiting as she fell to her knees in her haste to stop.

Emily gasped for oxygen as the dog tilted his head to one side. She hadn't heard him move and had never seen him flash past to get around her. A normal predator wouldn't wait for their prey to come to them, not if it was just a simple task of running them down.

The cold, bitter truth was as sobering as the ice crystals digging into her fingers.

She didn't know what was real anymore.

"Go away," she sobbed, bowing her head as the dog closed the final few feet between them. "Please go away."

Looking up into the snout now inches from her face, Emily saw herself reflected in a pair of glittering eyes as clearly as she saw horror bloom across her own expression.

Very hot and very real breath ghosted over her lips.

And at that moment, Emily realized she would die right there.

Something changed in the animal's face, the mouth dropping open as a black and shriveled tongue flopped out, the doggie smile looking anything but joyous. The sleek fur rippled with muscle as it moved, completely silent, the dog looming over her. Emily waited, still on her knees, their faint exhalations mingling together as the strange, sightless eyes looked on.

She wanted to cry, to sob and beg for her life, but she never had the time.

The maw that opened up before her was far larger than should have been possible, and the dog leapt forward, closing his jaws over her head and shoulders, growling as she reflexively struggled. Digging claws into the snow, the dog braced back until he felt the soul tear loose from the fleshy prison. Spitting out the limp body, he shook his head as the incorporeal soul settled at his side.

The body that had once held Emily Peterson's essence sprawled on the snow in front of him. There were no teeth marks and not a single drop of blood marred the white expanse around them. Nothing betrayed his presence that night.

And nothing ever would.

Satisfied for the moment, the black dog sat back and let loose a single howl, the sound long and slow as it spread through the night.

Even the stars seemed to shiver.

CHRISTMAS DAWNED CLEAR AND COLD, the world silent as people woke and continued the celebration from the night before. Smoke curled from chimneys and wreaths glittered with the trappings of hoarfrost and faux flowers. The roads were silent and mostly empty, save for a collection of police cruisers and one black van all clustered down a narrow side road just down from the lodge.

Snapping another picture, Gary Taggart shook his head at the woman lying dead in the snow. Shame. And on Christmas Day too. He marked another piece of potential evidence and took another picture, wishing, not for the first time that morning, that he was still at home with his girlfriend.

"What have we got?"

Gary looked up at the pair of detectives who'd appeared. Grace and David were a longtime team he'd worked with many times before, although neither looked to be particularly thrilled at their current assignment. The former came prepared with winter weather gear while her partner wore only a suit and overcoat.

"My bet is accidental," Gary replied. "She looks like she had a tumble recently." He pointed to some scabbed-over wounds along the woman's hairline. "Might be an aneurism, but we'll have to wait for the coroner to confirm. We've got witnesses stating she was acting strangely last night and she probably got confused and wandered off."

Gary watched as the taller detective left his partner's side, crouching down to look into the dead woman's face, her glazed eyes sightless and staring. "There're a lot of 'ifs' in that theory." David considered the body again. "She looks terrified."

"Cold," Gary shrugged. "Does funny things to muscles."

"Right," Grace said, rubbing her hands together. "It does funny things to the living, too."

"There's still a unit up at the lodge," Gary said. "They should be about done if you've got additional questions."

"Did they contact next of kin?" Grace asked.

"She doesn't seem to have any."

"Well once you're done with the coroner, go home," David said. "We can pick this up tomorrow, especially if there aren't any signs of foul play." He shook his head as he looked down at the dead woman. "So much for a jolly Christmas."

Grace snorted. "Shut up."

Not about to argue, Gary nodded, turning back to his

work as the two detectives made their way back up towards the main road, exhalations frosting together as they conversed.

It didn't take long to process the rest of the scene and Gary was packing up his equipment, only looking up when he realized he was alone. He'd been to plenty of crime scenes in his career, some far more gruesome than his current one, and never once had he felt such unease.

Hurriedly, he shoved the last of his camera equipment back into his case, shouldering the backpack as he glanced around at the dark tree trunks that rimmed each side of the road.

He wasted no time in heading back up towards the waiting patrol cars, eager to get on with his interrupted holiday plans. The unsavory feeling began to dissipate the further he got from the body, and he thought no more of it.

She was someone else's problem now.

No one noticed the pair of dim eyes watching the proceedings from the shadows, or the faint paw prints that ran along the very edges of the service road. Turning his head to the wind, the black dog lifted his nose, catching the scents of cider and pine as the soul he'd bound to his presence followed dutifully along beside him. He would leave her at the dark place and return to await the next calling.

Turning away, he took several steps along the freshly fallen snow, taking one final breath of mortal air as he angled them both downwards and back into the shadows.

WAISE'S REVENGE

H.H. CARLAN

A small puff of air burst in front of her eyes. Remmie breathed rapidly, each breath as brief as the daylight these days. She steadied her breathing so she wouldn't fall asleep. Christmas was yesterday, but Christmas was every day now. Had it just been a day? Maybe it had been a week. She awoke this morning to experience Christmas again, but the roast continued to rot, and the torn wrapping paper smelled of cat pee.

Remmie looked over at her brother. She turned nine a few weeks before Christmas, which meant Winston turned thirteen in a few months. They still shared a room, but their daddy promised Winston could move into the basement after winter ended. Remmie dreaded the change. She slept soundly with Winston in the room.

Winston lay curled up in his bed, sound asleep.

As much as she wanted to wake him, Remmie couldn't bring herself to do so. She closed her eyes and tried to go back to sleep. The same puff of air formed every minute or so until she fell back asleep.

"Are ya there? Can ya hear me?"

Remmie opened her eyes quickly. She must have fallen asleep. She glanced around the room, confused, feeling as though she might be late to something.

"Rem? Ya there?"

She glanced over at the tin can sitting on her window. She leapt out of bed and ran over to the can.

"Micah? Is that you?" Remmie spoke into the tin can.

"Yeah! I'm here! Are you okay?" Micah's voice rang through the line like a warm hug.

Remmie held the tin can between her hands. She couldn't believe her luck. Her friend Micah had wanted to set up tin cans for winter break so they could still talk even if they were grounded. Remmie clutched the can, adorned with glitter and purple construction paper, in her hands. She forgot about Micah since Christmas. The power went out on Christmas. It started with the snowstorm, then it seemed like the world came to a stop. The power was out. No noise except for the wind. A pang of regret hurt Remmie — she forgot about her best friend.

"I'm here. I'm… scared." She croaked as she fought back tears.

"Me, too." Micah's sadness hung in the air.

"Is that Micah?"

Remmie turned around to see Winston sitting up in bed. He rubbed his eyes.

"Yeah," she nodded.

Winston slipped out of bed and walked over to the window. He looked outside, but the snow fell as one continuous sheet of white crystals cascading to the earth.

"Is your family okay?" Winston asked into the tin can.

"My dad went outside yesterday," Micah answered. The weight of his words hung in the air. "He hasn't… come back…"

Remmie sat down on her bed and held her pillow to her chest. Winston put his hand around the tin can and pulled it close to his mouth.

"Listen, you can't think like that. You can come over here if you want. I'll let you in."

"Really?"

"Yeah, go tell your mom. I'll come over to get you."

"Thank you," the tiny voice whispered through the line.

Winston jumped from the window to his side of the room. He pulled out his clothes from the closet and slipped on his jacket and his boots.

"Mama's not gonna like you doing that," Remmie warned.

"Mama's sleeping." Winston pulled on his hat and slipped out of the room without making a sound.

Remmie, of course, followed close behind him. With her robe on over her pajamas, she followed him downstairs.

The house remains dark and cold. Candles on the mantle and table burned out days ago, and whenever Winston attempted to go to the wood pile out back, Opal pulled him back inside. She told him there was more wood inside, oblivious to the empty racks.

Winston found a flashlight and whacked it until the pale, yellow light flickered to life.

"I'm gonna walk over to Micah's house."

Remmie nodded.

"Wait!" She began to rummage around inside the mud room

"Daddy used to keep rope in here." She pushed the toolbox to the side to reveal a round of rope and a pickaxe.

"Here," she said as she tied the rope around Winston's waist.

"What are you gonna do with the other end?"

"I'll... umm... tie it to the door handle."

As Winston opened the door and a cold burst of air pushed into the house, Remmie quickly tied the rope around the door handle. Winston hugged Remmie for a brief moment before he slipped outside and disappeared into the blizzard. She couldn't imagine being out there. The fearsome cold made you want to die.

Remmie pulled herself up onto the counter and tried to peer outside through the snow. Winston disappeared through the curtain of snow.

"What are you doing?"

Her mother's voice cut through the darkness like a dull razor blade.

"Winston... he w-w-went... to g-g-get Micah... and her f-f-family..." Remmie only stuttered around her mother.

Opal Cutter stood in her kitchen and looked outside. The fabric of her nightgown became yellow from days of wear, and her skin seemed crusty and cracked. Her hair, pulled back many days ago, appeared slick from grease even in the low light.

"That boy... he shouldn't have gone outside. Don't open the door." Opal started to open cabinet doors.

Remmie's heart sank as she watched her mother shuffle through the items in the cabinets. "That boy..." she repeated as she found a dusty bottle of Wild Turkey at the back of the cabinet behind a food processor she never used.

Remmie stayed on the counter and didn't respond. Winston had told her the truth months ago. Daddy didn't leave because Remmie stuttered. Daddy left because he didn't love Mama anymore.

Remmie turned back to the window to look for Winston. *I wish he had taken me with him*, she thought.

She studied the snow and ignored the sounds of her mom

in the kitchen. Eventually, Opal left, only taking with her the bottle of bourbon.

"C'mon Winston," Remmie murmured against the window.

It felt like hours passed. She thought about Christmas – the horrible things her mother had said and the moment Remmie muttered aloud that she hated Christmas. Of course, Remmie knew she didn't hate Christmas – not really. She hated what her mother did to her family. She hated her father leaving them with their drunk mom.

Remmie's knees began to ache, but she stayed right where she knelt on the counter. Her stomach rumbled, and she made her way to the pantry. She found a box of crackers with a few packs left, and she took one pack out.

Winston had told her not to eat all of the crackers at once, so she left the pack on the other end of the counter. Remmie chewed slowly, savoring every dry morsel of cracker as she struggled to swallow it. She rubbed her nose, unaware as it leaked down her face.

Suddenly, she saw movement in the snow.

Winston pushed open the door, snow stuck all over him like a quilt that could kill you.

Behind him, two small people and a taller woman entered the house. Snow coated them in its deadly quilt.

Remmie hopped off from the counter, her legs aching from the quick movement.

"Here, let me help," she whispered. Remmie started to pull off the coats from the other girls and placed them around the mudroom to dry.

Micah and her twin sister Isla hugged each other.

Remmie didn't notice that their mother held a bag, and Winston held a similar bag under his coat.

As they shed their coats, Remmie took the bags. Food.

Lots of food. Both fresh ingredients and boxed foods. A warm wave of relief washed over her.

"Thank you," Remmie whispered.

Penelope smiled down at her. "Thank you for letting us come over. Is your mom down here?" Penelope glanced around the kitchen and reevaluated the state of Remmie and Winston. "I bet not," she added.

"Mama told me not to let you back in," Remmie confided in Winston.

He rolled his eyes.

"Why were you gone for so long?" Remmie asked as she knocked the snow off their boots into the sink.

"I was gone ten minutes," Winston glanced at her as he unpacked the grocery sacks.

Remmie blinked a few times. It had felt like hours.

Micah and Isla sat together at the bar and continued to hug each other.

"Do you want something to eat?" Remmie asked.

"No, we're okay." Micah answered.

"Do you wanna play Monopoly?" Isla loved Monopoly, and Remmie liked playing even if she always lost.

Remmie saw Isla was clutching her Christmas book, her favorite storybook. A twinge of pain struck Remmie's chest. *They deserve a better Christmas*, she thought.

"Yeah, it's in there." Remmie started walking toward the living room when a pair of strong hands grabbed her from behind.

"What are you doing in here?" Opal had been hiding by the stairs and quickly pulled Remmie behind her as she raised a shotgun to her eye.

Micah and Isla hid on the other side of the bar.

Penelope and Winston stood still.

"Opal," Penelope started, "put the gun down. We're here to try to survive this together. No need for a gun."

Opal looked at the food on the counter, and she rubbed her chin on her shoulder.

"Leave the food and get out," she shouted as she shook the gun.

"No, Mom." Winston gripped the side of the counter. "We need to help them. They're our friends."

"They aren't my friends," Opal sniffed, the gun still pulled up to her eye level.

"That's not our fault," Winston countered.

"She's why your daddy left," Opal spat, her eyes narrowing on the other mother.

"You know that isn't true," Penelope whispered.

Remmie looked around behind her for something to use. Her mom wasn't stable.

"She used to call your daddy in the middle of the night. Fix the water heater. Fix the sink. He'd go. Every time. Come back smelling like rosewater and vanilla." Opal shook her head as she kept the gun leveled at her neighbor.

"Opal, Sawyer didn't run off with me. You know what really happened to him." Penelope swallowed hard as she realized that Opal intended to try to shoot her.

"Lies!" Opal shouted, unaware of the movement behind her.

Remmie took a fireplace poker, swung it quickly, and whacked Opal in the back of the head. As Opal slumped forward, Winston ran from the side of the room and caught the barrel of the shotgun before it hit the floor. Opal fell onto the floor and slowly grabbed the back of her head.

"We need to do something with her," Winston urged as Penelope walked over and helped lift Opal into a nearby chair.

Remmie thought for a moment and ran back to the mud room. She found the rope they had used when Winston went next door and brought it back to them.

"Would this work?" Remmie offered the rope.

Penelope nodded.

"Good thinking, Rem," Winston gently touched her shoulder as he took the rope. He and Penelope stood on opposite sides of Opal and handed the rope back and forth to each other. Penelope tied the ends and they left Opal in the chair.

"Are you girls okay?" Penelope walked around the bar to find her girls huddled together under the counter.

"Yes, Mommy," Micah whispered as she and Isla pulled their mom into a hug.

Remmie grabbed the fire poker and walked into the living room. She set it next to the bookcase, and then went to the board games. She found Monopoly, and she cleaned the papers, pop cans, and remnants of long-ago food off the coffee table.

"How was it outside?" Remmie asked as she opened the box. She spread out the board and started dividing the cards.

"It's a white-out. Impossible to see what's going on with the neighbors." Penelope answered as she held her girls in her lap.

Remmie picked up the figurines and held them out to the girls. Micah and Isla leaned forward and scanned their options. Micah picked the shoe, and Isla picked the dog. Remmie looked at her brother and Penelope. Winston leaned forward and picked the thimble, and Penelope picked up the top hat. Remmie picked the wheelbarrow.

The small group assembled around the coffee table. Micah, the trash-talker of the bunch, heckled the other players on their turns.

"Do you think investment is the best option right now? In

this economy?" Micah asked, her small, authoritative voice repeating lines from the news.

"Bankruptcy isn't a devil's bargain, you know," she added with a slight shrug.

Occasionally, as they played quietly, someone would get up to get something to drink or stretch. In the middle of the game, Penelope fixed sandwiches for everyone. She checked on Opal. She placed her fingers on Opal's neck; she still had a pulse. Penelope returned to the game and the small group of friends enjoyed their company.

"Can we talk about what's going on," Remmie whispered as Isla claimed more real estate and the rest of the players were almost broke.

"I don't really know," Penelope answered. Her mouth turned down at the corners, her expression pained as she reached over and hugged each of her girls.

"Is Daddy going to come back?" Isla asked as she clung to her mom.

"I don't know, baby," she answered honestly, tears stinging her eyes.

"I'm sure he's safe somewhere, just like you're safe here. The power has to come back on, too," Winston assured them.

"Do you remember anything happened on Christmas that was weird?" Penelope asked as she made a funny face at Isla.

"I yelled at Mama," Remmie confessed, looking down at the carpet.

"What happened?" Penelope reached over and gave Remmie's shoulder a comforting squeeze.

"She was being mean. Throwing stuff. Trying to destroy the presents Daddy sent over." Remmie started, tears slipping quietly down her cold cheeks. "I told her to stop. I wouldn't let her take my presents." Remmie pressed her lips together, remembering the look in her mother's eyes as she told Remmie she hated her.

"Mama told us she hated us, and she waited until we went to eat to destroy our toys." Winston let Remmie take a few breaths.

"I told Mama I hated her, too, and I hated Christmas." Remmie succumbed to her cries, her small frame shaking as she laid her sins out for her friends.

The memory stuck in her mind. Her mom drank too much, got angry at their dad, and she lashed out at them. Remmie knew her mom didn't love her, but to hear it said out loud — especially on Christmas — felt like a kick to her belly.

Penelope pulled the young girl over to her and hugged her.

"You're a good person, Remmie. You were born to a really mean mother. That's not your fault. She was mean before she had you."

Winston looked at Penelope. "Did you know our parents before us?"

Penelope nodded. "I have known them for years."

Remmie and Winston stared at Penelope.

She smiled back at them. She knew they needed to hear the story. It was time for a story.

"I moved to this block when I was ten. Your daddy was living down the street, and Opal lived here. Her parents died when she was a teenager. Their deaths were… suspicious, but soon after they died your dad, Sawyer, moved in. And probably a few months later, Opal was on the block with a visibly pregnant belly."

"That was you," Remmie looked over at Winston and smiled.

He was thinking about the timeline, though, and he shook his head.

"No, that wasn't Winston." Penelope interrupted.

Remmie's and Winston's eyes widened.

Micah and Isla also watched in amazement.

No one had heard this story before.

"So that November, after her parents died, she gave birth to a little girl. Trinity. One night, the night before Christmas, Opal woke up the entire neighborhood screaming about Trinity not being in her crib. Police showed up. The neighborhood went out in force searching through the house, looking outside. It was awful."

Remmie stood and walked over to Winston. She wrapped her arms around him.

"My dad told Sawyer that Opal was cursed. He believed, and many other people believed, she killed her baby. Your daddy told him that was crazy. It was an accident. Opal loved Trinity."

Winston shivered.

Remmie hugged him tighter.

"A few weeks later, there was Opal walking around the block, talking about how she was pregnant again. That was Winston. Sawyer had his mom, Grammy Maybelle, move in before Winston was born, and she stayed with him all the time. Opal didn't hardly go near either one of you after you were born."

Remmie loved Grammy Maybelle, but Opal made her leave when Sawyer split.

"Why don't we liven up the mood in here?" Penelope half-smiled at everyone. "Do you all want to go build snowmen?"

Winston and Remmie glanced at each other.

"Is… is it safe?" Remmie asked as she looked out the windows.

"Let's see," Penelope offered as she stood up. She threw on her coat and hat, and she cracked the front door. A two-foot snow drift begant to fill the frame. She turned her back to the door and pushed the door closed as the bitter wind tried to force it open.

"No, better not do that." Penelope huffed as she latched the front door.

A deep cackle echoed through the house. Everyone stiffened as they slowly turned their heads to the kitchen.

Opal woke up.

"Why don't you let them go outside? We're all going to die anyway," Opal suggested with an accompanying cackle.

Winston stood and walked solemnly into the kitchen. "You starting to sober up?" He asked as he grabbed a kitchen towel. He stuck it under the faucet and brought it to Opal. He tried to wipe her face, but she kept moving around. He finally plopped it on her head before walking away.

"Who would want to be sober during this," she added behind him.

"You wouldn't even know what that's like," Winston shot back.

Opal struggled against the chair. Her nightgown ripped along her leg. She whispered obscenities under her breath.

Penelope, still standing by the front door, walked into the kitchen.

"Well, Opal, how are you doing? Would you like something to eat? I fed the kids earlier."

"You should feed them to-" Opal tried to say before Penelope cut her off with a look.

"No. None of that. I'm not going to listen to that. You can sit over here and be quiet if you're going to be hateful." Penelope kept her tone calm but firm, putting her hands on her hips and shaking her head.

"You can't help to control things, Penny, like always." Dirty hair fell into Opal's face. She twisted trying to get it out, but the oily hair refused to budge.

Remmie watched her struggle to get the hair out of her face. She went into the bathroom, found an old comb under the sink, and cautiously walked into the kitchen.

"Here, Mama, let me help you." As she lifted the comb, Opal leaned over and tried to bite her wrist.

"Get away from me, wicked child!"

Remmie dropped the comb and moved several steps back.

"We aren't going to have any of this, Opal. Remmie go back with the others." Penelope walked past Opal to the mud room and started looking around. She picked up Opal's purse and turned it upside down, dumping all of the contents on the floor.

All of the kids watched eagerly from the living room.

Penelope walked up to Opal from behind and dropped the bag on her head. Opal struggled to look around, but no one could hear her mumbling under the weight of the bag.

She continued to the living room and sat down on the couch. "Would anyone like to play Scrabble?"

The children quickly joined around the table for a game of Scrabble. Winston, the spelling bee winner for the district, also sat down to play.

"I don't think it's fair to play Scrabble with Winston. He's older than us! He knows so many more words!" Micah protested.

"Sometimes you know the game will be difficult. You still play," Penelope assured her as she pulled her daughter's hair back into a braid.

With Winston in the lead, Remmie found her letters

looking quite familiar and unusual. She grinned as she placed her tiles on an open Triple Word Score.

Winston put his hands over his face when he realized she was going to win.

"Queen," she whispered.

Night approached quickly, and the last of the firewood burned away in the fireplace.

Winston and Penelope moved a few mattresses downstairs next to the fireplace, and the kids assembled in a blanket pile on the floor. Penelope curled up on the couch above them and kept watch. She got up occasionally to stoke the fire and add more wood. She went out to get more as soon as she thought the kids slept.

The chill in the air turned her breath to vapor against the dark night. The wind howled against the house, and the snow continued to pile up against the windows. Winston woke up multiple times and checked the windows. As he stirred to do so again, Remmie woke up.

"What are you doing?"

"Checking outside. Looks weird."

"What's going on?" Remmie sat up and pushed off her blankets. The air in the room felt cold, and her nose began to run again.

"Something's moving out there," he answered, putting his face directly against the window.

Remmie curled up on the couch next to Winston.

"Are you sure?" Penelope's voice croaked from the couch. She also kicked off her blankets and pulled up to the window.

"Yeah, something's happening outside," Winston pushed back from the windows and walked back into the kitchen.

"She's gone!" Winston shouted as the lights flicked on.

Remmie and Penelope leapt from the couches and crossed

into the kitchen. Remmie's hands clutched her cheeks as she gazed upon the empty chair.

"Where... did she... go...?" Remmie looked around the kitchen. The ties lay on the floor in a puddle, and she reached forward to touch the chair.

Cold.

"She's been gone a while," Remmie's voice cracked as she glanced at the others.

Penelope turned back to the living room. Her girls slept soundly under a pile of blankets.

"We need to find out what's outside. Maybe that's where she went," Winston whispered as he gathered his coat and boots.

"You can't go out there alone," Penelope countered as she reached for her own boots.

"We can go together, but they need to stay inside," Winston gestured toward the girls.

"Remmie, keep the girls away from the door, but you can look through the windows," Penelope instructed as she slid on her gloves.

Remmie nodded and went back to sit near the sleeping sisters.

Winston and Penelope looked at each other, assessing themselves.

"Are you ready?" Penelope asked him, as if she was really asking herself.

"I think we should stay on the porch and come back to the door before we go out in the yard. We should stay together once we leave the porch." Winston had a plan.

Penelope nodded and she slowly opened the door.

Snowy wind pushed the door back, and they fought against it as they walked outside, struggling to pull the door closed behind them.

Remmie watched through the windows to see if she could see them. The whiteout persisted against the house, and she eventually snuggled up on the couch and watched the girls sleep.

Shouting outside woke her. Remmie rubbed her eyes - she couldn't believe she had fallen asleep. She looked down at the girls.

Their blankets pushed aside. They were gone. Remmie felt her breath catch as she leaped off the couch and started looking around the house for them, for Winston... for anyone. She quickly swept through the kitchen, the dining room, and then came back to the living room.

With a deep breath, Remmie ascended the stairs. She knew it was likely her mom was hiding up here, sleeping or waiting. She couldn't be sure. Remmie slowly opened the door to her bedroom, empty bed and stale air greeted her. The foul odor reminded her she hadn't bathed in... a while.

She checked the other rooms, including the bathroom and finally — her mom's room. She opened the door knob slowly, and she finally saw her mom passed out on her bed. Remmie closed the door and headed back downstairs.

She climbed back on the couch.

"I need to think," she muttered to herself. A book was open on the coffee table, and something caught her eye.

Remmie picked up the Christmas book Isla had brought over, and she looked at the story. The drawing depicted a blizzard and a scared family, huddled inside their darkened home. A dark figure stood in the fireplace, a goat head with horns looking at the family. The figure had a menacing expression, and Remmie flipped a few pages to look at the title.

"The Tale of Krampus"

She quickly scanned the page. Punishes misbehaving children. Evil-looking goat-demon thing kidnapping the kids.

She looked outside. Penelope and Winston had disappeared into the snow, and it seemed likely that Micah and Isla disappeared, as well.. Outside, a bright yellow glow started to come from the street.

"It can't be morning," Remmie whispered to the windows. Forgetting the sunlight, she turned back to the couch and the book in her lap.

She thought about her mom - her sad mom who never wanted to be a parent. She thought about her daddy and how much she missed him. She thought about Winston and how much she depended on him. Her friends, Penelope and the girls, they invited her over for sleepovers every weekend after her daddy left.

"There's really only one thing I can do," Remmie decided. She hopped off the couch and went to the mud room. She slid on her boots. She pulled on her worn coat, found her mom's gloves and slid those on. She needed water-resistant gloves. A pair of ski goggles sat on the floor, too, and she made a snap decision to put them on. She found a couple of knit hats and put those on her head. Finally, one of her dad's old scarves lay hidden, curled up on the floor behind the end table. She reached for it and wrapped it around her neck.

Just having a piece of her daddy with her made her walk taller.

She grabbed the fire poker on her way out.

"I'm ready," she whispered, as she opened the door.

The snow pelted her cheeks. The freezing cold air bit at her skin. She adjusted quickly to the freezing temperatures. She could still see, and it made all of the difference.

Through the darkness, one source of light burned on the street. A black sleigh, stopped in front of Remmie's house, lit by a barbed-wire string of christmas lights and a bright light in the back, illuminated the street from within. Goats and other strange creatures circled the sleigh. Remmie blinked. Taking a deep breath, she charged toward the back of the sleigh. As she walked between the jumping goats, she discovered two tiny bodies nestled together between black sacks.

"Isla! Micah!" Remmie rushed to the back of the black sleigh, and as she almost reached the girls, a goat pushed her over. She fell into the snow, and she turned back to see movement around the girls.

Light shone out from within the body of the sleigh, and slowly something began to emerge from the depths of the carriage.

Remmie's heart pounded. A robed figure emerged, and it set its hooved feet on the ground in front of Remmie.

"Another for the night," he laughed, the hood of his cloak sliding back and revealing the horned head of an old demon. Its beard was threaded with small bones, and its glowing gray eyes seemed not of this world. The storybook flashed through her mind.

Krampus. The Christmas night robber of bad children.

"I am a daughter of night. You will not take my friends." Remmie tried to shout her command. She stood tall in the snow; her hands balled in fists at her side.

"Are you sure?" Krampus asked, the goats frolicking and laughing behind him.

"I have someone better for you." The plan formed quickly as she stood before the demon of the night.

"My mother killed her baby daughter on Christmas thirteen years ago. Take my mother."

Krampus turned his head.

"I collect children. Why would I want your evil mother?" As he asked the question, Remmie looked over at the girls in the back of the sleigh. They sat up as they woke, and they watched in horror from the edge.

"Because you saved the baby. You took her in."

"I don't collect discarded babies," Krampus countered, his eyes narrowing as he quietly rubbed his hands. Winston rubbed his hands when he lied, and Remmie stood up straighter.

Remmie knew he was lying. "You collected her. You found this baby in the snow, left outside by a selfish mother. You picked her up and you took her with you, didn't you?" Remmie knew the story was wild, but it all made sense to her.

"And if I did?" Krampus spat his answer as he gestured toward the sleigh.

"Let her have her revenge. Let her collect her evil mother." As Remmie's final words crossed the dark and snowy street, a young girl emerged from the back of the sleigh. She looked remarkably like Winston, but her hair was braided into a crown atop her head. She wore a black robe, and chainmail hung from her shoulders and chest. A sword was sheathed at her side.

"I am the discarded child," she proclaimed as she stepped down from the sleigh. Despite her youth, her expression was severe, a seriousness found from seeing a thousand wars and a thousand more deaths.

"What do you wish for me, Grandfather?" The teenager's voice filled with kindness as she turned her attention to the old demon. She pulled the hair back from his face and searched his eyes for an earnest answer.

"You have earned your place. Exact what you feel you deserve, my dear Waise."

She nodded and murmured to the goats.

Remmie did not understand the language, but the rod of anger in her chest began to subside.

I can't really afford to lose my mother, too, she thought. Moments flashed through her mind: the times her mother hit her, when her mom came to school drunk and beat her in front of her class, and that night her daddy left when Opal screamed how much she hated them. No salve would heal those painful wounds.

A few moments later, noises echoed through the soft, snowy street. Opal's screams filled the air with expletives and confusion as the goats pushed her out of bed and forced her down the stairs.

Part of Remmie, a part of her she did not want to evaluate, felt pleased.

"Get outta here!" Opal shouted as the determined goats forced her from the house. Even in the darkness, her unwashed body and stained nightgown appeared foul and putrid.

"What... is... this..." she shouted as she finally observed the scene in the street. Krampus and Waise stood together and a parade of goats were frolicking around, eating random bushes and peeing on mailboxes.

Remmie looked at her sister, but the older girl remained stoic. No trace of emotion crossed her still face. Her eyes evaluated Opal from her dirty feet to her filthy hair. The mess in front of her wasn't a demon from her nightmares.

"Remmie! Get away from there!" Opal shouted as she tried to move back toward the house. A goat jumped and hit her in the face with its horns.

"No, Mother. Your reckoning awaits," Waise called as she crossed the yard. Goats flanked her as she approached the shrinking murderer.

"Muh... mother..." Opal repeated as she stared into a mirror wearing armor.

"You left me to die. You opened the window and dropped me outside. You killed me."

Recognition flashed across Opal's face.

"Trinity?" Opal's hands covered her own face.

"My grandfather saved me that night. I owe him my life… and my loyalty."

Opal kept her eyes covered.

"No! You were a wicked baby! You screamed and screamed and screamed! Wicked!"

"I was a baby. You were the adult. You chose a cruel and merciless fate for me, and I shall repay that debt to you."

Opal screamed and dropped her hands for a brief moment.

"Let me be the last face you remember," Waise murmured, and unsheathed her sword.

Krampus moved in front of Remmie, blocking her view. She didn't try to look around him, but she could tell from the screams that Waise showed their mother no mercy.

"This bargain has been fulfilled," he flicked his hand, and four bodies were lifted from the back of the sleigh. They slid out and landed hard on the snow.

"I will be back, and I look forward to seeing you again," Krampus pulled something from his robe and threw it at Remmie.

She caught it but kept her eyes on the old demon.

"Come forth, Waise." He shouted across the yard as he climbed into the sleigh.

Waise turned and immediately headed back. The goats carried Opal's body across the lawn. As Krampus lifted her into the sleigh, Remmie caught sight of her mother for the last time.

Waise held true to her word - Opal's eye sockets sat empty in her head. Waise's face would be the last thing her mother ever saw.

"Onto the night, my legion of reckoning," Krampus shouted as the sleigh and all of its inhabitants took off into the darkness.

As the final glimmer of light from their evil brigade flickered and went out, Remmie turned and looked at the bodies in the snow.

All four people - Winston, Penelope, Isla, and Micah - huddled together and watched the same scene.

Remmie ran to them, falling across their laps and throwing her arms out trying to hug them all at the same time.

"I'm so happy to see you all," she shouted as tears streamed down her face.

"We're so glad to see you, too" Penelope shouted as she hugged all of them together.

"Are you okay?" Winston asked Remmie, taking her small face in his hands.

"I'm okay," Remmie nodded. They all heard the lie in her voice, but none of them truly felt okay.

"Did that just happen?" Winston asked as he stood and looked down the street.

"Remmie saved us," Micah said as she held on to Remmie's legs.

"She did save us, my love. She saved all of us," Penelope affirmed, staring deeply into Remmie's young face. "We owe you more than you can imagine."

Remmie put her hands to Winston, and he pulled her in for a hug. They looked down the road again, expecting to see a demonic sleigh heading back to their house. Piles of fresh snow covered the street.

"We should get inside," Penelope suggested as she stood. The girls helped each other up, and they started crossing the street holding each others' hands.

They all started back to Remmie's house when Isla stopped walking.

"What's wrong?" Winston asked as the others turned to look at her.

"It stopped snowing," she murmured, her head turned to the sky.

They all turned, looking up at the clear night sky.

Slowly, the sounds of the city resumed.

A car started on a neighboring street.

An ambulance siren echoed in the distance.

"Penny?" A voice rang out from across the street.

Penelope and the girls turned as a man, Remmie recognized as their father, rushed toward the house. He held them close in his arms as they walked up to the porch.

"It was the strangest thing. It was like I took a nap over at the McGuire's place," he started.

They were almost to the front porch when a car pulled up to the curb. It came to a screeching halt and the group turned back to see who would climb out.

A silver sedan.

Winston and Remmie took off toward the car. They knew immediately who had come to them.

The door flew open, and the driver ran to them. Sawyer scooped up his kids in his arms.

"I've been trying to get here! I'm so sorry. I'm so sorry, my loves," he cried into their hair. Sawyer held his babies together, and they cried in each other's arms.

"Welcome home, Daddy," Remmie whispered, her head buried against his chest. "Please don't ever leave us again."

"Come inside with us, Daddy! We have so much to tell you." Winston urged him. He was back on the ground and heading inside.

"Where's your mother? I can't come inside until she allows me in," he attempted to clarify.

Remmie shook her head and lowered her eyes. "She's gone."

Sawyer watched her eyes carefully. He understood what she meant.

"I like this scarf on you, my darling girl," he kissed Remmie on the cheek.

"We'll tell you everything! Just come inside!" Winston pleaded from the porch.

"I'm coming," Sawyer answered, still holding Remmie in his arms.

They crossed the yard, and he slowly put her on the ground. Remmie looked down at her hand, remembering that she still held something.

"What's that in your hand," he asked, pointing to her closed fist.

"Something the demon gave me," she answered as she opened her fist. An old tarnished bell rested in her palm.

Sawyer dropped to his knees, and his face paled. He slowly pulled an identical bell from his pocket. The two stared into each other's trembling palms and terrified faces as the snow began to swirl around them.

GUARDIAN OF THE TREES

CHISTO HEALY

He watched from a distance. This was his forest, his woodland. It was his to protect. His father had entrusted him with this ever so important duty. He felt great pride stepping into those shoes, and he took it extremely seriously.

The trees were the true ancients of this planet. Some of them had lived for hundreds of years compared to the pitiful humans of thirty or forty that deemed themselves superior. Humans felt entitled to take and destroy anything they wanted. They put themselves at the top of the food chain. It disgusted him.

Unfortunately, the trees were unarmed and unable to defend themselves against the will and might of humanity. They just stood there proudly and took what came to them. As respectable as that was to him, he knew in his heart that they deserved to be protected. He was human too, just like those that thought to hurt the trees and the animals of his forest, but he was different. He was one with the forest, just like his father had taught him to be. He was special. He was a guardian.

Once again, a pickup truck pulled up, and a man got out with a chainsaw. He probably needed firewood now that Christmas had come. Each year at this time, the guardian struggled with anxiety and fear of failure, as it became so much more difficult to protect the trees. People came from everywhere, wanting to cut them down and display their carcasses in their houses. He couldn't believe that humans would partake in such a "disgusting" ritual, but they did, every single year. He would deal with it when it came. Right now, he needed to focus on the task at hand.

He raised his crossbow and fired. His aim was as true as always. The bolt went through the stranger's hand and he dropped his tree murdering saw, with a cry of pain. The guardian approached the wounded man and reveled in the fear that shone in the stranger's eyes. This man deserved to fear, to suffer, for the trees that he had killed.

The guardian lifted his axe and gave the killer of trees a few good whacks, sending his blood onto the forest floor. Then he put the axe back into the sheath strapped to his back and hooked the crossbow onto his belt. He would come back and get the man's truck and drive it far from these woods. He had learned the hard way that if he didn't, the authorities would end up prowling all over them. Even they didn't respect the trees, not like he did. There were too many of them for him to dispose of so he had opted to hide. It was better to live to fight another day and make sure that the trees still had their protector, then to go down fighting and leave the forest unprotected.

First things first though. He grabbed the dead man by his shirt collar and he dragged him through the trees. He took him through the dirt and past the noble ancients that stood tall all through the forest and the guardian only stopped when he reached his cabin. The guardian threw the dead man down long enough to open the door, then grabbed his limp form back up and pulled him inside to a dark green metallic pot that stood empty in the room's dusty corner.

The guardian put the body of the dead man in the pot feet first, placing a pole down the back of the dead man's shirt to hold him upright. Then he wrapped him with garland and tinsel. He put a layer of lights on him as well and plugged them in. They blinked and changed colors. He topped it off with a red ball Christmas ornament hanging from the bottom lip of the man's eternally fixed scream. He felt suddenly proud of his handiwork. It seemed he would be ready for Christmas as well.

He took the keys out of the dead man's pockets and went to go move the truck. As he walked, he thought about it. He had a huge open area back behind his cabin. He could get tons of those Christmas tree stands and set them up back there. Then, every time one of the trees he was tasked with guarding got cut down, he could find the person that did it, bring them back there, and add them to his collection; a tree for a tree.

The guardian pictured it in his mind, a forest of dead humans, decorated for the holiday season. He smiled to himself as he drove the dead man's truck down the road. It would be beautiful, he thought, absolutely beautiful.

SALLY RODE with her dads in the station wagon, her eyes watching the sky through the window with the hope of snow blooming in her heart. She still felt full from all they had eaten for Thanksgiving even though it was days ago, but her dads were ready to decorate for Christmas. It was by far their favorite time of year. Sally liked the presents and some of the carols; others were annoying, but seeing her parents happy was the most wonderful part of the holiday season for her. Their smiles never ended and they danced and sang, and hinted towards presents with a childish glee. Their happiness was contagious. There was no way for her not to feel it, even so soon after stuffing herself for Thanksgiving.

One of her dads, Ray, was a chef, like a for-real chef, the kind you see on TV, and everything he made was amazingly delicious and eye-catchingly beautiful. He was in charge of Thanksgiving and always made enough for an army. They had company sometimes, mostly family, but never enough to keep from having a week's worth of leftovers. She would have complained had it not tasted so good.

Sally couldn't wait until she could start working so she could buy presents for her parents. They didn't require presents from her, they were already happy as can be, but they were always so good to her and they gave her the best presents every year. She really wanted to be able to give something back. Unfortunately, at twelve years old, she still had a long way to go. She did try to make them cards and gifts with things she saw on DIY crafting videos, and they were never short of enamored with what she gave them, but she was still excited for the day she could do more.

Josh, her dad that wasn't a chef, was a really good artist, and sometimes he would help her to make something for Ray, but then she felt bad because Ray couldn't help her return the favor unless she wanted to cook something for Josh. She actually considered doing that this year because she saw a video about making these adorable Christmas appetizers that resembled the characters from Rudolph and she just knew he would love them.

Sometimes the kids in school were mean to her and made fun of her for having two dads, but they didn't actually bother

her. It probably would have hurt her feelings had she not been to most of their houses at some point and seen the way their families treated each other. It made sense to her that they would lash out at her. Their families were always arguing and yelling and seeming so unhappy with their lives, and her family was kind and loving and close, and they really enjoyed being a family. She supposed she would have been jealous and bitter if she had been in their shoes. Sally loved her dads and she wouldn't have traded them for anything in the world.

They had already gone to the Hallmark store and worked for an hour as a team until they agreed on the perfect ornament for the year. They got a new one every year. Now they were headed to the home repair store because they always had really big things to put on your lawn for the holidays. Last year they got giant light up candy canes and put them on either side of the porch, but this year, Josh really wanted to show his artistry. They were going to have a real Christmas party for the first time, not just a family party, and they wanted the house to look the best. Sally thought they also wanted people to see it and feel excited. Her dads always wanted to spread Christmas cheer to others.

She wished all of this could wait until they had fully digested Thanksgiving and there were no leftovers in the fridge anymore, but the party was before Christmas and she knew how much her dads liked to be prepared. They were always ready for everything and they were never late. That was them. They didn't enforce that kind of stuff with her, though she naturally picked up the habits. Her teachers always commended her for being on time with all her assignments. It was a benefit to her character to have two good influences at home, giving her something to be proud to be compared to as they were the happiest people she knew and were both successful in their chosen fields.

Josh wasn't an artist for a living despite being so good at it. He said that he didn't want to ruin his love for it by turning it into a job. That made sense to Sally. She told herself that she would take things like that into consideration when she was planning her future and choosing her own profession. For work, Josh was some kind of businessman that she didn't really understand, but she knew he dressed really fancy and worked hard and would come home really tired but so happy to see her and Ray.

Sally would have been a liar if she said she wasn't looking forward to giving him ideas of what to do with the outside of the house. She really wanted to put Santa and a sleigh on the roof, and maybe a snowman somewhere. They had this really beautiful tree in their front yard. The snowman would look really cute standing next to it under the over-hanging branches.

Traffic was low and the roads were virtually theirs alone as they sang happily on their way towards the home improvement store. Sally's smile was due to more than just this moment. She was excited to have a party. Her dads said if it went well, they would have one every year. That was something really cool and fun to look forward to. Her dads were such fun people. She knew if they were planning a party that it was going to be lit. They already told her that she could invite her friends, and she couldn't wait. The only part of the Christmas season, aside from Christmas morning, that could have possibly been better than that, was their annual trip to Santa Land. It was an entirely Christmas themed amusement park and the souvenir shop had the best candy ever. Ray had asked her if she was going to be too old for Santa Land next year, since she was turning thirteen and would officially be a teenager and not a kid anymore. Her answer was a very firm, "No way!"

As they were driving towards the home improvement store, Sally watched a deep blue pick-up truck headed in the other direction and met the passing driver's fierce stare. She felt uncomfortable. Something about the man was strange. He looked like the illustration of the woodsman in her Hansel and Gretel storybook. He turned his head as their vehicles passed each other and his gaze connected with her own. For some reason when she looked into his eyes, she felt scared. She shivered. Then he was gone, behind them, driving away.

"You alright, honey?" Josh asked her from the passenger seat.

Sally nodded to him and gave an obvious forced smile that made him frown in return. She gave a genuine smile then at how well he could read her. "I'm okay," she told him. "It's just that man in the truck. He was a little strange."

"I feel you," Ray said with a laugh. "He was a definite creeper. He looked like the type of guy that was perpetually on the naughty list growing up. A lifetime of coal has got to turn people bad."

The family shared a laugh, but down inside, Sally still felt a little scared. She turned in her seat and looked out the back windshield of the car, but the truck was gone.

SALLY WAS GIVEN the job of decorating the tree in the yard and she was excitedly performing that task as Josh assembled an elf's workshop on the lawn nearby. Hanging the garland and tinsel on the big tree made her think of something she had been wanting to ask. She wanted to ask both her dads at the same time, but Ray was inside baking Christmas cookies for them to eat when they sat down to watch a movie after all their hard work decorating.

She scrunched her face up thoughtfully and said, "Dad, can we get a real tree this year?"

Josh stopped what he was doing and put the elf and the toy car he was working on down. He turned to face his daughter. "You don't like the fake tree anymore?"

"It's not that I don't like it," she said, biting her lip. "It's just that the real ones are so much prettier and they smell nice and make it really feel like Christmas."

"I see," Josh told her with a smile. "Can we do something to make the fake one smell more like pine? Would that help with the feeling?"

Sally sighed. "I mean, I guess…if we can't have a real one, but I really want one. Just this year. It will be nicer for the party too, and I thought maybe we could plant a new tree so it wouldn't be so bad."

Josh looked at her like he was impressed. "You're a pretty good negotiator. I should take you to the office and let you work with me one day. Alright. Come on. Let's go see what your other dad thinks. I wouldn't feel right making this kind of decision without him when the life of a tree hangs in the balance."

Sally laughed. "Okay."

Josh politely asked the elves to wait for him to get back and led his laughing daughter up the walkway to the front door (decorated with a large Christmas wreath and red felt bows) and beyond it into the house. They crossed through the big living room and dining room areas into the kitchen where Ray wore a Christmas apron, working on the cookies. He smiled.

"They're not ready yet. I'll let you both know when they're done."

"I can't wait," Josh said to him."But since we have to, our daughter has a question for you."

"Oh?"

Josh tapped his daughter on the shoulder. "Go on. Tell him the whole pitch, just like you told me."

Sally smiled and nodded and then did as he asked. Then she and her father waited for Ray's answer. "Just this once?" he asked.

Sally nodded with a finger between her lips.

The sight of her being so cute and sweet made her father smile. Ray asked a follow up question. "And will you plant the new tree yourself?"

"Sure," Sally said. "That sounds like fun."

"Okay then. It's alright with me."

Sally's face lit up. She beamed with happiness and jumped up and down. Her dads shared a laugh.

Josh got his hand slapped for trying to reach into the batter bowl. They all laughed again. Then he said, "Two of the guys at the office were actually talking about this spot that would be great to get Christmas trees. It's virtually untouched. It won't be crowded and there will be tons to choose from."

"That sounds sad to me," Ray admitted, " but we can go. We'll get it tomorrow and then bring it back here and get it all set up before the party tomorrow night. How's that sound?"

"Just perfect!" Sally exclaimed. "I'm so excited. This is gonna be the best Christmas ever!"

"Well now that sounds like a lot of pressure," Ray said with a chuckle.

"Alright. We're gonna get back to work," Josh told him. "You hurry up and finish those cookies, because the smell alone is making my mouth water."

"What he said," Sally agreed.

Then she skipped, a dance in her step, as she followed her dad back outside to finish getting the arrangement ready for the big party tomorrow night. In her mind she was already daydreaming and imagining going with her dads to the special spot and picking out the perfect Christmas tree. It was going to be so beautiful, the most beautiful tree anyone had ever seen. She couldn't wait to hang the new ornament they had gotten on the new tree. She was so excited that she feared it was going to be hard for her to get to sleep tonight. Just like her friends and the kids in her stories, Sally felt the brewing anticipation of the morning's events. It wasn't exactly Christmas morning, but it was close.

———

AFTER POPCORN, cookies and family movie time, Sally had gone to bed and dreamed about Christmas. She woke up still in the spirit and ran to her dads who were happy to see her so happy but also needing their coffee before they could get going. While she was waiting, she went outside to the finished Christmas display. It was magical and truly made their lawn look like a winter wonderland. It was the North Pole. There was snow everywhere even though it hadn't snowed yet this year. There was a snowman under the tree, just as she had pictured it, and Santa's workshop where the elves were hard at work making toys. Mrs. Claus brought them a tray of cookies to fill their bellies with sugar as they worked. Sally was so delighted that her dad indulged her with Santa and his sleigh riding across the roof of their home. She beamed at the extra details he added, like the elves trying to catch the presents falling out of the overstuffed bag. Candy canes as tall as her lined the walkway up to the front door and made her feel like a Christmas princess as she walked between them.

Sally ran around playing and talking to the Christmas

characters. She named the snowman Chuck and then called the elves Linus and Lucy and Shroeder and Patty. The names were the names of characters from her favorite Christmas movie and she had actually been named after one of the characters herself. She realized what the display was missing then, a dog. It needed a dog which she would of course name Snoopy. She would have to inform her dads of this when they came out.

A little while later, when Josh and Ray were sufficiently caffeinated they exited the house ready to take her to go pick out her tree. Sally did a happy dance and then threw herself down and made a snow angel in the polyethylene faux snow.

"We have the coolest kid," Ray said.

"For sure," Josh agreed. Then they joined her in making snow angels and they all shared a laugh. "Too bad it doesn't stick well. It would be too much fun to have a snowball fight."

"I'm sure we will before winter is over with," Ray said with a smile.

"Come on! Come on!" Sally said, jumping up and down. As they piled into the station wagon she told them about Snoopy.

"Okay. One step at a time. Let's get this tree first," Josh said.

"But I think a Christmas puppy would be a great addition to Josh's display," Ray told her.

"Yay!" Sally squealed.

The drive was a bit far so they sang Christmas carols to pass the time, but only the good ones.

"Is there anything we can do to get the Mariah Carey song off of the annoying list?" Ray asked. "I really love her."

"No one can sing that song anyway!" Sally told him. "It's so high!"

"She's not wrong," Josh said to his husband with a smile. "I think this is it up here on the left."

Ray looked where his husband was pointing and he pulled the car over. He was dreading the part where they were going to have to actually cut the tree down. It felt like murder to him, but he knew when they decided to become parents that they were going to have to do some things that they didn't agree with along the way to make their child happy. There hadn't been many up to this point. This was really the first big one; he just kept looking at the happiness in her smiling face when he needed a motivational push.

He parked the car at the roadside and they all got out, stretching. Sally was exhaling heavily and enjoying how she could see her breath. Josh looked out at the wide expanse of trees and he asked, "There's so many. How are you going to pick the perfect one?"

"I'll know it when I see it," Sally told him.

Ray opened up the trunk of the station wagon and took out two big axes. He tossed one to Josh. "Don't think you're getting out of this tree murder," he said quietly so Sally wouldn't hear. "We'll chop the tree down together."

"As we do everything," Josh said, winking. "I wouldn't have it any other way."

THE GUARDIAN WATCHED them with disgust. They came as a family. They brought their child to witness such a heinous act. It went a step further even. The child was being allowed to choose which of his trees they intended to kill and steal. They were perusing them like the forest was a grocery store, walking down the aisles and deciding what they wanted. How could these people be so insensitive? So self involved? He would make them pay. All of them.

He had to wait on his moment though. As much as he wanted to run up on them with his axe and butcher them like they meant to butcher his trees, he knew that he couldn't. There were three of them and the two adults had an axe each. Add to that the fact that children are often spry and fleet footed, there were too many factors, too many things that made attacking them foolish. Fools never won. He was no fool.

As much as he hated it, as much as it made his stomach turn and twist into knots, the guardian was going to have to let them take one of the trees. He would pray for the ancient being's safe passage into the spirit forest and beg the stumped remains for its forgiveness and understanding. He hated losing even one but sometimes that was what it took to protect the many. War demanded sacrifice and as sad as that may be, Christmas time was war. With a hand to his heart, he snuck past them, staying low and hurrying through the trees.

The guardian made his way to the car that they had come in. He knew that they planned to tie the tree to the roof of the car. Unless they came in a pickup truck, that was what these killers had always done. He checked to make sure that they weren't looking back his way. Then he peered in through their windows. They had the twine in the backseat. The child probably wanted to hold it. They would still need to open the hatchback and put their murder weapons away. If they looked in and he was inside, they would spot him. He would have to wait on his moment once more.

The guardian ripped off a piece of his sleeve and placed it in the area where the trunk closed and latched. It would close but not lock. That way once they got back and put their weapons away, he could wait until they were not paying attention and climb inside. In the meantime, he needed to be close by but out of sight, so he laid down and slid underneath the car, out of sight, and there he waited.

————

SALLY FOUND the perfect tree but her dads convinced her to choose a smaller one that would be safer to drive home with. She reluctantly agreed and resumed her search. After a while she chose one at last, and her dads took turns swinging their axes until it came down. Then they worked together and dragged it back to the car as a family.

Sally hurriedly got the twine out of the backseat where she had been playing with it on their drive there. Her dads returned their axes to the trunk and then closed it. Then she helped Ray hold the beautiful tree in place while Josh worked to tie it to the car.

As they worked together like a good team, they failed to notice the hatchback pop open and slowly lift up. They didn't see the man that slithered out from under the car and up into the opening before quietly closing the door. He curled up against the backseat and covered himself in a dusty brown tarp.

With the tree secure and snugly tied to the roof of the car; the family got back into the stationwagon and resumed their caroling as they headed home.

————

THE CAR PULLED to a stop and still the guardian waited. If they opened that door, he would seize the axe and be upon them before they realized what was happening. He was ready, his anger honed to a fine point.

The trunk didn't open though. The family happily laughed and sang together as they worked on removing the hundred year old tree they killed in an instant from the top of their vehicle. He lifted ever so slightly to watch them through the back window as they carried the tree into their house.

It was then that he noticed that he was in some kind of strange winter wonderland scene. He had rested in the back of this car and arose to find himself in a child's Christmas movie. He had always hated such films as they never valued the trees as anything more than decorations. He felt like he understood how this family could be so nonchalant about murder. Well, he would be the same. He would avenge that tree and stop them before they could kill any others.

The guardian eased open the trunk of the car. He quietly slipped out into the snow covered yard. Looking around, he saw that the other yards were full of green grass. It was surreal. He felt confused and afraid, but no less prepared for battle.

The guardian stayed low as he moved forward, weaving through candy canes and elves to make his way to the house. When at last he did, he peered through the closed window that led to their living room. All three family members were now wearing gaudy ugly sweaters that matched the chaos of their yard. The tree was nearby, standing in a metal fixture at the room's corner. He watched as these careless heartless people bent the tree's limbs whatever way suited them, making it look like a toy rather than a creature that had lived and breathed for a century. He snarled quietly as he took in the sight.

Then the child turned and saw him. They stared at each other, her fear and his anger silently connecting through the gaze of their eyes. He recognized her then. It hadn't occurred to him when they were at his home, taking his tree, but he realized it now. They had crossed paths before. It must have been an omen and he missed it. He should have been watching for signs. He felt annoyed with himself for not seeing it when he saw her. They had passed on the road when he was driving to dump the dead man's truck. They had met eyes then, just like they did now. He should have known, prepared for them to come.

Still, despite his error the guardian knew that the girl would scream. She would alert the adults of his presence and these strange Christmas beings would come out after him. He didn't know what kinds of weapons they kept so he needed to be careful. He broke their stare and backed away from the window, dropping out of sight. It would only be a matter of seconds until they came out of the house, checking to see if her fears held any validity. He looked around for a place to hide in this overcrowded snowy landscape. Then he found what he was looking for. He took his axe and moved swiftly.

———

"ARE YOU SURE?" Josh said, standing on the porch and looking out into their makeshift North Pole. "It was the creeper from the pickup truck?"

"Yes. It was definitely him," Sally said. "He was staring through our window."

"Should we call the police?" Ray asked, his eyes scanning over the scenery before them. He nervously scanned the yard and the street beyond for any sign of the strange man. "If Paul Bunyan is hiding outside our house that is super sketchy."

Sally held his hand with one of her own. Her other was clutching his pant leg.

Josh shook his head. "No. He's obviously not out here now. People are going to start showing up for the Christmas party shortly. If we call the police it will be a big mess. Let's just keep an eye out. We'll call them if we see him again."

"I hope I never see him again," Sally said.

After a minute, they were back inside, putting the finishing touches on the tree and getting the food ready for the party. Sally wore the biggest grin as she took in the tree. It was gorgeous, a thing of absolute beauty and did have that piney Christmas smell. She loved it so much. It was too bad that they couldn't just keep it and use the same one every year. It would be hard to find one this perfect again next year. She hoped that the tree she planted ended up being this perfect when it got bigger.

The doorbell rang and she and her father jumped with a start after what she had seen moments ago. Josh laughed at himself and patted her head before going to open the door. His friend Murray was there, holding a Christmas gift and wearing a Santa hat and a smile.

"You're a little early," Josh said, "but come on in. Make yourself at home, and Merry Christmas!"

Before long, the house and the yard were full of people. There was music going and food everywhere and the place was full of laughter and joyful conversation.

———

THE GUARDIAN WATCHED all these happy people, singing and dancing, laughing and talking. It sickened him how many of them complimented the homeowners on their tree. The muscles in his face twitched and spasmed listening to these cretins talk about how beautiful the tree was in its death.

He was mortified and enraged on behalf of the ancient tree, upon seeing it decorated like some kind of dress up doll. His lip curled like an angry dog. He was barely able to contain such fury. He couldn't wait to turn them all into trees of his own.

The guardian was willing to bet that each of these people had a tree like the dead one he followed here. He knew down in his core that all of these Christmas loving people were murderers and tree killers. He felt it in his heart, that they were all evil. He could taste it in his throat like so much bile.

These horrid people deserved the worst that he had to offer, he felt like electricity sparking through his bones, and he would make sure they would get it. He just had to be smart about it, clever and unrelenting. He thought of his father and remembered the day the old man placed his hand upon his shoulder and said, "It's all up to you now. You must protect the trees."

The guardian knew how to be careful, to do this right and make his family proud. He needed to take his time, pick these killers off one by one. He refused to make a mistake. A mistake would allow them to find and stop him and then the trees would have no one left to protect them. He couldn't let that happen. He couldn't ever let that happen. He could feel his father's disappointment just thinking about it.

TWO PEOPLE SHARED DRINKS, spiked eggnog topped with nutmeg and cinnamon, and mingling over by the big tree in the yard. They didn't realize that the snowman under the tree was alive until it was too late. The guardian who stood within the hollow structure, stared out of the snow creature's eyes with rage as he lifted an axe in each hand.

With two well placed swipes of the axes, two glasses of eggnog splashed into the fake snow, turning it yellow. Behind the glasses, still intact, the snow was dyed a deep red and the guardian pulled one headless body with each hand clutching crimson stained shirt collars, dragging them through the yard towards the street.

The guardian found a neighbor's work van parked across the street. He decided that it would be perfect for him to steal and transport the bodies of his victims back home to begin his tree garden. He pictured it in his mind again, and smiled at the thought...all those dead people decorated in gaudy Christmas fashion. It was beautiful and poetic. He couldn't wait to turn it into a reality.

He popped open the van and dragged the bodies up inside of it, hoping the owner of the vehicle didn't notice from the windows of their own house. He suspected they wouldn't. They were probably at the terrible party. Once the bodies were inside, he threw the heads in after them, and he shed his snowman costume as well and threw it in the van too. Then he skulked back across the street to claim more lives.

There was a man getting presents out of the backseat of a car. The guardian's footfall was silent in the faux snow. He didn't even breathe. The man had no clue he was even in danger when the axe came down.

There were two people dressed like elves kissing against a workshop table. The guardian was repulsed by them. He could smell their sweat, hear the thumping of their sinning hearts. They would call this kiss love yet would show no mercy to his beloved trees. The kissers' eyes were closed and the guardian seized the opportunity to make sure they never opened.

He donned one of the elf costumes and dropped the bodies in the van across the way and then returned to claim more still. This was his duty, his oath, his purpose. The guardian wasn't satisfied and wouldn't be satiated until he had taken the lives of the family who had taken his tree. An eye for an eye. This was war. He knew that his father and grandfather were watching him from the heavens, expecting him to fulfill his sacred duty and succeed in his vengeance.

One by one, he took the party goers to the van. It was gradual and strategic and the others just assumed that people were leaving, bowing out little by little, trickling down as the night went on. They were right in a sense, but not completely. The guests were leaving but none of them were going to make it home.not this year. Each of them just ended up in the van, piled up with the others. It was going perfectly according to his plan. He was going to take the entire loathsome party... until he was spotted in the act of killing two dancing women spinning candy cane batons. The guardian growled at his mistake, knowing that the game had just changed.

"WELL, I'd say this was a success," Josh said happily. "What do you think?"

Sally gave a vigorous nod. "Yeah! Best Christmas ever!"

Ray had just come from the kitchen with a tray full of Christmas themed brownies, ready to join the conversation when Murray was running towards them, arms waving, a terrified look on his face. The family froze and stared at him with obvious dread as he approached them, his fear plain in his wide eyes and wild movements.

"An elf just killed Melissa and Maryann with an axe!" he screamed. "Call the police!"

Before the family could even comprehend what the terrified man was yelling to them, a Christmas elf rose up behind him and chopped him down with an axe. When he did, Sally saw the man's eyes, and she recognized them, shuddering with terror that she felt all the way in her bones.

"It's him," she said. "It's the creepy man!"

"Get inside!" Ray shouted, dropping the tray of brownies into the fake snow at their feet. Josh was digging his phone out of his pocket as he ushered Sally towards the front door. Behind them, the elf and his bloody axe marched towards them, eyes full of hate.

As they hurried to get inside and away from the axe wielding madman, they could hear him cutting down party goers behind them, screams accompanying the terrible chopping sound of the axe. They made it inside and slammed the door behind them, quickly engaging the lock. Through the window beside it, they could see him, still coming, his elf costume covered in the blood of their guests. This time Josh did call the police and he was listening to the ringing, waiting with bated breath for someone to answer, when the axe came crashing through the window, scattering shards of shattered glass over the carpet.

Sally screamed and Ray ushered her towards the stairs that led up to their bedrooms. Josh ran behind them, his phone to his ear, yelling, "Come on! Come on!"

As they barreled up the stairs, they could hear the front door fly open with a bang below. They quickened their pace. When they reached the second floor, Josh had finally gotten a hold of the police and was frantically filling them in on the situation while Ray was looking around nervously trying to decide where to hide with his daughter.

"Yes. There is a man, some kind of woodsman. He has an axe, two I think. I'm not sure. You need to understand... he's killing everyone," Josh went on to the 911 operator.

"Is the man still there?"

"Yes. He's here. Please. My family is in danger. My daughter. Please."

"Do you have somewhere you can go? Somewhere you can hide until the officers arrive, sir?"

"Yes. Yes. That's what we're doing, but I don't know for how long. Please."

"Where is the man now, sir? Can you see him or hear him?"

"No. I don't know. Just please hurry."

"There's a car on the way, sir. Just hang tight."

"He's coming," Josh said quietly. Then he hung up the phone. They could hear the blade of the sharp axe scraping the wall and the sound of the man's big boots clomping down on the stairs as he made his way up after them.

They went into the dads' bedroom. Ray took Sally into the large walk in closet and they huddled together in the back corner under the clothes. They worked to calm their shaking nerves as Josh pulled the dresser in front of the bedroom door. Then he worked to open the door of the safe where he kept his gun. His hands were trembling; he messed up the combination and had to start over. He could hear the woodsman stomping loudly through the hallway beyond the door.

Ray pressed his back against the wall and wrapped his arms tightly around his child. Sally, in turn, clutched to his arms. They were both trembling. They couldn't see or hear anything that was happening in the bedroom beyond the closet. Their hearts were thundering with the anticipation of something terrible.

Josh finally heard the lock on the safe click open and an axe blade came through the bedroom door. He jumped and started to shake. The axe pulled free and came down again. The wood splintered and chipped. Even with the dresser in the way, it wouldn't be long before he made it through.

Josh hurried to get the door open and retrieve his gun. He

could hear the sounds of sirens outside and he prayed they were coming there. The woodsman crashed through the hole his axe made in the door, his arms swinging, and his hateful eyes staring in Josh's direction.

Josh raised the revolver and squeezed the trigger. The boom was loud. Even his husband and daughter, hidden in the dark, deep in the closet heard it and squeezed each other a little tighter. The guardian fell away from the door. Josh got to his feet and inched towards the broken door on trembling legs that struggled to hold him up. His sweating hands clutched the gun tightly. He reached the door and knew that he was going to have to lean over the dresser and look through the hole. His breath caught in his chest.

Slowly, he moved forward, inch by inch, head moving towards the hole. He was shaking uncontrollably when he reached it. His heart jumped when he saw nothing but the floor beyond the door. He was hoping to see that his bullet had struck home and the woodsman was downed. Maybe it would still be okay. Maybe they could just wait it out in there until the police get inside. He knew that Josh was armed now. He probably wouldn't just come back, right?

Seconds ticked by that felt like hours. Then he heard Sally scream from inside the closet. Josh's eyes went wide. He ripped the closet door open and Ray was pushing their daughter ahead of him towards Josh and the open door. There was an axe blade through the wall. It pulled free and came through again. Plaster and sheetrock came crashing into the closet with a cloud of white dust.

"He must have gone into the other bedroom," Ray shouted as they ran past Josh into the bedroom. He slammed the door behind him.

"We've got to go," Josh said. "We can't keep him out of here." They could hear him still crashing through the closet.

Then the sound stopped. They all looked at each other with fear and horror. "Go, go, go!" Josh said.

Sally climbed over the dresser and through the hole in the door. Josh and Ray worked to drag the dresser from the door. They could see their daughter through the hole, looking terrified. They knew she would be trapped if he doubled back and came out the next door over, so Ray told her. "Go. Hurry. It's okay. We're right behind you."

She looked hesitant. Josh nodded to her. Sally bit her lip but then she turned and ran down the stairs to the first level. Her dads got the dresser out of the way. As they got the bedroom door opened, the closet door opened behind them. With a scream, the axe wielding maniac ripped into the room, swinging his blade. Ray ran through the open door and Josh raised his gun and fired as he followed behind him, narrowly avoiding a killing blow as the axe whiffed by his head.

He didn't have time to see if his gun shot hit anything. He just kept moving. If it did hit the madman trying to kill them, it hadn't been enough to take him out because they could still hear him behind them, breathing heavily and growling like an animal. Josh reached back without looking and fired twice more as they made it to the stairs and turned the corner, heading down. He heard a wild scream and hoped he had finally connected, but the scream turned out to be a battle cry and the blade of an axe sliced his cheek on its way crashing into the wall.

Josh reached back and fired again and again as he followed Ray down the stairs. The booms of the gunfire tore through the house and the neighborhood beyond. When they reached the bottom they could hear the killer tearing down the steps after them. He was so close behind them.

Josh and Ray reached the living room and the man behind them roared his hatred. They spun around to face him and

Josh raised the gun and squeezed the trigger, realizing the hard way that he had already fired all six bullets. The crazed woodsman looked from them to the decorated tree beside them. He snarled like a mad dog and raised the axe over his head in a two handed grip.

"Drop it! Now!" a voice yelled from behind Sally's parents.

The guardian froze. He stared beyond these murderers at the police that had entered the house, led by the young girl. He knew she was trouble when he first passed her in the truck. He should have followed the signs. He couldn't push it. If they shot him, there would be no one to protect the other trees. He could avenge this tree later. He had to think ahead and look at the big picture. Sighing, the woodsman dropped his axe and slowly put his hands behind his head. The police moved around Josh and Ray to handcuff him.

Ray and Josh hugged their daughter tightly as the police dragged the murderer from their house. "You saved us," Josh said.

"One second later and we were toast," Ray agreed.

"It's not what I'd hoped but I'm glad I finally got to give you something for Christmas," Sally said. She was trying to joke but she started to cry. Her dads cried with her and they all hugged. Soon there would be police everywhere, and forensics. They would realize just how many of their friends and family had lost their lives at their party. They would deal with the emotional weight of that later, together, but for now, they were content to see the madman being put into the back of a police car and taken away.

WHAT THEY DIDN'T SEE WAS that the police car didn't make it back to the station. Just up the road from their house it swerved and crashed into a tree. The guardian saw the smoke and steam billowing from the hood. He could see that the driver was face down on the steering wheel and smell that the car was on fire. It tickled his nose; the door was broken and no longer kept him locked in, and this made him smile.

Only one man emerged from the wreckage, and he was the prisoner from the back of the car. He moved around the damaged vehicle to the broken tree and he placed his palms gently on the bark.

"Thank you for your sacrifice," he said softly, his eyes closed. "You have saved many other trees tonight. I will not forget you."

Then he started walking back down the road. He wasn't going to try to attack that wretched family again with all those police around, but he did intend to retrieve the van across the street and its contents. It was too far to walk home anyway. He would take those that he cut down and bring them home and plant them, decorate them for the coming holiday. He would return for the family later. He would never stop. This was his sworn duty. He was the Guardian of the Trees.

THE GOBBO AND THE HORN

GARY POWER

Archibald Bland, executor for the estate of August Conroy, was a miserly looking man with a narrow, pointed nose and a spasmodic tic beneath his left eye. With the build of a fleshed-out skeleton and his oversized suit, he took the appearance of a gaunt crow. His face displayed little emotion as he peered furtively over his spectacles at twins Daniel and Seth Conroy.

In a tedious, droning tone he told them, "As beneficiaries of the last will and testament of the late August Conroy, the following conditions were stipulated by your father."

The brothers were handsome young men and, at first glance, appeared uncannily alike. Under closer observation, though, Seth's eyes possessed a glint of mischief and Daniel appeared incorruptibly innocent.

A faint scuttling sound from within a small box on the desk caused a momentary distraction. The young men glanced first at each other and then towards the mysterious container.

The elderly solicitor, now somewhat vexed, continued his instruction with a little more urgency: "It is a condition of your father's will that you are to go your separate ways on this day December 21st, 1858, the anniversary of the 21st year of your birth." He tugged a finger at his collar and, much to the amusement of the twins, took the resemblance of a tortoise craning its head from its shell. "With an inheritance of five hundred pounds each," he continued, "you are to return to this office in Arundel's Market Cross in the county of Sussex five years hence to learn of each other's experiences. Upon confirmation of that meeting the considerable residue of the estate will be divided equally between you."

Another flurry of scratching came from the box, this time causing it to shudder on the table.

Barely able to contain his amusement, Seth remarked, "... and which of us is to inherit the mouse?"

For that, he received a sanctimonious glare from the sour-faced executor. The old man appeared increasingly uneasy as he continued to read the conditions of the will. Raising a hand to conceal his worsening tic, he told them, 'I have an amulet for each of you that your father stipulated should be worn until we reconvene five years hence.'

Hesitantly, he opened the box from which had come the perplexing sound, but no small animal, nor any other cause for the noise emerged; instead, what appeared to be two pieces of jewellery lay within.

To Daniel, the lawyer gave a small, gold hunchback figure on a chain and to Seth a crude red horn set in a silver base that was no bigger than a fingernail.

Reading from the will the old man continued, "My gift to you, Daniel, is a 'Gobbo,' an Italian talisman known for banishing malignant forces and bringing good luck. To Seth, I bestow a red coral horn or as it is better known a Cornicello, bringer of fortune and protector from the malevolence of the evil eye."

Archibald's eccentric appearance and the absurdities spouting from his mouth caused Seth to be unable to contain his amusement. "Gobbo?" he roared and burst into an uncontrolled fit of laughter. Daniel watched his brother with a stifled grin while struggling to suppress his own laughter. Archibald, not impressed by his client's unruly outburst, stared in silence until Seth had composed himself again.

Clearing his throat noisily, he continued, "If you will have a little patience, our business will soon be finished gentlemen. These pendants will afford you protection on life's journey. As you are aware your father had a fervent interest in the occult and accumulated many such curiosities. He acquired the Gobbo and the Horn while on a visit to Italy, specifically to the infamous Piazza Statuto in the city of Turin and, I might add, at great expense. Your father held passionate belief in such things and it would be a mark of respect that you honour his final wish. The spiritual energy within these two pieces of jewellery is not to be taken lightly."

And so, after agreeing to the conditions of the will, and following a brief conversation, Daniel and Seth Conroy went their separate ways.

Seth soon found himself in the company of a bunch of local rogues who promptly accompanied him to the St Mary's Gate Inn for an evening of hard drinking at his expense. Having foolishly boasted of his good fortune he swiftly fell into a drunken stupor. Several hours later he found himself rudely awakened by two thugs brandishing iron bars. Shelagh Byrne, a local woman of fearsome reputation, stood behind them with her hands placed defiantly on her hips.

A brawny, dishevelled man with a deep scar on the left side of his face looked towards her. She nodded once and obediently he struck the side of Seth's head with such force that his left eye exploded from its socket. The next blow shattered his jaw and sent several teeth flying from his bloodied mouth. The other man, a scrawny individual by the name of Saul, set about him with a relentless and frenzied assault. When Shelagh told them to stop, the two men, like servile dogs, backed off.

Taking a closer look, the feisty Irish woman lurched back when Seth opened his good eye and spat blood and phlegm into her face.

Gripping the Cornicello about his neck and with a glowering grin, he told her: "You'll pay for this one day, lady, then you'll really know what suffering is."

Prising his fingers away, Shelagh tore the pendant from him. "You save your threats for those that might be frightened." she told him.

With one final rasping cough, Seth breathed his last.

"What do we do with 'im now?" asked the scarred man.

"Bury him in Slindon wood, Frank. Make it deep though, don't want no animals sniffing 'round." She sauntered over to the other man and clutched her fingers tightly about his throat.

"Y'know, Saul, put a bit of meat on your bones and there's a definite likeness between you and this man, Seth. How do you fancy slipping into his shoes and inheriting a fortune in a few years' time?"

With a nervous grin, he reluctantly replied, "…yeah."

"He lived in that river shack down from the Black Rabbit Inn. A right recluse, he was. Make an appearance in town now and then. Drink an' curse and show your face occasionally an' you'll do fine. Five years' from now and even his own brother won't know the difference. Then we'll all be rich."

Shelagh's men took Seth's body by horse and trap into Slindon wood, burying him deeply and celebrating their future fortune by drinking several tankards of strong mead before slipping into a drunken stupor beneath the shade of a nearby Oak tree. By morning's first light, they found the horse and trap gone and Seth's grave empty. The soil had been pushed away as though from the inside.

Too frightened to consider any other option, Saul spluttered, "Foxes, got 'im...or...or wolves. Dragged 'im out the ground and eaten 'im, they 'ave."

Frank, visibly pale and shaking, stared into the hole and muttered inanely to himself while considering what to do next.

"We can't say nuffin'. Shelagh will 'ave our guts." he replied, "We'll tell her, we did what she said an' keep this to ourselves."

"We got a long walk home." moaned Saul as he studied the tracks made by the trap. "There's footsteps comin' from the grave. I reckon someone stole 'is bones and our cart while we was sleepin'. Body snatchers most likely. Got to be bodysnatchers."

The rumble of distant thunder and a fine mist of rain penetrating through the forest canopy didn't bode well for their return journey.

Looking like he might actually burst into tears, Frank just shook his head.

SAUL, for his part, made a convincing job of being Seth over the intervening years, making an occasional appearance as his alter ego but staying clear of any meaningful conversation with the townspeople. A steady diet of Absinthe, Laudanum tincture and the occasional visit to 'Madam Vida's house of Veniality' helped him pass the time.

Shelagh continued to wear Seth's Cornicello about her neck, hidden amongst a heaving bosom and an abundance of other jewellery. She recalled that Seth had drunkenly mentioned wearing it being a condition of his father's will. When the time came she would get Saul to wear it so that he might conclude the business of the Conroy brother's inheritance.

She couldn't help thinking that the future looked decidedly rosy.

ALMOST FIVE YEARS LATER, on a bitterly cold December evening, Shelagh Byrne's brutish henchman, Frank, found himself staggering drunkenly away from St. Mary Gate inn.

The cumbersome man relieved himself against the looming castle battlement walls when he became distracted by a grief-stricken cry emanating from a derelict building close by.

Carefully stepping across the icy road and pushing open the front door, he called out, "You alright in there, lady?"

The childish whimpering came from the first floor but the old wooden stairs leading there were splintered and rotten. He climbed them anyway, treading as cautiously as a man of his stout build could in such poor light. Moving warily into a darkened room, he glimpsed the silhouette of a shadowy figure standing in the corner.

"What's up, love? Someone not been nice to you?" he asked.

Her whining sobs drew him closer, but the stench of something long since dead made him wretch. Probably a cat or rat rotting away somewhere beneath the floorboards, he mused.

"I won't let nuffin' 'appen to ya." he said, "...but I do think we ought to leave sharpish. It's cold and damp in 'ere... you'll catch y'death y'will."

The figure shuffled into the light and revealed, to Frank's horror, the face of a brutish man. His craggy face had about it a pale, deathly sheen and his left eye was covered by a blood encrusted patch.

"Hearing things are you, Frank?" growled the man, "Sure sign of madness, that is. Maybe I should put you out of your misery." And then lifting the patch to reveal a festering, eyeless socket added, "Remember this do you? You did it five years ago, almost to the day. Looks like you didn't quite finish me off properly though, did you?"

"Seth." gasped Frank. "You wus dead. We buried you in the woods. You wus just a stiff, an' the animals ate ya."

Lurching forwards, Seth grabbed the big man by the throat and lifted him easily from the ground with one arm. With a thick, calloused thumb pressing against Frank's left eye he told him, "...an eye for an eye, Frank. That seems fair, doesn't it?"

The big man howled with the pain as Seth slowly increased the pressure. The more he struggled the more Seth tightened his grip on Frank's throat.

"I just did what I was told..." cried Frank, "...it...it was nuffin' personal. It was you or me. You know what Shelagh's like." and then he let out a jarring scream as Seth ground his eye into the back of its socket.

"*Nothing personal.*" chuckled Seth, "Well, that makes me feel so much better."

Frank begged him to stop, but still Seth pushed harder and harder, laughing as a congealed, bloody mess oozed from his socket. "I've been biding my time, Frank; experiencing life in the big city; a dilettante of fine living, if you like. It looks like that pigeon-livered mate of yours, Saul has made a fine job being me while I've been away. I was a nobody in London, Frank. I did things that would've seen me hanging from a yardarm, but back here I had the perfect alibi. Seth Conroy was alive and well and living in Arundel, courtesy of Shelagh Byrne's idiot henchman, Saul."

Frank's cries became whimpers as consciousness abandoned him. When his body went limp, Seth lowered him to the floor into a spreading pool of his own urine.

"Dear me, Frank, I thought you were made of stronger stuff. I can't stand here chatting to you all night though. I've got far more important matters to attend to, so I'll bid you farewell and leave you in the company of some friends of mine."

Pausing to look back as he made his exit, he watched as several sewer rats scampered over to Frank's body and started tearing at his flesh.

"Don't be greedy, boys," he called as the door slammed shut behind him, "There's plenty of him to go around."

On Monday, 21st December, 1863, Daniel Conroy woke early in his hotel room to a flood of winter sunlight and an icy gust of wind. He'd arrived the previous evening and booked into the Norfolk Arms, a Georgian coaching inn set under the ruined battlements of Arundel castle. A gruelling detour had taken the carriage through barren and desolate woodland in the county of East Sussex. In a place known as Duddleswell he shared company with a boisterous gathering of revellers sitting about a huge bonfire. They were drinking and listening to a storyteller read bawdy tales of iniquity and wickedness. Bidding them farewell and crossing himself with the sign of the Lord, Daniel continued his passage to the market town Arundel. The seven-hour stage-coach journey from London, much of it through thick snow and treacherous ice, had been uncomfortable and exhausting.

After a breakfast of salmon kedgeree and fresh coffee, he kissed the charm about his neck as he did every morning and trudged through several inches of crisp, virgin snow to the market cross. In the small square, the tradesman set up their businesses for the day, ignoring the lone traveler passing through.

Noticing a commotion by the river, Daniel investigated and learned that a local woman's eviscerated body had been found under the bridge. Her name was Shelagh Byrne and it soon became apparent that few, if any, were going to miss her.

With an inquisitive crowd gathering, the police cordoned off the murder scene and attention was diverted towards the seasonal festivities in the square. By midday, the town bustled with families and shrieking children throwing snowballs, ignorant to the brutal crime that had been committed.

The aroma of hot mulled wine and roasted chestnuts filled Daniel with a euphoric sense of Christmas. A lively choir sang 'The Holly and the Ivy' with zealous enthusiasm and he found himself breaking into strident song as he passed by. After a while, and with hopes of meeting his brother dwindling, he decided to pay a visit to a tavern for some lunch.

As he crossed the square a hooded man with a patch over his left eye stepped in front of him.

"Mr Conroy, I have some news for you." declared the man gruffly.

Daniel was intrigued but cautious. He could see little of the stranger's appearance, just a glint of bedevilment in his good eye and the evidence of a hard life on his weathered face.

"Do I know you sir?" he asked.

The man seemed hesitant in his reply.

"Quite possibly," he muttered, "…it's my belief that we share a common interest."

Even from a distance the stench of his putrid breath and reek of stale sweat disgusted Daniel. If Seth sent this man, he had certainly fallen into bad company.

After an awkward moment of silence and with a raucous burst of laughter the man pushed the hood from his head. Daniel found himself looking as though into a mirror, but the reflected face he saw looked pale and sickly.

"It's me, Seth," the man declared.

Shocked by his appearance, Daniel took a step back. With a grey, sickly pallor and his discoloured teeth mottled with decay; he looked more like a penniless beggar.

"Fortune it seems has not found you brother, nor you it. The world has changed you, I fear." he remarked. It pleased him to see that he at least still wore the red Cornicello about his neck.

As though embarrassed, Seth looked to the ground and pulled the hood back over his head.

"I have had time to organise the business that we have here. That old crow Archibald Bland is waiting for us in his office in Tarrant Street. Best we go now before he croaks it."

The meeting went quickly and to the brothers' satisfaction. With the final part of their legacy secured, they moved to an alehouse by the river Arun so that they could learn of each other's experiences as stipulated by the will.

Daniel found his eyes welling with tears as Seth recounted lurid details of his life. The intervening years had not been kind to him although much of his hardship had been of his own volition. At such close quarters the stale stench of his unwashed body made the air about him quite suffocating. His eyes were bloodshot and his skin had a ghostly sheen. There was an iniquity about him that made Daniel feel quite uncomfortable.

"My story is brief brother," said Seth, "...but none the less dramatic. So many times since we last met my destiny has been decided on the turn of a card, but as you can see that luck is no longer with me. Love has eluded me, but whores and gamblers have not. I fear much of my inheritance is already owed to rogues and money lenders."

Seth grasped his brother's arm and pulled him closer; his bony fingers gripped tightly and pinched his flesh. "I have waited patiently and dreamed much of this moment."

On the underside of his wrists Daniel noticed several scars and on his left forearm a tattoo of what appeared to be a crude and unholy depiction of a goat's head.

"I saw you singing along to the Holly and the Ivy." he scoffed, "How amusing to see a Christian man glorying in a carol with such Pagan roots, or were you in ignorance of that?"

His sickly eyes revealed the look of a man who indulges in too much liquor. Already it seemed the ale made him bawdy and peevish.

"So, tell me of *your* life Daniel and while you do I'll get my favourite wench, Jan, to fetch more ale. She is from Liverpool, brother, and if you tease her, she will lash you with her spirited, scouse wit." Pulling the woman onto his lap, he wrapped his arms about her waist and slurred, "She has fulsome breasts don't you think? If I squeeze her tightly, then perhaps they will overflow just as the ale does from the tankards that she holds."

Equally drunk patrons laughed at his vulgar comments while more temperate folk looked on in disgust.

Daniel drew a deep breath as he observed the sad desperation of his brother's ways. Seth's feral eyes narrowed to a squint and he stared into the distance, as though lost in another world. His lack of social grace and appalling manners caused Daniel much consternation.

With a heavy sigh, and to satisfy his part of the bequest agreement, Daniel recounted his own life.

"I had the good fortune to share lodgings in London with a bright and scholarly gentleman and learned much of the way of finance. With my inheritance I invested my time and knowledge to great success. I have acquired much property and wealth."

Seth set his tankard heavily on the table.

"...and of women Daniel...have you indulged yourself in the company of many women?" His coarse tone and roguish manner drew disparaging looks from those nearest which pleased him. He mocked their attention with a leering chuckle, hawking phlegm into his mouth and spitting it into the sawdust on the floor.

Daniel winced at his brother's crude behaviour.

"I am a God-fearing man Seth." he said, and then after a moment of thoughtful silence continued, "I married a wonderful woman, Eleanor, the daughter of a respected clergyman." Tears welled up in his eyes, "Consumption took her life just 6 months ago." Resting a hand on his brother's arm Daniel solemnly told him, "She was with child, Seth. The grief that followed almost broke me."

The memory left him staring into space and for a moment lost for words. Seth showed little interest and even less compassion.

"The lord moves in mysterious ways." he muttered

sarcastically, taunting his brother by sniggering at Daniel's ignorance of such elemental irony.

Ignoring his cynicism and with a reflective smile, Daniel continued. "I live alone in a townhouse in the London borough of Greenwich. It is a large property; I rattle around like a stone in a bucket." He reached into his pocket and handed Seth a parchment card. "This is my address - you should visit me one day; I have the resources to set you on a righteous path."

Seth snatched at the paper, scraping his skin in the process. His overgrown fingernails, ingrained with dirt disgusted Daniel and it became obvious to him that his brother had developed a bestial quality to his nature.

"I've noticed that you look at me in a critical way, Daniel. With pity I think." he scowled.

Daniel tutted.

"It is with love that I look at you, Seth, and concern. How you conduct your life is your affair. I suspect that your anger is a sign of deeper pain."

Seth shook his head, "You fear that with this new wealth, I will once again spend my time with gamblers and whores. Is that it? Well let me tell you, brother, my plans run far deeper than you could ever imagine."

"Your destiny is in your own hands." replied Daniel, "I have no wish to be your keeper. But I am your kin; if you need me, then I will be there."

Seth laughed scornfully at his words. He drank heartily and boasted tales of gambling, fighting and lurid exploits with street women as though proud of his debauched existence. Seeing the look of disgust on his brother's face, he slapped his hand noisily on the table.

"I can see that I disappoint you Daniel, so let me bargain with you. Allow me to use the facilities of your lodging tomorrow and I will show you the seed of a changed man."

Reluctantly, Daniel agreed.

"You can choose some clothes from my wardrobe, Seth. Perhaps when you look like a gentleman you will start to behave like one."

When time was called at the bar the two men stood up to leave, but Seth hesitated at the door.

"Come with me, Daniel, to the place on the river that is my home. See how I have lived these intervening years and perhaps you will experience a side to life as yet unknown. On such a glorious winter's evening I will show you that the countryside is like another world."

"I *will* come Seth, but on one condition – that tomorrow we secure comfortable lodgings for you and then together embark upon a journey of salvation."

"If that is what pleases you Daniel, then we will do just that. Tonight though, I will take you to a place that will leave you a changed man."

In his heart, Daniel doubted that he would see his brother again. Within a week he would be gone with the spoils of his inheritance, and on the road to ruin.

Once beyond the town and away from the lurid glow of the gas lights the track became treacherous and difficult to follow. The countryside held a dark and savage beauty. The glassy surface of the river and the frosted countryside reflected the silvery glint of the moon. It looked like a winter wonderland. Just as Seth had described.

Seth's mood eventually lightened and it was with a wry grin that he told his brother: "You can walk on the water if you like." He picked up a stone and skimmed it across the icy surface. "I'm sure it won't be the first time you've performed such a miracle."

Daniel couldn't help smiling, but mounting concern tempered his amusement.

Seth carried with him a pewter flask from which he took regular swigs. He talked constantly to himself, sometimes as though to an unseen companion. The bitter cold caused Daniel to shiver, but his brother seemed curiously immune to the numbing chill.

"The moon shall be your guide back Daniel." he said in a moment of lucidness, and then with a chuckle added, "...it has been so for me many a drunken night." Several times Seth slipped from the river bank and clambered back with all the grace of a circus clown. Daniel could only wonder what kind of miracle had prevented him from falling to his death.

"Have you no desire to escape the drudgery of your life Seth?" Daniel asked. His patience was dwindling and now frustration tempered his words. "If I am honest I fear the devil has taken grip of your soul. Have you learned nothing of value in these past five years? Compassion and humility perhaps? Or maybe to at least be honest and respectful of your fellow man?"

Seth didn't answer but instead scowled at the ground and continued with a mumbled tirade of blasphemy. They walked for a while in silence, crossing a bridge and following the river east from the town. Daniel stamped his feet as he walked in an attempt to relieve the numbness that crept into his toes. When they reached the ruin of a ramshackle building set back from the river, Seth stopped and turned to his brother.

"This is where I live Daniel. I thank you for coming this far but with your damning words I feel it's time for us to part. If I am honest, we have little in common to keep us together. I shall light a fire inside and it will keep me warm until the morning. I have survived this far without your virtuous meddling."

Daniel observed Seth and shook his head. It pained him to see his brother living in such squalor. The absent years had driven a considerable wedge between them. Here, the crumbling abode's walls held newly painted obscenities and symbols of blasphemy beneath an overgrowth of twisted ivy. Most disturbing was an inverted pentagram, an unmistakable sign of his brother's spiritual decline. Animal carcasses littered the ground, half covered by snow. The malevolence of the ruin caused Daniel much unease. In his heart he could feel the sacrilegious nature of the place.

"I told you before; I am a religious man now, Seth. I know Satan's sign when I see it. I fear your descent has surpassed even my worst fears."

Seth looked back in a way that disturbed him. There was menace in his gaze. He edged closer and at the same time lifted something from the ground which he concealed behind his back.

Clutching the talisman about his neck, Daniel backed away.

Seth liked that, chuckling and fixing his brother with a wide-eyed stare that suggested insanity. He moved closer, like a slavering wolf, his eyes burning in the gloomy light.

"Are you foolish enough to think I invited you here just to talk of old times brother...are you truly that naive?"

Daniel appeared visibly shocked by Seth's outburst, but Seth had not finished his brutal tirade.

"I want everything you have, and to be everything you are. But on my terms. You see, Daniel, I have learned much of father's amulets. They will bring us together in a way you couldn't possibly imagine."

"And what of the stipulations of father's will and our meeting with our solicitor, does that mean nothing to you?"

Seth scoffed at that, demonstrating his contempt with ribald laughter.

"Hah! That old crow Archibald Bland is on my payroll. He stands to make a tidy sum if things go according to plan."

Daniel tripped over a large object in his haste to make his escape. He fell heavily and hit his head on the cold, hard ground. As he struggled to his feet, concussed and shaken, he saw he had stumbled over the half-frozen corpse of a man.

The flesh of the hapless victim's abdomen had been opened as though with a surgeon's knife. His intestines, glistening and raw spilled from his ruptured belly. The man had a look of crazed terror about his staring eyes, as though he had survived just long enough to witness the moment of his own evisceration.

"Ahh." chuckled Seth, "my other self, Saul, another of Shelagh's cronies who underestimated the potency of the amulet and my association with, let us just say, unholy forces."

Daniel tried to crawl into the shadows but Seth pounced with shocking speed. A glint of metal flashed in the moonlight. Instinctively Daniel held up his hand and felt a rusty blade slice through his palm.

He stared in horror at the blood streaming from the gaping wound in his hand and then incredulously at Seth. "You are truly possessed, brother. You need more help than I can afford you."

Seth lunged again, this time striking Daniel's chin with the butt of the knife. Daniel fell heavily to the ground. The blow left him stunned for a few seconds. When he came to, he found Seth standing over him with a crowbar in his grasp.

"How similar we are and how *that* likeness will be my

fortune.I was murdered, Daniel," he told him, and then gripping the pendant about his neck continued, "...but by this token, my life was returned, and soon your fortune will be mine."

For a moment Seth stood motionless in contemplation of his final murderous act. Turning his head, he looked at Daniel through black, soulless eyes.

"The river will be your final resting place, brother. I have made a hole there just for you. The water will freeze and you will remain there for the duration of winter's solace. After the thaw your bloated body will no doubt be taken as mine; few will mourn or be interested in my apparent demise. I imagine many will even celebrate."

Holding the iron bar threateningly before Daniel's face, he chuckled and declared, "I will take residence in your Greenwich home, the prodigal son returned if you like. Archibald has already been working on the finer details of father's legacy and you, or rather I, will inherit all. Worry not though brother, for I will be a spirited replacement for you; the women there will find you a much-changed man," he mocked as he clutched a hand to his crotch.

Daniel could feel his strength returning but feigned weakness to lull Seth into a false state of confidence.

"You have become a heartless man, Seth." he replied, "But my love for you, like the Lord's, is unconditional and I will pray for your soul, for you act in ignorance of the consequences."

With eyes closed, and raising his right hand he declared, "*The kingdom of God is within you already - Luke 17, verse 21*"

Daniel's virtuous words and propitious manner filled Seth with rage. He brought down the iron bar towards his brother's head. Daniel looked back without flinching, showing no fear in the face of such diabolic evil.

The weapon struck ground just a hair's breadth away. "You think you're so perfect, don't you Daniel?' sneered Seth, 'Not for long though. Our time for talking is gone. Time stops for no man – not even a saint such as you."

Seth dragged him like a rag doll to the edge of the frozen river. Daniel knew not to resist; on land his brother had the advantage of his unnatural strength - on the ice though, things would be different.

Once on the glassy surface of the river, Daniel kicked Seth's feet from beneath him. Seth's chin took the full impact of the fall, but Daniel underestimated his brother's unnatural resilience. Seth was a man used to brawling and quickly recovered, continuing to drag him towards his watery grave. Daniel kicked out again but Seth caught his foot and twisted it back on itself. With his brother screaming out in pain, Seth pushed him beneath the ice and into the freezing water.

Daniel's fight was not yet lost. He reached up, grabbed Seth's arm and, using his own weight as an anchor, took his brother with him. Entangled and struggling, they descended into the deep unforgiving darkness of the river.

With ironic timing a thick bank of clouds passed like a veil before the moon and brought an eerie silence to the land.

The tranquillity, lasting only a few minutes, shattered as ice and water erupted into the cold night air, and with a lingering, resonant growl, a solitary figure emerged from the river.

SNOW FELL in sweeping waves as a horse drawn carriage pulled up to the entrance of the Norfolk Arms. As though to greet them the wind whipped up a spiralling funnel of snow that for a moment took the appearance of a swirling ghost and then disintegrated into a soft explosion of white cloud.

Aided by a stick and limping to his left side, a cloaked figure descended the icy steps from the foyer followed by a young porter struggling with a weighty case. Thick, treacherous ice coated the steeply-inclined high street.

The man, who had several abrasions on his face and a livid bruise on his chin, reached into his pocket and handed the porter a handsome tip.

The young man's eyes opened wide at such extraordinary generosity. "Thank you, Mr. Conroy, thank you. I...I hope you enjoyed your stay with us. Perhaps if you return to Arundel you'll remember me; my name is Thomas."

The man returned an amused grin. "I did enjoy my stay, Thomas. My time here has been very enlightening."

"Did you fall sir? I noticed that you are walking with a limp...and your face..."

The boy's unrelenting curiosity entertained the gentleman.

"On that matter, all I can say is that ice is an unforgiving adversary. My advice to you is that you give it much respect."

"...and your brother? You mentioned that you might learn something from your brother?"

"You *are* full of questions." Conroy replied, grinning broadly as he climbed into the carriage.

Despite his lean stature, the young porter eventually managed to heave the passenger's bulky case onto a luggage shelf. The bitter wind whipped about him and chilled him to the bone. He waited patiently until the man settled in comfortably. Someone was already inside; an older man with a bony face and large crook nose. It intrigued him that the two men greeted each other with a cordial handshake as though already acquainted.

Grasping the unusual talisman around his neck, a small hunchback figure from the base of which protruded a vulgar red horn, Conroy beckoned the porter over and told him, "I did meet with my brother, and I benefited much from our time together." And then, leaning forwards so that the young man alone could hear, he spoke briefly to him before slinking back onto his sumptuous leather seat.

A sudden gust of wind whipped the snow into a blanket of white that smothered the carriage causing it to rock from side to side. With a resounding crack of the driver's whip the horses reared onto their hind legs and broke into a brisk canter forcing the young porter to retreat swiftly from the road. When the snow settled, young Thomas found the carriage to be gone. But the haunting timbre of Conroy's parting words still lingered in his ears.

"I learned that the Devil looks after his own."

NAUGHTY CHILDREN BEWARE

HARPER BARROW

DECEMBER 14

Eva pulled her rolling suitcase up over the door jamb with both hands, then stopped to catch her breath. She propped her hands on her lower back and stretched, trying to take some of the weight off her pregnant belly.

"Oh, no, let me help you. You're much too huge for that." Her sister grinned and pointed at the living room sofa. "Go sit down. I'll get your bags."

Despite her first inclination, which was to tell her big sister to leave off, Eva appreciated the break. She had been on the bus all morning, traveling to her sister's place in Denver, then she had to wait at the station for three more hours until Salka got off of work to come pick her up. She wanted to lay down, put her feet up, and catch some sleep. With any luck, she could get twenty minutes or so before the baby started to kick again.

Eva made it to the sofa and used the armrest to lower herself slowly. Her body sank into the cushion, and she closed her eyes in relief. Ignoring the receding sound of suitcase wheels and doors banging, Eva let her sister be responsible for once. Only when it grew quiet and she sensed she was alone did Eva breathe easy. She placed her hands over her belly and smiled as her son's little foot pushed against her palm.

She would never be alone. Never again. She still told herself that several times a day.

And at least she had landed in a soft place.

'Though she enjoyed her sister's suburban home, Eva missed her apartment.'It had been cramped and noisy, but it had felt like home. How badly Eva had hoped she'd be able to renew her lease, but she couldn't swing it. Not without Aron. On her own, on a hostess salary, she could never afford her own place, especially when she had to stay home for several weeks with a newborn baby. She had only started looking into daycares and nannies before she gave up and accepted her sister's offer to let her stay in the guest room. *At least stay through Christmas*, Salka had said, but both of them knew it would take much longer than that for Eva to get back on her feet. Literally and figuratively. When Aron disappeared four months ago, Eva had been devastated.

First, she had called both of his friends, the only two people Aron had ever introduced her to since he had no family. Then, she called all the hospitals and jails in the area. She checked the internet and newspapers for any sign of him. She even filed a missing person's report but the police didn't take her seriously. To everyone, Aron appeared to be just a scared young man, unable to face being a father. He had run away. From her. From their baby.

He didn't want them. Simple as that.

Although Eva tried to accept his absence, she still searched every day and obsessively checked her email and phone for any word from him. Their relationship had been special. She just couldn't believe he would purposely throw that away.

Salka and Brian's home felt a little too Crate and Barrel for Eva's taste, but liked it's coziness. It looked like a page from a catalog, except for the toy box in the corner that overflowed with Barbies, toy cars and an open juice box leaking red fluid onto the rug. The Christmas tree in the corner fit perfectly, with an oversized white angel on top, tinsel and ornaments made by the kids at school. She saw presents under it. Eva made herself lean forward and read the nearest tag.

Yep, she thought so. The tag had her name on it. She hadn't bought them anything.

She started crying.

DECEMBER 15

The soup pot was overly large, almost like a witch's cauldron in a fairy tale.

It was full to the brim with the thick, dark liquid that smelled delicious. She stirred it with an oversized spoon, the heavy chunks at the bottom of the stew gliding over each other. No vegetables. Just meat. Occasionally, she'd pull a gob up to the surface and touch it to her tongue. She'd add more salt and pepper. It was coming together nicely.

As she stood stirring slowly — this much stew would take hours, if not days, to fully cook — she felt the heat from the open fire against her fetlocks. She stepped back slightly, to be sure the flames wouldn't catch her long skirt, and continued stirring. This stew was the culmination of all her hard work and it made her nearly giddy with expectation. And pride. She was a mother who provided for her many children.

And the lads loved her in return. In their own way.

Stir, stir. Sniff, sniff. Lick, lick. Smoke from the pot perme-
ated her hair, coated her skin. She wiped at her brow, used
her apron to dab at her nose. It was long, as was her chin,
but she didn't mind. It was a family trait and one that she was
proud of.

She heard a ruckus at the entrance to her cave and she
smiled to herself. The lads were home. They'd be hungry, but
she'd have to fight them back with a stick, make them wait
until it was done. Just as she did every Yuletide.

With a grunt, she pulled the spoon through the thick
chunks at the bottom and pulled one to the surface. The
easiest way to tell if the stew was done, besides the mouth-
watering smell, was to look at the meat. Properly cooked, it
was a dark pink, firm but not hard.

She pulled the chunk to the surface and lowered her long
nose to sniff it. It was a thumb this time, perfectly pink and
swollen.

She smiled. Soon.

HER HEART POUNDING, Eva opened her eyes and tried to
focus. The dream had been so real. She could still feel the
itch of the meat in her nose, the sting of smoke in her eyes.
Her mouth still watered in anticipation of a thick, meaty stew.
What was in that stuff? Was that really a finger? Someone
had once told her pregnancy dreams were strange, but that
was ridiculous.

With a sudden wave of nausea, Eva reached for the small
trash can beside the bed. She heaved and rolled, her belly
hanging off the edge of the mattress, the baby kicking as she
bucked, and emptied her stomach. Her hand trembled as she

looked in the trash can, half expecting to see partially chewed and digested human fingers. Thankfully, all she saw was normal vomit and some old used tissues.

Eva wiped her mouth with the back of her hand and lay back in the bed.

As the seconds ticked by, the dream seemed less nightmarish. She closed her eyes and focused on her breathing, as her psychiatrist had taught her years earlier.

There in the chilly bedroom, Eva counted backwards from thirty and soon fell fast asleep, a smile on her face.

DECEMBER 16

Brian was working late again, so Eva sat in his chair at dinner. Eva's niece and nephew chattered on and on about sugar cookies and Santa Claus, ugly sweaters and sledding on the weekend. They both talked so fast, their eager words tripping over each other, Eva had to smile. She remembered what it was like to be a child around Christmas, the intoxicating feeling of excitement as the day drew closer. She missed it.

Eva watched the children as they shoveled mashed potatoes and applesauce into their mouths, talking over each other to anyone who would listen. At first, she tried to ignore the half-chewed food that splattered from their mouths and really listen to what they were saying, but it quickly became impossible. With growing anxiety that she would dampen the children's enthusiasm, Eva glanced at her sister. Salka didn't seem to be following the conversation at all. She simply nodded and sipped at her wine.

But Eva couldn't avoid the wide eyes of her six-year-old niece as she described her role in the holiday show.

"And I get a cape!" Lisa grinned, a bit of potato peel in

her teeth. "Tanner wanted the lead snowman, but I'm it. I'm the lead snowlady!"

Eva nodded and tried to smile. "When is the show?"

"That's dumb," Josh piped in. "There is no lead snowlady. Only regular snow people." He spooned up some potatoes and looked at Eva. "I was Rudolph in the first grade show. Way better than —"

"Shut up, Josh," Lisa shouted. She glared at her brother. "You're just jealous." Her bottom lip quivered dangerously.

The baby kicked and Eva tried not to wince as she looked to Salka, who just shrugged and took another sip. Children were exhausting. Maybe her baby would be different.

Apparently satisfied with his sister's hurt feelings, Josh changed the subject. "Hey, Mom. I'm almost done with my report." He didn't wait for her answer before he gulped at his water and looked to Eva. "We have to write a report on ancient Christmas folklores, and guess who I picked."

"Santa Claus?" Eva guessed.

Josh rolled his eyes, surprisingly rude in his innocent eight-year-old face. "No. Duh. So obvious. Although, I did think that Krampus would be kinda cool. Teddy stole Black Peter, though I don't know if the teacher will let him do that one —"

"Aunt Eva, look at me!"

Lisa's shrill cry ripped Eva's attention right away from her big brother, exactly as she had hoped. Eva turned to see Lisa balancing a spoon on the end of her nose. She held her hands out to the side like a tight rope walker.

"See?" Lisa said, barely moving her lips.

"Lisa, I was talking. Don't interrupt." Josh glared at this sister, then turned back to Eva and waved his hand in the air. "Never mind, you'll never guess. I'll just tell you." Sensing all eyes were now on him, Josh leisurely spooned the last of his applesauce into a pile and scooped it up. "Her name is Gryla."

"Who?" Eva asked.

"The Christmas Witch. You ever heard of her?"

Eva looked at Salka, who had stood up to refill her wine. "No. Who is she?"

Even Lisa had stopped to listen to her brother. He leaned forward like a boy scout telling campfire tales. "She's a giant ogress who lives in the mountains of Iceland. Every year at Christmas, she comes down and finds all the naughty boys and girls, takes them back up to her castle, and cooks them into a stew!" He ended by banging both his hands on the table top.

Lisa and Eva both jumped. Then Lisa giggled.

Eva suddenly felt sick to her stomach. She looked down at her half-eaten dinner, but didn't see her sister's mashed potatoes. She saw a child's thumb, half cooked and bloody, soaking in bone broth. She closed her eyes and pushed back her plate.

"Aunt Eva, are you okay?" Lisa asked.

Eva nodded. When she opened her eyes, she didn't see a thumb.

DECEMBER 17

"So, are you getting nervous?" Salka tossed her sister a sock and turned back to the pile of clean laundry without waiting for an answer. "I was so nervous at the end of my pregnancies. Both of them. Though Josh was worse, because I didn't know what was about to hit me." Salka winked and continued folding. "My crotch tore apart like *Texas Chainsaw*

Massacre. I had to have eighteen stitches and couldn't sit straight for two months. But don't worry, I'm sure you'll be fine."

Eva nodded and picked up the yellow sock with pink flowers, looking for its mate. She didn't want to think about labor pains or the baby that was about to enter her life — take over her life, if what everyone said was true. But there really wasn't anything else to talk about. Eva noticed Salka opening her mouth to start again, no doubt to explain the severe trauma Eva's nipples would soon be suffering, when Eva seized on the first thought that popped into her mind. "Josh sure seems excited about his project," she said.

With a grin, Salka tossed another sock to Eva. "Here's the other red one. Yeah, it's fun to see him so excited about school. It's just too hard to get the kid to focus."

"What made him decide on the Christmas Witch?"

"You mean Gryla?" Salka reached across the pile for a towel and held it up in front of her. "His teacher gave them all a list to choose from. Of course, he chose one from Iceland."

"What do you mean?"

"I mean because we're Icelandic."

This was news to Eva. Maybe Salka was joking around. "We are?"

"Both Mom's and Dad's sides are originally from Iceland, a couple generations back." Salka dropped her hands holding the towel and gaped at her sister. "You didn't know that?"

"No, they never told me." Eva placed the two red socks together, rolled them into a ball and tossed it into Josh's pile. "We never talked about where we were from, at least as far as I remember. Did they tell you?"

"Well...yeah." Salka shrugged and placed the folded towel on the pile. "I think it was actually a school project when I was a kid. The assignment was to research where our names came from. Mine is very obviously Icelandic. It means Princess." Salka beamed at Eva, blinking her eyes and tossing her hair.

Eva ignored her, wondering if her name was Icelandic as well, or if her parents had abandoned tradition by the time she was born. They certainly didn't care enough about their heritage to make it an issue while she was growing up. Then she had a new thought. "That's weird," she mumbled to herself.

"What is?" Salka asked, tossing her another sock.

The sock hit Eva in the chest and rolled down. She ignored it. "Aron is from Iceland."

"Who's Aron?"

With one hand supporting her bulging stomach, Eva squatted to pick up the dropped sock. "His father."

Salka's mouth dropped open and she turned to Eva with her hands on her hips. "So you're telling me that your ex, the father of your child, is Icelandic, and you're one hundred percent Icelandic, and you never knew? What are the chances of that?"

A slight taste of bile tickled the back of her throat. It was probably just heartburn from the pregnancy. Eva didn't answer her sister. The chances were rather slim, she thought, unless one were living in Iceland. For some reason, it gave her a feeling of uneasiness, like she had been a part of someone's plan. A pawn in her own life. The stress of the pregnancy and Aron's disappearance and then moving in with her sister's whole family at Christmas must be getting to her.

She shook off the uncomfortable feeling and rolled the matching socks together.

Folding the last towel, Salka shook her head. "That's crazy, sis, but I gotta ask. Are you going to name the baby something Icelandic?"

Eva rolled another sock set before answering her sister. "I haven't decided yet. But Aron had always liked the name Stekk."

"Stick?"

"No...Stekk." She spelled it for her. "It was a family name, short for something. I can't remember what."

Salka laughed and tossed her another sock. "That certainly sounds Icelandic."

It certainly did.

DECEMBER 18

The frigid wind blew through her gnarled hair and under her skirt. Her footsteps crunched in the snow as she followed the trail to the village, the hoots and laughs from her boys fading into the distance.

"Don't scare away all the children before I get there," she grumbled, knowing the lads wouldn't hear her. But she wasn't truly concerned. There were always enough naughty children to feed the entire family. In fact, though the Yuletide season was the most plentiful, she and her family found enough brats to keep all of them plump all year round.

She had no reason to think her days, or the days of her lads, were numbered. For centuries they had served the villagers below, collecting the young troublemakers who would only grow into adult troublemakers. For all she knew, the villagers adored her. She served a purpose. Her lads, who were boisterous and mischievous themselves, were usually a great help to her, though she did have to fight to keep them in line.

For centuries, she'd made the journey along the long

rocky trail to the village, until her feet eventually hardened into hooves and she no longer needed boots. To survive in the harsh northern winds, her skin had thickened into dark leather, her nose covered in warts and calluses from years of standing before the fires. She only wore clothing because she liked the way her capes hid her stooped shoulders and her skirts hid her fifteen tails.

The lights of the village rose in the distance, casting a faint glow across the valley. She grunted and adjusted the empty bags over her shoulder. Nearly a hundred empty bags, all of them reinforced and cut proof, each of them big enough to hold a child up to fourteen years old. They'd be heavy tonight for sure, when she and the lads left before dawn.

Her stomach grumbled in anticipation.

DECEMBER 19

Eva barely slept all night. Each time her exhausted body finally drifted off, she'd be awakened, either by the disturbing images of her dreams or by a tiny foot into her back or her bladder. As the sunlight crept through the curtains, she lay there hugging her belly and staring at the crib Salka had bought her.

Sleeping had become impossible. And if the nightmares ever stopped, she'd have a newborn to take care of. All by herself.

She'd better get used to being exhausted.

With that thought, Eva pulled herself out of bed and slogged out to the living room. Being the last Saturday before Christmas, Salka's kids were up, and the television blared *Santa Claus is Coming to Town*. They shoveled sugary cereal into their mouths as both of them looked up to see their aunt coming down the hall.

"Aunt Eva!" Lisa screamed, milk dripping down her chin.

"Hey, Aunt Eva," Josh said, a smirk on his face. "Did you sleep good?"

"None of your business," Eva growled. Her back ached, and her tailbone had a new throbbing pain that she thought might have something to do with the hormones relaxing her pelvis before labor. She'd read all the books, they just didn't really make sense. Her body had been taken over by the baby for months, why was it revolting against her now? Even more disturbing, her mind seemed to be following along.

"Wow, what's that on your nose?" Lisa asked, pointing to Eva's face.

Confused, Eva touched her nose with her forefinger. She felt a raised lump, firm and round, right on the tip. She pinched it, pushed it, but it didn't budge. She back tracked to the bathroom and looked in the mirror.

The face that reflected back to her was unrecognizable. She looked tired, with dark bags under her eyes, as she expected. She found puffiness in her neck, thin and dry hair, and yes, a brand new wart right there on the end of her nose. It had grown there overnight.

With a jolt of anger, Eva flipped off her reflection and waddled back out to the dining room.

Josh set down his spoon and tried not to stare as his aunt pulled out a chair and settled into it.

Lisa's tiny voice asked, "Eva, are you okay?"

"Leave me alone, you little brats," Eva muttered as she reached for her sister's laptop.

"Jeez, that was harsh," Josh muttered.

Eva ignored him and opened the computer, logging in with her sister's PIN. This seemed like more than normal pregnancy changes. She needed to know what was happening to her. "Josh," she said, clicking open the internet search bar and trying to ignore the baby pushing against her back bone. "What was the name of that Christmas Witch again?"

DECEMBER 20

Eva kept to herself most of the Saturday before Christmas. Salka's family had left for the day to go to some kind of Christmas market downtown. Salka had asked Eva if she wanted to go with them, all the while giving her the side eye, and Eva declined. She knew Salka, Brian and the kids needed private family time, and Eva didn't want to be in the way. She felt too exhausted, too sore, too…angry to try and pretend to have Christmas spirit. Her heart lacked goodwill towards men, her sister, or even her own niece and nephew.

Eva spent her quiet hours alone trying to sleep, but she didn't have much success. She watched a few rerun episodes of Jerry Springer and some holiday baking show, but she mostly killed time searching the internet. She read pages and pages, clicking on countless images of Gryla and the other figures in Icelandic Yule folklore. Gryla's husband, Leppaludi, who was apparently the first spouse she hadn't eaten. Her cat, who apparently had something against people without clothing. And especially her thirteen sons, the Yule Lads, who were obnoxious and each had a specific role in wreaking havoc around Christmas time.

Eva had a particularly hard time when she came across the name of Gryla's first-born son — Stekkjastaur. The name Aron wanted for his son. It couldn't be a coincidence, and Eva slammed the laptop shut and returned to bed. She stayed there until the family came home, pretending to be asleep when her sister came in to check on her.

The hours of lying in bed, half awake, half asleep, images of human stew and cold cobblestone streets intermixed with reality show contestants throwing chairs at each other or baking the perfect fruit cake took a toll. Eva woke up around three in the morning completely starving, her baby kicking wildly at her insides. She rolled out of bed, her stomach rumbling, and shuffled as quietly as she could into the kitchen.

The bright light from the open refrigerator made her wince, but she quickly found what she had been looking for. Salka's husband, Brian, had filled the fridge with things from the supermarket. She saw new cartons of milk and cream on the shelf, bundles of fresh vegetables in the drawer, and right there beside them, two fresh steaks. Wrapped in clear plastic and styrofoam, the steaks were pink and thick, and expensive, as she could see from the price tag.

Still in the dark, Eva found a large soup pot in a lower cabinet and filled it halfway with water, set it on the stove and turned the temperature to high. Her heart felt lighter than it had in days, and she found herself humming a tune. She unwrapped the steaks one by one — licking the inside of the cellophane wrappers before she tossed them to the ground — and lowered the steaks into the boiling water.

Eva was stirring and humming in the dark when her sister came in and flicked on the light.

"Eva?" Salka asked, clutching her bathrobe across her front. "What are you doing?"

Eva froze, her spoon in the air, and slowly turned to her sister. "Salka?" she whispered and stepped back.

"What the hell?" Salka said, then stepped over and turned off the stove. "It's the middle of the night. You're gonna set the house on fire." She looked in the pot and whirled on Eva. "Is that Brian's steak? What the hell?" she said again. "He's gonna be pissed."

Eva stood silently, confusion at war with anger, trying to think of what to say to explain herself. How could she tell her sister the baby was hungry? That they needed food and only meat would do? That her body was out of her control? Salka had had babies before, she must know what this was like…

"Eva," Salka said, her voice a harsh whisper. "Did you hear me? I said, what the hell is wrong with you?"

"I…I don't —"

Salka interrupted her with a wave. "You know what? I don't care. Clean this up. We'll talk about it in the morning." She started walking out of the kitchen, then turned back to her sister. "You have lost your mind, you know that? You're gonna have to buy Brian some more steak." She took a deep breath and shook her head. "And take a shower. You smell like a barn." Salka turned off the light and stormed off down the hall.

Eva stood for a moment in the dark, her mind racing. Her sister was right. But also…she wasn't.

Slowly, Eva turned to the pot and lowered her hand into it. Her skin burned and reddened instantly as she felt around in the water wrapped her fingers around the edge of a steak. Part of her mind screamed, telling her to pull her hand out, she was hurting herself, but part of her mind loved it. She felt alive. Pain was life.

Her skin steamed and blistered as she pulled out the half-cooked steak. The smell of the meat, and even her own hand burning made her mouth water. The baby kicked.

Eva took the steak to bed with her. She was still hungry.

DECEMBER 21

Her hand throbbed beneath the bandages, but not as bad as the rest of her body. Cramps radiated through her back and belly, down through her legs and up through her chest. The soreness near her tail bone had grown into full-blown stabbing pain. Her feet were stiff and numb, and she swore she could feel two hard bumps growing through her hair, like tiny horns. Intermittent headaches throbbed behind her eyes and she felt hungry no matter how much she forced herself to eat. Never in her whole life had Eva wished she could just go to sleep and never wake up.

She spent most of the day at the hospital, first for her forty-week prenatal care visit, then to the urgent care on the other side of the building to have her burned hand looked at. Both doctors had said she would be okay, the agony was temporary, and sent her home with strict instructions to take it easy, ointment for her hand and medication for the pain. Eva refused to take it.

Instead, she cowered in bed, hugging her bandaged hand to her belly. Her mind turned inward. She had been a bit depressed, she realized, feeling alone and abandoned. But as she cried and throbbed, shivering in pain with every false labor pain and hard kick the baby delivered, she realized something else. She wasn't alone. Her baby was inside her.

From then on, it was her and Stekk. "My Stekkjastaur," she whispered, her hand over her belly.

The beginning of a family.

With that comforting thought, Eva's pain lessened somewhat and she fell asleep, smiling to herself.

THE STORM WAS FULL FORCE, blowing stinging ice and snow sideways. The houses, made of stone, wood and turf, blocked out most of the weather as she and her lads stalked the township. She paused, her keen ears listening through the wind for naughty children. Her tails rustled and squealed behind her, most of her bags full already, and she slammed them on the ground to make them quiet. There, to the south, she heard another child, his voice mocking and rude, refusing to feed the sheep as his parents had asked. With a smile, she picked up her sword and turned toward the sound.

To her surprise, when she knocked on the door, ready to harvest the naughty child, a father answered, his own sword in hand. Before she could resist, or call to her lads, a net was thrown over her shoulders. The villagers cut the bags from her tails and tied her arms down. She struggled, her hooves whipping, her horns jabbing, but she was outnumbered.

As the townsfolk led her up the mountain, she tried reason with them. "The children have no respect! I am helping you," she cried, but none of them stopped. Before she could struggle herself free, or make them listen to her protests, she was at the top of the cliff overlooking the icy sea below. With a gust of wind and a shove, she went over.

All was dark.

DECEMBER 22

Bed rest must have agreed with her because Eva started feeling better almost immediately. For the first time in days, she felt mentally strong enough to get out of bed, take a shower, and join the family.

The kids buzzed around the living room, circling the tree,

shaking the presents, high on sugar cookies and Christmas spirit. Salka and Brian eyed her carefully as she settled into the sofa.

"Hey," Salka said. "You feeling okay?"

Eva nodded and smiled at Lisa, who was trying to tie a white cape around her neck. "A little better. Here, Lisa, let me help you."

"My show is tonight, Aunt Eva. Are you coming?" Lisa said, squirming as Eva tied her cape. "I'm the lead snowlady, remember?" Lisa bounced away without waiting for an answer.

Eva looked at her sister. "Can I come with you?"

The five of them barely fit in the minivan, especially with Eva's huge belly taking up more than her share of the seat, but they made it with time to spare. Lisa skittered off to the back stage to join her class while the rest of them wandered toward their seats. Red bows and plastic holly boughs decorated the elementary school auditorium.. Classic holiday songs played over the system. Eva hovered silently behind her sister and brother-in-law as they greeted the other parents and exchanged the requisite small talk. She smiled and shook hands as expected, but she soon overexerted herself. She took their coats, and she and Josh went to save seats.

The show started late, which was only a problem because Eva began to realize she had made a mistake almost immediately. Stuffed into the hard folding seat, Eva's back and belly began to cramp once more, her head throbbed like someone was jabbing ice picks into her temples. By the time the children walked onto stage, their wailing young voices fighting with the ear-splitting sounds of the out-of-tune piano, Eva felt halfway into a full-blown panic attack. She tried to wait for the appearance of the lead snowlady but found she just couldn't do it. Out of breath and cringing in pain, Eva excused herself in the middle of some song about candy canes.

She didn't remember shuffling her way up the dark aisles, didn't remember hobbling through the bright lobby to the parking lot. Only once outside, in the frigid mountain air, did she finally calm herself. She lowered her massive body to the curb on the side of the building where no one would see her or bother her. She leaned her belly on her knees, her elbows on her belly and rested her head in her hands. She closed her eyes and breathed in and out, silently speaking to the baby inside her, who silently kicked back.

Eventually, the pain in her back and head subsided, lessening to the dull ache to be expected of a hugely pregnant woman resting on a curb. She continued to breathe as her psychiatrist had taught her. In. Out. In. Out.

Then, with a bang, a backstage door off to her left crashed open and hit the wall behind it. Like a deadly flood, the children poured out, each of them in bright colors and glitter, their voices piercing and raucous. Eva's pains came back in a rush and she clapped her hands over her ears. Still, the swarm of naughty children continued, their ruthless sounds filling the air, their bodies blocking her escape.

With anger and pain erasing all thought, Eva picked up the nearest weapon she could find. It was a metal pipe, fallen from the nearby dumpster. She gripped it in her good hand and struggled to stand.

The naughty children must be stopped.

———

DECEMBER 23

She laid in bed again. Eva thought she might never leave the padded prison of her sister's guest room again.

She wasn't alone. There were people standing just inside the door. And they were talking about her. Eva kept her eyes closed, pretending to sleep, waiting to hear who they were and what they wanted from her.

"— under a lot of stress," Salka said. "The pregnancy and Aron taking off...it's just too much for her."

Of course one of the people would be her sister. That woman had to meddle in everything.

"She hit a child with a pipe. That seems excessive." The other voice belonged to a man. Not Brian. Eva cracked her eyes open slightly to see only blue jeans and brown leather boots. "You're lucky the other parents aren't pressing charges," he said.

"I know. I told them she tripped, it was all a big misunderstanding." Salka sighed. "By the time I got her out of there, she was crying and screaming so hard, it wasn't hard to convince them she was going into labor and I had to take her to the hospital."

"Why *didn't* you take her to the hospital?"

"I told you, I tried. She wouldn't have it. I've been on the phone all morning, looking for an office that's open this close to the holidays, but they're all closed." Big pause. "Anyway, I don't know what to do with her. Thanks for coming on such short notice, Trent."

Eva didn't remember meeting anyone named Trent, but the last eighteen hours or so had been a blur of pain and confusion. Now, as she lay there, pretending to sleep, she was having trouble telling the difference between reality and her dreams, here and there, now and then. Maybe they were all actually the same.

The baby kicked and she grunted unintentionally.

"Eva?" Salka rushed over and sat on the edge of the bed. Eva could feel her sister's weight on the mattress and her hand on her shoulder.

Reluctantly, Eva opened her eyes. "Hey," she whispered. "What happened?"

Salka hesitated, then she glanced at the man still standing by the door.

Eva followed her sister's gaze to a balding man with a beard and thick glasses. "Who are you?" She struggled to push herself up to sitting.

"Hello. My name is Dr. Troyer." He smiled warmly.

A flare of anger coursed through her chest and Eva glared at her sister, then back at the man. "What kind of doctor?" Though she thought she knew.

"Eva, don't be mad. Trent is a psychiatrist and a friend of mine from college. He came here to talk to you because I called him."

"You called him? Why?"

"Because I was worried about you!" Salka rubbed at her eyes. "You've been acting nuts. Don't you remember? Last night you attacked those kids with a pipe —"

"They were being naughty. They needed to be punished." Eva's voice sounded harsh to her own ears, but she didn't care. Her stomach rumbled.

Salka stared at her.

"You just don't understand. I'm getting out of here. I'm going home." Eva pushed against the mattress with her elbow, but a shock of pain careened across her back and belly. With a cry, she fell back down against the pillow.

"Stop it, Eva. You have to calm down or you'll hurt the baby. Besides, where can you go?" Salka asked. "You don't have an apartment anymore. Aron is gone. We're all you have now."

"That's not true." Eva breathed hard, clenching her teeth against the cramps. "Leppaludi is coming for me." She grabbed at her belly. "For us. To take us home, so we can be a family again."

"Leppaludi?" Trent asked Salka.

Eva answered. "My husband." It came out like an angry hiss and he stepped back.

"This is what I was trying to tell you before. Eva thinks she's Gryla, the Christmas Witch of Iceland. She's talking in her sleep about it almost constantly." Salka explained. "And look at her. She hasn't washed her hair or changed her clothes in days."

The cramps were beginning again, at the bottom of Eva's belly, then up her back and down her legs. "When the children are naughty, they must be punished…"

"See?" Salka said.

"Why Gryla, of all people?" Trent asked.

"I'm right here, you idiot," Eva growled. She pictured the man's head in a pot and smiled, her lips tight against her teeth. "I can hear you talking about me…"

Salka ignored her. "Josh was writing a report on holiday folktales last week and ever since her name came up, Eva has been acting crazy, stealing Brian's meat, burning her hand, attacking the kids —"

"I'm not crazy —" Grinding her teeth together, she could barely get the words out. "I'll cut your guts and boil your bones!"

With a look of concern on his face, Trent pulled Salka back to the doorway to talk in private. As the cramping subsided, Eva could make out most of what they were saying.

"With her history…worried about…could be serious —" Trent said.

"— should I do? Force her…police?"

Trent looked at her, a frown on his face. "Might have to."

"No," Salka said, then "— something to calm her? Help her sleep…"

In between cramps, Eva had been able to work her way to sitting. Now she sat with her legs over the edge, watching them talk about her. Hate filled her heart. How dare they try to stop her from reaching her family? From returning to where she belonged? She had the powers of a hundred centuries, the force of the ancient land of ice and fire in her soul.

If they tried to stop her, they would pay the ultimate price. The man named Trent especially needed to be punished. She glanced at his fat fingers, clutched together in front of him. Juicy.

Her stomach rumbled and she smiled again.

Salka glanced at Trent, then back to Eva. "Eva, are…are you alright over there?"

"Hungry," Eva growled.

Salka looked at Trent, who nodded. "I'll be right back."

DECEMBER 24

Eva didn't dream of home. She didn't dream at all.

She woke up many hours later, in the same room. Wearing the same clothes. The sun's light shone, but the fogged windows bore a coat of ice on the outside. If she held her breath and listened, she could hear the snow falling against the window. It made her homesick.

Struggling to sit up, Eva looked around. No sign of Salka or Trent. On the end table, she saw an empty plate and an empty cup.

Swinging her legs over the edge of the bed, Eva pushed against the headboard until she stood. Testing her balance, she let go and took a couple of steps. She felt a dull but manageable aching in her midsection. Her head swam, and she felt a bit dizzy, but no pain. She couldn't quite focus her eyes.

They had drugged her. The insight hit her like a blow to the head. If she caught them, they would pay.

Step by step, Eva walked out of the guest room, down the short hall to the family room. The lights were off. "Hello?" she called, her voice scratchy. Slowly, she hobbled to the kitchen sink, ran herself a glass of water and gulped it down.

A cramp, stronger than the others, seized her belly. It radiated out to every inch of her body, taking her breath away. Eva stood still, clutching her spasming belly, leaning on the counter, until it passed.

A brief feeling of peace. Then nausea. There on the counter, a note from her sister.

Eva,
  Went to see Christmas lights, be home by six.
  XOXO Salka

Off to make merry again. Leave the crazy, evil sister at home. Typical. Eva slapped the glass into the sink, smiling as the broken shards caught the light from the kitchen window. She peeked out. It was snowing hard.

Another cramp hit. Eva rode this one out, too. These cramps were different. They were contractions. She was in labor. Eva grinned as the contraction subsided and she started walking back down the hall. Stekk was coming. Which meant Leppaludi would be there soon. She was going home.

EVA DIDN'T WAIT for the family to come home. They were dead to her. She pulled her largest sweater over her belly, zipped her puffy coat over that, then balled up the duvet from the guest bed into her arm. With a last thought, she grabbed a package of smoked turkey lunch meat and crammed it in her pocket before heading out into the snow.

Deep down, in some part of her brain, Eva thought the smart thing would be to call 911 or go to the hospital. If she was really in labor, medical assistance would be needed. That idea, the last remnant of Eva, got shoved aside. As quickly as her swollen feet could carry her, she hobbled down the front walk.

The suburbs east of Denver were spread out, acres of cookie-cutter houses stacked side by side clear to the prairie. She hobbled towards the open space, the sting of the wind in her face, the snow packing on her bare feet. She breathed in deep, feeling the life pour back into her.

She hobbled along slowly, stopping for each contraction, breathing in and out against the pain. The sidewalks, empty in the snow storm, gave way to trails, then nothing. A sea of white snow opened before her and she paused, breathing in the frigid air. Behind a hill, beside a snow drift, she stopped again. Only the snow in the wind would be her midwife. As it should be.

For the next couple of hours, she labored alone, squatting over the snow drift, as generations had done before her. As she herself had done dozens of times. Grunting and pushing in silence, she rode each contraction with a grin on her face, sweat pouring down her face and between her breasts, mixing with the blood, freezing at her feet.

She only screamed once during the final push as her son's body followed his head. Her bandage had fallen from her burned hand long ago. She picked up her son and cradled him to her chest. She ground her teeth through one last contraction. One last spill of blood and tissue and the placenta dropped to the snow. Briefly, she considered gathering it up, taking it with her, but then reconsidered. She had no time.

She filled her eyes with her baby, his angry red skin, the full head of black hair. Two little arms. Two little legs, straight as swords. He had no knees. He was perfect.

"I missed you," she whispered as she wrapped him in the bloody blanket and held him to her breast. "Your father will be here soon."

Humming softly, she sat down to wait.

DECEMBER 25

Her footprints were buried under inches of new fallen snow. To all who cared to look for her, she had just vanished.

But those who paused in celebration, to set down their presents from Santa and their morning ham long enough to gaze across the snow-covered prairie, saw her last.

In a flash of lightning and fire, she returned to the hinterlands to resume her duty, satiate her hunger, and avenge exhausted parents everywhere. Only in *this* life, this go 'round, she'd not stay confined to the north.

Naughty children the world round were safe no longer.

RECEIVING IS BETTER THAN GIVING

VILLIMEY MIST

I ripped the wrapping paper apart and tore the box. A pale blue button up cardigan with tiny silver stars twinkle out of it. My excited smile disappeared.

"Oh, Brynjar! Isn't it pretty?" Mom cooed, snatching the cardigan and lifting it up for all to see. It felt like the winking stars were mocking me. I tucked my arms at the sides, shrinking under the fanfare. Could she be more embarrassing?

Helga, my little sister, snickered before grabbing another present from underneath the Christmas tree.

Heat burned deep in my cheeks and my chest tightened in embarrassment. "Mom, this is a *girl's* sweater. I'm not wearing that."

"No, Grandma told me that the salesperson told her that it was unisex. It suits both girls *and* boys. So, of course you can wear it and you will, won't you?" Mom folded the cardigan like a professional retailer and handed it back to me. Her narrowed eyes dared me to object.

I hitched up a fake smile and flushed down the disappointment. "Fine, then."

"Then you better call your grandma later tonight and thank her for the lovely gift," Mom said while stuffing the wrapping paper into a large, black garbage bag. I got the biggest urge to sneak the cardigan into the garbage bag, but Mom guarded it like a dragon would a treasure.

I looked at the loot next to me and then drifted to the cardigan on my lap. The crime noir books, the video games, even the towel my dad's girlfriend gave me were better than that ugly cardigan.

I had been adamant. No clothes for Christmas. It was a pact everyone in my environmental class had agreed on. The teacher had shown us dozens of pollution documentaries and had asked us what we could do to halt climate change. Our protests at Alþingi had gained us nothing except a few hundred likes on our social media. But that wasn't enough. We had to become more proactive but nothing to the extremes. Sigrún, the girl I liked, suggested that we deny ourselves new clothes for three months, leading to the new year. Clothing factories were one of the most polluting industries in the world and after watching a particularly invasive documentary about the *H&M* factories in South East Asia, we felt guilty. Besides, we would be able to show the baby boomers that we're capable of saving our money and use it for a better cause.

But apparently, Grandma didn't get that memo, or she chose to ignore it because she always gives us clothes for Christmas. I asked Mom why and she said that Grandma held on to traditions. Like inviting us to eat putrefied skate on December twenty-third, which is utterly disgusting. Our traditional food sucks. To make matters worse, Grandma also used to tell Helga and me the old Christmas stories. Every year she would recite the poems about the thirteen Yule lads, their heinous troll mother Grýla, and the huge Yule Cat. She used to threaten to write Grýla and beg her to come down from the mountain and take us if we were ever being naughty. She always told us to appreciate the clothes we got for Christmas because then the Yule Cat wouldn't come and eat us. As little kids, we believed her. But then we grew up and knew that it was all make-believe and just part of our Icelandic tradition. Traditions aside, she got *Helga* nice pajamas this year. I poked at one of the stars on the cardigan, as if it were a piece of boiled sheep's eyeball. My lips curled. Maybe Grandma's dementia had kicked in. No way this was going to look good on me!

"Are you going to wear it?" Helga whispered as we both assisted Mom tidying up our small living room.

I wheeled toward her, thrusting my chest out. "Hell no! I'm going to pawn it off to Ragnar as a back-up to the prank gift I gave him. It's his style, so he should be thrilled." I only used two fingers to stuff the sweater back into the box. I'm not touching it more than I have to.

Helga took a step back and goggled. "Are you meeting up tonight?"

I nodded. "Same place as usual. Paradísardalur park."

"Can I come with you this time? Please, pretty please?" Helga danced on her toes and tugged my sleeve. It wasn't the impromptu choreography that got me, though. It was her deadliest weapon. The one that killed all hope of a sweet, uncomplicated party with my pals. The one that wouldn't help me get closer to Sigrún tonight.

Puppy-dog eyes. Damn.

I hesitated, glancing toward the kitchen where Mom prepared the traditional, homemade Christmas ice cream. Helga was only fifteen, two years younger than me. The

Paradísardalur party was an opportunity for my friends and I to blow off some steam after the whole stress from work and school. The kind of party that involved alcohol—bought by an older sibling among our friends. Helga wasn't ready for something like that.

I leaned away from my sister. I tried to ignore the slight tenseness of my muscles. "I don't know, Helga. I'm not in the mood for babysitter duty tonight."

Helga's eyes narrowed. "If I can't come, I'll tell Mom what you guys really do at those parties."

I folded my arms, pressing my lips together into a thin line. "You wouldn't."

The breath whistled through Helga's nostrils as she inhaled, tilted her head in Mom's direction, and dropped her jaw, ready to shout.

My stomach dropped. Shit, she was actually serious. I clamped my hand to her mouth. "All right, all right. You can come, you little squealer!" I hissed.

An abrupt bang against the living room window interrupted her muffled giggles. Both of us jumped.

"What was that?" Helga asked, pushing me away.

I shrugged. "Dunno."

Helga stayed put, staring at me.

"What?"

"Aren't you going to check it out?" she asked. "It could be a burglar."

I snorted with laughter. "Yeah, like burglars would break and enter a house on Christmas Eve, when everyone in Iceland is at home. It was probably a bird or something." I walked over to the living room window, pulled the blinds apart and scanned the area. The colorful lights decorating the bushes in the yard revealed nothing. However, I noticed a dirty smudge in the middle of the window. It looked like a paw print. The yard was covered in pristine snow. Where had that dirt come from?

A pair of glowing eyes met mine.

My heartrate quickened. I squinted against the glass.

It was a small, dirty cat, hiding within the bush. I tried to conceal the tiny breath of relief that escaped my lips. I chuckled. Man, cats are eerie at night. I've never liked them, and apparently no one liked that one, considering how tangled the fur was and how thin it looked. Probably a stray cat or something. I'm definitely not letting it in, no matter how many times it begs for food.

"What was it?" Helga inquired, still rooted to the spot.

"It was nothing. It was probably some kids throwing snowballs at windows. Remember, we used to do that." I lied. Helga would have brought the cat in. We'd spend hours cleaning it and giving it leftovers. It would have ruined my night off. No, thanks.

Helga's mouth twitched at the memory. "Stupid kids."

I nodded as the two of us went into the kitchen to devour Mom's homemade ice cream.

SNOW HAD BEEN PILING on the streets of Reykjavík all December. Some days it reached up to people's knees, but the roads were cleared up daily, thanks to the city's snow plowing trucks. My small Honda Civic wouldn't have been able to reach Paradísardalur without their efforts.

Driving through Miklabraut main road was peaceful; No brown, icy sludge splattering against the windshield through the daily traffic. The warm light twinkled on the white fluffy hills that flanked the road. The colorful lights adorning each and every house on every street repelled the ever-lasting darkness. It was one of the few things that I liked about winter. Christmas really became a celebration of lights in Iceland. No one was outside at this time of night. Everyone usually retreated to their rooms after eating ice cream, snuggling in bed with the latest book they got for Christmas. Some would get together in the living room and play the board game they got as a price for finding an almond in their cinnamon rice porridge that afternoon. I wished I were there right now as a grunt of complaint came from the passenger seat.

Helga blew air on her hands. "Can't you turn on the heater? It's freezing in here."

I scowled. "It's already on. It just takes a while for it to heat up. You should have dressed warmer."

She tapped on the box that was crammed between her legs. "Gee, maybe I could have borrowed your *awesome* sweater."

I took my foot off the accelerator and the car slowed down as we approached Ártúnsbrekka. "Do you want to walk the rest of the way?"

Helga pouted a plump lower lip and hugged herself tight against her thin, neon pink windbreaker. "No. Besides if I wore that stupid sweater, Haukur won't lend me his coat. He is coming, right?"

I rolled my eyes. Haukur was in my year. He played football. He was a total jock and always tried to be funny by playing crude jokes on everyone. The girls in my year really liked him, and my sister was no exception. "Yeah, he is."

Helga squirmed in her seat, giggling. "I'm so excited. My first Christmas Eve party."

My eyes narrowed till my eyebrows formed a straight line. "You remember our deal, right? No drinking and no wandering out of sight. I don't want Mom chewing my head off if you get lost and freeze to death."

Helga gazed up the ceiling while she tapped her finger on her chin. "I think she'll do more than that. Take your car, maybe? Feed you nothing but boiled sheep heads? Destroy your phone?"

My hand slid down to my jean pocket. My phone was thankfully still there. The thought of it made me shudder. "Enough! Are you going to stick to our deal or not?"

Helga nodded eagerly. "Don't worry. I'll stay close...to Haukur."

I drowned out her shrieking giggles by whacking the radio volume to the max and suppressing a snort. Like Haukur is *ever* going to be interested in my geeky little sister. I mean, look at her. Who wears a neon pink windbreaker when everyone in Iceland wears a 66° North parka? And even if he did, it was going to be the most awkward *menage a trois* ever because I'd have to chain my little sister to my leg.

The Honda Civic's little engine whined as it trudged through the snow. I clenched my hands on the steering wheel, foot nailed to the accelerator as we climbed higher toward the small Rauðavatn Lake. The frozen water of the lake trapped the moon in its slick, mirrored surface, holding it fast. Like all the old folks and their dumb traditions. An irritated fingernail worried at the leather of the steering wheel.

It would be gone when the spring thaw came. Melt away. Maybe then I'd stop getting stupid presents like girly sweaters.

I looked again at the immobile moon shining in the lake. Then I blinked. For a moment, a shadow floated above it, as if the last cloud of the race had reached the finish line. I tilted my head up, squinting through the frost-framed windshield. The shadow, cloud, whatever it was, was gone. Only the stars winked down at me. My hands tightened on the steering wheel, then relaxed. It was probably just an abnormally big goose or something. I hummed with the song, pushing the uneasy feeling to the back of my mind.

We parked in the Morgunblaðið Newspaper's factory's near empty parking lot. The grey building, absent of festive decorations except for the lights within the windows, looked bleak compared to the houses that blinked red, green, and white across the hill. I scoffed at the sight of few cars scattered around it. Even though it's Christmas Eve, people still have to get their newspaper ready for tomorrow. How sad is that?

Helga stamped on the snow and slapped mittened hands on her thin arms. "How much further?"

I wrapped a scarf around my neck as I picked up the box containing that ugly cardigan. "It's about a twenty-minute walk from here."

Helga groaned. "Why didn't we park closer to the party?"

"Because it's way off in the woods. Now quit bitching and help me carry these bags." I handed her two of the lighter bags, filled with snacks and a metal canister of mulled wine. Sigrún, the girl I liked, enjoyed drinking that in the winter. I overheard her say that to her friends in the school's hallway. I'm sure to score points when I give her a glass.

Helga frowned at the canister. "When did you make this?"

I shrugged. "When Mom was working. You even think about telling her and I'll drive you back home."

Helga ran after me, the bags bouncing in her hands. "Cross my heart and hope to die."

I scowled at her over-enthusiastic grin.

Let's hope it doesn't come to that.

EVEN THOUGH IT was only a twenty-minute walk, it felt a hell of a lot longer when carrying a box and a heavy bag full of beer. The snow hadn't been plowed away from the trail, so Helga and I were knee-deep in leg-numbing frigidness.

I squinted through the dim light, searching for familiar markers on the path. Helga yipped like a frightened dog as birch branches snagged her hair. The thin white sentinels guarded the trail, knotty fingers groping through the inky black of night. But that's not how I saw the forest. No, I saw a winter wonderland. Snow dusting the limbs of the trees, like sugary peppermint sticks. A cautious rabbit nosing through the snow for a morsel of food. Though, come to think of it, I actually hadn't seen any of the woodland creatures I usually saw out here. Not a mink, nor a rabbit. Not even a rat.

I shrugged and cast a glance through the skeletal fingers of the tree-tops. Stars hung across the velvety blackness of the sky like twinkle lights. I grinned. Perfect for a Christmas Eve party.

I looked back toward the path and scowled.

It was also perfect for getting lost.

My toe caught a rock hidden under the snow. I stumbled. Helga rammed right into me.

She rubbed her nose. "Hey, what's the big deal?"

I frowned as I looked down. There should have been foot-prints from all my friends. I wasn't expecting a deep hole in the snow. It was a massive crater, like a group of people had all cannon-balled into a drift of powdered white.

"Brynjar, I'm freezing. Let's go." Helga whined, pushing me ahead.

I glanced behind my shoulder at the hole. It was the second weirdest thing I'd seen tonight if you counted the sweater. At least the sweater could be explained by Grandma's bad taste. Nothing explained the bizarre void in the winter snow.

———————

THE LONGER WE WALKED, the brighter the horizon became. The birch trees gave way to pine. Orange lights danced across them. An audible sigh escaped Helga's lips as we heard upbeat music drumming ahead. The pine trees swayed, beckoning us to the party like sirens.

"Yo, Brynjar!" Ragnar called. The crowd gathered at the small bonfire within the clearing cheered.

The gnawing unease I had felt over the hole in the woods dissolved in an instant. I was happy to see my friends, but I was ecstatic to see *her*.

Sigrún chatted with her friends by the fire. Her ginger hair looked like an extension of the flames. She looked like a fire spirit. I wasn't even close to the bonfire and yet heat enveloped my entire body when I stared at her smiling face.

Our eyes locked. Her cheeks pinked. She waved and jumped into a hurried conversation with her best friend.

I made a decision. If I got some alone time with Sigrún tonight, I'd man up and ask her out. It'd be a bold move. No one had successfully asked her out. She reminded me of our Hidden People, the elves and fairies of Iceland. If you wanted to see one, you'd have to be patient and make a wish. Well, I made a wish when I made that mulled wine. *I hope it comes true tonight.*

Helga nudged me in my elbow. "Where am I supposed to put this?" She held up the bags with an annoying pout.

I shook my head, dispelling the early punch-drunk love. "Right by the fire. That way the drinks won't freeze."

Ragnar came over and gave us hearty hugs. His cheeks

were dull red from both the cold and booze. "Merry Christmas. P.S, loved the pecker condoms you gave me for Christmas. They're not my size, but they gave my family a good laugh, though."

I chortled. "Sorry, I couldn't resist. Here, I got you a proper gift."

Ragnar took the box, lifted it up against his ear and shook it. "It's not a game or a puzzle."

Sudden regret tugged at me. My brilliant regifting plan had a flaw. We'd all agreed not to accept clothes for Christmas. I grit my teeth. He removed the lid. His blue eyes lit up. "Hey, that's pretty nice. Thanks, man."

I unclenched my jaw. In his intoxicated state, he seemed to have forgotten about our pact.

"Glad you like it." I patted him on the shoulder.

Ragnar put on the cardigan over his coat while Helga and I unloaded the bags. He looked ridiculous, but at least he was happy.

The snacks were immediately snatched up by hungry classmates. There was barely anything left for me. I chuckled. Never underestimate the bottomless wells of the teenage stomach.

"There's Haukur." Helga indiscreetly pointed at a guy with a shaved undercut who was surrounded by girls.

I sniffed as I opened a can of beer. Helga didn't stand a chance when most of the popular girls in our year were in the way. But I admired Helga's courage as she joined the girls and laughed at Haukur's jokes.

Since Helga was within sight, I grabbed the mulled wine and hurried over to Sigrún. I slipped on a patch of ice in my haste. She giggled. The sound of her sweet voice dissolved my lightheadedness, but it didn't ease my rapid heartbeat.

"Hey, Brynjar. I thought for a minute that you wouldn't come." Sigrún breathed.

"Sorry, I had to help Mom tidy up and Helga insisted to come as well. So that took time." I kept the canister hidden behind my back. No need to reveal it just yet.

Sigrún glanced at the group of girls, spotting Helga in her neon pink windbreaker. Her brows furrowed. "She's got competition. I hope she can handle it."

I waved a dismissive hand. "Don't worry about Helga. She'll be fine. She's tough."

Sigrún nodded, a smile tugging at her lips. "Like her older brother." She softly touched my arm.

An electrical jolt ran through me at the slight touch. My heart banged in my chest. *Is this for real? Is she interested?* I mean, she touched me first, so that must mean I've got a shot. *Now's your chance,* the daredevil within me cheered.

"I brought you something." I fumbled with the lid of the canister. The pungent aroma of cloves, nutmeg and cinnamon mingled with red wine wafted through the air.

Sigrún inhaled deeply. "I love that smell. Where did you buy it?"

She thought I had bought it? I bit my lip as I poured her a mug. My heart shrunk a tiny fraction. I tilted my chin down and had to bite the inside of my cheek to conceal the frown. "Oh, I, um, I made it myself."

"You did?" Sigrún's nose wrinkled from the first sip. She quickly disguised it into a smile. "Oh, it's great. Thank you."

"You think so? I can send you the recipe if you want. *Tasty* has some great ones." I rocked back and forth, a sudden giddiness taking hold. She liked my wine. Score one for me.

"Thanks, I'd like that. You can send it to me now if you want." Sigrún pulled out her phone. "Wait, I don't have your Snapchat, do I?"

My heart resumed doing jumping jacks. My palms became moist within my gloves. I never had the courage to ask her for it, even when the class went around claiming each other's handles. There's also the fact that my Snapchat handle was stupid.

She looked up expectantly, phone and app at the ready. I shuffled my feet in the downtrodden snow. "Oh, it's, um, brynjar_the_stud," I mumbled into my scarf. Heat gathered in my ears.

Sigrún smirked but she didn't say anything else. She was kind that way. Unlike the other girls, she kept it to herself. "Found you and added to my group."

My phone pinged in my pocket. I pulled it out and gazed at her handle. It was normal, just her full name and her birth year. But it suited her. "Thanks."

Her sweet smile returned. "Don't mention it."

I rubbed the back of my neck. I found it hard not to stare at the cluster of freckles that resembled the stars of the sky on her nose and cheeks. "So, what did you get for Christmas?" I cringed. Oh, *that* was original.

"I got lots of nice books. I can't wait to read them in bed tomorrow. What about you?"

I almost didn't hear her question. I was preoccupied with something over her shoulder. Haukur and the gang of girls were going deeper into the forest, away from the bonfire. Helga tagged along.

"Helga! Where are you going?"

"We saw a cat, but it didn't seem to have a leash. We're going to search for it." Her voice trailed off as she disappeared into the darkness. A cat? Rabbit, sure. Mink? Nasty little creatures, but yeah, okay. But a cat? I bristled. The only animal I was really worried about was a fox. Not the furry Arctic kind but the sly kind. The ones called Haukur.

I took a step forward, my brotherly instinct hovering on the attack switch. Sigrún's hand touched my arm.

"They'll be fine It's not like you can get lost here." She chuckled.

I joined in, although half-heartedly. My eyes scanned the tall pine trees. A shadow flitted between them. I blinked and rubbed my eyes, trying to clear my vision. When I opened them, it was still there, swaying. I breathed. It was just the shadow from the bonfire. The bright light seemed to dim. My gaze shifted upwards. Clouds gathered in the sky. That's odd. The weather forecast had said that the sky would be clear.

One by one the stars disappeared, snuffed out by the thick clouds. Even the moon said goodbye. The sky turned pitch black. Our only source of light was the bonfire that was losing embers by the second. Ragnar poked at the dying flames with a long stick.

"Hey, any of you geniuses remember to bring dry wood?" he bellowed to an emptying clearing. He stumbled a bit and plonked on a log. He looked down at his feet where Helga had dropped our bags.

"No? That's all right, then. At least we've got the beer."

He fished out a new can. The crack of the pop top echoed, and he chugged it back.

I tugged at my scarf, wrapping it closer around my neck. A chill, much deeper than could be explained by a dying fire, seeped through my skin. My scalp prickled.

My glance darted among the remaining party-goers. No one else seemed affected by the pervading cold. Everybody continued to chat, drinking their beer, as if nothing was wrong. But something was off. Or maybe I was just too sober.

A blood-curdling scream pierced the night.

Ragnar fumbled with the radio, turning off the music.

Confused silence fell upon the group. My heart clenched. The scream came from the direction of Haukur and the girls. Of Helga.

A second scream echoed through the woods.

My classmates muttered among themselves, shuffling closer to the perceived safety of the fire.

"Helga!" I bolted to the woods. Dread burned through my veins like acid.

Someone collided with me. One of the girls. Eyes bulging and out of breath.

"What happened?" I gripped her arms before she could bolt.

"I-I don't know. Something grabbed Haukur and pulled him into the trees. He screamed. We screamed." The girl sobbed, yanked herself free and ran away toward the clutching birch. Anything to get away from whatever she had seen.

The rest of my classmates weren't too far behind. Sigrún and Ragnar ran up to me. Soon, it was just us alone with cans of beer littered around the clearing and the sparks of the dying embers.

Sigrún stayed close to my side. Her shivers reverberated through her whole being. The red patches on Ragnar's cheeks had dissolved and his eyes were more focused than earlier.

"What the fuck was that?" Ragnar asked.

"No idea, but I have to find my sister." My mouth went dry, like I'd eaten a mouthful of the Sprengisandur black beach sand. Clenching clammy hands, I fought my flight instinct and ventured into the darkness. Helga needed me.

The quiet smothered. My breath choked in my throat. Why wasn't anyone screaming anymore? My mind went through haphazard scenes from the crime noir books I got for Christmas. Like how the villain buried a young woman alive near Esja mountain. I shook my head. Iceland doesn't have any serial killers, I rationalized. Haukur must have just played a cruel joke on the girls.

"If this is Haukur's idea of a joke, he's being an asshole right now," Sigrún whispered, mirroring my thoughts. Her hand clutched my arm so hard it felt numb.

"I'm sure they're fi—"

Something stubbed my toe. I involuntarily gasped. It must have been a branch, hidden beneath the snow. I turned on the flashlight app on my phone. The artificial light beamed down on speckles of crimson on the snow.

My pulse jumped up. I guided the light further ahead. I saw an arm. Only an arm. I dropped the phone. The cold snow swallowed the light.

Sigrún clamped her hand on her mouth, muffling her horrified gasp. Ragnar swore under his breath. "It's probably just a prop from the school theater."

Cold sweat gathered in my armpits. My rapid breath crystalized in the air and my heart thrashed in my ears. It didn't look fake to me. I scrambled in the snow for my lost phone. Ignoring the cold soaking through my gloves, I dug until I gripped stiff fingers around its case and pulled it from the drift.

"I see something. Over there, to your left." Sigrún tugged on my coat and pointed into the darkness.

I turned it to the left. A torn off leg hung in one of the branches. The dripping blood tapped a disconcerting rhythm on the exposed tree roots below.

"Let's get out of here, Brynjar." Sigrún's tugging became more aggressive and her whispers more hoarse.

A whimper sounded to my right. I shone the light there. One of the girls, Heiðdís, lay on her stomach, her hand outstretched toward us. There were ugly, long scratches across her back.

"Help me," she wheezed.

"What's going on? Who did this to you?" I asked.

Sigrún hurried over to her, scrutinizing over the wounds with a grimace. "She's hurt really bad. We need to call an ambulance."

"Wait, I want to know the bastard who did this. Was it Haukur? Is this some kind of sick joke?" Ragnar's voice rose higher as he circled the two of them.

Heiðdís's eyes squeezed shut, shaking her head. "It was huge... furry...yellow eyes...it's real."

I moved closer to her. My mind recalled the hole I stumbled into earlier. Thing was, it hadn't just been a single hole. As I had looked back over my shoulder, I now remembered seeing four smaller indentations curved over one edge of the larger one. A paw shape.

"Brynjar, please, before it comes back," Heiðdís crawled toward me. Sigrún bent over, sliding an arm under her shoulder.

I kneeled, ready to hoist her up.

A gigantic paw slammed down on Heiðdís. Bones crunched. Heiðdís spewed blood. It splattered my coat. Sigrún screamed.

Teeth chattering, I looked up.

Glistening eyes met mine. Full of malice. Brimming with hunger. Fur, matted with earth and blood, blended in with the trees as it crouched down on all fours. Stringy drool, tinged pink from blood traveled down from its opened maw. Its hot breath reeked of dank and rotted flesh.

A cat. Not the cute cuddly kind they make YouTube videos about. It took a step forward. The ground trembled under its massive paws.

"Brynjar," Heiðdís's gurgles were near inaudible.

"Brynjar, help me," Sigrún sobbed as she stretched out her left arm. Her right one was trapped under Heiðdís's crushed body.

The cat kept its gaze locked on mine. At the same time, it bowed its head and ripped the girl in half. It didn't even bother to chew. It swallowed Heiðdís's upper half whole and took Sigrún's arm along for the ride.

Her agonizing wails punctured my soul.

Ragnar bolted, screaming. The cat's pupils dilated as it followed him. The ground shook with each of its steps. The blank snow canvas splattered with pink as drool fell from its mouth. It raised its claws and swiped at Ragnar's back. Ragnar hit a pine tree and crumbled like a rag doll. It towered over my friend and the hideous purr resounded through the forest. It bent down its head once again, ready to swallow him whole. Ragnar whimpered. Then it stopped and sniffed him. The cardigan over his coat tugged with each inhale. It gave a nasty hiss, but it turned away, strolling to where Sigrún and the rest of Heiðdís' body was.

Warm urine cascaded down the inside of my pant leg. I wanted to help. I wanted to run. I wanted to snap out of it and realize this was all just a fucked-up nightmare. The weight of hundreds of years of tradition rooted me to the spot. This can't be real. This thing was only a myth. A cautionary tale to appreciate what you got during harsh times. I've never heard of people actually getting eaten by a humongous cat here. Something with an appetite that huge would have undoubtedly left a scar on the planet's face. You'd think we'd have noticed.

The cat yowled as it pushed the ripped lower half of Heiðdís's body around. Sigrún clutched at the stump where her forearm had been, tears streaking her freckled face, her blood painting the ground crimson. The cat's whiskers bristled as it touched the gore. Sigrún shook her head and pushed backwards.

"No, please don't," she begged.

The cat cocked its head to the side, as if considering mercy upon the girl. Then it bent low on all fours, ears tucked away, and pounced.

I clamped my hands on my ears, shutting out the bone breaking as it feasted on the girl I loved. With it, it ate my heart. I kept muttering, "This can't be happening, this can't be happening," as I took cautious steps backwards. Careful not to alert the damn cat.

Then, my mind connected the dots. Heiðdís, Sigrún, Haukur and the others were all in the environmental class with me. We all had agreed on no clothes. The old poem Grandma used to recite to us when Christmas neared flooded into my mind:

> *You all know the Yule Cat*
> *And that Cat was huge indeed.*
> *People didn't know where he came from*
> *Or where he went.*
>
> *He opened his glaring eyes wide,*
> *The two of them glowing bright.*
> *It took a really brave man*
> *To look straight into them.*
>
> *His whiskers, sharp as bristles,*
> *His back arched up high.*
> *And the claws of his hairy paws*
> *Were a terrible sight.*

He gave a wave of his strong tail,
He jumped and he clawed and he hissed.
Sometimes up in the valley,
Sometimes down by the shore.

He roamed at large, hungry and evil
In the freezing Yule snow.
In every home
People shuddered at his name.

If one heard a pitiful "meow"
Something evil would happen soon.
Everybody knew he hunted men
But didn't care for mice.

It all clicked. The small cat in the yard. It could have been working for the Yule Cat or maybe it had been the cat itself. The flitting shadow above the sky as we cruised to the park. The damn cat must have known. It must have been waiting for all of us to gather. This party had been an easy target.

The Yule Cat didn't eat Ragnar because I had given him the cardigan that Grandma gave me. For some reason, it doesn't eat people who receive clothes for Christmas. My fingers tingled. He was safe from its clutches. But what about Helga?

Not moving an inch, I scanned the area. A pair of frightened eyes within a neon pink windbreaker stared back at me, concealed within a clutter of birch to my right. I couldn't help exhaling in relief. Tears welled up behind my eyes. If I had any urine left in me, I would have expelled all of it right now.

Thank God! Helga was safe. Grandma had given her pajamas for Christmas. The Yule Cat couldn't touch her. That was all that mattered.

"Run, Helga. Take Ragnar and get to safety."

Helga shook her head violently. Her bulging eyes seemed to say, *what about you?*

I let out a weak chuckle that ended in a long exhale. "It's too late for me. For any of us who didn't get clothes tonight. We got what we deserved. Honor the old ways. Never forget that and spread the word. Go to Hagkaup and buy mittens, socks, any clothing for the rest of the class. Save the rest of them for me, if you can." My teeth chattered. I clenched my fists. "I'll stay here and hold it off."

A choked sob caught my ears as Helga crawled out of her hiding spot. I watched her pull a possibly-concussed Ragnar from beneath the pine tree and the two of them ran away. Both looked back, their eyes wide in fear and disbelief.

My muscles softened to jelly. Numbness enveloped my whole being. My chin trembled. I could no longer tell if it came from the cold or from fear. I glanced at the puddle of blood where Sigrún had been. Nothing was left of her. I couldn't save her. I didn't get my wish. My stomach threatened to empty the contents of it onto the already splattered snow. I could smell the Yule Cat's fetid breath and see the torn flesh hanging from its yellowed teeth.

In a weird, nasty way, my mind reminded me that I had forgotten to call my wisest relative and thank her for the gift before I left for the party. A huge lump lodged in my throat. Next time, we'll be wiser. Next time, we'll really listen and heed the words and traditions of the old.

"I'm sorry, Grandma," I whispered before the cat's stinking jaw unhinged and obscured the world.

WITHIN THE WICKER

BRAD ACEVEDO

FRIDAY, NOVEMBER 30

When winter frost bites at your nose
you'd better run and hide
For through the cold he'll find your home
you'll wish you'd gone and died

Through sleet and rain on blood tinged snow
the Old One rings his bells
For when the Krampus comes tonight
your soul he'll take to Hell

T he words echoed through the thirteen year old mind of Tim Ridenhour as he splashed through the mud-flecked snow. The poem had been found in a book of world-wide mythology he had been assigned in English class. It gave him just the slightest of pauses before he kicked a splash of dirty water at Sera's pants.

"Damn it, you little Devil!" the teenage girl cried out. She immediately regretted her outburst and pulled the young boy in for a damp hug, purposefully smearing the mud against his pants in the process. "Sorry, Tim. I didn't mean -"

Tim knew what she was going to say and he couldn't fully blame her. That was what siblings did, right? They bickered and teased and fought even when...things emerged in the heat of the moment. Moments like a young boy learning of his true heritage from the couple he had previously known as his birth parents.

It had been a classic moment of his father, Michael, calling him into a "family meeting." The boy knew enough to realize that it usually meant they had heard him dropping F-bombs on Fortnite or seen his search history or any other kind of mischief a young man his age might get up to. But this most recent one...this was something different. He still knew them as his parents, but in that one moment, he knew the woman by her name Justine and not as Mom even as she took his hand in her own delicate grasp. They told him then that he was old enough to know the truth. His real mother wasn't known to them nor to Sera (who had been told the very same tale years before, but with a much happier ending).

Tim had thought the worst part had been the revelation of his birth name: "Tuefel." A quick Google search later however, proved it much darker as he learned the meaning behind such a weak, diabolic sounding moniker. What woman would name her child "Devil?" Unwanted, unloved, a curse to her life; surely that's why she had surrendered him.

"Devil Devil Devil little hellion rancid beast."

Voices, from where? From within? He had no way of knowing if his mother had actually uttered those words to a helpless baby. Sera knew better, though, and he knew that his big sister really did love him, no matter how much street water he splashed on her. It was all in good fun, it wasn't like he needed to "be good for goodness sake." Fairy tale shit like that was...well, precisely that. He had steam to let off and what better way than to be an occasional -

"Little mischief maker!"

The Ridenhour siblings squinted across the sleet of Cold-brook Road towards an old white, single level house with a peaked roof. An elderly gentleman stood out front, tapping an aged mahogany walking cane on the front walk as a hefty looking black cat scurried about his feet. He wore a loose fitting green wool vest over a white button up shirt and a fashionable pair of slacks that strained as he bent low to try to scoop up the errant feline.

"We should probably go help him, right?" Sera asked, looking down at the boy for validation.

"Well, maybe-" he hesitated. He was old enough to know that in this day and age, one could never be too sure. But then the old man tumbled to the front walk with a startled cry.

The siblings quickly scampered across the street. Sera briefly stumbled on the sleet, too, before righting herself and joining her brother by the old man. The pair reached out and gently lifted him by his frail, bony arms even as the cat yowled in protest.

"Oh my, danke, danke," the old man gasped in a German accent.

"You okay, sir?" Sera asked.

"Yes, dear, yes, I shall be fine. My footing isn't quite what it used to be, I used to be so fleet of foot like a springy little mountain goat," he chuckled and stood up.

Tim shielded his eyes briefly as a glint of sunlight pierced the swollen clouds overhead and reflected off of the man's face. A passing shadow revealed a metal protuberance affixed where one would usually find a human nose amidst a light speckle of grey whiskers.

The old man quickly caught direction of the boy's gaze, dusted himself off and tapped the metal knob for dramatic showmanship effect: "1st Infantry Private Nikolas Bell at your service, young ones. Lost this little beauty on Normandy fighting against my own countrymen. Oh children, I've seen horrors that would twist your hearts...like when feisty little Hela here brought me back a headless rat!" He chuckled with a high pitched wheeze that brought to mind braying beasts of burden and silverware on old dishes.

Tim nodded politely and introduced himself and his sister. "We live just across the street."

Nikolas Bell strained his jaundiced eyes and peered at the two story grey Ridenhour house. "My children just helped me move in. I'm afraid I haven't had the pleasure to see much of the neighborhood. I'm sure it's a fine house, boy, but my vision, much like most of me, isn't quite up to snuff."

Sera smiled politely, a half hearted attempt to mask the air of unease that emanated from their new neighbor. She bent low to pick up the old man's cane and pondered what it was that brought such discomfort. It might have been his eyes, yellow as rotten egg yolk with a curious subtle indentation in the clear blue irises. She might have attributed it to the vaguely stuffy scent that whisked from his body, like the smell of livestock or rotted hay. No; it was certainly the deep breath she caught him taking, the old man leaning a bit too close to her (and more alarmingly, her young brother) as a sharp inhalation echoed through the metal confines of his nose. Could he even smell through that? If so, the old man seemed to like what he had picked up as she caught him subconsciously licking his lips and quickly glancing down at his cat. A call emerged from inside his home, a shrill cry of a songbird just distorted enough to raise a fresh coat of goose-bumps over Sera's cocoa-colored skin.

"I should probably get inside and put this little one to bed," Bell said as he ran a rough hewn hand over the squirming cat. "She does get cranky, and when Hela gets upset, there's no telling what hell there might be to pay." He smiled and grasped his walking stick tightly. His hairy knuckles bristled and grew taut around the dark wooden stick. Another whistle escaped his nose and he swiftly spun around with an abrupt start and began to close his front door. "Until next time, dear ones. And Danke, once again."

TUESDAY, DEC 4

The next few days passed along as days normally do for teenagers in Midwestern suburbia. Their parents, good people almost to a fault, prepared flyers for a forthcoming community winter festival. Sera continued to practice her softball skills, always ready for a challenge even in the frosty off season. Tim however, fixated on something entirely different than expected for a boy on winter break: he had filled his search engine with genealogy sites and a plethora of open tabs focusing on the culture of Southern Germany and other Alpine regions. Amidst the sea of information, the boy found another blighted beacon in that same hair-bristling poem from the book. He had heard about the Krampus before; the beast seemed to be growing in popular American culture ever since that movie had come out. Now Tim found himself drawn to other dark traditions, following breadcrumbs of knowledge into a surreal and twisted yuletide woodland.

Devils indeed, frolicking in the corrupted snow, no longer innocent and pure, new knowledge to gain and glean on a cold winter's night; things he hadn't known but now couldn't escape. Tuefel (Was that really so bad? Was it?) became engrossed in the culture he had never before experienced outside of a few history classes and one less-than-enthralling trip to Epcot. These tales rang like bells beckoning him into the further reaches of his past.

They summoned something darker still beyond the reaches, dark and foul things that were closer than he realized. The bell sounded again, pleasant and melodic, synchronized perfectly to the twinkling candy colored lights that coated the Ridenhour house in festive cheer. As Nikolas Bell pressed the doorbell again with one weathered, crooked finger, a cold wind began to blow and the glow of the lights surrounding him on the doorstep dimmed ever so slightly. The door opened to warmth and lovely smells beyond the threshold. Greetings were exchanged, frost dipped coats were removed and an elderly man from far away presented a bottle of spiced mulled wine to his hosts as the night's festivities began.

"I don't even know how this happened, dear," Justine Ridenhour smirked with all the good natured patience she could muster. She wiped a fleck of mashed potato from her husband's salt-and-pepper hair.

"One of life's little mysteries, I suppose," Michael Ridenhour chuckled, eliciting rolled eyes from his children.

"Indeed," Justine said. "Just like the mystery of how a glass of this delightful spiced wine ended up in my underage daughter's hand." She pulled the glass away from Sera and replaced it with a glass of non-alcoholic wine.

"I was simply trying to honor our guest and his lovely gift," Sera smirked and took a nibble of her tofurkey. She was grateful that her parents had prepared a separate meal for her particular tastes. She knew to be grateful for many things, even as she cast a wayward glance at the old man.

Bell nodded in the girl's direction and grasped his fork with a shaking hand. "This is very lovely, Mrs. Ridenhour and I thank you all for inviting a lonely old man over for dinner."

"Tell me, Mr. Bell," Michael started, plucking out one more fleck of potato. "Where is your family around the holidays? If I may be so bold as to ask."

Bell waved a gnarled hand dismissively. "No trouble, mein freund. My family is, well, it is complicated. There are many of us and some are very old while others are...very young and loud. Brash, if I am saying this correctly? Not like you fine kinder." He gestured towards the teens. "I moved here to find...new friends, new family, shall we say? Someone who doesn't bite and claw if I don't feed them when they demand it." He chuckled, wheezing through his metal nose. "The young people, they make ME feel young, you see, yes? I love to see the glow on their faces this time of year. Hearth and kin. The spice of life, as it were. Yes?"

"I think we can toast to that," Justine smiled warmly at the eccentric old man and raised her glass of spiced wine. "To the spice of life."

Warm smiles abounded on this cold winter night as the family and their guest supped and drank and made merry, even as curious thoughts ricocheted with violent fervor within two young minds. Pleasantries continued to be exchanged, anecdotes shared (Bell cordially offered a polite grin at Michael's proud recollection of passing by Steven Tyler in an airport) and invites were levied for further celebrations of the holiday season. Nikolas Bell accepted these invitations with gratitude as he finished his meal.

"Tim, I thought we agreed to no phones at the dinner table, especially in front of our guest?" Justine scolded as her adopted son made one more hurried glance at a long languished family tree diagram.

"Sorry, just-"

"Come on now, Tim," Michael said sternly. "I'll take it and hide it where you can't find it."

"It goes in your pants pocket, we all know," Tim smirked.

"Then I'll put it in my gym bag," Michael said, his eyes glinting with mischief. "After a good long leg day. Before I shower."

"Oh God," Tim groaned with a grimace of horror. He quickly stowed the device, but not before Bell managed to sneak a glance.

"Really, Dad?" Sera grimaced and dropped her fork down into her gluten free pumpkin pie.

"I'm just saying, it's best not to be rude-"

"Yeah, but while we're eating-"

"And why would you even-?"

"Tuefel?" Mr. Bell broke through the bickering. "Who then, is this Devil that we speak of? Oh, you children and your handheld telephone internets."

An uncomfortable silence pierced the warm air. The tension was as thick as the pie's flaky crust.

Justine took a deep breath. "Mr. Bell, I'm sorry. Tim, apologize to him for being rude."

"I'm sorry," Tim said. Shane flooded him and tears sprang from his eyes, knowing he would have to explain the story of his name to a complete stranger. He wouldn't though, he refused. There was no reason. "I was...researching something for school."

"So studious, ja, to do his homework during the family dinner hour. Not-so-idle hands do the Devil's work at this time when we should celebrate one another. No matter where we're from."

"Like I said-" Justine offered.

"No matter where we're from, even if we're not wanted," Tim said through reddening prism eyes.

"Well now, I hope you do not speak of this to me," Mr. Bell frowned and ran a hand through his thinning white hair.

"No, of course not," Michael said. "Tim – well, he-"

Sera took a deep breath. "He meant his assignment, of course. I mean, what kind of teacher assigns a report over winter break, right?"

Bell nodded and squinted his yellow eyes. "Yes of course." He took a deep breath, air whistling through his nose followed by two swift inhalations. His eyes seemed to light up in unmistakable pleasure. "Yes, yes, ja indeed." He wiped his thin lips on a cloth napkin and stood up suddenly, leaning on his cane. "Ridenhour family, I'm afraid I must take my leave. Uh, young Timothy, won't you escort an old man to the door?"

"Are you sure, Mr. Bell? We were going to watch *Christmas Vacation*," Justine said.

"C'mon, Mr. Bell, Cousin Eddie's antics will cure what ails you," Michael grinned goofily.

"While that sounds, ah, delightful, I really must go," the old man said. "Hela does get lonely and I promised I'd give her a nice, warm saucer of cream tonight. Thank you for the lovely meal."

"Tim, go help Mr. Bell home," Justine instructed.

"Oh no, no, just to the door, that's all I request," Bell said.

Tim sighed and stood up, leaving behind an untouched plate of pie that swiftly fell to the conquering invader of Michael Ridenhour's fork.

As the elderly man stood creakingly from the table, his walking stick tumbled to the floor. Tim reached down to pick it up, but Bell moved alarmingly fast, shrugging off the boy's attempt at aid and clutching the stick with determined ferocity.

"My apologies," he whispered as he stood. "It is a special piece, an antique from my homeland, you understand."

Tim shrugged off the incident as more eccentricity on Bell's part and helped the elderly man into his coat. As Bell shrugged on the tattered shroud, he took another long inhale. He reached forth, took the boy's hand, and patted it gently before pulling him forward in a rough manner.

"Young man, young Tuefel-Devil," he hissed softly.

"What the fu-"

"Do not say naughty things, boy," Bell whispered. "I know you are angry, I can tell these things, yes? This time of year, it is a special time. But sometimes, boy, and listen closely: sometimes a man's home is not what it seems. Sometimes you have to crawl a little further in before you see what really lies within a man's heart. Trust me. You want to know about your true family? They are called the Wagners. I offer this little morsel and hope you'll come see me tomorrow. I'll tell you more about your lineage, dig further into your roots than any man's spade could hope to reveal."

"How could you know these things?" Tim whispered back. The hairs on the back of his neck rose up, alerted with fear, maybe intrigue. How could one tell at this point? His nostrils filled with that earthy goat scent and he looked into the yellow eyes of the old man from across Coldbrook Road.

Bell tapped the side of his head, generating a curiously hollow knocking sound. "This old goat knows things, young man. June 20th, a summer solstice. That is when the light of this world first shined upon you and now, on a winter's eve, you'll see that light shed ever further than before. Tomorrow night, yes?"

Tim thought quickly, impulsively. The old man was

already out the door and into the cold and dark before the boy could give his answer.

Sera had always had a strong intuition. She knew from a young age that the Ridenhours were not her birth parents, but she also knew that her own lineage was more cut-and-dry than her adopted brother's. It had simply been a moment of a couple becoming pregnant a bit too early and not ready to raise a child. In fact, she planned to track down her birth parents after high school and the Ridenhours were very supportive of these plans. But on this night, she wasn't going to focus on herself. No, her brother was hiding something and she was determined to uncover it.

She knocked on his door and he invited her in. Tim took out his headphones and set aside the anime he had been streaming on his phone. He raised one hand in silent greeting and sat up against his headboard as she took a seat on the foot of the twin sized bed.

She ran her hand over the plain blue comforter and bit her lip softly, pondering how to begin. "So, how do you think Dad ended up getting those mashed potatoes in his hair?" No, stupid, she cursed at herself.

Tim smirked and deflected, knowing exactly why she was there. "He invited me over tomorrow, you know? The old guy, Mr. Bell. He says he knows a lot about German history and knows about my family – my biological family."

"And are you...going to go see him?" Sera asked, twirling and tracing her polished blue nails in the whorls stitched into the comforter fabric.

"Yeah, I think so. I mean, the worst case is that he gives me a bunch of bullshit and makes something up."

"And why do you think he'd go through the trouble of doing that?" Sera asked.

Tim knew what she meant and admittedly, he had caught

wind of the potential danger himself. "I'm not dumb, Sera. He's a creep. I think everyone but Mom and Dad know that. They're too blinded by 'the rigors of hospitality' and 'being good hosts.'. But you know I'll be careful, right?"

"Of course I do, Tim-Tim," Sera said, raising her eyes to meet her brother's. She always wondered about Tim's eyes, such brilliant blue contrasting the brown of hers and their parents. Surely he had to have had some suspicion?

Tim picked up his phone and punched a single key before putting it back down.

"Shortest text message ever?" Sera asked.

"No, that's just me keeping track of all the times you piss me off or annoy me. I figure if you don't make the weekly quota, then you're not living up to sibling standards."

"Oh, I didn't know I was being scrutinized so harshly," she said in mock offense. "What am I up to now?"

"Well, between calling me that heinous nickname and getting me data mined for My Little Pony crap, that puts you at 5 for the week. Well behind the curve, you need to step it up a bit, kid."

Sera giggled. "Oh don't worry, I'm sure I can think of something. After all, my pants are still covered in mud thanks to your oh-so-mature antics."

Tim spread his hands and smirked again. "I do what I can, you know? I work with what I got." He chuckled, feeling a bit better. He could always count on her to cheer him up. He knew that she had his best interests in mind but this was something he wasn't fully sure she'd be able to help him with.

"Sera, I have to try. I know we don't really know the guy but if he can help me, just a little bit or at least point me in the right direction-" he trailed off, not knowing how to finish the sentence.

"I get it, Tim, I do and...I'm sorry. I'm just- I don't know, I couldn't even imagine." It was true; she had some time to come to grips with learning of her adoption. She thought it was remarkable how quickly Tim had come to terms with the Ridenhours but...the business with his birth name had really rattled him. She couldn't imagine being given away with such callousness, such coldness.

"He's an old man with a cane and a cat," Tim said. "What could he do?"

"You never know, Tim. You really don't."

"Don't...tell them about it, okay? The Ri- Mom and Dad. Don't tell them. Please."

Sera had contemplated this. Had she received validation about Tim's plans, she might have gone to them to inform them of what he planned to do but...she tried to place herself in his position. No, she still couldn't do it, still couldn't imagine. She couldn't keep him from at least taking a chance and after all, he was right. Bell was just an old man in seemingly poor health. Even if he had ulterior motives, he'd be limited in what he could do. Her brother's plans were safe with her and she was sure to let him know.

What harm could possibly come from it?

WEDNESDAY, DEC 5

Tim Ridenhour kept his word. He told his sister that he would be careful. Michael and Justine were at a town meeting with the contractors who would be setting up the Christmas festival and Sera had gone out with her friends to see the new Tom Hardy movie. He hurried to get out of the house, making sure to bring along something to defend himself with. He didn't anticipate anything to go down, but the old man did creep him out. In any case, Tim set out across the street, anxiously traipsing among the sun dappled street slush with a pair of crafting scissors in his pocket.

The front door of the old grey house opened just as Tim set foot on the front walk. Nikolas Bell stood there, clad in the same clothes as the day prior and clutching his walking stick with ever increasing fervor. The old man's gnarled grip seemed to mesh with the cane, flesh and wood congealing as one. He smirked; his metal nose glistened, his whiskers twitched in the brisk winter wind, and he tilted his head back into the confines of the domicile. Tim hesitated ever so slightly before breaking into a neighborly smile and stepping across the threshold.

The inside of the house contained but a few simple furnishings. The living room consisted of roughly scoured hardwood flooring and only two gray armchairs. Between the two chairs sat a large, oval shaped beige wicker basket, turned upside down with a silver tray set upon the solid bottom. A battered tin pitcher and two equally dented tin mugs sat upon the tray. Bell took one of the chairs and motioned to Tim for the other.

Tim grinned and nodded a silent greeting as he took in the rest of the home. A hallway branched off from the living room, leading undoubtedly to a kitchen, bathroom and bedroom, maybe an office where he... hell, Tim didn't know what Bell would be doing. Building a ship in a bottle? Collecting teeth from the neighborhood kids?

He had been so transfixed by the odd furnishings that he hadn't noticed the wall décor. As he took a seat in the sagging armchair, the boy gazed upwards past his host at the veritable legion of wooden hand carved cuckoo clocks adorning nearly every surface of the walls. Each clock was festooned with decorations, some simple carvings and some more complex.

The clocks shone in a variety of colors, some black, some mahogany, and some with a reddish hue. Not a tick nor a tock nor an obnoxious electronic bird sounded in an attempt to shatter his eardrums. The silence of the room pierced his ears as Nikolas Bell picked up the pitcher and poured a steaming drink into both mugs.

"Lotus-Wort root tea, from the Black Forest," the old man explained, speaking for the first time. "Trust me, it's better than it sounds."

Tim picked up the mug and took an exploratory sniff. It smelled delicate, floral and citrusy. Not what he was used to. He set it back down. "Do you have a soda, or something?"

Bell frowned at the boy and twitched, a sudden jerk of the head. He took a whistling breath through his metal nose and Tim regretted the rude request.

"I have some sugar if the young man would like to indulge in excess," Bell said, bristling.

"No, no, I'm sorry sir," Tim tried to backpedal. "It's just that I'm not used to something this...exotic." There we go, he thought, that's a good way to put it. Don't be a jerk, Tim. He took a sip and actually found the tea somewhat tasty. Like hot lemonade, but more appealing than he would have imagined that sounded.

"My boy, the ways of this world are still exotic to me, even after all this time," Bell mused and gazed overhead at the assortment of silent clocks. He seemed lost in his own arcane words, staring past the room to a memory long past.

Tim decided to break the silence and bring the old man back to the present: "So, Mr. Bell, what can you tell me? Please." He took out a small notepad and pen, fumbled it, reached for it and fumbled it again.

Bell blinked and refocused on the boy, grinning a serpent's smile as he drank his tea. Tuefel Wagner, the boy before him, began to slump downwards and lose the bright focus in his youthful eyes. Bell sniffed again, shivering in delight at a miasma that danced tantalizingly in the still air. "So polite," he said to the boy. "Perhaps there might be hope for you yet?"

"I hope you can hellll and telllll me all I nnnnn," Tim drawled. He blinked rapidly, each closure of his eyes lasting slightly longer than the one before. The room began to blur as the old man moved and spoke, words that began to hiss and meld within one another in a cacophony of hideous nonsense.

Nikolas Bell removed the tray from on top of the basket and titled it upright, exposing the hollow interior. He stood up, reached to his scalp and ran a jagged nail across the skin, peeling it back even as he began to speak. "Yes, young Tuefel, I do know your family. I know many families from the old country, more so by scent than anything else."

Bell smoothed back the hard, gnarled horns that spiraled forth from the ragged remnants of his man-skin. He ran his nails along his sallow cheeks, removing the flesh in small strips. "History shows that some family blood tends to exude a rather odorous scent, yes? Bad blood, tainted by hate and malice and ill-will. And yet, dear boy, there are rare occasions where one branch in the rotted tree might bloom a little bit brighter."

He kicked off his shoes and flexed the hooves within. Bell leaned a bit closer to the boy; his eyes began to close and his breathing grew shallower. A tongue unfurled from within the beast's maw, remnants of hanging flesh dancing with wicked revelation to expose the face of barnyard animal; a bovine beast slavering with anticipation. The tongue grew forked and reached out with savage hunger to lap at the boy before withdrawing back into the stinking abyss. Even as the flesh continued to slough, the metal nose remained affixed to the snout of the goat.

Had Tuefel Wagner had the capacity to see, hear or smell, he would have heard the clanking of chains and the yowling of a cat, the sight of a dark recess drawing ever nearer and the smell of blood, bile and sweat emerging forth from Bell's own portable Hell.

The goat lifted a well muscled, fur leg that burst out from the old man slacks, and he took one step into the basket itself.

"Young blood tastes the best," came a hissing voice from somewhere beyond a shaded veil, as Bell lifted the dazed boy in its powerful grasp. "I told you, kinder, we will crawl further in to see what lies within a man's heart. I anticipate discovering what lies in yours, even as I pluck it from your body. Be kind to an old goat, won't you? Help me with this task and I'll show you your ancestors. I promise you this. Ich halte immer ein versprechen.

Der Krampus always keeps his promise."

SERA RIDENHOUR DRUMMED her nails on the faded Milwaukee Brewers steering wheel cover of her dented, white Kia. She had been sitting here, parked in her family's drive-way, facing the Bell house and contemplating if she should actually do what she planned. She had afforded at least two hours time, two hours of Tom Hardy's rugged good looks charging across the silver screen, before she decided she might check up on Tim. Might.

Yes, be a good sister. Be a good sibling and watch out for your younger brother. But then, he was his own man, wasn't he? No, screw that. He was barely a teenager. She decided to compromise and park here, keeping a silent hazel eye on the old man's house. But she didn't want to ruin this for Tim, on the off chance that Bell could actually provide some light on Tim's family. What were the odds? What were the odds that he was actually just a helpful old eccentric? What were the odds he would drug her little brother and do unspeakable things?

No. Sera couldn't take that chance. She couldn't imagine what might happen. Screw this.

Sera strode across the old man's walk with purpose, one hand tapping anxiously against her jeans while the other clutched the can of mace on her keychain. She tapped politely on the door, waited but a moment and then pounded with more intent.

Silence. Sera sighed, took a deep breath and navigated a narrow hedge to peer in through an uncovered side-set window. No sign of the old man or her brother. Just an over-turned basket, two chairs, an obscene amount of cuckoo clocks and...a pile of the old man's clothes heaped haphazardly on the floor.

Sera pushed back through the hedge and thrust forward with two swift kicks to the door jamb. She had slid into home base on multiple occasions and was well used to using her legs for force. One more kick and she was rewarded with the shattering of wood and the burst of warm, rural air.

Sera grimaced at the strong scent of manure and animal musk. She called out into the silent house: "Tim?!"

Silence. And then: a faint noise. A cry of pain, fear. A shifting clank of metal. The howl of a cat and the squawk of a bird. It was all far off, as if filtered through a barrier that she couldn't see. It took only a moment, though, for Sera to pinpoint the location of the din.

She couldn't imagine, but then she might have to. She possessed a more practical mindset; seeing is believing. Even as the holidays approached she didn't hold much in the way of anticipating a visit from Santa or celebrating the birth of a Christ figure. This world was a world ruled by laws and physics. Softballs fell to the ground due to gravity, genetics determine whether one would be born with darker skin like hers or the fairer skin tone of her adoptive parents. Science and logic wouldn't dictate the existence of a pocket dimension contained within a wicker basket lying on the ground within an old pervert's home.

But then, sometimes one must set aside what they think is right and move down the rabbit hole to a world of beautiful nonsense, one that shatters all notion of what they believe to be reality. And so, licking her lips and drumming her chipped nails on the rough hardwood floor, Sera Ridenhour dropped to all fours and crawled headfirst, diving deep within the Wicker before her.

She re-emerged exactly the way she had entered: defenseless and terrified at what had befallen her brother. Sera stood up and gazed around at the new room on the other side of the basket. The room was roughly the same shape as the last, supplanted with the same legion of clock décor but the hardwood floor beneath her was burned and scoured with an elegant design resembling an enormous tree. The branches spiraled off to several corners of the room, the most predominant containing a blazing furnace. The heat felt nice amidst the bracing cold of the outside world, but such little comfort was alleviated by the sight of a rusted chain affixed to a metal rivet before the furnace. The links of the chain snaked off down the single hallway and she knew immediately what path she must follow.

The air felt still and uncomfortably quiet. The army of cuckoo clocks remained silent and unmoving. Then she heard a noise, the unmistakable clanging of dishware and running water. Sera glanced around for any type of weapon other than the mace in her pocket but, finding none, continued cautiously down the hall, following the chain.

The sound had come from the first room on her left, the chain weaving beyond the threshold. Against her better judgment, she peeked inside a partially open and unpainted wooden door. A pot was left unattended upon a metal countertop and a trio of white objects poked over the edge of the pot. It only took a moment to notice the curvature of the joints and the pinkish rim of dried blood for her to realize that the bones extending from the pot were not that of an animal. She let out an involuntary squeak of fear and stepped back into the hall. No, that wasn't Tim. It couldn't be, she couldn't ima- she didn't know what she could or couldn't imagine anymore. Not after all this.

She left the chain behind, even as if shifted with latent movement, tugged at the other end by an unseen force. Sera passed a few more doors before she moved to the last one on the right, drawn by a light whimper. She cautiously passed into the room, a workshop by the look of it. A large cabinet stood against the far wall containing an array of roughly carved, traditional toys. Marionettes, wooden trains and toy soldiers: it looked like the setting of a Norman Rockwell Santa Claus painting. In fact, the room could pass for Santa's workshop... if Santa's workshop had been covered in cuckoo clocks and possessed a wooden table with a teenage boy tied to it.

"Oh my God, Tim!" She cried in a hush, rushing over to her brother. Fibrous strips of wood fastened his wrists and ankles to metal rivets, leaving his body spread eagle on the table. "Where is he? Did he hurt you?!"

The boy blinked tiredly, still emerging from his stupor. "Cat," he murmured and pointed.

Sera followed his finger to the old man's black cat, sitting daintily in the corner of the room and surveying the scene before her. "Never mind the cat," She whispered. "Let's get out of here. Where is he?"

"Scissors," Tim whispered.

"Scissors?"

"Right pocket."

Sera reached into his pants pocket and withdrew the crafting scissors. "Okay, um-okay." she started and quickly began to work at the ropes with the blades. They snipped off surprisingly easily but the boy still moved with the speed and coordination of a drunkard. "Oh God, Tim, what did he do to you?"

Hela began to yowl loudly from the corner.

"Shit," Sera whispered and glanced around frantically. The cat would bring her master calling. There was only one suitable hiding spot in the room. She nudged the protesting animal aside, braced against the back of the work shelf cabinet and pressed herself behind it.

As expected, Nikolas Bell tramped his way into the room, the length of rusted chain connected to his ankle, dragging along with him. Sera couldn't see the old man, but she could hear him rustling and muttering about, cooing to his pet. She peeked around the edge of the shelf and swallowed a scream of fear.

The fiend stood with its humped back to her. It stood at least seven feet tall, sporting a powerfully built, black furred stature topped with spiraling horns. A sinewy tail curled about between two backwards bending legs which ended in grooved animal hooves. The creature gripped the old man's walking cane in its clawed hands, the stick now frayed at the edges and splintering into smaller fragments. It looked like a stiff broom and cut through the air with a whistle as the fiend slapped Tim Ridenhour with the stick.

The boy cried out as the beast plucked at the frayed rope fibers and spoke with an accented hiss: "Naughty kinder, such clever tricks. Be naughty, boy, spices the meat and salts the soul. Köstlich seele. Köstlich kinder. Ja, ja, ja?"

It gripped the boy with its strong hands. The trauma of the unfolding scene seemed to generate more life into Tim, a cocktail of adrenaline cutting through the drug which dulled his senses. The beast swatted at the boy with the branch again. It turned away and approached the workshelf. Sera pulled back further in the darkness, staunching her breath at the sour scent emanating from the beast. It plucked a toy soldier from the shelf and held it before the boy tauntingly.

"Would kinder like a toy? You play while you wait to change. You not be boy for long." It pulled the toy away and tossed it into a far corner of the room with a hiss. "Only good kinder get toy. Frech kinder, naughty boy get Krampus!"

The beast picked its stick-switch up again and raised it high.

"You know stories, Tuefel, I know you read on me. Stories do not tell, I take your seele, your soul. I give to the Gods of Old Country, they set der Krampus free." He swatted the boy again. Sera cringed from her space, with each cry. She knew though, she had to pick her spot.

The beast continued to hiss and speak: "I give to Wotan, All-father, I give him boy as bird and he breaks chain. He lets der Krampus loose."

Swat.

"Krampus pay for sins of Motte and Vater, parents upset Wotan and Krampus is blamed."

Swat.

The beast tapped its metal nose. "Krampus smells the

child, smells the blood of the Wagner. Krampus gives you as bird and then moves on, rides winter wind to next town for more children."

Swat.

"-And then eats the leftovers, no more soul, must not let körper body go to waste. So yummy with salt and spice."

Tim flailed about and, in desperation, caught a grip of the stick. He fell back to the table, wrenching a single shard off of the stick-switch. The beast suddenly fell backwards against a wall, clutching its arm with a howl of unexpected agony and dropping the switch in the process.

The perfect time for Sera to strike.

Sera leaped from behind the work shelf, a silent streak of fury and rage. She barreled her shoulder into the chest of the beast and plunged the scissors deep into the beast's hide. It pierced the flesh and a black substance poured forth as the Krampus goat thrashed about, knocking cuckoo clocks down with a crash.

The clocks suddenly sprang to life, the mechanisms grinding and shifting. From within the clocks emerged their denizens, small black ravens that burst forth on their pedestals not with a musical cuckoo but fear laden shrieks that pierced the souls of the Ridenhour children.

Amidst the fray, Sera pulled her brother to her feet and Hela the cat pounced into the chaos, swatting at the ravens even as they dislodged themselves from their perches. She caught one and sank her fangs into its thrashing neck. The others began to fly about frantically, casting feathers into a bed of unthinkable mayhem.

"Grab the- grab the stick!" Tim called out.

Sera grabbed the frayed switch and gripped her brother's hand as the Krampus regained its composure and lashed out with a pain-blinded swing of its claws.

"Frech kinder!" It bellowed aloud.

The ravens righted themselves after their initial confusion and began to assault the beast, pecking at its fur with vengeful fervor. The siblings took advantage of the confusion and dashed into the hall.

"Hela, mein freund! Bring Krampus switch!"

The children ran down the hall. Sera dragged Tim along as he continued to recover from his ailment, carrying the switch and scissors with her other hand. A soft mewling sound caused the kids to turn around for just a moment. Hela emerged from the other end of the hall. The cat dashed forward, growing larger as it ran. It charged at them, now the size of a rottweiler and baring red stained, feather bedecked fangs as it leaped into the air.

Sera hurled her brother down, planted her feet, squared her shoulders and leaned into the swing. She swung the switch and it collided with a wet thunk into the charging animal, knocking it back down the hall with a thud. Krampus howled with fury from the workshop.

"Nice one," Tim murmured, picking himself up.

"Thanks, you good to go?"

"Yeah, let's move," he said. "We need to get rid of the stick, his lifeforce is tied to it."

"What, how?"

Tim didn't answer. He grabbed the scissors from his sister and began to snip at the branches. Each snip elicited a roar of pain and fury from the room at the end of the hall.

"No, that'll take too long," Sera said. "I know what to do, let's get going."

As they reached the apex of the hall, the workshop door crashed open and the old goat stumbled into the hall, bleeding black from various cuts and dragging the chain along behind it. The room beyond stood silent. Der Krampus paused in the silence of the room. Never before had it been taken by surprise. It had always been so careful about the children it selected. The Old Ones had demanded those with bad blood, those who rebelled against the yuletide festivities and pagan rites, those children that had given rise to the corruption of the yuletide. The Sinter Klaus, the Christ child, gift giving; The obscenity of it all. Der Krampus delighted in plucking the souls and salting the flesh. Yet for all its malice, the beast craved freedom and it had a contract to live up to. Somewhere, its father, the trickster Loki, lay in eternal torment beneath a venom dripping snake. When it had delivered enough souls, Krampus would break from its chains and slay Wotan, free his father and set upon feasting wherever it desired. As long as it could eliminate these two pathetic, horrendous smelling and naughty children. They would burn soon enough. They would-

Krampus' fur became engulfed in flames. The fiend shrieked, the cry of a wounded and startled forest predator. It charged forward, stumbling about, beating off the white hot licks of fire with its claws, knocking down cuckoo clocks as it flailed. The fire tapered off to manageable gouts of flame as the burning beast stumbled into the parlor of its lair.

It hissed through a blackened maw and gazed about at wondrous chaos. The house filled with the sound of shrieks, alive with frantic bird-calls emitted from husky throats, sore with disuse after having been confined to a prison of whimsical wood and rot for years untold. The ravens lashed about through the air, encountering barred windows and no escape route until...

No, this couldn't be. The Wagner child, the boy, had knocked each clock off of the wall and tipped the wicker basket back upright. The portal to the mortal world had been unlocked and Der Krampus' soul-children were flying

315

through it at a rapid pace. As each feathered soul fled its realm, the beast could feel the chain around its ankle growing tighter, hotter. It wasn't fair, what were the souls of a few hundred naughty children against its own wants and gain?

A shard of pain shot through its abdomen, fire as piercingly white as the snow beyond its hearth. The girl stood next to the furnace, part of the stick dipped into the flames as she clipped off great bunches of reeds from the other end. Each snip sent a bolt of pain down the beast's haunches, a lifetime of thoughts, misdeeds and memories embedded within each fiber. No more, this would end here, it would end now.

Der Krampus lashed forward, smoking and stinking like burned meat. It grasped Sera with one smoldering claw and the heated flesh made her cry out in pain. Sera pulled the small canister of mace out of her pocket and raised it. The beast caught it with its other claw and smashed the canister in an iron grip, shaking its head and snuffling like a dog at the burst of acrid fluid.

"Naughty kinder!" Krampus snarled and grabbed the girl around the throat with both hands. It snarled, unfurling its long serpent tongue as the world began to bloom into a great, deep blackness within Sera's hazel eyes.

And then... relief, the loosening of the powerful burned paws and a flood of oxygen back into her throat. Krampus grabbed its own horned head in pain as Tim stepped back, shards of a broken cuckoo clock at his feet. The boy reached down and hefted the great iron chain. He began to spin it in spools, encircling the beast.

"Quick, the stick!" He cried out to his sister.

Sera didn't hesitate. She pitched the remnants of the stick into the furnace. The flames engulfed the stick and with it, Der Krampus. The siblings stepped away from the burning beast even as it fell to the floor, writhing in flesh licking fire, ensnared within its own eternal iron prison. The chain pulled taut on its own accord and pulled itself back in, encircling rapidly around the post in the floor. The sudden impact of the chain hurled the beast, still ensnared, into the belly of the furnace itself.

The room around them lit on fire, great bursts of oxygen depleting blue flames even as the yuletide beast howled in the last remnants of its physical being. Neither sibling spoke a word, communicating solely through frantic glances and tear-streaked gasps. They grasped wound and smoke streaked hands and, holding their breath against the encroaching smoke, stepped one by one into the Wicker and the salvation beyond it.

Tim Ridenhour blinked back reddened blurs and opened his eyes. He flexed his fingers and grasped the rough hewn fabric below them. The Bell house still stood, no worse for the wear, save a pair of shattered windows. The walls were barren, all of the clocks having vanished and a pile of ash sat before him. The setting sun outside caught a small glint off of the ash. Tim reached down and touched a small shard of hot metal. Sera blinked herself back to reality dazedly, herself having been seated on one of the armchairs. Tim pocketed the metallic shard and pulled his big sister to her feet. He yanked her quickly into a hushed embrace. They broke apart and glanced around the quiet house.

Sera kneeled down and brushed her hands through the ash pile. "This is all that's left," she whispered.

They both knew this to be true. A smoldering pile of waste would have sealed off the realm beyond with no way to return even if the beast had survived the flames. But that didn't matter now. They were family, they were safe, they were together.

"Come on," Tim whispered and grabbed her hand, leading her towards the door.

The siblings exited the house, Sera Thompson-Ridenhour and Tim "Tuefel" Wagner-Ridenhour, and stepped into the welcome burst of cold winter's air. In the snow surrounding the house, shards of broken glass glistened like opalescent jewels. Scattered amongst the glass were a heap of tiny black feathers and three toed, clawed footprints. As the siblings walked hand-in-hand down the walkway, the bird prints shifted towards barefoot, five toed and altogether human impressions.

Both knew that they had performed an unexpected good for the wayward souls of the many, but both also had no clue how they would assimilate into society. How long had the children been there? Where were their families now? How much time had passed for them deep within the Wicker? What did they remember...if anything? Curious thoughts for curious minds from a place that existed on an even curiouser fringe of reality. Questions to be answered, perhaps in due time.

The pair crossed Coldbrook Road and Sera ran her hands along the paint peeled surface of her father's old blue Acura. Good, they were home. They needed the comfort of loving arms and the warmth of their true parents.

But first: "I love you, Tim-Tim, you know that right?"

"Yeah, I love you too," he replied. The pair walked into the house, arm in arm. "Now I have to think of an annoying nickname for you."

"Yeah, good luck with that."

A voice echoed from the living room, alight with cheer: "Merry Christmas, the shitter was full!"

"Mike, don't quote the movie out loud, you know I hate that."

"I have to babe. I have to. I mean, if I don't then what am I even watching?"

"All I want to do is watch the movie in peace-"

The siblings left the good natured bickering to their parents and headed off to their respective rooms.

"Hey," Tim called after Sera. She turned around. "Nice stance, by the way." He mimed a softball player swinging a bat. Sera smiled and mimicked the motion back.

Back in his room, Tim sat down on his computer and pulled up his search browser. The window was still open to a genealogy search and name explanations sites. He bit his lip and studied the monitor for a moment.

"Tuefel: An intrepid or aggressive, adventurous person. From Middle High German meaning Devil".

He hadn't noticed the first part of the line before or more likely, hadn't bothered to note it. He had focused solely on the negative connotation. He closed out the search windows and shut down his computer. Tim reached into his pocket and withdrew the one thing his sister didn't know about: the lumpy shard of metal, hooks fastened to the back as one would use as an archaic prosthetic device. The metallic nose of the beast had remained perfectly intact and traveled through the Wicker with the pair.

Tim regarded the trophy for a moment and set it upon his desk. Outside the window, the sun began to set and the winter's twilight was greeted by a dapple of electric and festive rainbow hues as the Christmas lights twinkled on. A harsh wind began to blow; the lights briefly dimmed and the metal shard began to twitch. And yet, Tim felt at peace.

He would keep a watchful eye on the remnants of the yuletide beast; he would keep a watchful eye over his family and any innocent children. It was the most that he, the intrepid and adventurous soul that he was, could do.

One could hardly imagine what had occurred on that cold winter's day to the Ridenhour siblings but Tim believed, as did his sister. They had made bonds stronger than blood with the fear they'd eclipsed beyond the tainted snow, deep within the darkness of the Wicker.

ABOUT THE AUTHORS

E.D. Edwards is a journalist, filmmaker, and the author of many books, short stories, and articles. In 2016, she wrote *Bars, Blues and Booze: Stories from the Drink House,* a collection of bar and gig stories from across the South, which also served as the inspiration for "Dark Harmony."

Kelly Gould's work has appeared in anthologies from Lycan Valley Press, A Murder of Storytellers, Deadman's Tome, Aphotic Realm, Lycopolis Press, Soteira Press, and Weirdbook. His most recent story, *Platinum VIP*, was included in Strangely Funny VII, an anthology from Mystery and Horror, LLC.

Sinéad McCabe comes from Lancashire, where they have some interesting Christmas traditions and the high crags are creepy at night. She lives in London, teaches English as a Second Language to make a meagre living, and writes scary stories for fun. Her work has previously appeared in Disturbed Digest, Pennyshorts, Fantastic Horror, and the Best of Fiction on the Web Anthology.

K. A. Miltimore lives in the Pacific Northwest and writes paranormal cozy mysteries, modern witch lit tales, and historical fantasy fiction in the wee hours of the morning. She loves mid-century fashion, 80s music and nachos (not necessarily in that order). With her husband and son, she loves exploring quirky local towns, including Enumclaw, WA (the setting of her Gingerbread Hag series). Perhaps she will succeed in dragging her family to Iceland for a tour someday. She fancies herself a crafty person, both in projects and devilish schemes. In addition to a love of writing, she has a Masters in Labor & Employment Law that she is still paying off, a fondness for great Washington red wines, and re-watching the movies that she has forgotten over the years. K.A. loves reading about Ancient Rome and historical fiction set in the Tudor and Victorian periods.

DM Davanti. Between spurts of haiku and micropoetry, DM Davanti is a historical fiction and horror writer. With several works being published this year, he has appeared in Headline Poetry and The Organic Poet.

Della Sullivan is a mother of four adult children and has written short stories for years. She has one published poem, and within the past year has had several stories accepted into published anthologies. She is the proud owner of two gigantic Maine Coon cats. A self-declared voracious reader, she enjoys genres of all kinds.

S.C. Fantozzi. They say people are strange, and let me tell you, S.C. Fantozzi fits quite well under that heading. She is a horsewoman, a rock hound, an artist and a landscaper. She lives in the wonderful state of Idaho and possesses far more animals than she does sense. She believes that if you're not trying to type with a cat on your keyboard, you're doing it wrong.

H.H. Carlan is a TRPG designer, consultant, and novelist. She has several best-selling products on the Dungeons & Dragons DMs Guild, and she is a co-author on the hardcover adventure *Icewind Dale: Rime of the Frostmaiden*. H.H. is a lore consultant for the Forgotten Realms setting for Hasbro, and she continues to work on TRPG projects for various companies. She spends her spare time writing fiction. Formerly of Seattle, she now resides in Maine with her husband and tiny humans.

Chisto Healy has been writing since childhood, but he only started following his dreams and writing full time in 2020. On top of the award nominated self published novels from his earlier days, he now has 80 published stories. You can find out what is out to read at his blog as there is new stuff constantly coming out. He lives in NC with his fiance and her mom, his daughter Ella who has inspired stories that have been published, and his daughter Julia who has been published alongside him in this very book, and his son Boe who thinks the world is his drum. Blog https://chisto-healy.blogspot.com

Gary Power is an author of short stories that have been published in respected anthologies such as When Graveyards Yawn (Crowswing Books), Spinetinglers (Spinetinglers publishing), 3 times in 'The Black Book of Horror' (Mortbury Press), The Horror zine (as featured author of the month), The Year's Best Body Horror 2017 (Gehenna and Hinnom publishing), Volume 6 of Dark Lane books Anthology series , 'I'm Dead?' anthology from Zimbell House Publishing ,Twistit Press and 'Father of Lie's in 'Dig Two Graves' from Death's Head Press (USA) . He has also been e-published with Penny Shorts, 50 Word Stories, the

Ham Free Press and Sein und Werden amongst others. He has a podcast play currently being adapted by Manor House Audio (USA).

Currently, he has a novella, 'The Art of Anatomy', being published by Mannison Minibooks (USA).

Harper Barrow. Eternal optimist Harper Barrow is a veterinarian and mother by day, writer and roller derby player by night. Her non-fiction articles have been featured in numerous local publications, her blog on scarymommy.com and her fiction recently won third place in the NYC Midnight Short Story Contest, second place in the Rocky Mountain Fiction Writers Colorado Gold Contest and was accepted into the Pikes Peak Writers Anthology *Fresh Starts*. She received her undergraduate and graduate degrees at Colorado State University and currently lives, works and plays in Parker, Colorado. You can find her and read her blog at harperbarrow.com.

Villimey Mist has always been fascinated by vampires and horror, ever since she watched Bram Stoker's Dracula when she was a little, curious girl. She loves to read and create stories that pop into her head unannounced. She reads horror, listens to horror, watches horror and writes horror. She lives in Iceland with her husband and two cats, Skuggi and Robo-Cop, and is often busy drawing or watching the latest shows on Netflix. She has written a vampire horror series. Two of the books, Nocturnal Blood and Nocturnal Farm, are available. She is currently writing the third book in the series, Nocturnal Salvation which will come out in January 2021.

Brad Acevedo is a tech support specialist who writes out of the lightning blitzed shores of Clearwater, Florida. He lives with his wife, a collection of horror memorabilia and an obscene amount of vinyl pop culture figurines. When not writing, he can often be found in the Florida theme parks or braving the woodlands in search of local lore and geocaches. He has an Associate's in Film Analysis and is currently pending publication with the *Tattoo Shop of Horrors* collection.